FROSTHAMMER: THE DWARVES OF NAGDOR

AETHEAON CHRONICLES: BOOK THREE

LEONARD D. HILLEY II

For my wife, Christal, our two children, and our two grandchildren. My love always.

Aetheaon
Misty Seas of Reus
Isles of Welkstone
Snowton
Evenfar
Gharlou
Icebourne
Highwale Plains
Raven's Fall
City of Hoffmang
Nagdor
Sparrows Point
Icevale
Wanderroot
Haunted Forest of Dorden
Tharmost
Leander
Glisten Ridge
Ironbone River
Crows point
Vale of Frozen Tears
Glasslyn Lake
Mithalis
Bridgethorrow
Raybourne
Falls Lake
Vylon
Elvendale
Black Chasm
Woodroe
Sylianthanu
Westroyan
Spellhaven
Tauran
Kingdom of Legelarid
Shadeport
N
W E
S
Kingdom of Ovaloth

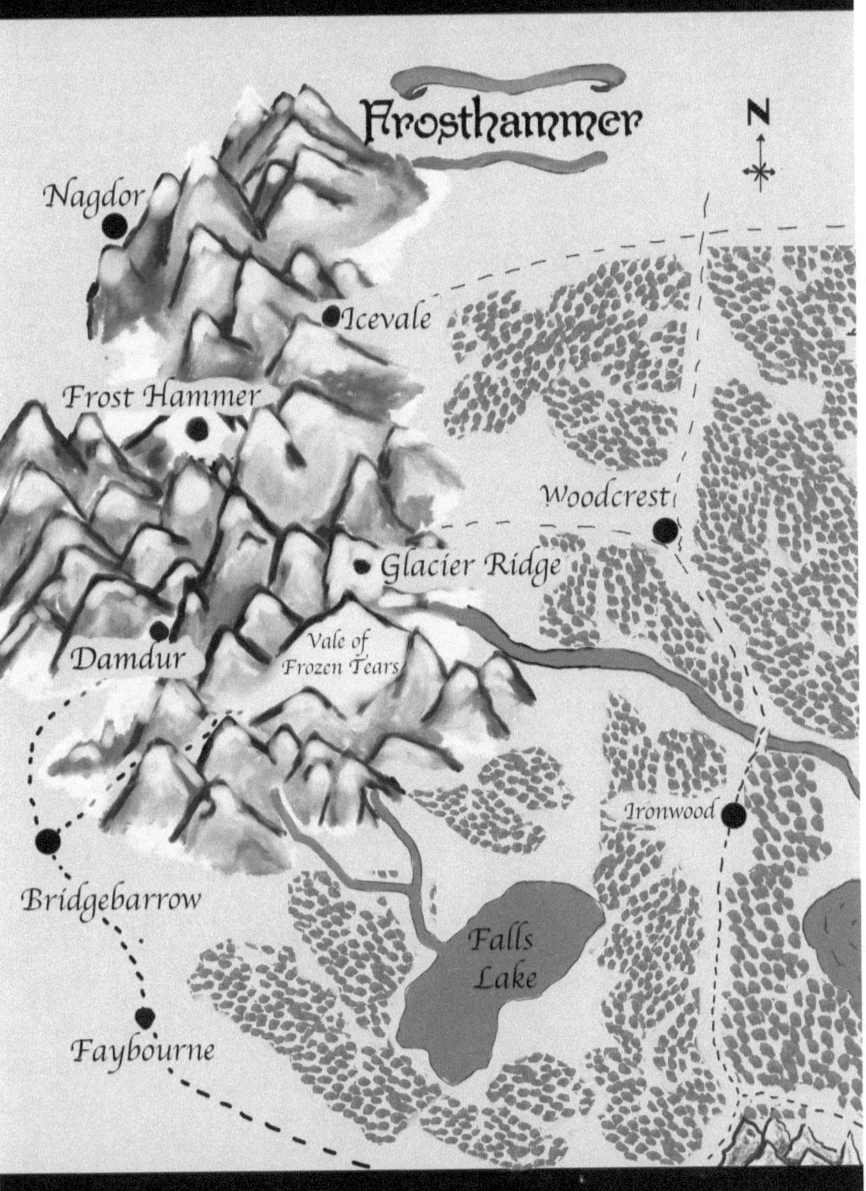

Frosthammer
N
Nagdor
Icevale
Frost Hammer
Woodcrest
Glacier Ridge
Damdur
Vale of
Frozen Tears
Ironwood
Bridgebarrow
Falls
Lake
Faybourne

CHAPTER 1

Boldair—Nagdor's newly appointed Dwarven King—marched through the dungeon halls beneath Hoffnung's Castle, escorted by Drucis and Dwiskter. Their chainmail tunics clinked in riveting waves against their steel plate-legs. Their hair was tied into long braids down their backs.

Reading Boldair's emotions was difficult, despite his narrowed brow and hardened face. His eyes indicated the internal stormy struggles his weary mind endured. Neither Dwiskter nor Drucis offered any words as they strode down the hallway, but occasionally, they gave brief side-glances to Boldair. During times like these, silence offered more assurance than words.

Their heavy steel armor and steel-covered boots rattled, echoing their unified purpose as they walked in equally timed steps. Since they weren't in a hostile environment, they left their helms with their mounts in the Royal Stables.

Near the steel prison gate, two of Hoffnung's guards stood at attention. Their heavy long shields were propped against the wall. Both guards were armed with two sheathed short swords. When they noticed the three Dwarves marching in their direction, their eyes widened momentarily, and they grabbed their shields.

After recognition set in, the guard to the right of the gate placed his shield against the wall again. He took a heavy key ring from his belt and unlocked the door.

"Welcome, King Boldair," the guard said. "Queen Taube sent word of your arrival earlier today."

The guard swung the gate open. He took a torch from a barrel of viscous pitch and touched it to the flaming sconce. The torch ignited with a quick engulfing swoosh, hissing for a moment before curls of black smoke rose.

Boldair paused to look at Dwiskter and Drucis. "You two wait here."

"Are you certain?" Dwiskter asked with a frustrated frown.

"Aye," Boldair replied. "I won't be long."

Dwiskter and Drucis exhaled heavily but didn't relax. Their massive hands rested on the hilts of their weapons. Their eyes stared into Boldair's momentarily. Without words, the new King recognized their devotion. Should events somehow go awry, the prison gate could not prevent them from rushing to his aid. Not that Boldair expected any true danger. His father was enclosed inside a cell, after all. The Hoffnung's guards were no threat, being close allies. However, entering any prison offered unforeseen dangers, because no prisoner could be trusted, especially not his own father and Nagdor's former king, Ulthor.

Boldair shook his head with disappointment. How horrible to have a father he couldn't trust.

Ulthor, now dethroned, might still have loyalists determined to free him and return him to his former throne. Even the worst vagabond rulers had ardent followers who were blinded to their transgressions. Some Dwarves in Nagdor might've believed Ulthor's constant condescending insults about Boldair and viewed Boldair's reputation as too weak to rule Nagdor successfully. And if so, those Dwarves were his greatest threat and camouflaged enemies that held an advantage over him since he didn't know who they might be.

"This way," the guard said, pointing to the right.

The dungeon prison in this castle was, by far, more *comfortable* than any prison Boldair had seen in other kingdoms. Some of those prisons he remembered viewing from the other side of the bars. Such was the price of a drunken boastful Dwarf telling tales of treasures so vast that the lesser treasure hunters angrily called his honesty into question. Nothing angered a Dwarf more than accusations of dishonesty, and Boldair's temper flared whenever tavern patrons attacked his veracity. He seldom lost a tavern brawl, but at times the guards in some of the major cities subdued and arrested him. The following morning, he awoke in a lightless acrid cell filled with mold and uncertain sticky, disgustingly greenish brown wastes that he dared not examine closely.

Boldair winced and choked back his nausea.

Hoffnung's prisons would've been more welcoming a stay for him before he had taken his father's throne.

Sconces blazed soft dancing fires outside each prison door. No cries of anguish echoed, which meant none of the prisoners were being tortured. None ever were in Hoffnung. Such was contrary to Queen Taube's nature but not necessarily unbecoming in a Dwarven prison.

No rats scurried along the corridor. Strangely, the prison lacked the acrid odor of the sewers or the gagging aroma of decaying flesh; all common traits in the prisons in other kingdoms.

No barred sections interrupted the thick rock walls on either side of the hall. The dim passageway seemed to go a half mile or more at an underground depth Dwarves found suitable for habitation. The heavy wooden cell doors were spaced every ten feet along the walls, but not directly across from one another, so that even if a prisoner looked through the small barred window, he couldn't view a prisoner through the window of a cell across the hall.

For a few moments, Boldair thought about the miserable prison cell where he had awakened at the top of the mountain peak before Taniesse had a change of heart, spared his life, and hired him to lead a battalion into battle.

The wrinkles around his eyes creased and a half grin spread on his face but faded with his next breath. From having been a prisoner shackled beside a crisp decaying corpse to becoming Nagdor's next king, Boldair found the switch of fate more than unusual and somewhat satisfying. He'd witnessed a lot of odd things in his life. Not once did he ever consider visiting his father, the former King of Nagdor, inside a prison cell.

In many ways, months earlier, he half expected the tables might've turned the opposite direction except Ulthor's uncontrollable selfish greed caused him to deceive the Dwarves of Nagdor and the surrounding Dwarven kingdoms. His father's deceit was something Boldair never anticipated. He found it difficult to believe even after receiving valid proof. His father was the last soul Boldair would've ever thought to possess a traitorous demeanor.

The guard led Boldair past a dozen cells before finally stopping outside the door. "Do you wish, Sire, that I open the door so you can speak to your father face-to-face?"

Boldair pursed his lips slightly as he thought. His eyes narrowed beneath thick bushy eyebrows. He ran a hand through his long beard and slowly shook his head. In his gruff authoritative voice, he said, "No. Speaking through the window grate is more than enough."

"As you wish," the guard said. The guard spoke several Elven words, and a glowstone inside Ulthor's cell lightened the prison room. A moment later, the guard turned on his heels and marched toward the gate.

Boldair rose slightly on his toes to look through the barred opening. Ulthor stood in a long-sleeve, aged, sweat-soiled undershirt and pants. He was stripped of his armor, his weapons, jeweled rings and necklace, and worst of all, his crown, which now belonged to Boldair. By all measures, Ulthor was no more than any of the filthy peasant prisoners in the neighboring cells. Had his name been unknown, most would've viewed like the other prisoners.

The former king's gray hair was untied and frazzled. His dark-skin was abnormal and ashen like a corpse. The knots in his long beard were loosened, looking more like frayed rope than the pristine style an honorable Dwarf wore. The strength his gray eyes once possessed was gone, resembling the hopeless eyes of an aged soul near the threshold of death. His weakened resolve was progressing, but Ulthor wasn't a Dwarf to readily admit his defeat.

His father's thick knuckles were bruised and bloodied from repeatedly punching the solid prison walls to diminish his anger. At least Boldair speculated such to have caused the injuries. It wasn't so Ulthor could escape. Even with the best blacksmithing hammer, these rock walls could withstand hours of the hard strikes without cracking or allowing a flick of the rock to chip.

The stones were carved from sea deposits composed of petrified layers of seashells and oyster shells. The stone was not only capable of resisting the blasting sticks Dwarves used to open new underground tunnels, this odd stone could stop the harshest cannon fire from the best Dwarven cannons. The only weak points were the cell doors lining the inside dungeon halls. So it was highly unlikely the outer prison walls could ever be breached.

Boldair stared at his father a bit too long and pricked his father's awareness. Ulthor turned his attention toward Boldair with a fury that'd send Hellhounds to the Lava Pits in mere seconds. In spite of his father's indignant stare, Boldair didn't flinch. Instead, his eyes narrowed with an unleashed inner fury of his own.

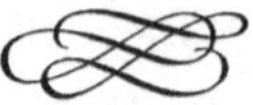

CHAPTER 2

"Come to gloat, have ye, ol' son of mine?" Ulthor said through gritted teeth, peering through the barred square window. Anger creased Ulthor's brow. A slight craziness loomed in his tired eyes. His wild eyes indicated he had slept little, if any at all, since his incarceration.

The shock of how far his father had fallen within the matter of several days weighed upon Boldair. All the zeal and power the former King displayed before the Battle of Hoffnung was buried deep under his wallowing and loathing in self-pity. Had Boldair passed this version of Ulthor on the street, Boldair wouldn't have recognized his own father. He would've assumed Ulthor was a beggar.

"No, father," Boldair replied in a near whisper. "What's to gloat over?"

"Have you already forsaken the crown?"

"No."

"Then where is it and why are you not wearing it?" Ulthor asked.

"It is in a safe place."

Ulthor eyed Boldair with great suspicion. "Have the guard open the door or do you not even have the courage to stand face-to-face with me? Bah! Figures, as you've always proven yourself a coward."

"I have no fear of you," Boldair replied softly. "Or your mocking words."

"Because I have no weapons?"

"I've *never* feared you. I once held respect for you, but that has faded."

"Then have the guard open the door, if you possess no fear."

Boldair stood firm, unflinching. His hardened stare focused on his father's eyes, boring heated anger. "I came to say me good-byes, father. Nothing more."

"I suppose you're looking forward to your father's hanging?" Ulthor said with a sudden fiery glare in his eyes. In two steps, he stood at the prison door, looking at his son. His hands tightened around the steel bars of the window. He hoisted himself slightly until his face was in full view. For a moment, Ulthor's desperate eyes glanced to the Boldair's sheathed ax before returning a look of disdain toward his son.

Boldair held his father's furious gaze without fear or faltering backwards as he might have done a few years earlier. Boldair had suffered several swift backhands from his father during heated arguments, but he never sought or considered retaliation since Ulthor was not only his father, but he was the Nagdor's king.

Boldair rested his hands on the hilt of his heavy ax. His jaw muscles flexed, but no words escaped his mouth. His lips barely moved. His anger faded and he looked at his father like he would a stranger.

Ulthor sneered. "A worthless son once under my rule now possesses my throne. Ah, ye shall boast well, adding fury to your drunken bard tales in the taverns. The taverns are where you belong. Not on *my* throne."

"I've never desired the throne."

"Bah! You've waited a long time to find a way to steal it. Owning the city's wealth legitimately as King is a quicker reward than your gambles to find hidden and lost treasures. You never proved your valor on the battlefield. Not to me."

"No?" Boldair said. He pointed a thick stubby finger to the Dragon Skull pendant riveted to his steel collar. "You see this? Lady Dawn honored me, Dwiskter, and Drucis as Knights of the Dragon Skull Order because I led them and my troops through Hoffnung's gates. I fought the Vyking horde, alongside every other warrior, to regain the throne."

"Bah! *Any* Dwarf could storm a city without fear when aided by a trio of dragons. Even a halfling or sprite could defeat a city with dragons. But those dragons won't be there to protect Nagdor's throne should any outside forces attack my kingdom."

"Your actions are why you've been dethroned. Your execution is an unavoidable consequence. The blame falls on you. No one else. You're a traitor to Hoffnung. Most likely, *your* lust for gold is the reason Erik's dead."

"A trait you've inherited, you ungrateful scamp. You think robbing the dead isn't unscrupulous?"

"At least I didn't cost a king his life," Boldair said gruffly.

"It's interesting you favor the Dragon Skull pendant over wearing the crown, or did ya sell it for gold?"

Boldair's eyes narrowed. "That's enough with your insults."

Ulthor chuckled deep in his throat. "Well, you'll have the satisfying glory in seeing ya father hang in the gallows."

"Bah, I won't be watching," Boldair replied.

Ulthor's eyebrows rose. His wearied, bloodshot eyes widened in despair. Ulthor never sought pity. Did his father actually expect Boldair to hold sorrow after his father's treacherous actions?

"What were ya hoping for?" Although Boldair's face was stern, his eyes glistened tears in the flickering sconce light. "All me life I've held you in the highest esteem, even when you belittled and taunted me. After you degraded my reputation with Nagdor's council, I still viewed you as a king with great valor and thought I'd never be near your equal. A braver heart I'd never known. My judgment was in error. You 'ave no valor. You're a traitor and a scallion. No king could fall any lower than you."

"You dare judge your father?" Ulthor's face tightened with bitterness. Spittle flew from his mouth and sagged at the edges of his mouth, coating his wiry beard.

"I didn't until the truth emerged," Boldair replied. "As king, I've the power to judge you openly."

"Taniesse cannot be trusted," Ulthor said. "If you believe she's innocent in all that's transpired, you've been deceived."

"She and her two sisters fought to reclaim Hoffnung's throne for Lady Dawn."

"As did I!" Ulthor said, gripping the barred window tightly. "I brought my best troops, or 'ave ya forgotten already?"

"I didn't forget, but your betrayal outweighs every good deed you've ever done. Every time someone mentions your name, I'll be reminded of who you really are."

Ulthor spat on the floor. "Bah! Ya think yourself sanctimonious now, do ya? What? 'cause you led a small battalion into war after years of refusing to carry a battle ax to prove yourself worthy of being a Nagdor warrior? You think yourself better than those who served and sacrificed their lives in my armies for a hundred years?"

"I might not've been in your armies, but I've proven myself. Even had I followed your every detailed command to the utmost perfection, I'd have never been worthy of your acceptance or praise. You've held contempt for me my entire life. Perhaps you be more angry that I've become something you've not? An *honest* king?"

Ulthor's eyes narrowed and darkened like obsidian. The flickering sconce reflected on the moist sheen of his eyes, making the flames appear as a part of his internal, raging fury boiling to the surface. His reddened face glowed like metal inside a hot forge. If Ulthor was a mechanical pressure gauge, he'd have exploded. "Says the Dwarf that robbed the great dragons' treasuries of Aetheaon and the dead! Which, by all accounts, is treasonous to Queen Taube."

"Taniesse has settled the issue with me. The grievance was between she and I! No one else. Not Hoffnung. Not *you* nor any Dwarf, Elf, or human! She and I." Boldair's lips snarled. "One cannot be a thief by taking treasure from the dead. They've no use for gold."

"But she and her sisters were *not* dead," Ulthor said. A sly grin spread on his face.

"Aye, tis true, but you told me a barrel of lies about her demise, didn't you? You convinced Nagdor into believing your lies. Some probably still do. But not much longer."

Ulthor shook his head but didn't respond with words.

Boldair said, "When Taniesse revealed herself, I offered her treasure and that of her sisters back to them without question."

"Did ye now?" Ulthor said. "Or was it the threat of her scorching breath that persuaded you the most?"

Boldair huffed. "Have you knowledge of any Dwarf that's ever survived the fiery breath of a dragon?"

Ulthor roared with a belly laugh. "Aye! Yes! A coward through and through. Not something you can say about me though. I fought her. I stood boot to boot against ..."

"Dragons don't wear boots," Boldair said.

"You know what I mean!" Ulthor said. Clenching his hands into tight fists, his moment of laughter ceased and his boiling anger resumed. "I risked my life and fought to strike a deathblow!"

"She meant no threat to you," Boldair replied. "Not until after you attacked her. She was on that mountain peak looking for King Erik, as you should've been. But you feared she'd discover your true reason for being there. *That's* why you tried to slay her."

"Still—"

Boldair shook his head. "No, she could've killed ya after windblasting you unconscious. Instead, she spared you."

"No matter," Ulthor said, releasing the bars and turning from the door. "There's no escaping me death now."

"Death comes for us all," Boldair said. "Regardless if one is a peasant or a king, Death comes. It's how we're remembered *after* our demise that counts da most."

"Aye," Ulthor sighed. He glanced away from Boldair. "Tis true, son. Perhaps you hold more wisdom than I ever credited you."

"Indeed, father, that's true as well. No treasure hunter survives this long without quick wits."

Ulthor looked at his feet. His shoulders slumped. "I've failed as a king, and worse yet, I've failed ya as a father."

"Too late for apologies," Boldair said with an even glare. He sighed and turned to walk away. "I've said what I had come to say."

Boldair stepped away from the prison door.

CHAPTER 3

"Wait, son." Ulthor's voice was a stern whisper overcome by grief.

Boldair turned toward the cell.

Ulthor gripped the bars of the window. "Will Nagdor's battalions escort you back to Nagdor?"

"Dwiskter, Forboud, and Drucis accompany me."

"That's *all* that travel with you? Son—"

"It's enough."

"No." Ulthor shook his head. "Where's our battalion?"

"I sent them ahead with King Staggnuns and King Thorgum."

Uneasiness settled upon Ulthor. Fear widened his eyes. "It's a long journey to Nagdor. You're the king. Surely, you understand the dangers an unprotected king faces. Never journey without an army? Any fool knows the saying, *'a King's ransom'*, comes from that aspect. Any tyrant that takes you hostage will demand wagonsful of gold for your safe return. Don't risk the gold and silver coffers of Nagdor due to your foolishness."

"I suppose you value the loss of the treasuries more than your own son's? I've spent years scouring Aetheaon, ancient dungeons, and abandoned dragon lairs, often by myself. Finding treasure isn't a risk-free pastime."

"That was *before* you were King," Ulthor said with a tightly knitted brow.

Boldair shrugged his thick shoulders. "Besides, Forboud has always watched me back whenever he's assisted me. More so, now that I'm King."

Ulthor sighed and looked away. "Forboud was the one I'd have chosen to take the throne."

"Why's that?"

His eyes peered hard into Boldair's. "I trained him. I've seen him in the heat of battle."

"'ave you now? Where was he during the Battle for Hoffnung? He wasn't amongst us, nor was he knighted into the Dragon Skull Order."

Ulthor stood silent for several moments. "No matter. Staggnuns and Thorgum had no right placing you on my throne. They've their own kingdoms to rule."

"Your crimes gave them little choice."

"Bah! I've never stuck me nose into their affairs. They've no—"

"What's done is done, father. Their choosing me was no doing of me own."

Ulthor sighed. "Forboud's always been more worthy. That is, until he began scouring Aetheaon with ya to find treasures. That's when he disappointed me the most."

Boldair's eyes narrowed. "He's never spoken an ill word about you."

"He didn't need to say anything."

"What do you mean? You'd disown your own sons because we've chosen to walk different paths than you'd hoped?"

Ulthor's broad nose scrunched. Bitterness oozed with his words like poison dripping from the fangs of a Rusktin bat. With maddened eyes, he stared at Boldair. "Sometimes actions speak louder than words."

Boldair stood in silence while he studied his bitter father. Delirium was overtaking Ulthor. Boldair shook his head. "Words of truth, father. Your actions have gotten you exactly where you stand. You've disgraced even your father—my grandfather—The Mighty Thorseg, by your betrayal. If rocks could weep, a new river would rush beneath Nagdor, but even that won't cleanse the filth you've brought upon us."

Redness flushed Ulthor's ashen face. His pale bloodshot eyes narrowed, and his jaw trembled.

"I pity what awaits you after death, for it cannot be good." Boldair lowered his gaze, turned, and walked away.

"Wait, son!" Ulthor cried. His thick hands wrapped around the bars. The desperation in his voice equaled the panic in his eyes. "Don't leave yet! I've more to tell you!"

"I'm done listening," Boldair said in a gruff whisper, waving a stern dismissal without glancing over his shoulder.

"Don't be a blasted fool! It's more than *your* life you risk! It's the Kingdom of Nagdor that's at stake. You must listen! The war isn't over!"

"Aye, father it is! And we won!" Boldair took fierce steps.

"Not *dat* war! Another one stirs, it's in the making, and it'll be a great war unlike anything Aetheaon has witnessed!"

"More lies, father?"

"No lies."

"You're delusional."

"Turn around and listen to me, you blasted fool!"

Boldair's jaw tightened. He kept marching toward the gate where the two Hoffnung guards stood. He refused to reply, even though Ulthor kept shouting, pleading.

"You've no knowledge of how to rule Nagdor, Boldair! Don't be a fool and think the council will serve ye! You need Forboud at your side for guidance. I admit I've failed you as a father and disgraced our alliance, but don't fail our kingdom! The Dredgemen never left Snowloch. Their city is further underground. Much deeper than our own."

Boldair paused his stride for a moment at the last statement before shrugging off the comment. His fuming father loved a heated argument, and being confined inside the small prison cell didn't allow Ulthor any physical means to burn off his rage and frustration. Of course, his father could be telling the truth, but he might've only said the words to capture Boldair's attention, hoping to lure Boldair back to the cell where their arguing might ensue.

Boldair flicked his gaze to the guard who had opened the gate previously. The guard unlocked the door and swung it open. The guard acknowledged Boldair for a moment before he glanced down the corridor toward Ulthor's cell. Ulthor bellowed.

"Does he prattle like that often?" Boldair asked.

The guard, hearing Ulthor's tirade, shook his head. "No."

"If he continues, thrash him. He'll calm down. He's not so brave without an ax and shield. But unarmed, it'd still take the two of you. Normally, you can't do that to a king, but a *former* King who's lost his glory—that be a different tale. You've my permission." Boldair gave a quick wink.

A slight smile tugged at the guard's lips, but he kept his composure in check. "Sire, I'm certain that's not necessary."

"Ah, ya never know," Boldair said, shrugging.

The guard secured the gate and stood at attention once more.

Boldair glanced at Drucis and Dwiskter and fought his urge to glance back in the direction of his father's bombastic insulting shouts. Boldair wondered if Ulthor was telling the truth about the Dredgemen and their underground dwelling at Snowloch. He wanted to know. Yet, he resisted. He was tired, hungry, and needed stout. "Ah, now. We're a long way from home. Tis best we journey to Nagdor."

They nodded their agreement.

Forboud approached the gate where the other Dwarves stood. "What's our father shouting about now, Boldair?"

"Utter nonsense," Boldair said in a low tone. He tapped the side of his helm with a firm finger. "Father's deranged. More so now than ever. I suppose he doesn't take too well to confined quarters."

"Perhaps I should speak with him?" Forboud said, turning toward the gate.

Boldair shook his head and grabbed the ruby-encrusted bracer that covered his brother's left wrist. "No."

Forboud scoffed. "He's still rambling endlessly down the hall. What *did* he say to you?"

"He mainly pointed out repeatedly how unqualified I am to be the new king."

Both Drucis and Dwiskter cocked a brow and turned toward Boldair. Their anger was instant.

"He didn't!" Drucis said.

"Aye, he did," Boldair said.

"I don't doubt you, brother," Forboud said. "Father's held no secrets about his feelings toward you."

"Ulthor should speak," Dwiskter said, chuckling. "Tis *he* who stands on the wrong side of the cell door."

Forboud cast an angered gaze at Dwiskter. "Yet, he *was* our King. Hold some respect instead of mockery."

Dwiskter turned toward Forboud and placed his hand on the hilt of his heavy ax. "Once Ulthor was king, but no more. His misdeed outweighs all the good he's ever done. He was dethroned for a reason. Your brother is king now. Ulthor deserves less respect than being spat upon. He's the reason King Erik is dead, lest you so easily forget. It be I who rang the alarm bell in Hoffnung when the Vykings stormed and invaded the docks. I took up arms to help Lady Dawn reclaim the throne. I willingly risked *my* life to save a kingdom to which I was an outsider. I'd do it all again. I serve your brother, Boldair, as the rightful King. Where do *your* loyalties lie? With your father or your brother?"

Forboud stared into Dwiskter's fierce gaze and then glanced at Dwiskter's tight grip on the battle-ax. Forboud huffed and looked away.

Down the long corridor, Ulthor shouted more obscenities. Within a few seconds, his voice lowered in defeat or perhaps he fell asleep. Nothing was worse than a disgraced king stripped of his rule and former glory, especially for a Dwarf.

Dwiskter pulled his ax partially free of its sheath. "Well?"

Forboud stepped away from Dwiskter, eyed the locked gate with the Hoffnung guards, and then he faced Boldair. "Brother, I'd never question your authority as king nor protest your seat on the throne, but father's *never* behaved in such a maddened behavior. Surely he discussed more than his disapproval of you being king."

Boldair's lips tightened. His eyes narrowed. "What was said between a *former* king and Nagdor's *new* king has nothing to do with you."

Forboud read the anger in his brother's eyes. Boldair's bluntness cut quickly. Forboud lowered his gaze. "Aye, brother."

"Now, let's not waste any more time in Hoffnung," Boldair said with a more optimistic tone.

"And leave father?" Forboud asked. "Are we not staying for his execution?"

"Stay, brother, if that be your wish. You're entitled to do so, but I've no want to view his last moments. It'd make no less the bad memories of his ill-treatment toward me," Boldair said firmly. He turned to Drucis and Dwiskter. "Time to fill our bellies with some hearty stew and tankards of stout before we make our long journey back."

"Now you're talking!" Drucis said. "I'm all for that. But it best be something powerful enough to coil my beard hairs tighter."

Boldair laughed and placed his hand on Drucis' left pauldron. "In a few days time, I'll buy you a drink that'll make ya think your insides are boiling."

"Bah! Nothing's *that* good!" Drucis howled before offering a sly grin. Eagerness set in his eyes and drool hung at the edges of his mouth.

Boldair didn't offer the slightest smile. He held a dead serious stare the other Dwarves recognized. Whenever Boldair boasted of a new treasure discovery, his eyes gleamed. Although Boldair embellished his treasure hunting events, he never lied about the loot. He might lie about *how* he obtained it, or exaggerate the obstacles he overcame to retrieve it, but he never lied about the quantity or quality of the gems or gold he had found.

"Oh?" Drucis said. His broad grin shrank. He wiped drool from his mouth with the back of his hand. "Such a drink exists?"

"Aye, it does," Boldair said. "The harshest drink I've ever swallowed. Its kick will drop ya to the ground. When you fade into the blurry darkness of the stupor, it kicks ya again."

"Sounds like good stuff!" Dwiskter said, grinning and combing his red beard with his hand.

Boldair coughed to clear his throat. Tears burned his eyes as his memories recalled the drink's painful burn. "Ah, it's the most powerful drink I've ever had. Thought the blasted stuff was going to kill me. I swore I'd never drink it again. But these past few days, I've craved it for some reason."

"Ye got me curiosity up now," Drucis said. "Where's the tavern that sells such a drink?"

"Not a tavern as we're used to. It's a small vendor's camp on the winding Meadwyrm Pass," Boldair replied.

"Odd way of serving brew," Dwiskter said.

"Meadwyrm Pass?" Drucis said. "That's a long way *out of the way* to Nagdor."

The four Dwarves stopped at another locked gateway and waited for a guard to unlock it. They turned to the right and ascended a short set of rock steps where they faced another locked gate, which opened to the final ascending spiral stairs.

"I've a feeling we could've already been at the camp you mentioned for as long as it's taking us to get out of Hoffnung's prison," Drucis said.

Boldair chuckled. "Aye, tis a long ways down and back again. But perhaps the cleanest prison I've ever seen."

"True," Dwiskter said. "Peasants should 'ave it so good."

"At least ye father's in a comfortable place," Drucis said.

Forboud frowned. "He's still going to be put to death."

"Traitors usually are," Dwiskter said evenly.

"And he's a traitor to whom?" Forboud asked angrily. "He's king. A king serves no other king or he's no king at all."

Dwiskter turned sharply, clutched Forboud's throat with his thick hand, and hefted the prince off the floor and pressed him against the wall. Anger narrowed Dwiskter's eyes and leveled heated hatred at Forboud. "Your father *was* king. While I agree no king bows before another, one that betrays another ruler simply to gain wealth isn't fit for *any* throne. That's who your father is. It's what he is that has him locked in a prison cell."

Forboud used both hands in an attempt to pry Dwiskter's viselike grip off his throat but couldn't. He gasped, and his face reddened.

"Dwiskter," Boldair said softly, shaking his head. "Release him."

Dwiskter opened his hand, allowing Forboud to land on his feet. Forboud coughed and rubbed his throat. Boldair stepped between Dwiskter and Forboud and stared intently into his brother's eyes.

"Do ya wish to travel to Nagdor with us?" Boldair asked. "Or are your loyalties to father too strong to accept me as your new king?"

Forboud took a deep breath and cleared his throat. "Aye, me loyalties are to you, brother. It's—simply too difficult to fully accept father as a traitor. Where's the proof?"

"The words came from his own mouth," Boldair said. "On the battlefield."

Hurt saddened Forboud's eyes.

"Aye," Drucis said, "I was there when he spoke them."

Forboud's shoulders slumped. Glancing at the floor, he shook his head.

"I know it's hard to accept, brother, and something I wish were not true. Such disappointment cuts to the heart," Boldair said. "But our kingdom must redeem itself for what he's done. Understand that I never requested the crown. King Staggnuns and King Thorgum gave it to me."

"What gives them the right to dictate such an order?" Forboud asked.

"They've every right, as our kingdom is joined with theirs in the Northern Dwarven Alliance. That means that whenever one kingdom suffers attack, the other two join the battle to defend the city. As kings, they're bound to hold one another accountable for derisive actions."

"Should we not hold a public hearing for father?"

"He admitted his own guilt," Boldair said.

Forboud swallowed hard. "You'd have held him guilty regardless. The animosity between you and he was too great, which makes you bias."

Boldair gently placed his hands on Forboud's shoulders and stared into his eyes. "Look, father'd rather have had you crowned king instead of me, but *that's* not what our alliance decided. For whatever reason, they've placed me on the throne, even though I've never desired to reign. If it's too much for you to 'ave your brother reign over you, perhaps you should stay behind until after father's execution. Damdur or Icevale could readily accept you into city."

Forboud frowned. A tear trickled down his cheek into his beard. "You're exiling me?"

Boldair smiled and shook his head, still keeping his hands on Forboud's shoulders. "Not at all, brother. But you've some decisions to make. Decisions not to be taken lightly."

"I'd like to speak to father," Forboud said.

"Aye," Boldair said with a simple nod. He removed his hands from Forboud's shoulders. "Then you've made your decision."

Forboud's brows rose in confusion. "I 'ave? What decision did I make?"

"To stay behind and find a new home," Boldair said.

"I never said such a thing!"

"You don't 'ave to. Since father wants you on the throne, he'll do everything in his power to convince you to take it. You're my brother. I know you quite well. I know you covet the crown."

"Dat's not true," Forboud said, shaking his head. "What crime is it for me to talk to him, especially since he's to be executed? I can't talk to him *after* he's dead."

Boldair smiled evenly. "You were given a choice to make. You've made it."

Forboud shook his head. "No, if that be the choice, I won't speak to him. I'll follow you to Nagdor. I hold no grudge against you and will gladly serve you as my king without any malice. It's just you never had the bond with father like I 'ave."

Boldair looked at Dwiskter and Drucis and nodded. "Tis true. Perhaps this was why Staggnuns and Thorgum chose me to assume the throne. If you remain behind to speak to him, you are not welcome in Nagdor."

"You don't trust me?"

"I don't trust his influence over you," Boldair replied. "Especially not in his current state of mind."

"Then tell me what he said to you before I arrived? It had to be more than him wanting me on the throne instead of you."

"He prattled about random nonsense, Forboud. Nothing more. Perhaps he's edged closer to senility than what we realized. He might've been bewitched or poisoned. Whatever the case, he's shown me his mind is no longer rational."

Forboud rubbed his bearded chin. "His mind wanders from time to time. That always concerned me. I assumed it merely meant too much occupied his thoughts."

"Murder can derail a mind," Boldair said.

"We don't know he murdered King Erik," Forboud said.

"We know he did *nothing* to rescue Erik," Drucis said. "And dat's essentially the same thing."

"What is your choice?" Boldair asked.

"I travel to Nagdor with you."

Boldair smiled. "Good to hear, brother."

"What other choice did you leave me?"

"Come." Boldair motioned up the spiral stairs.

"Ah, blasted it all to Hell!" Drucis said with a gruff growl. "*More* stairs!"

"You think they'd might consider building a lift to the prisons, eh?" Dwiskter said with a sly grin. "For you?"

"Bah! They never took into consideration a Dwarf's short legs with all these endless stairs." Drucis cocked brow and shook a stubby finger.

"Why should they?" Boldair asked. "They're humans. Ever notice that we never build high ceilings in our tunnels for their convenience and comfort?"

Dwiskter howled with laughter. "Aye, tis true! Never seen a human visitor brave our mining tunnels to emerge *without* a bruised forehead."

Drucis laughed. He glanced at Forboud. Forboud wasn't amused by their conversation. In the light of the burning sconce, he appeared rather sickly. "You okay, Forboud? You look a bit under the weather. Maybe the high altitude of Hoffnung is making ya lightheaded?"

Forboud grumbled.

"Oh, let 'em be," Dwiskter said. "It's not often he's ventured to the heights of Hoffnung's cliffs."

"He's a lot on his mind," Drucis said.

"I do," Forboud said in a harsh whisper. "But nothing you'd understand."

"You're still young," Dwiskter said. "Wisdom increases with age. Whether you believe me or not, I understand you being torn inside concerning your father and Nagdor's transition. But the change will strengthen the city."

"I still think more could be done," Forboud replied.

"For father?" Boldair asked with a shrewd stare.

Forboud didn't make eye contact. "Aye."

"When crimes go unpunished," Boldair said, "chaos goes unchecked. Greater problems emerge."

"I understand, brother, but it doesn't make it any easier."

"No," Boldair said softly. "It doesn't."

They reached a door at the top of the spiral stairs that opened to the east ramparts overlooking Hoffnung Bay.

"Oh, praise be," Drucis said, placing his hands on his knees and leaning forward. "Level land, at last."

CHAPTER 5

Boldair stood outside the door. Drucis and Dwiskter stepped into the courtyards and admired the towers of Hoffnung's Castle.

When Forboud stepped through the door, Boldair placed a hand on his brother's arm. "Come, let's speak privately."

Forboud wiped sweat from his brow and nodded. "Aye."

Boldair walked with Forboud to the edge of the wall near the lifts. They stood overlooking the bay. Few ships were in the harbor. The charred ruins of several Vyking ships bobbed near the docks.

"You said that you've noticed father's mind slipping?" Boldair asked.

"Aye, from time to time."

"Did you notice anything else unusual about him?"

"Like what?"

"His complexion."

Forboud frowned. "What about it?"

"Like me, he's dark-skinned. But today his skin is ashened. Has he been sick?" Boldair asked.

Forboud shook his head.

Boldair rubbed his bearded chin. "Hmm."

"What?"

"Don't rightly know," Boldair said. "He and I 'ave always kept a wall wedged between us. Seldom 'ave we seen eye-to-eye, but he seemed out of sorts more so than normal."

"In what way?"

Boldair squinted as he thought. He folded his hands together and rested his elbows on the rock wall. His eyes wandered from ship to ship, and then he watched the workers on the docks. "He seemed—given to a fear dat everyone was out to get 'em."

"Would you not, given his current situation?"

"I'm not referring to his imprisonment."

"Then what?"

"Ah, his mind is in disarray, thinking a Great War is coming," Boldair said.

Forboud's eyes widened. "He said dat?"

"Aye, he did. You believe 'em?"

Forboud rubbed his bearded chin. "It's not the first time he's mentioned such."

"Then you know what we're dealing with? The details?"

"No, I don't," Forboud replied. "He's never said more. But, each time it's slipped from his lips, it's been when he studyied the land maps bordering Nagdor. Whenever I've asked what he meant, he shrugged off my question and changed the subject. He's never told me more."

"Never?"

Forboud shook his head.

"He insisted that you remain by my side and aid me with your council since I was appointed king."

"That brother, I can do."

"But given that he's never told you more about this coming war, you think maybe his mind has a few cogs loose? We have no true evidence."

"Perhaps." Forboud sighed. "What should we do?"

Boldair shrugged. "The only thing we can."

"And that be?"

"We return to Nagdor."

"Like that?" Forboud asked. "Leave him to his death?"

"Nothing more we can do here."

"We could send a medic to examine him."

"For what purpose? He'll be dead before too long anyway. Perhaps, he's caught a blight of some sort with all the undead they battled?" Boldair replied. "Or perhaps his madness stems from the rich unmined veins along the mountain ridges?"

Forboud frowned. "Shouldn't his trial take place before the Dwarven Council and *not* before a half-elf queen? Her throne does not supersede ours."

Two Hoffnung guards turned toward Forboud and Boldair with their hands placed on the hilt of their sheathed blades.

"Be careful, brother," Boldair said with a firm gaze. "Speaking ill of Queen Taube will have you in the dungeon with father. Even though the war against the Vykings has ended, the Hoffnung Guard remain on high alert. Probably will be for quite some time to come."

Forboud glanced toward the guards, shook his head, and lowered his voice. "Having father's trial in Hoffnung won't settle well for Nagdor, and you know it."

Boldair sighed. "Bah! It'll have to suffice."

"Why?"

"Because I'm not about to attempt transporting father across Aetheaon for another trial. Staggnuns and Thorgum agree that father's execution takes place *here.*"

"And I suppose you cast the third vote?" Forboud asked.

Boldair frowned. "I do not oppose their judgment, which by every means is sound through and through."

Forboud shook his head. Tears burned his eyes.

"I know this is difficult, Forboud," Boldair said. "I wish there be a better way, but there is none."

"Your heart isn't as heavy as mine."

"Your assumption's correct," Boldair replied. "I've no doubt in the future that today will turn to one of regret. A time will come when I'll wish to consult his advice, and I won't be able. When a father dies, his children become true adults. We must make our own decisions and hope they're correct."

"Boldair, you don't know Nagdor's council like I do. Should word get to them of your quickness to allow father's execution without an outright protest and petition before the Dwarven Council, you'll lose favor with them. Father never spoke highly of you to them."

"Ah, dat's no secret."

"They'll view you with utter hostility, brother. Mark me words," Forboud said.

"I've the feeling you do already," Boldair said.

"Not true."

"Isn't it? You're 'aving difficulty hiding your loyalty to father."

Forboud formed fists and hammered the top of the wall. He grunted and struck a fist to his chest. "Aye! I'm torn in me feelings. I don't want to believe our father's a traitor. I can't fully accept it but know I must. Dat part saddens me most. I spent more time with him than you. He trained me. We talked daily, except when I travelled with you. And somehow, at some unknown time, his mind altered. You'd think I'd have seen it long ago. Blasted! I can't even see it now!"

Boldair placed a hand on Forboud's shoulder. "Aye, he's not the same. Though you may not believe me, I ache inside. Nowhere as deeply as you. Regardless of he and I's differences, he's still me father."

"Then 'ave compassion enough to remain for his execution," Forboud said. "He's betrayed Hoffnung's crown, but if we're not there during his last moments, we've betrayed him as well."

Boldair let his hand slide from Forboud's shoulder. He shook his head. "Brother, it's not the same thing. I cannot wait behind to see his final moments. It's not something I wish to see, and not a memory I wish to keep, either."

Tears brimmed in Forboud's eyes until they spilled and trickled down his cheeks, soaking into his thick beard. "Brother, me heart is heavy at your decision."

"I'm sorry, Forboud. Truly, I am."

"As am I. But I'll honor your wishes and return home with you. No animosity, I swear it. But my grief will burden me for some time to come."

"I understand."

"And if it seems I hold anger and hatred, that be toward me-self. Not you."

"Good to know. Perhaps in time, we'll understand the truth behind our father's actions and what distorted his mind beyond return."

"Aye." Forboud gave a firm nod.

CHAPTER 6

"*L*et's gather our belongings and make our way to Meadwyrm Pass. Drinks are on me," Boldair said.

Forboud stared at the bay from the lift's ledge. His blue eyes shimmered, greatly resembling the water, but without enlightened radiance. His eyes toiled darker, like a storm brewed overhead and a destructive whirlpool was forming beneath his feet. Despair consumed him.

Boldair frowned with concern. "Did ye hear me?"

"Aye, I heard," Forboud whispered. "Drinks plummet the sorrow of a heart far deeper than it should suffer. Leave me to me pain."

Boldair left Forboud to stare at the bay. He walked to where Dwiskter and Drucis stood talking to an old peddler. The old man wore a tattered robe with a hood pulled over his head. His wiry white beard twirled down his soiled frayed tunic. He gently patted the side of his packhorse's head. The horse was weighted down with heavy wares.

Drucis raised both hands in the air as he spoke. "Aye, that be when the Horned Beastlord hefted up his ax and came at me full speed. His giant hooves beat the ground with such vibrating force that I almost lost me footing. His eyes blazed like hot coals and smoke streamed from his nose. In seconds, he was upon me."

The peddler puffed his pipe with a half grin spread on his face. "What happened then, Dwarf?"

Drucis leaned forward with wild eyes and flushed cheeks. Spittle flew from his mouth as he told the tale. "Ah, I sidestepped him. He brought down his ax and sliced through his right knee, causing him to topple forward with a bleating cry. He turned his head toward me and flames flickered from his blackened mouth. A second later, I lopped off its horned head, which is now mounted in the Gorefest Tavern."

"That's all?"

"What do ya mean, is that all? You think you'd do better?" Drucis asked. "A crazed Beastlord? Nah, there's no way—"

"No, I meant, was his head the only trophy you took?"

"*Oh?* Oh, no," Drucis said, shaking his head. He turned the hilt of his battle ax to show two large polished topaz stones and a blood ruby. "These I found in his coin pouch."

The peddler cast a greedy gaze at the gleaming gems. His shadowed eyes flashed a brief glimmer of red.

"Ah, now, don't be coveting these."

The old man held his pipe and gently shook his head. "Those don't draw my interest."

"Rare gems draw anyone's interest," Dwiskter said, stepping closer to Drucis.

"No?" Drucis asked.

"No," the man replied. "I'm more curious where you happened upon one of these Beastlords since they're a rare creature to encounter."

"There be more common than you might think," Boldair said.

The peddler regarded Boldair with sudden interest. He pointed an aged, crooked finger. "You … you look familiar. Perhaps I've seen you during my travels. A tavern, maybe?"

Boldair offered a bold grin and chuckled. "Aye, I've visit a vast number of taverns. Some are like second homes."

"Before he became king," Drucis said.

"King?"

The man bowed slightly. "Your Highness. I am honored."

Boldair regarded the man suspiciously. "Forget the formalities. We're not in Nagdor."

"Nagdor?"

"Aye."

The peddler stood in silence for several seconds. The hood prevented any of them from seeing his eyes or the clear details of his face. "But are you not still a king, regardless of what kingdom or hamlet you visit?"

"Aye," Boldair said with a simple nod. His face reddened. "Still not used to the title. That's all."

"I see," the man said. "How long have you been King?"

Dwiskter frowned and stepped between Boldair and the peddler. "What business be it of yours?"

"Pardon?" the peddler asked, taking a step back and pulling the packhorse's halter to keep it close to him.

"Dwiskter," Boldair said firmly but softy, shaking his head. "It's all right."

"No, he asks too many questions, Sire," Dwiskter said. He frowned fiercely at the old man and placed his hand upon the hilt of his ax. "You've another game at play, don't you?"

The peddler studied Dwiskter for a few moments before finally shaking his head. "No, honestly, I don't. Sorry to have troubled you. I'll be on my way. Lots of wares to sell and no need to waste *my* time or yours by being held suspect by Dwarves outside their own kingdom."

"Hey!" Dwiskter said, pulling his ax slightly out of the sheath.

Boldair placed his hand upon Dwiskter's and squeezed. "Let 'em go."

Boldair pulled Dwiskter to the side of the cobblestone path and allowed the peddler to pass with his packhorse. After the peddler was out of hearing range, Boldair said, "What be the meaning of dat?"

"Not sure," Dwiskter said, sheathing his ax. "I've an uneasy feeling 'bout him."

"He didn't pose a threat toward me," Boldair said. "Not in any regard."

"Perhaps not," Dwiskter replied, "but we can't take that chance being so far from Nagdor."

Boldair nodded. "Perhaps, but let's not be so ready to alienate passersby. After all, a King must show diplomacy. No need to create unnecessary enemies."

"Aye," Dwiskter said. His shoulders drooped slightly. "I want ya to know that I've got your back."

"No need to tell me," Boldair said with a broad grin. He patted a firm hand upon Dwiskter's shoulder. "I know ya do, and I greatly appreciate it."

The peddler led his packhorse through the morning tradesmen without offering a glance over his shoulder. The citizens approaching the lifts were dressed in finer linens than those often seen in the market square. They were merchants who came to the port, perhaps to trade or wait for goods unloaded from the ships. Some were more arrogant than any aristocrat.

"That sight should fill anyone with delight," Boldair said, looking off the lifts' ledge at the harbor.

"What?" Drucis asked with a curious smile.

"Every kingdom knows the devastation the Vykings caused, but merchant ships haven't abandoned Hoffnung. The charred Vyking ship hulls stand a reminder to the victory Taniesse and her sisters won in this harbor."

Dwiskter grinned. "Aye, I watched the filthy Vykings rush from their ships the night they invaded. I was down there when their ships slipped into the harbor. I must admit, moments of fear almost paralyzed me. *Almost.*" He cackled. "But me fury overcame it. I took down a few Vykings before getting to the lifts. I missed seeing their ships and sails burst into flames. That'd 'ave been a glorious sight."

Boldair laughed heartily and nodded. "Aye. But we saw the aftermath."

"Yes, it shall be a long time before the Vykings recover from their losses," Dwiskter said. "But dat night … one thing still haunts me."

"What's dat?"

"How close I was to the Plague-bringer but I was unable to get to him before he vanished."

"We'll cross paths with him again," Boldair said.

"Dat I've not doubt," Dwiskter replied. "But it could've ended dat night, had I reached him."

"Possibly," Boldair said, nodding. "Or worse, he'd 'ave inflicted you with the plague, and you'd be one of his."

Dwiskter thought about Boldair's statement for several silence.

"The good thing is dat Mors has been weakened. We can hope others find a way to destroy him while his power has diminished."

"Perhaps we should've gone with Riese and Prince Manfrid to attack King Obed," Dwiskter said. His eyes gleamed with the thought of returning to battle. "Obed's tied to Mors."

"I know. I greatly considered joining Riese's battle," Boldair said. "If not for other commitments."

"Taking the throne in Nagdor?" Drucis asked.

"Aye," Boldair replied. "'Tis time I took my role more seriously. Less drinking and tavern tales, though I will sorely miss such occasions. It's time I settle down and seek less adventures."

"Wait now," Drucis said. "You're not saying that we're skipping the Meadwyrm Pass drink that sets your insides on fire now, are ye?"

"Goodness sake's, no!" Boldair said with a broad grin. "A King mustn't go back on his word, now should he?"

Drucis released a heavy sigh. "Good. You got me worried there for a moment."

"Sorry," Boldair said. "No, I'd not make a Dwarf suffer such worry, especially over the promise of drinks. I'd almost wager you only manage half a shot of the molten drink."

"Bah! If it's a wager ya want—"

"Boldair!" a female said.

Boldair turned to see a tall, muscular woman dressed in armor with her midriff exposed. The golden dragon belt studded with various gems encircled her waist and hugged her right side. Her black-bladed sword hung on her belt.

"Taniesse?"

"I'm surprised you've tarried in Hoffnung. I suspected you'd departed for Nagdor days ago," she said.

Boldair nodded. "Aye, we planned to be gone before sunrise this morning, but I needed to visit father one last time before his execution."

At the mention of his father, Forboud turned his brooding attention away from the bay and joined them.

Drucis and Dwiskter stood to each side of Boldair and studied Taniesse's face.

"Far be it for me to offer bad news concerning Ulthor's execution," Taniesse said, "but the four of you need to accompany me."

"To where?" Boldair asked, cocking a brow.

"We need to discuss your father's destiny," she replied.

"Why?" Forboud asked, stepping behind Boldair.

"All will be explained, but not here. Not in public."

"Then where?" Boldair.

"Come," she said.

The Dwarves followed Taniesse from the lifts and through a narrow alleyway. She stood a good three feet taller than them so she lessened her strides as she walked.

"So tell me, treasure-hunter, do you feel differently now that you're King?" she asked.

Boldair stared at his feet while walking. "Ah, it be no different."

"None?"

"No."

"I suppose it's too early for the realization to set upon you, but you'll feel a King's weighted burden soon enough," Taniesse said.

"What do ya mean?"

She laughed but never slowed her pace. "You'll see. You've yet to sit upon the throne and give the commands or enact judgment. You're far from your kingdom, but I assure you, your life will forever change once you've ascended the throne."

"*Now*, ye have me worried."

"Worried? Actually, worry's the best frame of mind for a new king to possess."

"How so?"

She grinned and glanced down at him, staring into his curious eyes. "Because it means you're less likely to make hasty decisions. It *means* you're finally understanding what true wisdom is. You've actually matured since our first meeting, which impresses me."

"Bah! I don't know about dat." Boldair shook his head. For her every step, he hurried two to keep up, and the other Dwarves worked hard to match his pace.

"Every decision you make as king has consequences, so you must weigh each mandate for its advantages and disadvantages before finalizing any resolution."

"'Tis true," Boldair said.

Forboud rolled his eyes. "Phht!"

Boldair's jaw tightened and his eyes narrowed, but due to trying to match Taniesse's pace, he didn't bother to turn toward his brother. "Where are you taking us, Taniesse?"

Taniesse turned right onto Market Street. "Queen Taube has requested your presence."

"Me?"

Taniesse nodded. "All of you, actually."

"Why?" Forboud asked.

"To further discuss your father's fate," she replied.

"What?" Boldair asked, his brow furrowing. "I thought the decision had already been decided."

"In ways, it has," Taniesse said, "but an execution is never rushed."

"Why not? Even if the crime has been proven?"

"Even if the guilt has been proven," she replied.

"Father confessed before Staggnuns and Thorgum," Boldair said in a gruff voice.

"Yes, we know."

Boldair huffed his disdain but offered no words.

"You're not wishing to rush his death, are you?" Taniesse asked with a side-glance.

"He is," Forboud said.

"Is that true, Boldair?" she asked without a tinge of judgment.

"No," he replied. He turned and pointed a sharp finger at his brother. "If I need your input, Forboud, I'll ask ya. Now, pipe down!"

Taniesse glanced at Boldair without slowing her steps. "I sense great hostility between you and your brother, Boldair. Is this because the Northern Dwarven Alliance named you king instead of he?"

"Partly," Boldair grumbled.

"Aye, it is!" Forboud said. "Nothing partly about it."

Taniesse shook her head. "I never expected such."

"What?" Boldair asked.

"That the two of you would come to odds over the throne."

"I'm not at odds. *He* is. I never asked for the throne," Boldair said. "Forboud believes he deserves it because father trained him as a warrior and potential diplomat."

"I see the logic in his ambition," Taniesse replied.

"But tis not true, O' Great One," Forboud said. "I don't covet the crown. I don't feel entitled to replace father. The roots of this go much deeper."

Taniesse nodded slightly. "I see."

"Oh, *much* deeper!" Boldair said.

"In what way?" she asked, staring at Boldair.

"Forboud's against father's execution, even though father is guilty. He wishes to turn a blind eye to father's crimes."

"That's *not* true!"

"Forboud," Taniesse said softly. "You had a more intimate relationship with Ulthor than Boldair?"

"I wouldn't call it *intimate*." Forboud snarled the word with bitterness. "But he and I spent a lot of time hunting, training, and discussing Nagdor's defense. I know the mining maps like the back of me hand. Father even discussed the plans for digging deeper mines to find better ore veins."

"So his execution is more costly to you than Boldair," she said.

"Aye."

"Boldair," she said, "you and your father weren't close?"

"Never," he replied in a low voice.

"So the division between the two of you is jealousy over his affections?"

"Affections! Bah!" Boldair said, balling a tight fist. "Father has no affections. None except for himself. And the way dat I see it, for his crimes he should pay the price. So I don't see what this meeting we're being led to has to do with dat. He's admitted his guilt. Death is his price."

"No one's questioning his guilt or his sentence," Taniesse replied.

"It seems dat way," Boldair whispered.

Drucis gave a side-glance stare at Taniesse. "Didn't Staggnuns and Thorgum already place the sentence?"

"They did," Taniesse said.

"So is dat going to change?" Dwiskter asked.

"Probably not," she replied.

"Then what's to discuss?" Boldair asked.

"That will be acknowledged once we sit with Queen Taube," Taniesse replied.

"Is there any chance he'll escape his fate?" Forboud asked. "Or that his sentence could be lessened?"

"That's doubtful," Taniesse said. "Let's discuss this no further, until we've met with Taube."

CHAPTER 7

Boldair and Taniesse stood at the railing of the high balcony that overlooked Queen Taube's Royal Garden.

"The city's destruction is barely noticeable," Boldair said, studying the gardens and streets below. "Can barely tell that a war took place."

Taniesse smiled. "The peasants and citizens have worked hard to erase the damage."

"Aye," Boldair said.

"Elven artisans from Woodnog offered their services to replace the statues and the decor the Vykings destroyed."

"Icevale and Nagdor 'ave metalworkers to reinforce the archways and gates," Boldair said. "The scorched ramparts are almost repaired."

Dwiskter and Drucis sat on a stone bench with various Elven runic symbols carved in the artwork. Forboud stood near a fountain with his hands clasped behind his back. His sad eyes warned of the unsettled turmoil churning in the depths of his soul.

Queen Taube entered the upper patio, adorned in a sparkling gold gown. A deep sapphire stone set in gold hung on a thread of silver around her neck. She wore a glimmering ruby ring on her right hand, and an onyx ring on the left. Almost hidden by the long sleeves of her gown were several turquoise tattoos of protective runes.

Dwiskter and Drucis stood, offering slight bows of reverence and respect for the half-elf Queen. From the corner of his eye, Forboud noticed their homage, turned, and did the same.

Boldair and Taniesse smiled in response to Taube's radiant smile. The Queen's eyes glowed brightly like the sparkling gems she wore. A web of magic enveloped her. Tendrils of her magic swept outward, reaching and searching, it seemed, to detect the slightest trace of unseen malice or inner hostility any of her guests might harbor.

Although Boldair was unable to cast magic, he was more than capable of recognizing and sensing it. When he stepped within several feet of Taube's proximity, the magical gems set in his weapons glowed for a moment in response to Taube's magical aura.

Taube's expressions didn't hint of any uneasiness or fear, but the magic leaping from her toward her guests indicated she was still on high alert, even though she reigned on Hoffnung's throne.

"Please," Queen Taube said, "be seated."

Boldair and Taniesse left the balcony and approached the table. Taube motioned two of her servants with a graceful wave of her hand. The servants carried heavy wine pitchers, and promptly filled the prearranged tankards on the oak circular table.

"I extend my thanks to you, Taniesse," Taube said, "for finding King Boldair before he and his party left Hoffnung."

Taniesse acquiesced a nod.

Boldair lifted his tankard and sniffed its contents. Despite his want to snarl his nose in protest to the drink offered, out of respect for Taube, he took a sip of the wine. He greatly wished it contained Dwarven Stout or something stronger. To his surprise the wine was pleasantly sweet, but not enough to mask the bitter taste of hops, causing his sip to progress into a larger gulp. He set the tankard down hard on the table, and out of habit, wiped his mouth with the back of his hand.

Amusement danced in Taniesse's eyes and she bit her lower lip, holding back her laughter for the new king's rude mannerism. Boldair's gaze met hers, and he blushed.

Under his breath, Boldair huffed, "Sorry."

Taube smiled. "No apologies necessary. I wish to thank you, King Boldair, for your aid in the retaking of Hoffnung's throne. Taniesse and Lady Dawn informed me of your bravery, as that of your fellow comrades seated at the table, and how you fought against the Vyking tyrants that ransacked my kingdom. Dawn is truly impressed by your valor."

"Aye," Boldair said with a sheepish grin. "Happy to help. How's Lady Dawn?"

Taube's eyes met his for a moment. She smiled briefly before laughing softly. "Proud to *not* be Queen, I suppose. The last message a raven delivered stated that she and Caen are exploring every crag and forest in Aetheaon. Her spirit's too wild for her to settle herself with the obligations of a throne. For now, at least, and of course, I cannot blame her wanting to see more than the inner castle walls. Her wanderlust is far greater than I ever had."

"Oh, but she's a valiant fighter through and through," Boldair said, raising his empty tankard in a toast.

"Aye!" Dwiskter and Drucis said in unison.

Forboud observed in silence, not offering any physical response.

"Her need to avenge your betrayal by Lord Waxxon was ruthless and boosted our morale," Boldair said. "I fought proudly beside her."

"As did I!" Dwiskter said.

Taube's face beamed with pride. "A princess gown … she's outgrown. She never seemed to fit into the role of a princess. She was more like her father than me. She's rambunctious and free-spirited." She laughed. "I cannot count the number of times she snuck from her room to hunt rats with the sewer rat-killers. Wearing one of her best dresses, too. She once brought back a string of dead rats and showed them to me with great pride."

Boldair, Dwiskter, and Drucis roared with laughter.

Taube shook her head. Her eyes were lost in memories. "No matter how much I tried to explain what it meant to be a princess, she paid me no mind. Nessa had a difficult time keeping track of her. Dawn was like the son Erik never had. Perhaps with her, he got the best of both, a daughter who served as both. He took her stag hunting in the forests many times when she was little, thinking I didn't know where they had gone." She sighed. "I cannot rightly call her a princess now. Perhaps I never could with complete honesty. I still find it difficult calling her a warrioress, though that's what she is in heart and spirit."

"Indeed," Boldair said, staring into Taube's eyes. A slight grin parted his thick beard.

"Dawn insisted that you be knighted into the Dragon Skull Order, and rightly so." The radiant smile on her face faded. Sadness filled her eyes. "In spite of your father's betrayal to my husband, my heart holds no animosity toward you. You're not responsible for Ulthor's actions."

"Aye, milady," Boldair said. "I knew nothing of my father's state of affairs. To put it bluntly, I still don't. Rest assured that once I return to Nagdor, I'll overturn any of his affairs that are damaging to Hoffnung or our other peaceful kingdoms. And, because of his greed and the ... his contribution to King Erik's ... death, I expect you'll carry out his execution promptly."

Various emotions struggled on Taube's face. "In time he'll be executed, but I'm afraid not in the *immediate* future."

"How's dat?" Boldair straightened in his seat. His eyes narrowed. "And why not? He confessed and admitted his guilt to his hand in King Erik's demise."

Taube and Taniesse both nodded.

"He did," Taube said.

"Then what reason delays his punishment?" Boldair asked.

"While it's true he confessed to his crimes and involvement in the battle where Erik met his end," Taube said, "it's ... well, I need *more* than his confession."

Dwiskter downed wine, set the tankard on the table, and winked at the female servant. The servant blushed, filled his tankard, and offered a slight curtsy.

"What more do you need?" Boldair asked.

"A trial," she replied.

His eyebrows rose. "A trial? Why?"

Taube folded her hands and rested them in her lap. "Regardless of his admission of guilt, a trial is necessary."

"What do you expect to discover from a trial that you don't already know?" Boldair asked.

"That's just what I hope to find. Discovery."

Boldair frowned.

"Ulthor didn't act alone," Taube said softly. "He couldn't have."

Boldair thought for several moments. His brow tightened. His eyes brightened and he looked into hers. "You think others in Nagdor aided him?"

"It's possible," Taube replied.

Boldair placed his fists upon the table and leaned forward. "I shall find them."

Taniesse shook her head. "Undisclosed enemies are not readily found, especially when they don't wish to be discovered."

"Father knows more of what happened," Boldair said, "but he'd never confess it to me."

Forboud adjusted in his seat and cleared his throat. "He might to me."

Boldair glared at his brother and pointed a stern finger. "Oh, you'd like dat, wouldn't you? Father's scheming to have you upon the throne. Perhaps you've conspired with him and dat's why you're so insistent to talk to him?"

Forboud shook his head.

"No, brother, I forbid it," Boldair said. "I cannot risk letting you speak in private to him."

Taniesse raised one brow. "I understand why you don't trust your own brother but you need to set your differences aside, at least for now."

"I wish I could. Father told me that he'd rather have Forboud on the throne than myself. Ever since I went to the prison and spoke to father this morning, Forboud won't stop his insistence to visit him. Like me brother said earlier, there's something *deeper* at hand."

"You think they're in cahoots?" Queen Taube asked.

"I won't put that past them."

"You don't think Forboud can get the answers you need?" Taniesse asked.

Boldair spread his stubby fingers wide and his hands to the sides of his head, adding his dramatic expression like he did when telling his tavern tales. "Father's mind is scattered. Forboud knows it, and apparently Thorgum and Staggnuns do, too. Otherwise, I don't think they'd have declared me as the one to succeed my father."

Taube frowned, looking from Taniesse to Boldair. "Do they have such a right?"

"Aye, they do," Boldair said with a firm nod. "The Northern Dwarven Alliance oversees all three of our kingdoms. But to answer your question, Forboud would be no more successful in getting honest answers from Ulthor than myself."

"There are ways to get answers from him without a trial," Dwiskter said. His hand rested on the hilt of his ax. "Give me a half hour with Ulthor. I'll make him talk. I swear it."

"You're speaking of the *former* king," Forboud said. His eyes narrowed, his face flushed red, and he placed tight fists on the table, slightly rising from his seat.

"Yes, *your* former king," Dwiskter said. "Now, he's nothing more than a Dwarf without a crown and without a throne. He's no longer king. He tarnished the crown, and now, the punishment—"

"No!" Taube said, rising to her feet. "I won't allow Ulthor to suffer such treatment while inside *my* prison. That's *never* been tolerated in the past, and it most certainly will not come into play *now*."

"You've my permission," Boldair said, gazing at Dwiskter.

"It's not permission I seek," Queen Taube said. Her eyes narrowed with anger and wrath.

Boldair flicked his angered gaze to Taniesse. "And you're okay with this?"

"Why shouldn't I be?" Taniesse shrugged.

"My father tried to kill you in order to keep his ties with the Dredgemen a secret."

"Believe me, Boldair, no one else seated here would like to see your father executed for his actions more than Queen Taube and myself. We have every right to seek his death. If I relied upon revenge, I'd side with you, Boldair. But as you already know, had I wanted your father dead, I had ample opportunity to char his body on the snow-covered mountain without anyone having knowledge of his demise. Perhaps sparing him at that moment wasn't the best decision, but killing him, and believe me I fought hard not to, would not have gained me any better advantage. And had I done so, we'd have lost the truth. Forever. We'd have never known of his secret alliance."

"Then let me propose an alternate solution," Boldair said, relaxing his fists and then placing his palms upon the table.

Taniesse stared at him in silence for several long moments. "And what's that?"

"*You* visit him in his cell. Reveal to him who you are and what you will do should he not give you the answers you seek."

Taniesse entertained a smile for several seconds. Her eyes indicated her mind was tracing possible outcomes of visiting Ulthor in private. But then the coldness of a serpent darkened her eyes. She shook her head, shaking herself from her imagination. "I'm sorry, but I have to decline such an opportunity."

"You'd kill him, wouldn't you?" Boldair asked with a shrewd grin.

Taniesse flicked her gaze from his, and she folded her hands upon her lap. "That would not be my first solution."

"Then what?" Drucis asked. "You thought of something."

Taniesse nodded slightly. "My meeting him would never come to the proper fruition."

"And why not?" Boldair asked.

"Because Ulthor would say practically anything to *make* me kill him. He'd arouse my anger beyond the point of no return, and sadly, he'd suffer less by my fire than he does by staying alive and being confined in a prison cell."

"Meaning?" Queen Taube asked.

"His death would be instant," Taniesse replied coldly.

"It'd save us the agony of a trial," Boldair said.

Taniesse shook her head. "Never act in haste, Boldair. Your father is more stubborn than you and less likely to offer information, no matter how severely Dwiskter or I tortured him. He'd probably die before he'd divulge further confessions."

"Trust me," Boldair said. "A trial won't get you the desired answers, either."

"Perhaps not," Taube said, "but my conscience will be clear."

Boldair placed his elbows on the table and leaned forward. "So dat's what this is all about, eh? *Your* conscience?"

Taube's jaw tightened. Fury darkened her eyes.

Taniesse shook her head. "Careful, Boldair. You're both rulers. There's no need to breach your relationship with the Queen this early in your rulership. Your kingdom needs hers as well as she needs yours."

"Aye," Boldair said with an abrupt sigh. "My apologies, milady. I've let me emotions get the better of me."

Taube took a deep breath, held it, and slowly released it. Her anger subsided and tears crested in her eyes. "As have I."

Taniesse offered an aristocratic smile. "I think it's fair to say, with all that has occurred over these past few months, our emotions are all running high."

Taube straightened her gown with her hands, nodded, and seated herself. "You're right, Taniesse. Some of my wounds are still tender."

"Aye," Boldair said.

"Is it necessary that I be present for his trial?" Boldair asked.

Taube shook her head. "No. Not at all."

"Good," Boldair said, standing. He eyed Dwiskter and then Drucis. "Let's go."

"Boldair," Taube said. "By no means am I attempting to place you at odds with me. I must at least attempt to get necessary answers, if possible. Should he refuse to comply, judgment falls in the courtyard. There'll be no further delay."

"Aye, no bitterness or anger from me, Your Highness," Boldair said.

"One thing you should understand," Taniesse said, rising and placing her hand on the hilt of her sword.

"Yes, Ol' Great One?"

"Whatever secret alliances your father holds are not only Queen Taube's enemies, they're also yours. Which means, most likely, these enemies reside nearer to Nagdor than to Hoffnung. They might not take too kindly in your assuming the throne. In fact, they might want you dead."

Boldair frowned and chewed his lower lip. "Aye. If father doesn't give the information you seek, I highly suggest you take Dwiskter's suggestion to find the answers we all seek."

"Whatever becomes necessary will be decided in court," Queen Taube said.

Boldair's eyes narrowed. He nodded his disgruntled agreement. "As you wish."

"Boldair," Taniesse said. "Where shall I find you, should I need to speak with you?"

"We be headed to Nagdor, although not immediately. I have a few … side places I wish to visit first."

"Then you need to understand my warning."

"What warning? Dat there could be enemies within Nagdor?"

"Yes," Taniesse said.

"Aye! I've taken that to heart."

"No," she said. "What I mean is that until we find who's aligned themselves with your renegade father, you cannot return to Nagdor. Until they're removed, there'll be no coronation for you to assume the throne."

Boldair cocked a brow. "What?"

Taniesse nodded slowly. "Do not return to Nagdor until I deem such is safe. No sense having a king murdered before he's properly placed on the throne."

"If I don't return to Nagdor, I'll be viewed as a coward," Boldair said. "I'll have no one think such of me."

"How will your death prove otherwise?" Taniesse asked. "Nothing's foolhardy by avoiding unknown enemies."

"Then I should reside as King in secret?"

Taniesse shrugged. "For now."

Boldair shook his head and grumbled under his breath as he left the table and headed for the stairs. Dwiskter, Drucis, and Forboud followed.

"Dat went well," Boldair said, marching through the palace gate. Dwiskter eyed Drucis with a confused expression. "Ya think so?"

"Bloody hells! Of course not!" Boldair said, clenching his fists and growling.

"So what now?" Drucis asked. "Are we leaving Hoffnung?"

Boldair waved his finger in the air. "You bet your arse we are. I'd rather shave me beard than listen to more of dat—"

"Just go on an' say it, brother," Forboud said. "You want father dead. Admit such and get it out in the open."

Boldair spun in an instant with his double-edge battle-ax drawn and the razor-edge blade inches from Forboud's face. Boldair's cheeks flushed red and his eyes narrowed in fury. "I've had enough of your meddling."

Forboud's eyes widened. His hands rose to his sides in surrender. "Have I offended ye with me words? Is dat it? Or does the truth make you despise me even more?"

"Ya know not what ya talk about," Boldair said, stepping closer. "There's no truth in your words, so stop your prickling and prattling. Else, you're going find out what my anger and wrath are really like."

Dwiskter placed his hand against Forboud's chest and eased him back. Dwiskter stepped between Boldair and Forboud, shaking his head furiously while staring at the ax. "Boldair, this is not like you. Sheath your ax. King or not, I'll not allow you to slay your brother."

"Then bloody keep him the hell away from me, and if he presents such lies again, neither you nor Drucis or the both of you combined shall stop me."

"What lies have I told?" Forboud asked. "Explain, brother."

"Aye," Dwiskter said. "I agree with Forboud."

"As do I," Drucis said. "Explain or I refuse to accompany you any further."

Boldair glared harshly at Drucis. "Is dat so?"

"Aye," Drucis said with a firm jaw and an unflinching gaze.

Boldair huffed, and he ground his teeth. He turned his attention back to Forboud. "Explain what exactly?"

"You said dat I have presented mistruths," Forboud said with anger in his eyes. "I have done no such thing. And if ya think dat I 'ave, tell me what lies they are!"

Boldair took a deep breath, held it, and slowly exhaled. His jaw tightened. "Father told me dat he wanted you on the throne, dat he'd prepared you to take his place, and yet, you keep denying that. I 'ave no choice but to believe dat's why you want so badly to visit him in private. You deny it?"

Forboud gave a firm single nod. "I do. I doubt you believe me, but I've no reason to lie. But since your appointment set by King Staggnuns and King Thorgum to replace father, I've become your enemy. For the life in me, I don't understand your sudden hostility or why—" Forboud shook his head and looked down.

Boldair's shoulders slumped. He kept his eyes fastened on his brother for a few seconds more before glancing away. "Go on. What else?"

Forboud lowered his hands. "Explain *why* you want father dead so badly. I understand his betrayal and his lies being a reason for his imprisonment, but why do ye push so hard for his *immediate* execution?"

Boldair lowered the ax and sighed. He placed the head of the ax on the path and then rested his hands atop the hilt, propping himself. He shook his head. "It's not so much you, Forboud, dat bears me anger toward father or dat he'd rather you rule over Nagdor than I."

"Then what?"

Boldair stood in silence for several minutes. His eyes grew distant, deep in memory, until finally he snapped to attention and cleared his throat. "Unprovoked, father tried to kill Taniesse and there was the possibility that he might have been successful. That angers me greatly."

"Why does dat anger you?" Forboud asked. "He didn't succeed. Why does dat remain an issue for you?"

"*Why?* Had he killed her, I'd 'ave never known her. She wouldn't 'ave become my friend. I'd 'ave never led a battalion into battle for Lady Dawn to recapture Taube's throne. I'd still be tavern-hopping and telling tales to entertain drunken peasants. I'd not be king. Taniesse is the major reason I became king. Father tried to kill her. His failure changed my destiny. For his misdeeds, he should never be pardoned."

Dwiskter's eyebrows rose. "Pardoned? I understand your feelings. Dat's never going to happen. Ulthor won't receive *any* pardon. You heard dat, from both the Queen and Taniesse."

"Aye. Dat's what they *say.*" Boldair's brow furrowed with concern. "But the more Forboud presses the Queen and Taniesse—"

Drucis shook his head. "No. No amount of persuasion could alter Ulthor's judgment. Such a thing would spike a titanium wedge between the Dwarven Kingdoms and Hoffnung forever. That won't be happening."

"Aye," Boldair said. "Maybe not a pardon as we know them to be. But there's the chance he might somehow escape."

"From Hoffnung's prison? Are ye serious?" Dwiskter asked. "No. That's simply not possible. That prison's the most secure in all the kingdoms."

"From physical attacks, perhaps," Boldair said. "But ... magic ... magic could penetrate the walls, unlock locks, mesmerize guards—"

Drucis gave Boldair a shrewd stare.

Forboud placed his hands upon Boldair's shoulders. "Brother, I swear to you I've no interest in the throne. Never have I known you to worry such, nor have you ever threatened my life. You've faced numerous dangers when you explored dark dragon caves while searching for treasure, without ever a fear or worry. Our father has placed himself into condemnation. And yes, I ache with grief at his loss to me, but I've accepted what his fate has become. My last words dat I would 'ave spoken to him, had you allowed it, would 'ave been to express my sorrow for the reprehensible damage and divisions he has caused. Nothing more did I wish to disclose to him. I swear it. So, you 'ave no need to worry o'er what you thought I *might've* said. Let's go. Wherever you lead, I follow, and ye 'ave me axes at your disposal."

"What has you so uneasy, Boldair?" Dwiskter asked.

Boldair shook his head and stared at his thick hands folded atop the hilt of his ax. "Maybe father was right. I worry that placing me as king might've been a mistake. I fear I'll disappoint Taniesse, King Staggnuns, and King Thorgum. They might discover that I be a better treasure-hunter than a ruler."

Forboud slammed his hands firmly upon Boldair's steel pauldrons, causing Boldair to look into his eyes. "You'll do fine, Boldair. And ya got me at your side for guidance should you need it."

"Us, too," Drucis said. He winked. "Now 'bout that drink you were promising me."

"Aye!" Dwiskter said with a broad grin. "Don't think we've forgotten 'bout dat."

Drucis howled with laughter. "Aye, we best be heading on, eh?"

Boldair straightened, sheathed his ax, and nodded. "I could use a strong drink. I'll hold to me promise of buying the rounds, and let no Dwarf say otherwise."

CHAPTER 9

At the royal stables, the four Dwarves went inside to retrieve their mounts.

Boldair approached the giant dire wolf, Ember, that Ulthor had raised from a cub until mature enough to become the king's mount. The outer thick fur of the wolf was black with an orange-red undercoat. When brushed back, the fur's blended colors resembled glowing, wind-blown embers of smoldering coal. The contrasting colors were why Ulthor named the wolf, Ember.

Boldair reached for Ember's bridle. The wolf's eyes narrowed and focused on Boldair. Ember's huge muzzled snout snarled, exposing its huge teeth. A low growl rumbled deep inside its throat.

"He's taken a fondness for you," Drucis said with a wink.

Dwiskter laughed.

"He has," Boldair said, not offering the slightest smile. "At least he's stopped trying to rip my arm or leg off with his massive jaws."

"I think the muzzle prevents dat," Drucis said with a howling laugh.

Boldair laughed. "He has the muzzle for a reason. The first time I attempt to mount him, he bit and dented my steel bracer. He damn near dragged me to the lifts. It took six Hoffnung guards to pry his mouth open so I could get free. Bloody hell, I won't go into detail about what happened to one of the guards. His sacrifice to free me won't be soon forgotten."

Dwiskter shook his head. "So that explains the nasty bruises on ye forearm, eh?"

"Aye, it took two smiths to pry and cut the bracer off me forearm."

Drucis reared back his head and howled with laughter. "'ave you not informed Ember that you're king?"

"I don't think dat matters to Ember," Dwiskter said.

Boldair shook his head. "Probably not. I doubt any amount of persuasion will ever change his feelings toward me."

Dwiskter winked at the other Dwarves. "That wolf's temperament toward Boldair is the same as Ulthor's."

Boldair chuckled. "Now *dat* be true."

"I don't know, brother," Forboud said. "I think the wolf holds *more* affection for you."

Boldair turned to his brother. Forboud offered a slight, kind smile. "Maybe in time Ember will soften his outlook for me. Doesn't look too promising at the moment."

Drucis and Dwiskter chuckled.

Boldair took the reins, grabbed the steel handle welded to his saddle, and pulled himself up. Ember snarled and shook his head. "Settle down, you big heap of fur and teeth!"

"Are ya capable of getting him to obey?" Drucis asked, leading his giant gray ram from its stall. The ram was equal size to a full-grown horse. Its curled black horns were the size of a market vendor pushcart's wheels. The ram's goatee was braided neatly and looked freshly groomed. Drucis looked the ram in the eyes. "Someone's gone to a lot of effort to fancy ya up, Tusk."

The ram blew air angrily through its flared nostrils. Drucis laughed. "Aye, don't be getting mad at me, Tusk. Trust me, I never paid anyone to sissify ya."

"Nor I," Dwiskter said angrily, holding his ram's reins and shaking his head. His ram's horns were flat and were shaped like large pinchers with the sharp tips pointing forward. The beard of his ram was also separated into different braids. "Will ye have a look at this?"

Boldair looked at the pair of ram mounts and bellowed a hearty laugh. Forboud joined his laughter until he noticed that his ram wore similar braids.

"What in blazes?" Forboud asked. His face flushed hot red. "What dainty elf-kissing prancer's been messing around with our rams?"

Despite Ember's low rumbling growl, Boldair scratched the fur behind the wolf's ears. "Think I'm beginning to like having a wolf now."

Forboud turned and pointed a finger. "You? Did you have someone do this?"

"Me?" Boldair shook his head. "I had *nothing* to do with this. I've been with you the entire time."

"Doesn't mean ya didn't pay some peasant to do this though," Forboud said.

"With everything dat's been occupying my mind … such a prank never occurred to me. But, tis a good one, if ya ask me," Boldair said.

Ember growled and fought against his muzzle.

"What's eating him?" Drucis asked.

"Bah! I never know," Boldair said.

"Something's angering him a heap," Dwiskter said.

"Easy, Ember," Boldair said, scratching behind the wolf's ears even harder.

"Just get him out of here," a high-pitched voice said from behind a stall door.

"Who's there?" Boldair asked. "Show yourself!"

Drucis and Dwiskter placed their hands on their weapons, ready to draw.

"Come out, whoever you be," Drucis said, pulling his ax from over his shoulder.

"I can't unless you take the wolf outside."

"It's me you should worry about, more than the wolf," Drucis said. "Unless I remove his muzzle, that is. Of course, then we're probably *all* in trouble."

Ember growled fiercely. A small shadow moved behind the stall door and the furry face became more visible.

"Viorka?" Boldair asked. "What're you doing 'ere?"

"Trying not to get eaten by your wolf," she replied.

Boldair pulled back on the reins. "I'm holding him back. Come on out."

Dwiskter cocked a brow. "You sure you 'ave him under control? I tend to believe he's much stronger than you."

"Oh, I hold no doubts 'bout dat," Boldair said. "Come out of the stall, Viorka, but keep your distance from Ember."

Viorka, a magical catlike fynx that could turn invisible, stood a bit taller with a tad more bravery. She stepped from the door of the stall and walked a wide sweep away from the growling wolf.

"Why are ya here?" Boldair asked.

"I hoped to find Taniesse," she replied.

"Here? She doesn't have a mount. She doesn't need one."

Viorka offered an embarrassed smile and shrugged her narrow shoulders. "Have you seen her?"

Boldair nodded. "She's in the palace."

Her furry brows rose and her nose scrunched. "She is?"

"With Queen Taube," Drucis said.

"Oh."

Boldair stared at her with curiosity. "What'cha need her for?"

"Adventure, if she plans on traveling soon, and doesn't mind a tagalong."

"Ahh, little cat," Dwiskter said, "if it's adventure you seek, you should travel with us."

Viorka stared at Ember with wide eyes. "I've a feeling I'd be safer *not*."

Boldair grinned, tugging hard on the reins. Although Ember made no attempt to lunge toward Viorka, his resistance to Boldair's hold indicated he'd not given up on the idea. "I think you'd be right 'bout dat."

"The wolf likes him about as much as you," Drucis said, winking at Viorka.

She offered a sheepish grin.

"Were you the one who tied all the fancy knots in my ram's beard?" Dwiskter asked. His eyes narrowed beneath his furrowed brow.

She nodded. "I did."

Dwiskter frowned. "I oughta smack ya with the flat side of me ax."

"It was *you?*" Forboud asked. "What prompted you to do such a thing? Are you trying to soil our reputation? Or do you wish to shame our rams into thinking they be unattractive sheep?"

Viorka shook her head. "Sorry, I got bored."

"Bored? There be lots of things to occupy your mind, other than this!" Forboud said.

"Ah, let her be," Dwiskter said. "No harm done."

"Not until we meet other Dwarves," Forboud said. "We'll be mocked beyond scorn, especially if they've been drinking."

"By then, the knots will have unravelled."

"Doubtful." Forboud rubbed the bridge of his black ram's nose. He took the side of its bridle and led the ram toward the wide door to exit the stables.

Boldair looked at Viorka. "Be glad you didn't try to braid Ember's furry neck. He'd 'ave wolfed ya down. How'd you get past him, anyway?"

"I came inside invisible."

"Invisible?" Dwiskter asked curiously.

She nodded. "Yes."

Dwiskter smiled. "That's interesting."

"Then how'd Ember find you?" Boldair asked.

"I suppose he smelled my scent. I remained invisible the entire time I braided the rams' beards."

Drucis shook his head. "Do you habitually braid others' mounts without permission?"

"I can unbraid them if I've caused you trouble," Viorka said.

Drucis ignore her offer and glanced at Boldair. "What route are we taking?"

Boldair pulled the reins to turn Ember around. Even though the wolf obeyed Boldair's direction, it never took its hungry stare off Viorka. "North, toward Icevale."

"Icevale? Meadwyrm Pass is close to Damdur on the other side of Glacier Ridge. The quicker route would be to travel south, then head west to Bridgebarrow. We can drink our fill there and stay the night at the inn."

"Dat's true," Boldair said, "*if* we travel on the surface. But I know some underground tunnels—"

"Icevale has tunnels, but none burrow in that direction."

Boldair laughed. "Aye, I never said we were going to Icevale."

"Then where?" Drucis asked.

"It's a secret tunnel I found during one of my treasure hunts."

Dwiskter's eyes widened. "You must tell us!"

"I'll do better than dat. We'll travel through an abandoned goblin cavern that leads to Frosthammer."

"Frosthammer?" Drucis said. "Does that city actually exist?"

"You've never been?" Boldair asked perplexed.

Drucis scratched his beard. "No. I've always believed the place to be legend."

"As have I," Dwiskter said. "So it does exist?"

"Aye," Boldair replied. "Getting to Frosthammer is difficult. It requires more dedication and determination than what most surface-dwellers are willing to sacrifice. Ya got to cut into the heart of the frozen mountains. That's why most believe Frosthammer's nothing more than a bard's tale. But I've been there."

Dwiskter and Drucis looked at him in awe as did Viorka.

"Is it true that Frosthammer is the town o'er the edge of the Lava Pits?" Drucis asked.

Boldair rode a disgruntled Ember to the open stable doors. "I must confess that I didn't seek to venture to any plane lower than Frosthammer. I did see a gated off section on the wall that sealed off whatever lies on the other side. The titanium was riveted and chained, so either they don't want anyone passing through that gate, or they don't want whatever be on the other side to *get out*. But a river of molten Steel divides the great city in half."

"Ye have me curiosity now," Drucis said.

"Mine, too," Dwiskter said.

Viorka shivered.

Boldair chuckled. "We'll only pass through the city. No extended stay. They don't welcome outsiders too often. When I was there before, though, they requested my extended stay so they could hear my tales of treasure hunting."

"Since your king now, they'll more than welcome you, eh?" Drucis asked with a grin.

"Ahh, don't be mentioning dat," Boldair said, scratching his chin.

"Why not?"

"Let's just say that my departure wasn't on the best of terms and leave it at dat."

"Wait," Dwiskter said. "You expect us to pass through the city that holds hostility toward you? Do you want us on the other side of metal bars like your father?"

Boldair shook his head. "It's nothing like dat. The King of Frosthammer holds no grievance with me."

"Then what be the problem?" Drucis asked.

Boldair looked away and cleared his throat. "Perhaps it be nothing, but I'd rather not speak of it, for now. We best not waste any more time."

CHAPTER 10

*B*oldair rode Ember ahead of the other Dwarves on the narrow forest trail, but the wolf's temperament was no less forgiving. Boldair half expected the wolf to charge through low branched trees to dislodge him from his saddle, so he kept a tight hold on the reins, as a precaution. Boldair glanced over his shoulder. "I thought you wished to speak to Taniesse, little cat."

Viorka followed the forest trail near the rear of the Dwarves, out of Ember's sight, and stayed partially invisible at times. "I said that I wanted adventure. What could be greater than seeing a city I've never even heard of? That's the best adventure I could ever seek."

"What happens if you become Ember's supper?" Drucis asked, looking over his shoulder at her. A sly grin crept across his face.

"He'd have to catch me first," Viorka said, laughing nervously. Her fearful eyes glanced at Ember. The wolf turned his head, making certain she noticed his hungry gaze. "I plan to stay outside his reach at all times."

"I hate to tell ya," Boldair said, "but the goblin cave entrance and its first series of pathways before we even reach Frosthammer is tight and narrow. We'll be packed together and it'll be nearly impossible to turn around once we enter."

Viorka nodded. "Then I'll stay at the rear. If it's that compacted, Ember cannot possibly turn on me."

"This wolf's full of surprises," Boldair said.

Viorka's voice saddened. "If you'd rather I didn't accompany you, I won't be a nuisance."

"That's *not* what I'm implying," Boldair said.

"Ye aren't bothering me," Dwiskter said.

"Viorka," Boldair said, "You proved herself a great asset when you traveled with me and Taniesse before. I'm honored to 'ave you with us. Besides, you're the perfect scout. I doubt a Forest Elf could hide any better."

"Thanks," she said. A confident grin came to her lips and her whiskers twitched.

Forboud faced her. His face was stern; his eyes cold. "But you must promise not to tie fancy knots in me ram's fur."

"I 'ave to agree with dat myself," Drucis said.

"Deal!" Viorka said.

Dwiskter smiled at Viorka. "It might be handy to 'ave a fynx that turns invisible. Ya never know what type of creatures we might happen upon."

"Whatever help I can offer, I'll readily do so," she said.

Boldair tugged the reins, causing Ember to stop on the path. The other Dwarves followed suit.

"There a problem?" Dwiskter asked.

"We leave this path and head through the trees." Boldair untied his helm from the saddle pack and placed it on his head. "I advise wearing your helm."

"Why?" Viorka asked. "I don't have one."

"You have no worries," Boldair said. "Us, on the other hand, have to worry about bashing our heads on branches."

"Which wouldn't happen if you walked on foot like me," she said.

"Hey!" Drucis said, pointing a stern finger. "That might be true, but just cause you're shorter than us, doesn't mean you can poke fun at our height."

"I'm not poking fun," she said. "Sometimes, being shorter has its advantages."

"Don't I know it!" Dwiskter said. "In some ways, our height gave us the upper hand against those blasted oversized Vykings."

"Don't forget about those goblins and orcs," Drucis said.

"Aye," Dwiskter said. "Still trying to get that stench out of my nostrils from battles long ago."

"Is it necessary for us to leave the forest trail so soon?" Forboud asked.

"Aye," Boldair replied. "The forest floor is rocky and unpredictable the farther south it goes. With nightfall approaching, we'd best not take unnecessary chances."

"Viorka," Boldair said. "Do us the courtesy of traveling ahead through the treetops. Alert us should you find any bandit camps?"

"How great is that possibility?" she asked.

"Bandits and thieves don't like to be seen. The dark cover of the trees conceals them. You know that," Boldair said. "Once we enter the wilderness, we might encounter bandits or wolf packs. Receiving a forewarning from you could be quite helpful."

"What about … goblins?" she asked. "You mentioned the goblin cavern. Are any goblins still there?"

Boldair, Drucis, and Dwiskter all laughed. Forboud observed their response, grinned, and then reared back his head, joining in.

"We've ne'er seen a goblin in any of our underground cities in more than a century," Boldair said.

She shrugged and her eyes narrowed. "Doesn't mean they *don't* exist. How can you be so certain they're all dead? Look at me. If you asked anyone in Aetheaon about whether they'd ever seen a fynx, only a minor few could say they had. Most have never heard of my kind. Yet, here I stand. I've never encountered another of my species, but I'm not so foolish to believe I'm the only one. At times, when I've worried I might be the only fynx left, I'm overshadowed by gloom."

Boldair said, "You've never seen another fynx?"

She forced a smile. "No. We're good at concealing ourselves within our environment, which prevents hunters from killing us for trophies. Since I'm often on edge and stay hidden, others like me have done the same. I might never see another fynx. If I don't, I'll offer no offspring to continue my species."

"Goblins were obliterated during the Battle of Final Rest that is now known as the Vale of Frozen Tears," Forboud said. "That's when the three major Dwarven cities—Damdur, Nagdor, and Icevale—formed the Dwarven Alliance. All three cities sent massive battalions into the valley, trapping the goblins at the mountain base, where they were all slaughtered. So you needn't worry about goblins."

"Dat good enough for ya?" Boldair asked Viorka.

She nodded.

He pointed at the nearest tree. "On with ya, then. Into the trees. We need to reach Whirled Forest before sunset."

"Whirled Forest? Why?" Drucis asked.

"There's a bluff where we can take shelter and camp for the night."

"No tavern before we camp? Now, you're getting on me bad side," Drucis said.

"What's eating you?" Boldair asked.

"Need you ask? No tavern means no drinks."

Boldair smiled. "Don't get testy. I always pack a flask or two. Don't you?"

"Of course!" Drucis said. "But I don't aim to use them unless we're in dire circumstances, which we're not."

"We're headed to the Whirled Forest," Forboud said. "If that's not dire—"

Dwiskter nodded. "From what I hear, the climate's almost as bad as Glacier Ridge, except that Glacier Ridge *has* a tavern, an inn, and residents."

"No places to buy a drink is quite dire, if ya ask me," Drucis said with a slight frown.

"Not to worry. You shall all drink from my flasks," Boldair said. "Now, get off the road before highwaymen see us. We don't want someone trying to rob us after dusk."

"Ahh, let 'em try," Dwiskter said. "They'll breathe their last."

Viorka altered her appearance into a large cat and scampered into the underbrush that spread like carpet around the trees. She scaled the wide truck of an oak and disappeared into the foliage.

Boldair turned Ember with a gentle tug of the reins. To his surprise, the wolf didn't resist, leaving the worn forest path and stepping into the forest underbrush. He whispered, "Ah, there we go. Thanks for listening."

Ember growled deep inside his throat. The wolf's back muscles tightened under Boldair. He expected the wolf to bolt forward and attempt to dislodge him from the saddle. Boldair scratched the nape of the wolf's head, hoping to soothe the giant beast, but the wolf stopped in his tracks, arched his head partway around, and bore his teeth.

Boldair pulled back his hand and whispered, "Easy, I know ya don't like me. Perhaps you don't trust me? But for now, for *this* journey, we're sorta stuck together. I hope ya can see past your distaste for me enough to get us to our destination. We can reevaluate our relationship afterwards, if dat be all right with you."

"All well up there?" Dwiskter asked.

"Aye," Boldair replied.

"You're moving painfully slow," Dwiskter said. "Is that your doing or the wolf beneath ya?"

"A bit of both, if I can be honest about it. I guess you can say that we're slowly working through our differences," Boldair said.

Drucis laughed. "Have you reached a mutual understanding?"

"What do you think?" Boldair huffed.

"I think your courtship is a bit too slow, so hurry it up a bit," Dwiskter said.

Boldair glared at Dwiskter but said nothing. Drucis laughed.

"What do you expect, brother?" Forboud asked. "Ember was father's mount for nearly ten years. He won't easily forget father and possibly senses your resentment for father."

"I agree that Ember and I must come to terms somehow. I don't expect he'll forget father as their bond is still strong. I only hope his resentment is short lived."

"Give the furry bag of bones a chance to adjust to your … scent," Dwiskter said.

"You've poked your fun at my expense," Boldair said. "But now, it's time we listen more than we speak, just in case we're not alone."

CHAPTER 11

hirled Forest set atop a narrow ridge overlooking the steep descending mouth of the valley. The ridge divided the Frosted Peaks, separating Glacier Ridge to the southwest from Woodcrest directly east.

The harsh cold winds that cut through the valley blew fiercely upward, forcing the massive pine branches to whirl in unnatural directions. Because of the never-ending winds, the branches grew in irregular whirled patterns over time.

Massive icy roots clung to the cliff's jagged edge, making it impossible to climb. The cold winds were too severe and deafening for any Dwarf, Elf, or human to withstand for an extended period of time. Traveling parties that attempted to climb upward, hoping to shorten their journeys to Glacier Ridge swiftly fell to their deaths. Their deaths were reported by the few wiser travelers that refused to attempt the suicidal climb. The survivors' misfortune resulted in seeing their friends fall from the thick gnarled roots onto the frozen spiky rocks below. The witnesses retreated and found the warmth of a tavern and strong drinks and spun their sorrowful tales of the treacherous nature of Whirled Forest to anyone willing to listen.

Boldair remembered listening to a young drunken lad, Mosser, tell his tales in Bridgebarrow Tavern. Mosser's slurred words could've easily been a tale spoken to draw sympathy from the patrons in order to receive gratuity to buy more drinks. Boldair almost discarded the story, except for the haunted fear that possessed Mosser's eyes and withered his face. One couldn't fake such terror. Boldair experienced such terror from his own treasure hunts. With pity, he offered the young bard a gold coin for sharing his loss.

Mosser sat at a tavern table with Boldair for a short spell. He explained that the harsh winds were the greatest culprit. The wind's fierce howls whistling through the jagged rocks and through the whirled tree branches. Those winds whispered, too, Mosser said, encouraging his comrades to blindly disregard the dangers. The winds spoke and hinted of great treasures for whomever reached to the whirled pine plateau. But the whispering voice frightened Mosser so he chose *not* to risk his life.

The coarse wailing winds made it impossible to hear anything other than its banshee howls. That's why Mosser named the rough mountainside Banshee's Bluff. Unlike his friends, he heard and resisted the baleful summons. When the last of his dangling friends dropped and vanished into the valley below, Mosser ran through the forest and headed to the safety of Woodcrest.

Days later, Mosser's story plagued Boldair's mind. Boldair's curiosity gnawed at him enough that he decided to view the gruesome nature of the Whirled Forest for himself. Looking back, it had been a foolish endeavor.

It wasn't the hint of possible treasure that lured Boldair to the rough mountain's edge. He needed to know the tale was true. When Boldair found himself overlooking the mouth of the valley, he realized Mosser's fears were genuine. Although Boldair held no fear of the crude cliffside, he greatly respected the dangers. No amount of treasure was worth gaining if he were dead.

And yet, he imagined the bottom edge of that jagged bluff was littered with broken, frozen, bodies of those blinded by their obsessions and unable to ascertain doomed fate until after it became too late.

These were victims of their own demise, partly due to the arrogance of overcoming any obstacle that no one before them had ever achieved. This type of haughty stubborn nature was common with most Dwarves, Elves, and humans. The less intelligent races, like goblins and orcs, held more common sense whenever they approached such terrain. At least, Boldair would wager a large portion of gold that his assumption was true. But, he'd never risk his life to see if he could scale the wicked mountainside.

CHAPTER 12

The last fragments of the sunset smoldered over the mountain. Boldair dismounted. He led Ember by the reins while keeping a fierce side-glance on the wolf. Even though the wolf had not challenged Boldair after leaving the forest path, Boldair didn't fully trust the giant. Not this soon. He was hopeful the wolf's distrust and resentment eventually faded.

"Now what?" Drucis grumbled, climbing off his ram. "You led us out here for our deaths?"

Boldair ignored him and led Ember to the side of a large boulder that blocked the swirling winds.

Drucis shook his head and followed him. "I'm beginning to dislike the prospects of this powerful drink you have tempted us with. The price of *getting* to it is far too steep, and for a Dwarf, *steep* isn't something we like. Ya should have warned us that we might die *before* we ever wet our throats with this lava-like concoction."

Boldair glanced at him and leveled a stern frown. "Are you done with your Elfish-whining?"

"Hey!" Drucis said, pointing his finger. He released the reins of his ram and took several quick steps toward Boldair. His face reddened. "What's the point of leading us out to one of the most dangerous terrains in the Frosted Peaks? Blasted, we passed dozens of nicer places in the forest where we could've set up a cozy camp. Instead, you 'ave us facing winds cold enough to freeze the heart of an Ice Ogre."

"You can always turn back, if you like," Boldair said angrily. "The whole lot of you, if dat's the way you see it. But if ya remember, Taniesse warned that I should keep a low profile until we discover who's aligned with father that might want me dead. If you choose to leave, go back the way we came. I'm done with ya."

Dwiskter placed a hand on Drucis' shoulder. "Careful how you speak to our King, Drucis. It's easy to forget that he's no longer a treasure-hunter, but a ruler."

Drucis lowered his hand. He sighed and nodded. "Aye, forgive me, Your Highness."

"We're all beat. The path to the Whirled Forest is filled with pitfalls and low branches. But ye shall be rewarded for your efforts," Boldair said with a broad smile.

"How's that?" Forboud said, leading his ram to where they stood. "I agree with them. I can't see camping on this windy cliffside without freezing our arses off. The only ones of us capable to withstand this weather are our mounts."

Viorka scampered from the trees toward the boulder where they stood. The wind picked her up and flung her into the trees. With her second effort to reach Boldair, she clung to protruding roots until she was behind the boulder that blocked the wind's path. She pressed her back against the cold rock and rubbed her arms, shivering.

"Ya can't possibly get a fire roaring here," Forboud said. "Even with the boulder's protection, the whipping wind prevents it."

Boldair chuckled. "Aye, but this is not where we shall camp."

"Then where?" Drucis said. "Don't tell me we've got to ride in the dark alongside this wicked ridge."

"No-o-o," Boldair shook his head and sighed. "I've learned a few things over the years as a treasure-hunter."

"Well, if it be magic," Drucis said, "how 'bout whipping us to the Meadwyrm Pass now and save us further torture?"

"Everyone stand back," Boldair said, kneeling behind the rock.

"Why?" Forboud asked.

"I've got to release the traps," he replied.

"I can't move away from the rock," Viorka said. "If I do, the wind's going to carry me away."

"Okay, Viorka, climb on my back and firmly hold my armor. You should be safe there. The rest of ya, give me some room."

The other Dwarves backed away. Boldair ran his stubby fingers along a large flat rock that lie next to the standing boulder.

"Ah," he said. "There we go."

A distinctive click sounded and he rose quickly. He took several steps back, and the flat rock sunk. In the fleeting daylight, a set of stairs became visible.

"Everyone go down before we lose the last of the light. Otherwise, I won't be able to find a torch to light."

"What about our mounts?" Forboud asked.

"There's room for them, too," Boldair said. "Viorka, you go first."

"Why?" she asked.

"Ember's probably gotten fairly hungry carrying me all this way. To him, you're a tasty morsel. Put some distance between ya. Besides, you're the only one of us who can see in the dark. I need ya to find my torch."

"What's down there?" she asked nervously.

"Since I've disarmed the traps, there's nothing dat can hurt you," Boldair replied. "I promise."

Viorka climbed down from his back and dropped into the hole, landing promptly upon her feet. A second later, she disappeared down the steps and returned with an old pitch-covered torch.

"Thanks, lil' cat."

She beamed a smile.

Boldair glanced at the other Dwarves. "Forboud, if you'd be so kind as to lead Ember down the steps, I'll follow you and light the torch. Viorka follows me."

Forboud gave a solemn nod.

"Thanks."

Boldair and Viorka disappeared down the rock steps.

CHAPTER 13

The flickering torchlight brought strange contours to Boldair's face. After Forboud brought Ember down the steps, Boldair waited for the rest of them to descend. Then he walked to the side of the steps and pushed an iron lever up. The large stone that had lowered into the ground slowly rose until it was flush with the ceiling.

Forboud turned and watched the heavy stone move back into place. "Since when have you learned engineering skills?"

Boldair chuckled. "With all the traps and snares I've encountered through the years, you get a knack for how they work."

Viorka stood outside of Ember's reach, rubbing her arms briskly to warm them.

Boldair took the torch and touched it to a pile of dried firewood in the center of the room. "Ah, is this better?"

She nodded.

The fire rose in a matter of minutes. The smoke masked the dusty smell the room contained. A small hole in the ceiling near the outcrop of the bluff acted like a flue, quickly sucking the smoke from the room. Boldair grabbed a thick dry log and placed it on the rising flames.

The room was quite large with several hay-covered flat stones in one corner that could be used as beds. Near the center of the room was a table with benches made from stacked stones. Several unlit torches were inserted into crude rock sconces on the walls. Boldair made his way around the room, lighting each one.

"If you will," Boldair said to Forboud, "tie Ember near the far wall. The rest of ya can tie your rams along beside him. There's some hay in the corner for them to eat, and Ember's saddlebag has some dried meat you can feed him."

Drucis offered a shrewd stare. "How'd you find this place?"

Boldair paused from lighting a torch and smiled. "I built it."

Forboud studied the room. "*You* impress me, brother. How did ya do all this?"

Boldair laughed heartily. "You and father might think I never listened to the things I was taught, but that's not true."

"The stonework is quite good, considering," Drucis said, looking around the room.

"Thanks," Boldair said. "Give it a few minutes and the fire will take the chill out of the air."

"*Why* did you build it?" Dwiskter asked.

"Ah, have a seat, and I'll tell ya."

The Dwarves seated themselves at the table. Boldair rested his torch in a small hole at the center of the table, walked to Ember, and took two wineskins from the large saddlebag. He set those on the table, along with several strands of elk jerky, and a quarter wheel of hard cheese. He said, "Help yourselves."

As the Dwarves drank, Boldair shared Mosser's story about how the seductive siren winds disguised their true banshee screams and led the misfortunate to their deaths.

Dwiskter took a long drink, wiped his mouth with the back of his hand, and handed the wineskin to Drucis. "Knowing what happened to all the people who died on this cliffside, why'd you travel here to check it out?"

"Curiosity mostly."

Viorka peered at him with wide eyes. "Didn't you fear that these winds might lure you to your death, too?"

Boldair shrugged. "There's always risks when one hunts treasures. Certainly no greater than awakening a dragon inside its lair though."

"You've done that?" Viorka asked.

He shook his head. "No. But I've always feared the possibility. Now that Taniesse and her two sisters have shown their might in battle, I suppose the possibility of encountering a dragon now is far greater. That is, if they did like she did and made themselves look human. But perhaps it was a danger all along dat would've caught me off guard."

Drucis passed the skin to Forboud. "So what happened when you arrived at the Whirled Forest?"

"While the wind speaks harshly to the humans and Elves who have ventured here, the mountain spoke *louder* to me than the wind possibly could. Cause we're Dwarves, rock and stone are where our hearts belong, right?"

Forboud, Dwiskter, and Drucis nodded.

Boldair pointed a finger toward the ground. "Under the mountains are our homes. It's where we abide and where our strength is at its greatest. We're part of the mountains. But, something odd happened when I came upon this point facing the mouth of the valley."

"What?" Viorka asked.

"I wasn't dressed for the journey. The cold wind bit me arms and face. I'd been on foot dat day, too. I noticed the large boulder we stood behind that sheltered us from the wind. Then, it lay flat on its side, so with all my might, I pushed until it stood upright. I used it as a shield to block the wind. After moving it, I noticed a small crevice, so I took a blunt rock and dug. A bit of warmth touched me hands, so I dug faster. The next thing I knew, I fell into this pit."

"Nothing was set in 'ere like it is now, was it?" Dwiskter asked.

Boldair shook his head. "Before the large boulder had fallen flat, it's possible some type of creatures used this pit for shelter or to hibernate, but I found no trace of them. Luckily, I keep flint in me pockets. I broke off some dead tree roots to start a fire. I used loose stones to build those steps. I had fallen ten feet or more from the opening. It took me more than a day to stack enough rocks to reach the top. I traveled to Woodcrest and traded for masonry tools to chip and fashion the stones into smoother steps. Then I made this table and benches."

"But why? What purpose did you have to spend so much time making this place more hospitable?" Forboud asked. "Certainly, you didn't plan to meet your death by trying to climb the bluff. You've often taken great risks to find treasures, but nothing as foolhardy as dat would be."

"You're right, brother. I've no want to ever make such an attempt up that ridge, but having a hidden place to stay overnight on long journeys is always a plus."

Forboud frowned. "But there's nothing out *here.*"

Boldair smiled. "I came upon this place *after* I found Frosthammer. It's a midway point. Within a few hours tomorrow we shall come to the old goblin cavern, and a few hours after that, we'll arrive at Frosthammer."

"I see," Drucis said. "I'm surprised you never hid any of your treasure here."

"I thought about it, but carrying the masonry tools on foot was difficult enough. Gold and silver are much heavier, but this would be the perfect spot to hide treasure though."

"You built the crank that lowers and rises the stone platform?" Dwiskter asked.

Boldair nodded. "Aye. The iron lever I found discarded in an old cemetery sepulcher, but it proved useful to me. The gears and chains I found at the narrow creek we crossed. No telling why they'd been left there, but no one was coming back for them. The rest of assembly was simple mechanics. I've used enough gadgets in old dungeons and cemeteries to know how they work. That's also how I learned to set me traps. After disarming dozens of them, one learns how triggering mechanisms work. It doesn't take much more to build ya own afterwards. Hell, I reset some traps in the hopes of spearing a few of those nasty Ratkins."

Dwiskter and Drucis laughed.

"I've never heard your tales in the taverns," Dwiskter said. "But before we ever met, I'd heard plenty about you."

Boldair chuckled. "Word of me adventures travels faster than I did. Peasants and townsfolk enjoy my stories."

"Some say your a blowhard," Forboud said with a shrewd grin before sipping from the skin.

"Oh, do they now?" Boldair asked.

"Actually, brother, they do," Forboud said, nodding.

"He's right," Drucis said. "I've heard others whisper such names when they see you. Ha! They're probably jealous of the riches you've found."

"Bah, let 'em talk," Boldair said with a dismissive hand. "I pay 'em no mind. Besides, why should I worry about 'em now anyways? I'm King."

Dwiskter pulled out his pipe, tapped dried herbs into it, and lit it. A sweet scent lofted above the table. After a few puffs, he looked at Boldair. "Tell me how you hunt for your treasures? Do you have a process, or a secret for discovering large gold and gem deposits? Most Dwarven miners have a keen sense for which rocks contain rich ore deposits. Is it similar for you?"

"Thinking of becoming a prospector?" Drucis asked.

Dwiskter chuckled and shook his head. "No, just curious."

"I've never mined, so I cannot compare the two. However, whenever I'm near a large amount of gold, a strange feeling arises in the pit of my stomach," Boldair replied. "It's best described as a tinge of excitement. My heart hammers in me chest. I know treasures are nearby. This probably sounds strange, but precious metals and gems cry out a strange melody, like a song."

"Been hitting the hard stuff already?" Drucis asked. He rose from his seat, pressed his hands atop the rock table and looked around for a bottle. "Where'd you hide dat?"

Boldair shook his head. "No, I'm being serious. Gold and all these other treasures came from the earth. I believe they wish to return."

Viorka cocked her head. "In a way, that makes perfect sense."

"It does," Boldair said.

Dwiskter cocked a brow, looking at Viorka. "Careful not to inhale the smoke off me pipe. The herbs can disorient the minds of smaller creatures."

"Let her alone," Boldair said.

"You're agreeing with a cat," Forboud said.

"A fynx," she huffed, glaring with emerald eyes.

"Ah, no matter," he replied. "You look like a cat to me."

"Seems your brother, Boldair, has inhaled too much from me pipe. Viorka's isn't shaped like a feline; her body resembles a human too much," Dwiskter said.

"Boldair was the one who said gems and gold sing!" Forboud said. "Maybe's he's too close to your pipe, too."

Drucis laughed. "Bah! I wasn't going to say anything since he's the new king."

Boldair frowned. "Hey! Dwiskter asked. That's the best I can describe it. How else do you think I found the dragons' lairs that belonged to Taniesse and her two sisters? Treasure hunters searched unsuccessfully for years to find them. Their lairs held so much gold and gems that I was overwhelmed by the cacophonous volume. The excitement was so overbearing I almost collapsed."

"You returned all of dat to them, didn't you?" Dwiskter asked.

"Aye," Boldair said in a heartbroken voice, nodding. His eyes went distant, remembering the stacks of gold he once stood atop. Gems of every color. Silver. Tears formed at the sides of his eyes. He flicked his gaze to Dwiskter. Sadness of loss coated his voice. "But, it was the right thing to do. The treasure was theirs, not mine."

Forboud straightened slightly on the crude rock bench and lit his pipe. "And not one gold coin you kept for yourself?"

"No." Boldair shook his head. "None except the reward Taniesse gave me after we won the war against the Vykings."

"There's no way you hauled all of her treasure to Legelarid and Oculoth by wagon when you hire armies to march into battle," Forboud said. A tinge of angered jealousy flowed with the words.

"Of course not!" Boldair said. "I drew maps for her to follow to find the rest of their accumulated treasures. You think I'd be alive if I'd tucked away any portion of their treasure for myself? A dragon knows to the last pitiable shilling how much treasure it owns. They'll abandon their lair to scorch any thief that steals from them. The *only* reason I ventured into any dragon's lair was because it was long believed that all dragons were dead."

Drucis and Dwiskter looked at Forboud with narrowed gazes.

"Are you making accusations against Boldair?" Drucis asked.

"No," Forboud said, shaking his head.

"Because your line of questions seem headed to presume Boldair guilty of something," Drucis said.

Forboud cleared his throat and set his pipe on the table. "That was not my intention at all."

"Then what is your intention?" Boldair asked, rising from his seat.

"None, brother. I swear it! It's just I didn't accompany you on that trip. We got separated after we left Bridgebarrow Tavern."

"Doesn't seem you spent too much time looking for me," Boldair replied. He studied Forboud shrewdly.

"The lot of us ran for our lives when that warrioress threw fireballs at us. I did return to look for you."

"When?" Boldair asked.

"The following morning."

"That soon?" Boldair shook his head. "For how long did ye search for me?"

Drucis cocked a brow and took a puff from his pipe.

"A few hours. After not finding you, I guessed you headed north to Damdur or perhaps decided to hunt more treasure without me."

"And where did you go?"

"I joined others and we headed to Nagdor."

Boldair chewed on the tip of his pipe. "Seems I worried much longer about you than you did me."

"Surely, you jest," Forboud said.

"No. I thought you were the charred dead prisoner in the cell next to mine when I awakened. The warrioress you mentioned was Taniesse," Boldair said.

Forboud nodded. "I realized that when I saw you standing with her outside Hoffnung with Lady Dawn."

"So do ya think I'd be so foolish to horde any bit of her treasure when she lopped fireballs at all of us?"

"No, I suppose not."

"Ye *suppose*? While the rest of you fled from Bridgebarrow, she knocked me unconscious and took me prisoner. She locked me in a tiny prison cell at the top of a high cliff and waited for me to awaken. When I did, she told me the dead body in the neighboring cell was you, and I'd suffer the same fate if I didn't agree to give back her treasure. For the period of time I thought the charred body was yours, I grieved deeply. I wept. You only searched for me a few hours? Did you ever consider dat I might've been killed or taken prisoner?"

Forboud shook his head. "The thought never crossed my mind."

"And why not?"

"Because to my knowledge you've never had an enemy. The only one to view you negatively is our father, and he was nowhere around."

"And so now, you ask accusing questions of whether I kept any of Taniesse's treasures for myself."

Forboud opened his mouth to speak, but Boldair raised a stern finger and shook his head.

Boldair leaned forward, resting his elbows upon the stone table. "You saw those fireballs that came at us. No doubt her intentions were to frighten all of you away. She came to take me, to find where I had hidden her treasure. After she chained me to the prison wall, she hurled large fireballs at me. I figured I'd become a burnt corpse, even after I agreed to tell her where her treasure was, but she spared me. For her mercy, I'm forever grateful. And because of her mercy, I'd never in the remainder of my life ever give her any reason to doubt my loyalty to her."

Forboud lowered his gaze and shook his head. "I'm sorry, Boldair. I never saw her take you. To be blunt, I ran to save me own hide. I cannot apologize enough."

Boldair grinned. "Brother, I cannot blame you for dat. Hell, I don't blame you at all! She took us all by surprise. Not one of us had any idea what her itinerary was. I cannot rightly recall, but I'm fairly certain I ran off the path into the forest before getting struck in the back of me head." He laughed heartily. "Anyone would've fled. My point isn't to make you feel guilty. My aim is to ask if you noticed any hostility from Taniesse toward me when we sat with Queen Taube?"

Forboud lifted his head and looked at Boldair. "No. None at all."

"Dat's my point. I've been honest with her before I was released and even now. If she harbored any grudge toward me, or if she believed me to be a thief, she'd have never warned me not to return to Nagdor, nor would she have allowed me to leave Hoffnung. Dragons are not creatures you betray and not expect repercussions. I'm surprised she set aside father's attempt to kill her."

Forboud nodded. "That surprises me, too."

Boldair stood and grabbed another log to place on the roaring fire. "We'd best sleep as much as possible. Tomorrow's trip has its share of hardships."

"Unlike today?" Forboud asked.

"A bit worse in places, I'm afraid."

CHAPTER 14

The following morning Boldair stood at the bottom of the stairs. Dwiskter, Forboud, and Drucis brought fallen deadwood they found on the forest floor and handed them downward. Boldair took them and set them at the side of the stairs.

"And your purpose for this?" Forboud asked.

"So we have dry firewood ready for whenever we return. No sense tripping around while hunting for firewood should it be dark upon our return," Boldair asked.

"We won't be heading back this direction after we reach Meadwyrm Pass, will we?" Forboud asked.

"No."

Forboud shook his head. "Good, 'cause I've no intention of ever seeing this fierce mountainside again. I'm surprised we're not up to our necks in snow with how cold it is."

"The winds prevent snow from sticking," Drucis said, "but the ground is frozen solid. Beyond this peak are the snow hills of the Frosted Peaks."

Boldair set down the long log and dusted off his hands. "All right. Dat be enough."

"So much for staying warm throughout the night," Forboud said. "Gathering all this wood has gotten me cold again."

"Ahh, come back inside then," Boldair said. "There's still heat rising from the ashes."

"I'd just as soon be headed on our way," Forboud replied.

"If you weren't my brother, I'd swear you were an Elf the way you constantly whine," Boldair said.

"I'm *not* whining. I see no reason to take the path we're currently on. All for a drink?"

"It's not just *any* drink." Boldair hurried up the steps. "And what would you propose we do?"

"Since you're the new King, you should meet with the Northern Dwarven Alliance's council," he replied.

"You heard Taniesse. She advises against it."

"Yes, against us returning to Nagdor. She said nothing of visiting King Thorgum and King Staggnuns. Seeking an out of the way path for a rare drink is pure foolishness, if you ask me."

"I didn't ask, did I?"

Drucis laughed. "You fail to see the point, Forboud. The drink is a powerful one that tests whether you be worthy of claiming Dwarf heritage or if you have traces of gnome in your blood."

Forboud frowned. "I wouldn't go that far."

"Then let's see if *you* pass the test, eh?" Drucis' eyebrows rose, and he beamed a daring smile.

"Boldair," Forboud said. "Please reconsider this bizarre quest."

Dwiskter laughed and shook his head. "Quest? A quest would be us undertaking a series of Tavern-hopping to see which Dwarf's the most resilient afterwards."

Boldair turned a metal handle, which activated the gears to bring the heavy stone flush with the ground. After the stone set into place, he placed several smaller stones atop it to better conceal the opening. He rose and placed a hand on Forboud's shoulder. "My days of these *quests* as you call them are limited. Once I'm seated on the throne, my duties change forever. These next few days are the last of my freedom."

"Freedom?" Forboud asked. "Are you suggesting being king is like a prison term?"

"Isn't it?" Boldair said. "A king's bound to his kingdom, or have you never considered that before?"

Forboud rubbed his chin. "Not like that, I haven't. But, yes, I see what you mean."

"Good, then let's not continue shivering our arses off, and be on our way."

Dwiskter nodded. "I agree. But, might I ask a question?"

Boldair glanced toward him. "Sure."

"Do you perceive any treasure that lies in the valley's edge below or upward beyond the gnarled roots of those whirled pines?"

Boldair stood and faced the valley. The harsh breeze made his long hair flow like ribbons. The braids in his long beard struggled not to become untied. He stared toward the foggy bottom of the valley. After a few moments, he shook his head. "If any treasure awaits, it's small. The sound of the winds silences it. To risk death for whatever small amount of coins the dead carried … isn't worth it."

Dwiskter stared at the trees and nodded. "I agree. Such a shame others didn't heed the risks."

"Mount up," Boldair said. "The temperatures might not improve, but at least we won't have to contend with this fierce wind much longer."

CHAPTER 15

The Dwarves rode an hour before the wailing winds diminished enough to speak without shouting to be heard. Boldair untied and unrolled a mottled bear hide from his saddlebag and wrapped it tightly around his shoulders.

His blood-red cheeks were numb. "All well behind me?"

"Aye!" Drucis and Dwiskter shouted in unison.

Seated behind Dwiskter, Viorka peered around him and asked, "Where are we?"

"We're riding along the Lost Pass," Boldair said, straightening on Ember. The wolf's heavy paws kicked up snow with each step he took.

"Lost Pass?" Forboud shouted. "Determined to lead us to our deaths, are ye?"

Boldair let the question linger in the frozen air. Suddenly, his growing anger at Forboud's constant challenging remarks warmed him more than the thick bear hide draped around him. Boldair lit his pipe, puffed it, and then combed the bits of ice and snow from his beard, watching Lost Pass narrow ahead. Holding his tongue was painful.

The path scaled between two steep mountainsides. Hanging from the rugged cliffs were long bluish icicles that whistled like chimes in the higher breezes that gusted between the two mountains. Several brown eagles glided overhead, possibly looking for concealed snow hares. Their shrieks echoed between the ridges.

Although not a treacherous road, few ventured along this narrow pathway, as the Lost Pass led into the heart of the Frosted Peaks, which was frozen uncharted wilderness. The few prospecting Dwarves that had ventured deeper into the mountainous terrain, hoping to map the region to find rich ore veins, were never seen again. Such bizarre disappearances inspired bards to spin tales about flesh-eating Frost Giants and ogres or something far worse; like mysterious creatures never encountered before.

The unknown mysteries didn't concern Boldair. The darkening skies above the higher peaks indicated heavy snow would soon fall. His party didn't need to be trapped between these two towering mountains, as they were in desperate need to replenish their rations.

Boldair estimated another half hour of riding lie ahead before they cut northeast onto a smaller path. That intersecting side path was the farthest he'd traveled into the Frosted Peaks. Such bold expeditions were never wisely done alone, especially when previous explorers never returned.

"Shield your eyes!" Boldair shouted.

A harsh gust of wind whipped downward and swept a blanket of loose snow and ice crystals from the pass into the air, carrying it full force right at them.

Pellets of snow and splinters of ice bounced off the bear hide Boldair wrapped around his face, making a strange crisp tapping sound as it accumulated.

Ember growled slightly, bowing his massive head. He braced himself and refused to take another step forward.

As quickly as the gust passed, it faded, continuing in the direction they had traveled. These harsh gusts were probably why the Lost Pass pathway remained visible and didn't accumulate impassable walls of snow.

Boldair lowered the bear hide. Ember was covered in a thick layer of white ice crystals. The wolf shook his head and groaned with a long yawn.

"Not much farther," Boldair whispered to Ember. The wolf replied with an agitated growl. Boldair shook his head and chuckled and looked over his shoulder. "How are ya faring back there?"

The rest of his party dusted and shook away the snow from their hair and beards. For a moment his companions resembled the elder Dwarves that had advised Ulthor many years ago.

"Looking forward to a warm place to camp, or a small tavern where we can drink and perhaps eat warm stew," Dwiskter said.

"Ah, sounds great!" Boldair agreed. "We've not much farther before we cut off this pass."

"And then we have the warmth of a cozy goblin cave, right brother?" Forboud said.

Angry, Boldair turned in his saddle to stare at Forboud. "Nah, we've at least another three hours before we *reach* the cave!"

His voice boomed between the mountains. Several hanging icicles crackled. Small pieces of ice trickled downward, crinkling like broken glass at the base of the mountain ridges. Some of the icicles, larger than spears and capable of splitting an armored Dwarf in half, swayed slightly.

"Careful," Drucis said. "The mountains are sensitive. Let's not make our presence any more unwelcome. Might prove costly."

Boldair kept his fierce gaze fastened on Forboud until his brother looked away. Boldair shook his head and turned back around. *Must you increase this contention between us, Forboud?*

They rode in silence for the next quarter hour, listening only to the crunching steps of their mounts walking on the thin layer of snow and ice.

Boldair hummed a tune that he once heard in Bridgebarrow Tavern. He didn't know the words, as the song was in an Elven tongue, but the sweet melody endeared his heart, bringing him peace whenever strife sought to torment him, like now. The song had been sung by a pixie, and she lured the peasants and tavern patrons seductively with her physical beauty and soothing voice. Humming the tune led his mind to a place sorrow knew not. He smiled.

"What's that song?" Drucis asked, riding up beside Boldair.

Boldair shook his head. "I'm sorry. What did you say?"

"That noise. Did you hear it?"

"Oh, I—I was humming."

Drucis shook his head. "No, not that. I heard your melody, but no, the sound echoing along the ridge."

Boldair pulled back on the reins. A soft thudding riveted in the distance, almost like a woodpecker tapping a rotten tree. He shrugged. "I've no idea."

The sound held no constant rhythm and was sporadic.

"What's the problem?" Forboud asked, riding closer to them.

"That sound," Drucis said.

Forboud cocked his head to the side and listened. "I hear nothing."

"Wait," Drucis said. Again, the thudding echoed. "Dat."

Forboud frowned and shook his head. Dwiskter reacted in the same way.

"It's got me curiosity up," Boldair said. "Let's go see."

Forboud sighed. "Brother, it's best we be on our way to wherever it is you wish to take us. Side journeys not only place *your* life into danger, but *ours* as well."

"We've yet to reach the road that leads us away from the Lost Pass, unless of course you wish that we all head back to Banshee Bluff and then south? Or perhaps, maybe we should trek our way up one of these high peaks and cross over and down the other side?" Boldair said, frowning. "Or is that too much for your sense of adventure?"

Drucis and Dwiskter stared at Forboud with mild agitation.

Forboud looked at the steep mountainside and shook his head. "Head on, brother."

Boldair's eyes narrowed. "By what authority are *you* commanding *me*?"

Forboud stiffened in his saddle and lowered his gaze. "Apologies, brother."

"Still playing prince?" Boldair asked. "Perhaps exile from Nagdor is your best option as you seem unable to accept me as the new king."

Forboud bowed forward on his saddle while gazing into Boldair's eyes. "Again, apologies. I'm tired, cold, hungry—"

Boldair waved his hand and shook his head. "As are we all. No one else is complaining. Only *you*."

Forboud closed his eyes and sighed.

Boldair clicked his tongue twice, but Ember ignored the command. Boldair nudged the heel of his boot into the wolf's thigh. Ember released a low guttural growl of stubborn protest but stepped forward and walked. "Seems too many resist my requests as king."

Drucis frowned at Forboud, tapped his ram's side, and moved in behind Boldair. Dwiskter followed. Viorka sat on the high saddlebag behind Dwiskter with her back pressed to his where she kept sight of Forboud.

Another half mile and the terrain on both sides of Lost Pass drastically changed. Large stumps remained where trees once stood. Deep trenches cut away the side edges of the pass where the massive trees had been dragged away.

"Odd," Drucis said.

"Very," Boldair said, nodding.

"I smell smoke," Viorka said, scrunching her nose.

"As do I," Dwiskter said.

"A stew of some kind," she added. "An odd aroma that I don't recognize."

The thudding sound grew louder and more consistent around the bend.

"Bloody hells!" Drucis said.

Boldair tugged the reins. "So, you see it too?"

"Aye, and I swear that I've not drank a drop this morning."

CHAPTER 16

A pile of snow-dusted logs were stacked against the mountain base. Next to the logs stood a large sawmill with several stacks of planks on the other side. An iron kettle bubbled over a roaring fire. Black smoke curled upward.

Atop two large balance beams rested an almost completed hull of a large wooden ship. Visible inside a small section of the frame was a Dwarf hammering rivets into the wood.

"Greetings!" Boldair said.

The Dwarf paused in his hammering, startled, and with wild eyes, he looked at Boldair with a stern frown. Then he studied the party of Dwarves. His skin was dark with a slight icy, bluish tint. His beard and long hair were whiter than the snow. He stood and huffed. "Be on ya way!"

"Is that any way to speak to the King of Nagdor?" Dwiskter said.

"King? Ha! Now, if you said that he were *Queen*, that'd impress me far more. Be gone!"

Dwiskter, Boldair, and Drucis exchanged confused glances.

"You've no respect for our king?" Dwiskter asked, placing his hand upon the hilt of his ax.

Boldair placed his hand atop Dwiskter's and shook his head.

The Dwarf frowned and scanned the Lost Pass. "I see no throne. He wears no crown. As far as *I'm* concerned, he's not a king here! Be gone now, the lot of ya. I've work to do. No time to prattle!"

Boldair chuckled. "Why are you building a ship at the side of the mountain? There's not a body of water anywhere in sight."

The Dwarf flung his hammer against the side of the hull, cursed under his breath, and stormed to the edge of the platform, looking down at them. "What concern is it of yours, Ol' King?"

"No concern," Boldair said with a frown. "Just a bit …peculiar."

"No more peculiar than a *king* traveling unprotected with a party through the Frosted Peaks."

"Fair enough. What's your name?" Boldair asked.

"And dat concerns you, *how?*"

"I only ask out of curiosity."

Dwiskter leaned closer to Boldair and whispered, "He's a bit unhinged."

"I agree," Forboud said. "We should keep going, brother."

Boldair grinned.

The Dwarf retrieved his hammer from the floor of the hull and sighed. "My name's Ice'ik. What else do you need?"

"What kingdom are ye from, Ice'ik?" Boldair asked.

Ice'ik tilted back his head, stared toward the sky, and shook his fists. "I don't see how dat matters, but if you absolutely *must* know, Frosthammer was my home. But no more! The Dwarves there are daft!"

"As though *he* has room to talk," Drucis whispered with a smirk.

Boldair and Dwiskter laughed.

"Is dat funny?" Ice'ik asked. "You wouldn't think so, after you've tarried there long. That's why I'm building this ship, so I can get as far away from them as possible."

"Good luck with dat," Drucis said.

"I've no need of luck," Ice'ik said. "I'm a master carpenter."

Boldair stared at the ship hull with feigned admiration and scratched his chin. "I cannot argue with dat. Quite good. Tell me, are you building this ship by yourself?"

"What do you think?" Ice'ik said, crossing his arms.

"To be truthful, I'm not certain what to think of a Dwarf building a ship on the side of a mountain," Boldair replied.

"We have company," Forboud said, nodding toward a small party approaching on the path ahead.

Four Dwarves balanced and carried a midsize log on their shoulders. When they noticed Boldair and his party, they dropped the log. Their complexions were dark and tinted icy blue like Ice'ik. Their hair and beards flowed to their waists and were the color of snow.

"Is all well, Ice'ik?" one Dwarf asked.

"Aye!" Ice'ik said rather frustrated. "Just some *king* wandering around the Frosted Peaks. They should be on their ways now. Or does *Your Highness* 'ave more questions to delay our work?"

Drucis put his hand on the hilt of his ax, tapped his ram's side, and rode a few steps closer toward the ship. "I've had it with his disrespectful—"

"Ah, let 'em be, Drucis," Boldair said. "As Forboud suggested, we should head on."

"Perhaps, you'd sell us some of your stew?" Viorka asked.

"Viorka," Boldair whispered in a scolding manner.

"What?" she asked. "It smells good."

Ice'ik's eyes widened when he noticed the fynx. He looked to the Dwarves and said, "Fill 'em some bowls. No one will e'er say that Ice'ik refused passing travelers food in such freezing conditions. Of course, I'm sure Halmick would like to know if his stew's fit for a king."

Halmick laughed.

Dwiskter and Drucis roared with laughter.

Halmick handed a tin bowl of bubbling soup to Boldair.

Boldair nodded his appreciation. "I suppose you'll have your answer in a few minutes."

Dwiskter took the bowl from Boldair.

"Hey!" Boldair said.

Dwiskter raised a finger in protest. "Allow me, just in case."

Halmick looked hurt.

Boldair frowned and harshly whispered, "You actually think they'd poison me? *Us*? You think they'd keep a large cauldron of bubbling poisonous stew out here in subzero temperatures, just waiting for the first unsuspecting party to arrive? I doubt they've seen any travelers for weeks."

"We cannot take such chances," Dwiskter said.

Boldair yanked the bowl from Dwiskter. "My apologies, Halmick. Dwiskter has my best interests at heart, though his manners in the situation could be more proper."

"Boldair," Forboud said. "You really should heed what Dwiskter said."

Boldair blew the steam from the bubbling stew. He carefully placed his lips to the side of the bowl and took a sip. He chuckled. "Hot! But tasty. Is this rabbit?"

Halmick shook his head and a sly grin parted his beard. "Kobold with yams, ice-root, and secret spices."

Boldair gave an old side-glance at Dwiskter. "Never eaten Kobold before; not that I ever plan to again."

"How is it?" Halmick asked with eager eyes.

"Different. A bit … gamey."

Halmick nodded. "Aye, yeah. They're a bit stringy, too. Not a lot of critters around. Sometimes, we're lucky enough to trap an occasional snow hare. But the Kobold wandered into our camp and tried to kill and rob us. A mistake he won't e'er make again."

"Yes," Boldair said, swallowing hard and trying not to spew the tough meat from his mouth. "I imagine he won't."

Viorka held out her catlike hands for a bowl. "You have to make due with what you have sometimes."

"Aye," Halmick said, handing her a bowl. He looked at Drucis. "Come on. The rest of ya gather round. Eat before heading on your way. After all, you're hours away from any villa or city."

With a look of bewilderment, the rest of Boldair's party approached cautiously.

"It's really not bad at all," Boldair said. He pulled a long strand of curled white hair from his mouth, winced, and tossed it on the frozen ground.

The rest of his party took bowls of stew and leaned against the stack of logs. Each watched the other to see which was brave enough to take the first bite. Drucis sniffed the stew and then he jammed a large spoonful into his mouth. He chewed for several seconds, paused, and his eyebrows rose. He shrugged, swallowed, and took a second bite.

Ice'ik set his hammer on the hull floor, made his way down the ladder, and joined his group at the boiling pot. "What's your verdict, King?"

"I'll never tell anyone outside our circle that we ate Kobold. Considering how nasty and foul-smelling those creatures are, Halmick has done a remarkable job to make a delicious stew. No offense, but ... a Kobold isn't something I'd ever consider eating again," Boldair replied.

Ice'ik laughed. "Nor would we. That's chunks of snow hare in the stew, not Kobold. We set traps each day and get lucky e'er so often. You caught us on a good day. Kobold's stink worse than a skunk. Ain't ne'er a way we'd become *dat* desperate for food. Tree bark sap is far tastier. Besides, Kobold hide is quite tough. I imagine their meat is the same. They're filthy beasts ridden with disease."

After hearing the meat was hare, Drucis and Dwiskter ate the contents in their bowls with vigor, complementing Halmick for his incredible culinary abilities. Even Boldair ate a bit more at ease, but couldn't shake the thought of the long white hair, which must've been Halmick's.

Boldair set his empty bowl on a small table beside the cauldron. "Why'd you leave Frosthammer? Were you exiled?"

Ice'ik studied Boldair's concerned face for several moments. "The particulars for our being here aren't important. Do you plan to travel to the city?"

Boldair nodded. "It's where we're destined now, but only to pass through."

"No diplomatic appointments?"

"No," Boldair said. "We need a quick pass under the mountains."

"I see. Have you been to Frosthammer before?" Ice'ik asked.

"Aye, but a long time ago."

Ice'ik's icy blue eyes shimmered like sapphires struck by a bright ray of sunlight. "I wish you well on your visit, but do know things have changed in the underground city. If all you desire is to get through to the other side of the mountain, be quick. Tis a shame my ship isn't yet completed. I'd be honored to take your party to wherever your journey ends on our first voyage."

Boldair glanced at the ship hull. The bow and stern were virtually complete. Two large masts were set into place with unfurled sails. To Boldair, the ship looked near completion but then he looked at the narrow Lost Pass. After a few moments, he expected Ice'ik to burst into laughter, but he didn't. His blue eyes and facial expressions remained serious.

"How long 'ave you worked on this ship of yours? It looks almost finished," Boldair said.

Ice'ik sighed. "Aye. It takes a lot of time to build a ship, especially when I've only eight other carpenters who chose to flee Frosthammer with me. We've been working day and night for the better part of a year. If you tarried with us for a few more days, you'd witness our maiden voyage, perhaps even sail with us."

Boldair exchanged side-glances with Drucis and Dwiskter, and all three strained to not burst into laughter.

"Indeed, dat would be a fantastic … event to … witness." Boldair bit the tip of his tongue until it hurt, hoping the pain thwarted the rumbling laughs wishing to escape his mouth. After tasting blood, he attempted to redirect the conversation. "I doubt we could survive the cold nights."

"The ship is quite insulated from the cold," Ice'ik said. "Ya get used to the cold after awhile."

"You mentioned Frosthammer had changed. What made you *flee*?" Boldair asked.

"Lots of things, actually, the least of which would be political."

"Like what?"

"I'm afraid if I told ya, ye would not believe. Nor would I, had I not witnessed firsthand such abnormalities. It's why I spoke warnings to all who are dear to me. They chose not to listen and remained behind. But I pleaded with my broken heart for them to leave with me. That ache has not lessened, but I'm compelled to build this ship, so we can get far from here. It's my hope they'll come to their senses and join me before the ship is finished."

"What did you see?"

One side of Ice'ik's lips twitched. His eyes became haunted and their brilliance dimmed as though sunken beneath murky water. "King, I must bid you and yours safe travels. Don't tarry in Frosthammer. Be quick about your business. The only warning I shall give you is to remain on the higher levels where you'll be safe. Rumor is the Frosthammer gates shall be closed by King Rigrim's orders. Those caught inside, shall not be allowed to venture out."

"Why?"

"Some of the dead are alive once more," Ice'ik said. "But they're not the same. Some believe a plague. Others like me, a curse. A few suggest the magic of a dark wizard has created these undead. There be worse things, too, but until you see them for yourself, words cannot explain them. So heed my warning and be quick to reach the other side."

"You left Frosthammer a year ago?"

Ice'ik glanced over his shoulder at the ship. "Aye, about dat long."

Boldair marveled. "You've done that much construction?"

"Aye."

"With only nine of you, that's incredibly fast."

"When time's limited, you work faster and harder and through many nights. Unlike now, with you delaying us."

"My apologies," Boldair said.

"All is fine, dear king," Ice'ik said. "Of course, if you and your companions cared to use a hammer or two, we'd be done even faster."

"I'd love to offer my help," Boldair said. "But none of us are carpenters. Our *help* would only slow ya down."

Ice'ik chuckled. "I appreciate the candor. It's been nice to have your brief company, but we must return to our work. Again, I wish this was completed, so we could aid you in your journey."

Boldair appreciated the sincerity in Ice'ik's voice and in his mannerisms. He seemed completely different than when Boldair had hailed him a half hour before. He wondered if some sort of plague had occurred deep in Frosthammer. Was it the reason for Ice'ik's delusions for building a ship so far from the sea?

Boldair smiled and extended his hand. "You've done more than enough with your hospitality. I wish we could return the favor. Perhaps, whenever you complete this, you could visit me in Nagdor."

"I appreciate your offer. But I'm afraid once my ship is completed, I travel east toward the Hoffnung Sea."

"Might I ask one other question?" Boldair asked.

"If it won't take too long."

"No, it won't. Do you know if a man riding a black carriage ever arrived in Frosthammer?"

Ice'ik shook his head. "Frosthammer's a huge city with many levels, so it's possible but not someone I recall. Why?"

"This plague you mentioned could have been brought by him. He is Mors, and is known as the Plague-bringer. He has the power to make the dead come to life wherever he appears."

"Sounds like you've dealt with him before," Ice'ik said.

"Aye. He brought an army of undead to the surface and even an undead dragon. The Dwarven Alliance defeated him in battle, but he isn't dead. He escaped."

"I see." Ice'ik shook Boldair's hand firmly. "Safe travels, King, and perhaps one day we shall meet again."

CHAPTER 17

Once Boldair and his party traveled a half mile farther, the hammering on the ship returned to a hollow thudding echo, but was now a chorus of nine hammers instead of one.

"So Boldair," Drucis said, "what did *you* think of Ice'ik?"

Dwiskter laughed. "Yeah, he called others daft?"

Boldair kept his gaze focused on the path ahead of them. Other than the darkening clouds and different numbers of soaring eagles and swooping hawks, the Lost Pass hadn't changed. If anything, the path seemed endless.

His mind couldn't shake the brief moments of fear he'd witnessed in Ice'ik's eyes, especially after Ice'ik's dismissive and hardened attitude upon meeting set an instant barrier to keep the travelers moving forward, rather than to stop and visit. Perhaps, part of Ice'ik's stance came from the urgency of constructing a ship he believed could rescue them. But why and *how*? They were building the ship on the side of a mountain far from any body of water.

The idea was ludicrous, and nothing more than the dream of a maddened Dwarf. Farfetched as it seemed, one might accuse a human or Elf, more so than a Dwarf, of attempting such a preposterous monstrosity of a goal, as shortsighted as it was. Yet, Ice'ik's sincerity and devotion held more stubbornness than the silence of a monk. And as best as Boldair could tell, nothing about Ice'ik's intentions even hinted a religious tone.

"He's seems a bit deranged, don't you agree?" Drucis asked.

Boldair shrugged. "His actions are a bit … unbalanced … if you only judge from what you see, I suppose."

"Or perhaps he has drunk one barrel too many," Drucis said, grinning.

"I didn't see any barrels," Dwiskter said.

"Ah, my point exactly. Nor did he offer us a drink, which for a Dwarf lacks hospitality."

"Maybe rations are low?" Viorka said, rubbing her full stomach.

Drucis chewed his lower lip, thinking, and then he nodded. "That's probably true. Still, I'd wager that he's stashed several barrels behind the hull of the ship out of sight. Who could blame him? I must admit, though, dat in a matter of a few months, if what he'd said is true, they've accomplished quite a bit in a short amount of time."

"But building a ship on the side of a mountain? I suppose if ya pushed hard enough, it might slide down the ice-covered Lost Pass," Dwiskter said with a chuckle. "But once it broke free, there'd be no slowing or stopping it."

Drucis howled with a fit of laughter until a tear edged down his cheek. He grabbed a handful of his ram's hair to keep from falling off his mount. "My, what a sight dat would be! Can you imagine them tugging back on the ropes while the heavy ship dragged them down the slope! Of course, it'd simply crash into the mountainside or plow through the trees. And *he* thinks the Dwarves in Frosthammer are daft!"

Dwiskter wiped tears from his eyes. "Enough! I need to see where we're going." He tried to regain his composure but shook his head, still laughing.

"He's sincere in his beliefs, Drucis," Boldair said, in a quiet, serious tone.

"Oh, is he now?" Drucis asked.

"Aye, he is," Boldair said. "You remember the Plague-bringer?"

Drucis and Dwiskter nodded. Their laughter ceased.

"It's possible Mors has been to Frosthammer. Ice'ik mentioned dat the undead are roaming the lower levels of the city," Boldair said. "Dat's the biggest reason for why he left."

"Perhaps dat is what has driven Ice'ik to madness?" Drucis said.

"Perhaps. I can't think of anything more batty than building a ship in the mountains," Boldair said.

"And for what purpose did he give?" Dwiskter asked.

"He wishes to flee quickly."

Drucis cackled. "Walking would be much faster, don't ya think?"

Boldair nodded.

"Or crawling," Dwiskter said. The two returned to their laughing fits.

Boldair sighed but didn't join in their laughter. "He still has family in Frosthammer. Perhaps the deranged notion of building a vast ship is his way of prolonging his stay, nearby, hoping dat others in his family will leave Frosthammer to join him. At least it's shelter from the cold."

"It'd take a lot of family to hoist that ship," Drucis said.

"You're missing the point," Boldair said.

"That being?" Drucis asked.

"Leaving family behind," Forboud said sourly. "Even when they don't see things the same way. Or if their minds have altered slightly. Family is the strength of all Dwarves. It always has been and will always be."

"Aye," Boldair said. "But not all transgressions can be forgiven or forgotten."

"They should be, if one has the heart to forgive," Forboud replied.

"It has little to do with forgiveness, brother. Trust lost can seldom be earned back," Boldair said. "Such a division cannot ever be bridged together in the same manner as it was, either."

Forboud straightened in his saddle and puffed his pipe. "One needs to allow those wounds to heal."

"Wounds heal," Boldair said. "The scar, however, is the constant reminder of the injury and pain."

Drucis gave Dwiskter an odd side-glance. "I don't think we're talking about Ice'ik's dilemma anymore."

"You be right about dat," Dwiskter replied. "How 'bout sharing one of your treasure hunting tales, Boldair?"

Forboud groaned slightly.

"It'll help pass the time," Drucis said. "And let us forget other things for a while."

Viorka perked up. Her eyes widened with excitement. "Have him tell you how we destroyed the Orb of Misfortune!"

"Is dat a good one?" Dwiskter asked.

"Not about treasure," she replied.

"And not the way *she* tells it!" Boldair said fiercely, before turning and giving her a broad smile. "But I 'ave you know, had it not been for her bravery, I might not've survived. She looks tiny at times, but her heart is dat of a warrior. The worst part, though, is dat I nearly killed her."

Viorka smiled and blushed. "The orb held you under its spell. You weren't at fault."

"You tell them what happened," Boldair said.

"You sure? I wouldn't want to tell it incorrectly."

Boldair smiled. "You'll do fine. Besides, there's a lot of things that occurred dat I don't remember after I took the orb."

Viorka turned on the saddlebag to tell the story, which turned out to be a more optimistic tale than Boldair might've told.

CHAPTER 18

After several hours riding along the bottom edge of the Frosted Peaks, Boldair pulled the reins. Ember stopped, and Boldair slid off the saddle. The snow went above his knees. A chill shot through Boldair as he realized his back was exposed to Ember. The dire wolf growled and lunged at Boldair.

Boldair turned, trying to step out of Ember's reach, but the deep snow prevented him from moving. He raised his steel-gloved fist. "Wait until I get me back turned, eh? Back up, you mangy mutt! You want to wear that muzzle forever? 'ave some respect or find yourself missing teeth."

Boldair's heart hammered in his chest, but he stared fiercely into Ember's eyes without showing fear. The wolf's eyes glowed like red coals. Neither broke their gaze with the other. Boldair pointed his finger. "I'm a warning ya! Back up!"

"Ember!" Forboud shouted in a stern voice, sliding off his saddle. Fury reddened his face. "Yield!"

Ember's ears backed. He glanced from Boldair, and took a step back. The wolf lowered his head in submission and licked his lips.

"That's better," Boldair said, staring at the wolf. He glanced at Forboud and nodded. "Thanks, brother."

Forboud offered a slight shrug and loosened the wolf's muzzle.

Boldair turned his attention from Forboud and took a difficult step forward in the snow. Two fir trees stood at the base of the snowy mountainside. Snow weighted the tree branches, making them sag almost to the point of snapping.

"We're here," Boldair said. He grabbed a lower tree branch and shook it. Snow plummeted around the base of the tree in thick clumps. With several feet of snow covering the ground, at least they didn't have to contend with the harsh winds like they endured at Banshee Bluff.

Viorka sat on the back of Dwiskter's saddle, watching with wide cat eyes. She kept expressing her hatred for the snow, and since she was too short to walk through it, she didn't reject Dwiskter's offer to remain on top of his saddlebags while they traveled.

"This is it?" Drucis asked. "I don't see any cavern."

"Aye," Boldair replied. "The snow has hidden the opening. These two firs are the landmark I was looking for."

Forboud frowned. "They look like all the others."

Boldair nodded. "Except, for my carving on this one's trunk." He slapped his hand against the smooth bark. Above his hand was a dark colored groove cut deeply with the hammer symbol Boldair used in his signature.

"Ahh," Dwiskter said, dismounting. "I'd have never seen dat, had you not pointed it out."

Boldair walked to the snow-covered entrance, pounded his fist against it, and stepped back, allowing the snow to fall and build into a small pile on the ground. "Step back. I gotta release the trap."

"Do you set traps on everything?" Forboud asked.

"Only on things dat I value the most I do."

"You *value* an old goblin cave?" his brother asked.

Boldair laughed. "I value what's inside."

"O-oh," Dwiskter said. A smile spread across his face. "You've hidden treasures inside."

Boldair looked over his shoulder and grinned. "Not much, but some. The good thing is that no one's triggered the trap. At least not the one on the outside."

Boldair fumbled with a small device, removed it, and then slid his hand into a small hole. Boldair squinted tightly. A gear clicked. He exhaled a sigh of relief. "All is safe now."

"I suppose that's *until* we step *inside*?" Forboud asked. "Careful, all, it'd be a shame if the trap misfired. Nothing's worse than being killed by a king when no crime's been committed, don'cha think?"

"Dat's not going to 'appen," Boldair replied.

Forboud grinned. "How can ye be so certain?"

"I didn't find the switch for the second trap."

"What does *that* mean?" Forboud asked.

"Perhaps I didn't set it properly and it's already fired. Or, a rat triggered it from the other side. Bah, who knows? All I know is that it has fired. Dat good 'nuff for you?" Boldair asked, frowning.

"Didn't mean to rile ya up, brother, but it seems possible you're losing your knack for setting these traps. Perhaps it is time you retired from treasure-hunting to become king."

Boldair sighed. Forboud's tone defined the resentment in his voice. Regardless of how much Forboud insisted that he wasn't jealous or that he didn't want to be crowned king as Ulthor desired, Forboud continued spewing his disdain whenever he spoke. Boldair wondered if Forboud even realized it. The facial expressions Drucis and Dwiskter often displayed revealed they also detected the bitter undertone in Forboud's words.

It saddened Boldair that he might have to part ways with his own brother, because up until their father's imprisonment, the two always got along. Their interests were never exactly the same. Boldair was more inclined to hunt for lost treasures than to partake in military exercises. Despite their differences, they were still close.

Forboud often traveled with Boldair on the shorter journeys, but now, after discovering Ulthor's plan to place Forboud on the throne, Boldair wondered if Forboud was a spy for their father.

Protest all ye like, Boldair thought. *But, the truth's in your tone, Forboud. Can't you see the disgrace father has placed on our name and our lineage by his betrayal to one of our dearest allies? Will you ever realize how he has tarnished the crown?*

Boldair hated not trusting his brother, but until he could fully trust Forboud, Boldair needed to keep a watchful eye on him.

Boldair gave a side-glance to Ember. The giant wolf wagged its tail as Forboud scratched behind its ears. Forboud smiled, holding the muzzle in one hand. He fed the wolf a strand of jerky. Ember gulped down the dried meat and nuzzled Forboud's hand. Boldair's brow furrowed. A new worry came to mind.

The wolf hated Boldair, but held affection for and obeyed Forboud. What prevented Forboud from commanding the wolf to attack, maim, or kill Boldair whenever Dwiskter and Drucis were away? They knew the wolf's underlying resentment and distaste for Boldair. Should the wolf kill Boldair, no one could argue the wolf had not purposefully done so. The blame would never fall on Forboud because of the wolf's hatred for Boldair.

Boldair pulled a lever. A set of gears squeaked and turned. The faux rock door pulled slightly inward.

Viorka leapt from the saddlebag and landed facedown in the snow. The deep snow swallowed her, leaving only the visible outline of her body. Dwiskter waded through the snow to where she landed, reached in, and pulled her out.

Her lips shivered. "Uh, thanks."

Dwiskter laughed and shook his head. "Any deeper and I don't think my arm could've reached ya."

Boldair stepped beside the door. "Viorka, you go first."

She peered at the narrow opening with nervousness. "I—I don't know."

"Oh, come now," Drucis said, "Boldair's inside trap has been released. Nothing's gonna hurt you."

"I'd rather not," she said.

"And after I boasted so greatly of your bravery earlier," Boldair said, "you're going to simply prove me wrong?"

"Can you prove the goblins aren't inside the cavern?" she asked.

Boldair shook his head. "Ya don't believe Dwiskter and Drucis, either, then?"

"Or *me*," Forboud said with a firm brow. He tapped his pipe against the wall to dislodge the burnt herbs.

Boldair pushed the door farther inward, turned sideways, and walked through to the other side. He returned a moment later with an unlit torch. After several scrapes of his flint against the side of the rock doorway, the pitch on the torch flared. A ribbon of smoke curled upward.

"There," Boldair said, with a broad grin. "Satisfied?"

Viorka nodded. "Mostly, yes, but that doesn't prove there aren't goblins inside."

"I'm afraid I misspoke your bravery, lil' cat," Boldair said.

"I see no reason to risk *my* life in a situation where bravery isn't called for. I choose not to die for *your* curiosity," she replied.

"You're not the least bit curious?"

"Not when I might get eaten by goblins. Besides, you don't know why the other trap has been released."

Boldair grumbled under his breath and entered the narrow doorway with Drucis and Forboud following behind. Dwiskter carried Viorka inside and set her on the dirt cavern floor.

"Boldair?" Viorka said softly.

"Yes?" he replied.

"I know how your second trap was disarmed," she said.

"How?"

"You might rethink your thoughts about the goblins being dead."

Boldair turned. "Why?"

Her eyes widened as she pointed.

CHAPTER 19

Boldair swung the torch in the direction Viorka pointed. Speared into the rock wall was a scrawny goblin. The spear wasn't what had killed it. Its shriveled skin stretched over its bones indicated the mottled green-skinned creature had starved to death.

Dwiskter and Drucis drew their double-edged axes.

"It triggered the other trap," Boldair said with a slight grin.

"I see no amusement in that," Viorka said with a frown.

"So ya know what dat means," Dwiskter said.

"What's dat?" Boldair asked.

"There's more goblins in the cavern," Dwiskter replied.

"Could be a straggler trying to find its way outside," Boldair said.

Drucis shook his head. "Doubtful."

Dwiskter glanced at Boldair. "Is what you hid still here?"

Boldair used the torch to scan the dirt floor. Old crates had been strewn and some had been smashed against the wall. Splintered fragments of planks littered the dirt. "Dammit! Thieving varmints!"

"What did you have?" Dwiskter asked.

"A few small bags of gold coins and some gems. Not a great loss, really," Boldair said. "But too much to have toted back to the city without a mount."

"Where had you found them?" Viorka asked.

"An abandoned goblin alcove deeper in the caverns," Boldair replied.

"You stole the loot from them?" Drucis asked.

"No. No goblins were there."

"Apparently, they were, brother. And they stole back whatever you took from them."

Dwiskter frowned and shook his head. "Dat's not good. They must've been hidden in other dens that you didn't see. If they followed you to the surface to take back their loot, they'll be more violent if we enter their cavern."

"Perhaps we should find a new route to Meadwyrm Pass?" Forboud asked.

Viorka nodded and pleaded. "Yes, let's."

Boldair shook his head. "No. We continue our route to Frosthammer. There's no turning back."

"Why?" Forboud asked in a challenging tone. "Can't you see the odds be far greater against us by entering a cavern where these goblins still live?"

Boldair crossed his arms. "No. If you wish to go back, then go. There's the door. I'll lock it once you're out. But understand, that as king, I need to know dat Frosthammer's not suffered their demise from these fiendish imps. We need to know how badly the undead infestation has become as well. *We* need to know. If somehow the goblins have returned in greater numbers, we need to warn the other kingdoms.The Dwarven Alliance needs to know."

Forboud pointed at the goblin speared to the wall. "You 'ave more than enough proof with dat corpse."

"One dead goblin isn't sufficient evidence to have our allies send troops to investigate," Boldair replied. "We're already here, so we can explore the cavern and alcoves."

Frustrated, Forboud headed toward the door. "I doubt the Alliance will be pleased with your decision to risk your life to explore this cavern."

"I've been through this cavern twice before and never saw one goblin," Boldair said. "I saw no recent evidence of their camps. Besides, their horrendous stink gives them away."

"It doesn't mean they didn't see you," Forbold replied. He walked to the crude entrance.

"Are ye leaving us?" Boldair asked.

"No," Forboud said. "If you're so foolish to continue downward into a maze of goblins, I cannot allow you to go without me. You're still King. I have no choice but to pledge my life to save yours, even if I don't believe in your purpose for ignoring our sound advice. Should we both die, though, who'll rule our grand city?"

Boldair ignored the snide comment. "Then why are you going outside?"

Forboud sighed. "To fetch my mount and Ember. So, Viorka, you might want Boldair and the others to stand between you and Ember. Even though I put Ember's muzzle on again, he can still hurt you." He studied the narrow corridor that led deeper into the cavern. "Judging by the low ceiling, we'll have to lead our mounts."

"The ceilings are higher once we get past the corridor," Boldair said.

"Until then," Forboud said, "we must lead them."

Boldair looked at Viorka and grinned. "Looks like you go first after all."

Her eyes narrowed. "I'm not certain *which* danger I prefer less; Ember or the possibility of goblins gnawing on me."

Drucis chuckled. "For now, we know Ember is real. Not sure about the goblins, but you alert us when they appear."

"I won't be *that* far ahead of Boldair," she replied.

"You'll smell them long before you see them," Drucis said.

"What do they smell like?"

"Acrid sweat and musty ol' rat-eaten rags with a hint of burnt oil and kobold feces. If their jagged blades don't kill ya, the smell most certainly will distract you."

She scrunched her nose and looked at the dark passageway. Frigid air flowed through the corridor and engulfed them.

Viorka rubbed her arms, trying to warm them. "It feels as cold in here as it does outside."

"Aye," Boldair replied.

"Most caves are warmer than this," Drucis said.

Boldair nodded. "Usually, they are. Even though we're going deep underground, the temperatures stay like the dead of winter. How do you think Frosthammer and the Frosted Peaks got their names?"

Dwiskter brought his ram and Drucis'. Forboud entered the cavern with Ember and his ram. After the wolf and ram were clear of the door, Forboud twisted the device at the side of the door. The narrow doorway sealed. Darkness consumed them. Boldair's flickering torch was the only light.

Ember's eyes glowed green in the swaying light.

"Viorka, head on," Boldair said, nodding toward the path ahead.

"No turning back now, huh?" she replied.

"Not unless you wish to be a tiny morsel for a hungry wolf," Forboud said in an ominous tone.

Viorka gasped.

"Pay 'em no mind," Dwiskter said. "Ember's muzzled. As little as the wolf likes Boldair, it's more likely to attack him first."

Boldair shook his head and chuckled.

Dwiskter smiled. "We won't let dat 'appen either."

Viorka took a few hesitant steps. Boldair held the torch overhead, offering the light to be cast around them. The flickering flame licked the frozen rock and melted ancient spider webs.

"Ya know," Drucis said, "there be times when I wish I could cast light spells."

"How long will we remain squeezed tightly together like this?" Dwiskter asked.

Boldair said, "Not too much longer. Twenty yards or so."

"I can't hold me breath dat long," he replied.

"Why would you need to?" Boldair asked.

"These rams' odors are quite gamey."

"I thought dat was you!" Drucis said, before howling with laughter.

Inside the narrow passageway, their voices and laughter echoed.

"Tease all ya like, Drucis," Dwiskter said, "but for a moment, I thought maybe dat stew had made its way through ya already."

"Ha! I'd never confess if dat is true."

"Shh-hh!" Forboud said. "The point of heading deeper into the cavern is to *not* be noticed."

"Ah, now—" Drucis said.

"You realize," Forboud said, interrupting Drucis, "dat any forces dat choose to rush us headlong while we're confined in this tight huddle can destroy us quite readily."

"Let 'em try," Dwiskter said, holding his ax over his shoulder.

"He's right," Boldair said sternly. "The least sound is greatly magnified inside this narrow passage, possibly booming outward into the cavern. If goblins still live here, they know we've entered. They'll be waiting for us."

The group walked in silence until they reached the end of the narrow corridor. Viorka stepped into a vast open room. The path ahead was a narrow stone bridge with no walls at either side.

"Wait," Boldair said to Viorka. He reached to the side of the corridor passage and grabbed an old torch stuck in a hole. He placed it against the lit one until the second torch flamed. He handed it to Drucis. "Dat should help some."

"Aye, much better."

"Watch the path carefully. One misstep and you won't escape death. I've no idea how far down the bottom is. I don't think any of us want to know."

"Shouldn't we mount up?" Dwiskter asked. "The rams are more sure-footed than we are."

"If you trust dat better, so be it." Boldair thought for a moment. "As for me, I continue on foot. Forboud, if you wish to mount up, tether Ember behind you. Should I attempt to ride him across this bridge, he'll find a way to send me to the depths below."

Forboud laughed softly. "You're starting to understand him better than I thought you might."

Boldair took a deep breath and held it. *I'm afraid I understand more about you and the wolf than you realize.*

Drucis climbed on his ram and held the torch. "You mind my asking you a question, Boldair?"

"What's on your mind?"

Drucis cleared his throat. "What e'er possessed you to journey beyond this point? With either side of this bridge dropping into oblivion is enough that I'd have turned back."

"Why would you enter such a place alone?" Forboud asked.

Boldair sighed. "My goal during those days was to find Frosthammer."

"What led you to believe it'd be through these caverns?"

"On occasion I've found old crude maps in the treasures I've discovered."

"Treasure maps?" Dwiskter asked.

"Sometimes," Boldair replied. "I found one particular map that revealed a passageway into Frosthammer. I wanted to know if Frosthammer actually existed or if it was indeed only a myth. That's why I chose to pass through here."

"Do you ever weight the dangers of your travels?" Forboud asked.

"Aye, I have. I do every time."

"I've difficulty believing that," Forboud said.

Boldair held his torch high, allowing more light to spill on the path ahead of Viorka and himself. "Believe as you wish. It's obvious you do anyway. But entertain me with why you think I'm not weighing the dangers now."

"Blasted! Isn't it obvious? You're leading us on a folly-fallen, fool-hardy trek across Aetheaon for a bloody drink," Forboud said.

"That be *half* true," Boldair replied.

"Then, brother, do tell. What be the other half?"

Boldair's voice deepened with anger. "Unfinished business I should've tended to in Frosthammer years ago, if dat's *any* of your concern."

"But you weren't king then."

"Right you be!" Boldair shrugged and nudged Viorka to keep walking across the bridge. "King or not, it's something I should've already take care of. It's none of your concern."

Forboud sighed. "Fair enough. But at least answer this, since I am part of your council. Did the map indicate this cavern was once occupied by goblins?"

"No."

"So other than the dead goblin at the entrance, what caused you to believe goblins inhabited it?" Forboud asked.

"Brother, the treasure I found in the alcove and hid near the entrance had several silver daggers with various rare gems in the handles." Boldair sighed. "They were goblin daggers. I wish I had taken them back with me. The jewels were worth more than all the gold coins combined. But the daggers … there's no mistaking their origin, as no other race crafts them in dat manner."

"What if these goblins had swarmed and killed you?"

"You'd be king," Boldair said with a short laugh. "Erm, wait. I'm wrong 'bout dat assessment."

"Why?"

"Because, most likely, father would still be King."

"Why do you say that?" Forboud asked.

"Everyone believed father when he boasted about killing Taniesse. It wasn't until after she revealed to me who she was that I let others know father had *not* killed her. King Staggnuns and King Thorgum pressed father about his lies and his purpose for lying about his *great dragon slaying*. Dat's when his lies about King Erik surfaced and *why* he was stripped of his reign. Are ya done with your questions? After all, you were the one who insisted we remained quiet, so the goblins can't hear us."

"You're right," Forboud said. "I did say that. But your actions for exploring these caverns seem careless, even now. Regardless of my warnings, you insist we—"

"Enough, Forboud," Boldair said, drawing his ax from its sheath. "I gave you the choice of following or leaving. You chose to follow, yet you yammer on and on. Why question my reasons for seeing if the map led to Frosthammer years ago?"

"I think any one of us would have had held major qualms of further exploration without seeking aid from others."

"I imagine *you* do," Boldair replied. "But you're not me. You don't have the fortitude necessary to search through the dark crevices deep inside the hearts of mountains. Dat's the huge difference between the two of us. It's also why I have the crown. If you wish to take this battle beyond words, me ax is ready. What say ye?"

"I do not wish to lift any weapon against you," Forboud replied. "Regardless of whether you're king or not, you're my brother. I couldn't ever attack you with a weapon."

"No weapon other than the sourness of your words," Boldair said. "The bitterness of your heart spills through your lips and your actions."

"Aye," Dwiskter said. "I can attest to dat! Forboud, I've bitten my tongue for some time during this journey about your questioning our King and his decisions. It's one thing to advise, but you're close to treason with your words. Whether you've noticed or not, my ax is drawn at the ready to remove your tongue if you speak any more ill words toward King Boldair. You know me reputation well enough dat it's not an idle threat but an action I *won't* hesitate to carry out. Do we 'ave an understanding?"

"Aye, duly noted," Forboud said.

"Boldair," Drucis said. "Could I ask you a question?"

"Go on," Boldair said.

"Why would Frosthammer allow goblins to live in such close proximity to them? Is there a treaty between the two?"

"None dat I know of."

"It does seem odd though," Dwiskter said.

"Aye," Boldair agreed. "It's a question worth asking. If nothing else, the goblins are a strong deterrent to prevent outsiders from finding Frosthammer."

"There's no way the Dwarves of Frosthammer couldn't know this goblin cavern neighbors their city," Drucis said.

Viorka dove forward on the narrow bridge. "What was that?"

"What?"

A small creature fluttered in the darkness outside of the torch's radius, swooped past Viorka, and then darted into the darkness once more.

"A bat," Boldair said.

She peered over her shoulder at him. "You're sure?"

"Yes. Quite harmless."

"How much farther do we have to worry about where we step?"

Boldair extended his hand to Viorka and helped her stand. "We've almost reached a giant column that descends from the cavern ceiling into the dark abyss below. A spiral path encircles the column. It's not much wider than the natural bridge ahead of us, but at least we can brace ourselves against the solid column while we get our bearings."

"What about our mounts?" Drucis asked. "Is it wide enough for them?"

"Aye," Boldair replied.

"Once we're on those spiral stairs, where do we go from there?" Dwiskter asked.

"We descend into the darkness below," Boldair replied. "We continue downward until we reach a level rock ledge. That's where another tunnel leads to Frosthammer."

"The map gave you detailed instructions for how far down we are to go?"

"Yes."

Viorka increased her pace. "That smell you warned about earlier?"

"Goblins?"

"Yes."

"I don't smell anything," Boldair said.

"Nor I," said Drucis.

"Trust me," she said. "My sense of smell is greater than all of yours combined. Goblins are nearby, unless there's something else that smells so badly."

Bursts of fires appeared at different levels of the cavern at the outer perimeters. Dozens of them. Mad squeals and angered growls echoed. Metal bolts fired at them, striking the rock bridge at their feet.

"They see us," Boldair said. "Move to the column quickly. Once we head down those stairs, we should be out of their view."

CHAPTER 20

Boldair tried to match Viorka's swift pace but was unable to keep near her. Metal bolts struck the rock bridge in rapid succession. Her keen night vision aided her nimble steps. She seemed capable of knowing where the bolts were going to strike, and her feet moved a second ahead of the bolts as they chipped off the bridge.

In seconds, she was at the column and turned, placing her back against the center column. A large circular, stone platform encompassed the stairs. Should they get down the stairs unharmed, the platform could block the goblins' view from overhead.

Boldair moved his stubby, muscular legs swiftly. Metal bolts struck his steel plate-legs and ricocheted off. He released a burst of crazed laughter, spun his two axes in windmill fashion, and thwarted several bolts that were destined to strike him above the belt.

Behind him, the ram mounts bleated in pain. Ember yelped and snarled. The hides of the rams and the giant wolf were thick, but their skin wasn't impenetrable.

Drucis, Dwiskter, and Forboud dismounted, grabbed the halter of their mounts, and hurried along the narrow bridge. Metal bolts continued to strike the mounts.

Boldair joined Viorka at the circular platform where two more stone bridges intersected into the platform that encircled the spiral stairwell. A line of torches came from each of these roads with at least two dozen crazed goblins growling and snarling. Their eyes glowed crimson, while a few were an odd, snottish green.

"So you *didn't* 'ave this problem the last time you were here, eh?" Drucis pulled his ram onto the circular platform.

"No!" Boldair said, readying his broad axes.

"Well, they've come to greet you with a hearty welcome today!"

"Let 'em come!" Boldair shouted. "I'll sharpen me axes with their bones."

"I'm with you," Drucis said, sliding his shield off his back and hefting his massive ax in his right hand.

Viorka screeched like a mountain lion and growled.

Drucis glanced in her direction. "What the—?"

She was no longer the smaller version of herself. She stood taller and more slender, nearly five feet in height. Her claws extended into long, needle-pointed nails, and her face altered. Her teeth were longer with sharp fangs. A madness swirled in his emerald eyes.

"You've not seen dat side of her before?" Boldair asked.

"Uh, no," Drucis replied with a furrowed brow. He pointed with the tip of his ax. "I'd remember *dat*."

Dwiskter and Forboud reached the circular platform.

"They'll be on us in the span of a few breaths," Boldair said. "Keep your backs against the stairwell! We've no time to descend. We can't retreat, so don't get backed to the outer edge. We're outnumbered, so they can overpower us and knock us into the abyss below. Goblins don't care to sacrifice themselves to kill their enemies."

Dwiskter led his mount to the center near the stairs. He hooked the reins around a metal bolt embedded into the rock column. Drucis did the same. Forboud held Ember's reins and his ram's and positioned himself near the other mounts, hiding in the midst of the rams and Ember.

The stench of the vile goblins was on them before the scuttling creatures even reached the platform.

"Steady yourselves!" Boldair shouted.

Dwiskter laughed. "Seems this trip has a few highlights before we get to Meadwyrm Pass."

"Keep telling yourself dat," Forboud said in an angered whisper.

"Tryin' to work up our thirsts *before* we get there?"

Dwiskter took his shield and positioned it to one side of Boldair to lessen the chance that a metal bolt might strike him.

The goblins' eyes glowed in the light of their torches. Their narrowed slits displayed their fury and demonic hatred. Their rapid footsteps thudded without any fear in their approach. Perhaps they viewed the odds in their favor?

Drucis and Dwiskter lowered their shields, preparing for the onslaught, but as the goblins neared, they leapt, snarling and swinging their daggers madly as they descended.

Before the first goblin touched the platform, Viorka sprang upward, spun, and sliced her long, sharp claws through a goblin's throat. Its squeal of pain ended in less than a second as its head left its body and bounced across the platform.

While still in the air, she spun again, dropped, and kicked her feet off Drucis' shield, propelling herself toward the next two goblins. Their angered expressions widened into brief fear. Viorka stabbed her claws into their chests, plunging deeply. She landed atop them, yanked her claws free, and readied herself for the next goblins.

"Hey!" Dwiskter shouted. "Leave some for me!"

Viorka glanced over her shoulder and grinned. "There's not a shortage from what I can tell."

"From the rear!" Forboud shouted.

Boldair turned toward the other rock bridge. A dozen small torches danced, lighting the eyes of the goblins carrying them. "Ye 'ave an ax, brother. How 'bout using it!"

Forboud released the reins of Ember and his ram and fumbled with pulling his ax from its sheath.

Boldair growled and rushed to the rock bridge, hoping to cut off the goblins' advance before they reached the platform. By the time he got past the ram and Ember, two goblins lunged from the bridge at Forboud.

Boldair growled in fury. He spun with both axes outstretched and jumped forward. When he landed, a goblin's arm dropped to the platform still holding its torch. The goblin squealed. Black blood spurted from it shoulder. Boldair kicked its chest and sent it toppling off the ledge into the darkness below. The second goblin clutched its throat, gurgling. Blood leaked profusely between its fingers. Even in near death, it gnashed its teeth. With the flat-side of his ax, he smacked it. It staggered backwards, slipped on its own blood, and dropped off the platform.

Viorka was midway down the other bridge, slashing through the goblins, dismembering them. Frustrated, Drucis hurried onto the bridge to help. Boldair chuckled. *Not that she needs any help.*

Dwiskter left the two of them on the bridge. He didn't have enough room to join them for fear he might knock them off the bridge by accident. He hurried past Forboud who still struggled to unsheathe his ax. Dwiskter shook his head in disgust and flung his shield upward in front of Boldair, blocking several metal bolts before they struck Boldair's chest.

Boldair and Dwiskter took turns swinging their massive axes, striking and toppling the approaching stream of goblins. As more and more goblins fell into the chasm, the goblins farther up the bridge slowed their paces, possibly realizing they held no advantage in their swarm tactic.

"Hold your positions!" Boldair shouted. He glanced at Dwiskter. "They're having second thoughts now."

"Seems so," Dwiskter replied.

Fireballs glowed from a higher ledge. Seconds later, the fireballs glided toward them.

"Bloody Hell!" Boldair shouted. "Sorcerer!"

Dwiskter lifted his shield and blocked two fireballs. Several metal bolts flicked off the shield immediately after.

"We've no way to stop their firing from this distance," Boldair said.

Forboud whispered, "Behind you."

Boldair turned and looked. On the ground was a goblin crossbow. He glanced at Forboud. "You know how to use it?"

Forboud nodded.

"Then do so. It's apparent you can't use an ax!"

Forboud frowned at the comment. He grabbed the crossbow and several bolts off the platform.

"Aim for the sorcerer," Boldair said.

"I can't see him," Forboud replied.

"Whenever he creates a fireball, dat's where you aim!" Dwiskter said, frowning. "Ya sure your father trained you for battle?"

"Quite," Forboud said.

"Then bloody hell prove it!" Dwiskter said.

Six goblins charged in pairs toward Boldair. They struck Dwiskter's shield, knocking him and Boldair backwards onto the platform. Another half dozen goblins scrambled down the bridge, trying to encircle them.

The crossbow twanged.

Boldair blocked the downward dagger attack from a goblin, catching its wrist with the handle of his ax. He shoved, sending the goblin back into the others.

Fireballs lofted on the higher ledge. Forboud fired again. The sorcerer shrieked in sudden pain, and the fireball engulfed the sorcerer.

Boldair and Dwiskter fought to hold back the goblins. But before he realized it, the goblins had taken the advantage of the Dwarves' brief distractions and were moving quickly to overpower them.

Boldair swung his ax, ripping a goblin in half. He glanced toward the other bridge. Viorka and Drucis backed their way to the platform as a huge wave of goblins pressed across the bridge. Viorka slashed but these goblins carried tiny iron shields, which prevented her claws from reaching them.

Ember howled fiercely, ripping the muzzle off its snout. The sound echoed greater than thunder, striking fear into the goblin mob. The wolf growled and lunged at the goblins surrounding Boldair. Its massive jaws clamped down on a goblin. The goblin squealed in pain as the wolf held tightly and shook its head. Bones cracked.

Ember flung the lifeless goblin onto the bridge, causing the line of approaching goblins to pause and inspect their dead comrade. Two goblins nudged the body with the tips of their daggers. With eyes widened, they peered at Ember and the Dwarven warriors fighting on the platform.

Ember snapped up the next goblin and repeated the process. Then in a frenzy, Ember mauled and bit his way through the remaining goblins standing on the platform. Several goblins jumped off the platform, preferring to fall to their deaths rather than being ripped apart. Ember stepped partway onto the bridge with a fearsome growl rumbling in his throat. He faced the line of goblins that stood frozen, contemplating whether to continue their attack or to turn and flee.

Boldair decapitated a goblin with a swift swing of his ax and pushed his way to the next one. Goblin corpses piled around his feet. Slick pools of black blood spread and dripped off the edge of the platform. With Ember blocking the approach of the frightened goblins, Boldair hurried to the other side of the platform to aid Viorka and Drucis.

"Some help here," Viorka said, panting. She leaned her back against the column. Blood dripped from her long sharp claws.

Dwiskter turned and stepped beside her, eyeing the blood dripping to the rock platform at her feet. "You okay?"

She nodded. "It's not mine, but … I'm winded. I've killed sixteen."

"Ah, now, I counted fifteen," Drucis said, teasing. "The one *jumped* to his death."

Viorka grinned. "It still counts. He jumped because I took a step toward him."

While Ember faced the perplexed goblins on the opposite bridge, Drucis, Dwiskter, and Viorka faced a determined line of partially armored goblins with daggers and shields. Although their armor was flimsy at best, it didn't allow for swift kills.

"How many have you killed?" Dwiskter asked.

"Erm, ten, I think, but *she*'s been blocking my path pretty much the entire time."

She grinned and shook her head. "Excuses!"

"Move aside and let me show you how it's done," Dwiskter said. He glanced at Viorka and whispered, "Catch your breath and rejoin us."

"Ah, find your own!" Drucis said, placing his right foot forward and readying his ax.

The band of armored goblins advanced in odd jumpy steps. They sprang upward from one foot to the other, bounding toward the column platform. They seemed to defy gravity, as though floating softly on unseen steps in the air.

Drucis and Dwiskter stood side by side and battered their axes into the goblins' helmets. The crushing impact bent the helmets into their skulls, causing them to collapse where they stood. These goblins, like those on the opposite bridge, realized that while they held a far greater number, they weren't capable of making a wide lunging attack due to the narrowness of the bridge. After the two Dwarves killed another half dozen goblins, the goblins halted, grumbling and shouting obscenities. As their heated bickering amongst themselves ensued, some of them fought each other.

Viorka screeched with a high-pitched growl of pain. A moment later, Ember yelped and whimpered in a horrible series of cries.

"Viorka!" Boldair yelled.

She lay on the platform, clutching her side, drawn in upon herself. Ember staggered away, wiping its bleeding left eye with its paw. His whining yelps frightened the remaining goblins, and they scurried away, deeper into the darkness.

Ember shook his head, spraying pellets of warm blood across the platform. The pain angered the dire wolf, causing him to growl and snap savagely at the air. His nostrils flared and he panted, sniffing across the platform until he found Viorka.

Already in pain, she pushed herself upright and moved backwards, scooting toward the column. Ember lunged at her again, his massive jaws barely missing her. In response, Viorka slid to her side and flailed her long claws into Ember's left shoulder, sinking her nails deeply.

Ember yelped and yanked back, dragging Viorka's limp body with him. She pressed her free hand against the rock platform for leverage and yanked her claws free.

"You shall die for this!" Forboud shouted with his ax held overhead with both hands.

Boldair leapt and caught the ax handle right beneath the sharp blade and yanked downward, causing Forboud to land on his back hard. "*Now* you choose to use your ax?"

"Look what she did to Ember!"

"The wolf's lucky *I* don't kill it," Boldair said.

"That damn wolf attacked me," she groaned. She winced with each breath. Blood leaked through her fingers.

Spittle flew from Forboud's lips. "A shame it didn't!"

Boldair placed his boot atop Forboud's chest and pressed the sharp edge of his ax to his brother's throat. "I've a good mind to slit your throat right here in front of our enemy. Viorka's my friend, and a friend of the King outweighs your loyalty to me; which, as it appears, has been next to nothing."

"How can you say dat?" Forboud asked.

"How?" Boldair cocked his head to the side. Fury reddened his cheeks and creased his brow. "Because you never lifted your ax to kill any of these goblins. You don't think I could tell dat you were leaving us to our demise? You hid amongst our mounts."

"I couldn't free my ax."

"You think me a fool, brother?" Boldair pressed the blade harder, cutting Forboud's skin and looked into his brother's frightened eyes. "I thought father taught you how to fight in battle, but it seems you're a coward to the core. And cowards on the battlefield must be punished for such weakness."

"Please, brother, don't."

"Other than striking the sorcerer with a metal bolt, you lingered away from the battle while the rest of us fought for our lives. Rest assured, Forboud, we *weren't* fighting to protect *you*. Are you wishing my death so you can claim the crown? Is dat why you refused to draw your weapon?"

Forboud opened his mouth to speak, but Boldair shook his head and pushed the blade harder. Tears formed in Forboud's eyes and spilled, running down the sides of his face into his ears.

"Now, you listen. Your words mean nothing to me. Your actions reveal everything about you, do they not?" Boldair asked. "Tell me something, brother. When Drucis, Dwiskter, and I fought for Lady Dawn, *where* were you? I didn't see you on the front lines, nor did I see you with father dat night. In fact, I'll wager dat if I ask King Staggnuns and King Thorgum about your whereabouts during the battle, they'll be clueless as well."

"I—I was—"

"Save your breath, brother," Boldair said, kneeling atop Forboud, peering deeply into his eyes. "Your lies cannot save you. Drucis, Dwiskter, did either of you ever see Forboud during the Battle of Hoffnung?"

They shook their heads, looking at Forboud with disdain. Both said, "No."

Boldair shook his head and ground his teeth. His breathing grew heavier with each deep breath he took. "See? None of us saw you in battle. You kept father fooled, didn't you? All those years of training with him, making him believe and boast about ye, and yet, none of dat ever gave you bravery to face an enemy on the battlefield. You can't even kill a stinking lil' goblin, but you can try to kill my friend after dat bloody wolf almost killed her. You're a disgrace to Nagdor. And as such, you shall pay the appropriate price."

Fear widened Forboud's eyes even more. Tears leaked rapidly. His breathing shuddered.

"Only if father could see ya now," Boldair said. He set his ax aside and it clanged on the rock. He drew a sharp dagger from the sheath on his belt.

"Brother, please," Forboud said with a shaking voice. "Please reconsider."

Boldair shook his head. "There's nothing to reconsider. Don't struggle. Just close your eyes, take a deep breath, and be quiet. It will end in seconds."

Boldair pressed one hand around Forboud's throat and placed the dagger to his brother's neck.

"Boldair," Forboud sobbed. "Please."

"Sh-hh-hh," Boldair said. "Close your eyes."

Forboud obeyed and offered a slight nod.

With one swift stroke, Boldair sliced with the dagger. Confused,

Forboud opened his tear-filled eyes. Boldair lifted his left hand. Clutched in Boldair's fist was Forboud's long braided beard.

A hurt sigh expelled from Forboud's mouth. He closed his eyes. His body fell limp. Tears flowed.

"Boldair," Drucis said, "Viorka isn't moving."

Boldair pushed himself to his feet, grabbed his ax, and clung to Forboud's beard with his other hand. "Dwiskter, take Forboud's weapons. Make certain he doesn't even possess a lock pick. Then bind his hands behind his back. If the goblins return to attack, leave him to their mercy."

Dwiskter nodded, eyed Forboud's beard in Boldair's fist, and stared at Forboud.

No greater shame was known to the Dwarves within the Dwarven Alliance than for one to have his beard removed. It showed everyone, regardless of rank or race, the Dwarf's great dishonor.

Boldair knelt beside Viorka and placed the back of his hand against her furry cheek. Blood leaked from her nostrils and at the edges of her mouth. Her breathing was shallow, and if they didn't get her to a medic or a healer immediately, she'd die.

Gently, Boldair scooped her into his arms and rose. "Have the goblins fled, or do we still need to defend our position?"

Drucis looked up from gathering coin pouches off the goblin corpses. He took a few moments to study the bridges. "They're retreating, for now. We probably killed a hundred of them by my estimate. They'll reconsider a second attack for a while."

"Good," Boldair said. "I must get Viorka to Frosthammer before she dies."

Dwiskter shoved Forboud toward the stairs. Forboud's hands were tied behind his back. "And what of him?"

"Tether Ember to walk behind him. Should either decide to jump, they both suffer the same fate," Boldair said, eyeing Forboud fiercely. "Not much of a loss either way."

"You could execute him here, if you so wish," Dwiskter said. "Toss his body into the ravine. You 'ave dat right. No one but us would know."

Forboud's eyes hollowed as he peered at Dwiskter and then flicked his gaze to Boldair.

Boldair nodded, pondering the thought. "Aye, I do. But living in shame is greater punishment than immediate death."

"I agree with you there," Dwiskter said, placing his hand against Forboud's shoulder. "Come on."

Boldair looked at Drucis. "I must go first. If you could, please lead our mounts down the stairs. You'll come to another platform like this except there aren't any bridges connected to it. Only a large double-door dat will lead us into Frosthammer. I'll await for you there. Please hurry."

CHAPTER 21

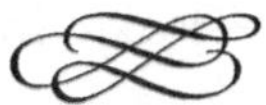

Two glowing Elven stones set at the each side of the double-doors offered enough ambient lighting to see from the entrance to the stairwell column. Boldair held Viorka in his arms and paced in front of the locked steel double-doors. He mumbled incoherently. Anger and rage shortened his patience.

Ember's harsh attack had left no obvious bleeding wounds, but the caked blood around her mouth and nose indicated she'd suffered serious internal injuries, and perhaps neared the brink of death.

No guards stood outside. On Boldair's last visit, the guards were inside the double-doors. To have them open the steel doors, he needed to rap the proper sequences of knocks at exactly the right pace. Since no one else in his party knew the proper code, he needed to wait until they arrived.

"You're going to be okay, lil' cat," Boldair said. "I promise. I'll get you help."

He shook his head and exhaled. Puffs of white flowed from his mouth. The frosty air bit his nose. Frozen tears filled the wrinkles around his eyes.

"Boldair!" Drucis shouted. "Are we near?"

"Aye!"

Their steel boots scuffed harshly against the steps as they came around the last spiral.

Drucis led his ram and Forboud's off the steps and onto the platform. He stared at the double-doors with uncertainty. "Don't tell me that we're locked out?"

"We are," Boldair said, "but they'll let us in."

"How can you be certain?"

Boldair shrugged, holding Viorka in his arms. "They opened the doors for me the last time I was here."

"Is she going to survive?" Drucis asked.

"I pray so."

"Is this her true form?" Drucis asked. He studied her face and gently touched the fur on her forearm. Raising her limp hand, he inspected her long needle-like claws. He shook his head, possibly thinking about how painful it'd be having those claws thrust into one's flesh.

Boldair said, "I'm not sure which form is dominant. She alters, based on the circumstances. She's a dangerous fighter when in this form."

"But she's not changed back. Is dat normal?"

"Perhaps it's because we're *not* out of danger. Her life's in the balance, so it's safe to say dat she's still in danger."

Dwiskter stepped on the platform, reached behind and grabbed Forboud's mail tunic, and tugged him to follow. Forboud offered no resistance or words. His eyes expressed his shattered spirit and loss of hope. Since Ember was tethered to Forboud, the dire wolf stood closely behind. Blood dripped from three deep grooves Viorka slashed through its left eye and into its skull during the few moments she had to defend herself.

Boldair guessed that Ember rushed her from behind and wrapped his powerful jaws around her waist, possibly shaking her like he had the goblins he'd killed. But she had done nothing to provoke the wolf. Raking her razor claws was her natural instinct to defend herself. It was possible her aim was off the first time she struck. But slashing through the wolf's eye was a tender vulnerable spot, enough to distort and disorient her attacker. It was enough to make Ember drop her due to his shocking pain.

During Ember's second attempted attack, Boldair figured Viorka's aim was for the wolf's heart, but she was too weak to accurately strike the proper spot or plunge her claws deep enough.

Boldair cradled Viorka in his left arm and did the series of knocks with his right from memory.

"You learned dat code from the map?" Dwiskter asked.

Boldair nodded. "Aye."

The double-doors rattled slightly and pulled inward. Two Dwarf guards stood dressed in armor fashioned from the scales of Ice Dragons, which were rumored to have lived in the highest elevations of the Frosted Peaks. From Boldair's previous visit, he learned that this armor was light weight and almost impenetrable to most weapons, other than those enchanted with fire spells.

The Frosthammer guards looked at Viorka with grave concern before they noticed who held her.

"Boldair!" one guard exclaimed. "I never expected you to return after such a long absence!"

Yotram! Brandrum!" Boldair said with a forced, hearty laugh.

"With your treasure hunts, I figured a dragon might have eaten you," Yotram said.

"Almost, my friends! Almost!"

"Good dat you've returned."

Boldair forced a quick smile. "Only hoped to be passing through, but my friend here has suffered a vicious attack. Her life is fleeting."

"This fynx is your friend?" Yotram asked, peering closer. He marveled. His icy blue beard was neatly tied into long braids. His hair was sheered short on the sides but a long ponytail tied into knots hung down the center of his back. "I've only seen paintings of these unique creatures. Never thought they really existed."

"It's obvious they do," Boldair replied.

Yotram shrugged. "No denials now, I must say."

"I don't suppose dat you're aware," Boldair said, "but there be an army of goblins in the outside cavern. You might consider placing more guards to stand watch at the gate."

Brandrum was bald with a dark bluish-black beard. He reared back his head and roared with laughter at Boldair's remark. His voice thundered deeply when he said, "Oh, now, Boldair, much too early and too little stout for ya to begin telling tales so soon upon arrival!"

"No, not a tale. Tis the truth. The goblins 'ave returned," Boldair said with a stern gaze. "In far greater number, it seems."

"You're not hoodwinking us? No lie?" Brandrum asked, cocking a brow.

"I never lie," Boldair said with a slight frown. "I might exaggerate from time to time, *after* a few tankards, but my friend, this isn't one of those times. I speak truthfully and without exaggeration. The goblins have somehow returned."

Dwiskter nodded. "Boldair speaks the truth. We killed a hundred of 'em before they retreated to the higher ledges of the cavern. In the pitch darkness, we've no way to properly estimate how many there are."

Concern overtook Brandrum's and Yotram's facial expressions.

Drucis held up several coin pouches and shook them. "This be some of the loot I retrieved off their stinking corpses."

Brandrum and Yotram cautiously watched the outside stairwell column while they hurried to shut the heavy doors. After sealing it shut, they latched several heavy steel planks into position and locked them. It was doubtful the best Dwarven cannon could destroy the gate; not that they need ever fear one from the outside, as it was impossible to get one through the cavern and up the spiral stairs.

"Goblins? Did they do this to the fynx?" Brandrum asked.

"No," Boldair replied. "The wolf mount tried to kill her."

"She's not faring well at all," Brandrum said.

"Aye," Boldair replied. "I need to get her to a medic or a healer quickly, please."

"Yotram," the guard said to his companion. "Could you escort him to Telsia?"

"Of course," Yotram said.

Two patrol guards approached the locked gate, studied Boldair for a few minutes, and broad smiles broke their stern faces. "Boldair! Come for more of our frostbitten stout?"

"At the moment, no," Boldair replied.

"I'm escorting him to the medic," Yotram said.

"Drinks at the Ice-Slurry Tavern later?" one guard asked. He carried a heavy hammer in his hand and had an octagon bronze shield slung over his back. He wore a patch over his left eye. A long scar began above his left eye and ended at his lower jaw, cutting a bare path through is bluish-gray beard. "Or perhaps, you'd prefer Hogshead Splatter Grog?"

"Perhaps later, Kairun. Let's see how things go with the medic first," Boldair replied.

The two guards nodded.

"Can I or Bathil aid you in any way?" Kairun asked.

Bathil crossed his thick muscular arms. Sheathed on his belt were two short swords. His braided beard and hair were dark blue, which appeared almost black in color. Several tattoos marked his face and massive forearms. He studied the fynx with great curiosity.

"Actually," Boldair said, "Forboud needs to be placed into a cell until we're ready to depart."

"Your own brother?" Bathil glanced toward Forboud and grimaced.

"Aye," Boldair said.

Forboud looked at Bathil questioningly. "And how do you know my name?"

Bathil ignored him and said, "What's he done to bring himself such shame?"

"Partly, what happened to my little friend here," Boldair said. "If you can place him in a cell until I can get Viorka help, I'd be grateful."

"Aye," Bathil said. He frowned at Forboud with disgust. "We'll make certain he's well taken care of."

"Good. Trust me, you cannot believe a word dat falls from his deceitful tongue. Almost cost us our lives by trusting him," Boldair showed the horrible bruising around his wrist where Ember had attacked him. "And it might yet cause hers. He'd best hope she survives."

"May I ask what he did?"

"He betrayed the King of Nagdor," Boldair replied.

"Your father? I thought the two of them were close?"

Drucis shook his head. "Boldair's the King now."

"Boldair?" Yotram said in disbelief. "You've taken the throne?"

Boldair held a grim gaze and nodded solemnly. "We've much catching up to do. Now's not the time. I'll share with all of you my endeavors since we last spoke. Drinks shall be on me."

Bathil nodded and laughed. "I hope you've deep pockets, if you're buying the stout."

Viorka's body shook. Boldair couldn't tell if it were due to the frosty temperature or if death was trying to claim her.

"Follow me, Boldair," Yotram said.

CHAPTER 22

Boldair followed Yotram. Drucis and Dwiskter walked alongside Boldair. He cradled Viorka in his arms. Other than her occasional tremors, she hadn't moved since they entered the gate. Her shallow breathing and profuse sweating were the only reasons he knew she was still alive.

They marched at a rapid pace. Their steel boots thudded on the metal roadway. Thick steel panels with tread grooves for traction were riveted to the roads throughout the upper levels of the city. They walked along the Pinnacle Path at the edge of a deep chasm, which divided the great city into nearly equal halves. The pungent scent of brimstone lofted in the air. Every eighth of a mile, a bridge crossed the divide. At the bottom of the ravine, the fiery river's radiant glow reflected upward.

The river's appearance was deceptive. Contrary to the heat the river should've provided Frosthammer, the city remained frigid. Braziers of fire set outside each shop and place of lodging. And yet, they offered little heat, unless one stood close to the flames. Lanterns hung from polished metal posts along the edge of the roadway, the awnings of buildings, and along the bridges.

The Frosthammer Dwarves were hearty. The cold didn't affect them.

The only ones standing at separate braziers were a few visiting forest Elves and some gnomes. The Elves regarded the passing Dwarves with slight suspicion, but when they noticed Viorka in Boldair's arms, they turned with keener interest.

Drucis peered over the edge toward the river below. "Ah, the legend be true?"

"What legend?" Boldair asked.

"That Frosthammer's built above the lava flows?"

Yotram glanced over his shoulder. A slight grin broke through his thick beard. "That, my friend, is the River of Steel. It's a river of molten steel that runs from our smelters. It flows and separates into different channels farther down into the lowest levels of the city. There, it's poured into various molds, depending on what we need."

"For dat much molten steel to be flowing through a vast channel, you must 'ave a mighty furnace for heat," Drucis said. "Either dat, or your using the heat from the belly of Hell."

Yotram laughed softly. He came to an intersection. The left path led to a bridge that crossed the River of Steel. He walked to the right, which led them to an open lift. The rising platform elevated and stopped right before them. "Come. We're almost at Telsia's shop."

Boldair and his party followed Yotram onto the lift. After several seconds, the lift lowered, descending at a moderate pace with the clicking of gears and chains. The lift stopped at two different floors, and when it stopped at a third floor, Yotram stepped off onto the street.

The glowing river beamed brighter. Several Dwarves pushed carts of goods. Some led burros packed with large sacks of grain and other odd and end wares. A couple of wagons passed with freshly sawn logs.

Dwiskter studied the passersby. "What cities do you trade with?"

Yotram turned right onto the next street. "Frosthammer's essentially self-sufficient."

"How?" Drucis asked. "We're far deeper under a mountain than any other Dwarven city I've ever been to. How do you maintain food and where did those logs come from?"

"We have farmers. A large pool of water has a variety of fish. Over time, we've adapted, learned how to obtain our own resources without the aid of outsiders, but we still trade some goods. There's not sufficient time to explain it all," Yotram said. "But if you're with Boldair in a tavern later, I'll try to answer your questions as best I can."

"Aye, thanks," Drucis replied. "Sounds like something worth listening to while downing a few tankards."

Yotram pushed the door of a small building inward. "This is Telsia's shop."

"Thanks," Boldair said, walking past Yotram.

Boldair stood before a polished wooden countertop that looked more like he was in a tavern and not waiting for a medic or healer. The only exception was the carved runes in the counter's surface. He studied them for a long moment. *Elven?*

"Where is she?" Boldair paced. He scanned the room.

Hanging directly over the counter was a chandelier made from four medium-sized dragon tusks. Large candles burned at each of the four flattened ends. Boldair almost cringed. Between the guards who wore their armor made from the scales of long-believed extinct Frost Dragons and dragon tusks used for ornamental purposes, he wondered where they'd obtained these materials. Had they discovered the burial grounds where these dragons once prospered? Or were they the ones who drove the Frost Dragons to extinction?

He averted his attention away from the tusks to prevent his curiosity and anger from increasing. Since his friendship with Taniesse, his view of dragons was far different than most of Aetheaon's. He wondered what Taniesse would do if ever she entered the gates of Frosthammer. Would she torch the city in an unyielding rage?

Boldair turned from the counter, and gazed about the room. Bottles of powdered herbs, dried leaves, and ground roots lined the shelves from the ceiling to the floor on two walls. Each bottle was labeled with penmanship unlearned by the hand of most Dwarves. The writing resembled that of the dedicated monks in the Ruins of Sturn, which had been destroyed centuries earlier by the dark Elves. However, some of the scrolls they'd written were kept in the libraries and temples throughout Aetheaon.

A double-sided bookcase acted as a partial wall to divide the main entrance and formed a tiny room in the corner. The decorative spines of the books were written in various languages of Fae, Elves, Dwarves, humans, and Gnomes.

Almost hidden in the nook was a small round table that set in the corner where the two shelves filled with the bottled ingredients met. A black cloth weaved from pure spider-silk draped the table. In the center of the table were Fae crystals, used to divine one's future or more commonly, to find a lost loved one. Sweet incense billowed in tiny streams from a silver burner shaped like a dragon's head. The eyes were deep red rubies that glinted ever so slightly whenever one gazed at them.

A silver birdcage hung from a golden hook on the ceiling. Several odd looking sprites hovered inside the cage. Their eyes shifted with mischievous curiosity as they studied the three Dwarves. Their hideous bitter faces prevented anyone from staring at them for more than a few moments.

Telsia pushed a hanging purple drape across a silver curtain rod, stepped through a narrow doorway, and offered an endearing smile. The brightness of her amber eyes was mesmerizing. "Sorry to have kept you waiting."

She wore a long, flowing black robe that shimmered when she walked. Like the delicate tablecloth, her robe was made from exquisite spider-silk. Her brown hair was tied into a series of knots down her back. With her given name and the decor of the room, Boldair had expected the medic or in this case, the *healer*, to be an Elf, *not* a Dwarf.

"Welcome." Her eyes darted at Viorka and her brow rose. She gasped. "A fynx? She's injured?"

"Aye," Boldair said with a firm nod. "Can ya help us? Quick?"

"My goodness," Telsia said, placing a hand over her mouth. "Bring her to the back, quickly."

She turned and hurried through the curtained door. Boldair followed without hesitation.

Telsia waved her hand toward a small cot. "Lay her there."

Boldair gently placed Viorka on the bed and stepped back. A gentle fire burned in a fireplace. More bookshelves with magical tomes lined the walls.

"What happened?" Telsia asked.

"A dire wolf mount attacked her," he replied.

Telsia placed her hand to Viorka's forehead. She shook her head. Tears moistened her eyes. "Fynxes are rare creatures. She's burning to the touch. Where'd you find her? Did you plan to sell her?"

Boldair shook his head. "Sell her? Hell no! She's my friend."

"Your friend?"

"Aye, she's traveled with me on a couple of journeys now, but nothing as tragic as this."

Telsia studied his eyes for several moments, possibly attempting to discern whether he was telling the truth or not. "I see. When did she last speak?"

Boldair shrugged and looked at Drucis and Dwiskter who stood right outside the door.

"More than a half hour ago," Dwiskter said. "Perhaps a bit longer."

"Hopefully, you've brought her in time," Telsia said. "Leave her with me and I'll tend to her."

"If it's all the same," Boldair said, "can we wait with her for a bit?"

Telsia smiled and offered a slight nod. "You may, but she'll be here for a while. A day or more at best, before she awakens. I'm sure you're all weary from your travels. Across the bridge you'll find an inn with a steam room and other amenities like a hot bath to soothe your aching muscles. Of course, we have dozens of taverns and pubs on each side of the chasm. But as for your friend, she needs immediate attention and lots of rest. She probably won't awaken for some time, as her body heals. May I have her name?"

"Viorka," Boldair said.

She looked deeply into Boldair's eyes. Her amber eyes soothed him, as did the gentle tones of her voice. "Rest assured. She's in good hands. You may come visit her at any time, day or night. My door's always open."

Telsia placed her warm hand on his elbow, and then looped her arm in with his, walking him to the door where Dwiskter and Drucis stood.

"Ya know," Boldair said. "When first told your name and then seeing all the various books ya 'ave in other languages, I never figured you to be a Dwarf. I thought maybe an Elf."

She laughed in a near seductive tone and squeezed his biceps. "While we do have the occasional Elves visit our grand city, we never expect any to set up shop in Frosthammer. We're tolerant of their kind, but not *that* tolerant."

"Many believe Frosthammer to be a mythical city," Boldair said.

"I did," Dwiskter said.

Telsia nodded and beamed a smile. "And we're not offended in that error at all. In fact, it's something we're rather proud of."

"Why's dat?" Boldair asked.

"Because it keeps us from getting involved with the skirmishes of the clashing kingdoms on the surface," she replied, rubbing the inside of his arm. "Of which, I'm certain all of you have witnessed. I'm certain the three of you have fought in a recent war?"

"Aye," Boldair said, nodding in agreement as did Dwiskter.

Telsia walked through the doorway with Boldair. "I detect great valor in you, Boldair. Your boldness has made you a leader, has it not?"

Boldair frowned. "H-how'd ya know dat? How'd you know my name? No introductions 'ave been given."

Telsia smiled softly. Her eyes held his in a warm gaze. "I see a lot of things, and I'm far more than a healer."

Boldair cocked a brow. "I-interesting."

Drucis stood near the exit, counting coins from a goblin pouch. He slid the coins back inside and pulled the drawstring tightly. He tucked the pouch behind his belt and pulled out another one. Frowning, he shook it. "What the—?"

He opened the pouch and looked inside. Carefully, with his forefinger and thumb, he pulled out a stack of dried leaves and held them up.

"What have you there?" Telsia asked. If she had wanted to mask her interest, she failed miserably.

"Leaves of some sort," Drucis replied.

"May I inspect them?"

"Of course." He shrugged and handed them to her.

She carried the leaves to the counter and set them down. Her eyes widened. "How'd you find these?"

"From a goblin's purse," he replied.

"Goblins?" she asked, turning her attention from the herbs to Drucis. Her brow furrowed with concern.

"Aye," Boldair said. "We had to battle our way through the filthy beasts in the cavern in order to get to Frosthammer."

"No goblins have been seen in … ages," she said. She spread the leaves on the countertop. "May I see the pouch?"

Drucis slid the pouch across the counter to her.

She looked inside the bag. "And the goblins had these leaves in their possession?"

Drucis nodded. "Most of their pouches held coins, but dat one had leaves. I probably should've 'ave tossed them rather than keep them."

"To the contrary," she said, "these are quite rare. In fact, if I used a sliver of one in my salve for Viorka, her healing might occur quicker. What's your price for these?"

Drucis shrugged. "You can 'ave them. They're useless to me. And if they can help Viorka, all the better."

"While I greatly appreciate your generous offer, I cannot simply take them. I'd become indebted to you. But, I'd gladly pay whatever your tab is during your stay in Frosthammer for all of you—that's the cost of the inn, your food, and all your drinks at any or all taverns."

Drucis' brow rose, and he exchanged glances with Dwiskter. They laughed heartily until tears formed in their eyes. "Ah, now, ye be puttin' us on. The tab we'd build on drinks alone would cost a fortune."

Boldair nodded. "He's not exaggerating."

"But, it's a price I'm willing to pay," she replied. She crouched behind the counter, clicking a few devices. She rose and tossed a heavy bag onto the counter. Gold coins rattled and spilled out of the top of the bag.

"What are the leaves?" Boldair asked.

"Frostroot."

"They're dat hard to come by?" Drucis asked.

"Yes, especially if the goblins have returned to reside in the cavern. These herbs grow in crevices along steep inclines, which are most difficult for a Dwarf to scale. An Elf or human could do so much easier, due to their thin statures. But whenever I've offered a high reward for Dwarves to collect them, the younger Dwarves are more adventurous and have fallen to their deaths. I quit sending Dwarves into the cavern to find them after we had learned how to cultivate them.

"But a blight of some sort wiped out our supply. The reason I'm willing to pay such a high price is because the pouch also contains seeds. With the proper care, I might be able to sprout some seedlings in my shop to transplant in the darker recesses of Frosthammer. Should I succeed, I'll be able harvest more seeds and replenish our cultivation." She placed her hand on the bag of gold coins. "However, I refuse to take these for free, so do we have an agreement?"

Drucis nodded and placed the loose coins back into the bag. "Aye."

"Good," she said before turning her attention to Boldair. "There's one thing more I need from you."

"What's dat?" Boldair asked.

"Stick your index finger into the pixie cage," she replied.

Boldair responded with a curious frown. "Why?"

"Trust me," Telsia said, smiling.

"No offense, but I find it difficult to yield my trust to anyone since I've been betrayed by my father and my brother. Both of which probably wish me dead."

"I understand betrayals within families more than you might think," she said. "Often one learns to rely more on strangers than those bound to us by blood. All the same, it's only a simple task and something you need to do in case I need to find you quickly. Frosthammer's a huge city. If finding someone based on chance alone, you could wander for weeks and our paths might never cross."

Boldair removed his glove and placed his finger through a small hole near the top of the cage. A pixie lighted upon the edge of his finger, jabbing his finger with a short quill. He yanked his finger from the cage. Blood pooled where he had been pricked. He frowned at Telsia. "What's the meaning of dat?"

The pixie placed the hollow end of the quill to its lips and tilted it back, drinking Boldair's blood.

"Now, if need be, should Viorka's health worsen, and we pray it doesn't, Frizt can locate you for me. Preferably, all shall go well for Viorka's recovery. But if not, I'll send Frizt to fetch you."

Boldair rubbed his finger and nodded. He looked at Drucis and Dwiskter. "Let's go."

CHAPTER 23

Boldair left Telsia's shop and walked onto the bridge that crossed to the other half of the city. Drucis and Dwiskter walked behind him.

"You trust her?" Dwiskter asked.

Boldair stopped mid-stride and turned, glancing at Dwiskter over his shoulder. Frustration creased his brow. He shrugged. "What choice do I 'ave? I'm not a medic, nor a healer, and to be honest, I don't know who else I could leave Viorka with. It pains me to leave. You 'ave any suggestions?"

Dwiskter shook his head. "No. I know no one here."

Boldair forced a tired smile. "Then the rest is fate."

"Know, King, dat I'm here for you, regardless of the outcome. My ax and shield are to protect you for as long as I breathe."

Boldair nodded. "I appreciate your devotion, but while we're in Frosthammer, let's not mention my being the King of Nagdor. Safety reasons and such."

"Aye, as you wish," Dwiskter said.

Boldair turned and walked halfway across the bridge.

"You've only been to Frosthammer once before?" Drucis asked.

Boldair stopped and stepped to the side of the bridge so the city's inhabitants could continue to their destinations without having to step around him. He nodded. "Aye."

"The guards know you quite well," Dwiskter said. "How long did you stay?"

"A couple of weeks."

"Why'd ya stay for so long?" Drucis asked.

"To be truthful, I was tired of searching for treasure after the map led me here. Getting to the goblin cave through the mountains exhausted me. After two weeks of *recovery* ended, I was almost out of gold. Drinks are expensive at most of the Frosthaven taverns, especially when you're *not* a citizen. With my funds depleting, I left to get more gold from my troves, so I to could stay longer."

Dwiskter leaned against the steel rail of the bridge and looked down. Icicles snapped off the rail and tumbled downward, melting before they were even close to the molten steel. "But you never returned until today?"

"No, I didn't."

"How many levels does Frosthammer have?" Drucis asked. "This is a massive place."

Boldair grinned. "Aye, it is. When I visited before, I counted eight levels on each side of the river." He laughed. "Of course, dat might not be accurate with all the tavern-hopping I'd done; the occasional blurred vision and all. If your goal is to drink at each tavern before we leave, we'd be here longer than an average Elf's life."

Drucis laughed. "In the heart of the mountains lives the hearts of the Dwarves, and in the hearts of the Dwarves live our love for hard stout. I could die a happy Dwarf in Frosthammer."

Dwiskter pounded his fist on Drucis' shoulder. "I'll drink to dat!"

From the rail of the bridge, Boldair counted the closest sets of bridges downward. Four levels of the city were below their position, as best he could tell since the floors got darker, the deeper the city went. Another three levels of the city were above them. Following the River of Steel into the heart of the mountain, he counted the number of bridges outward, but his limited vision prevented him from viewing the full distance the city expanded. Frosthammer seemed unending.

Of course, the colossal statue of King Rigrim Dragonbane stood with one foot planted on each side of the molten river and blocked the view of what else was downriver. Balanced in both hands was King Dragonbane's massive warhammer with simulated icicles hanging from the hammer's head. Atop his helmet were wings like a majestic eagle. His eyes were insets of enormous amber stones set in the sockets. Braziers burned behind these huge stones, causing the eyes to glow ominously. For any visitor, the statue was menacing because the city stood eight levels high, and the tip of the winged helmet rose above the rooftops of the highest level.

Most Kings possessed egos, but none, it seemed to Boldair, was greater than Dragonbane's.

During Boldair's previous visit, he never met or saw the King, but the Dragonbane's massive warhammer was the reason for the city's name. From stories belted by the bards in taverns, Dragonbane's hammer could not only crush his enemies, it froze their bodies seconds beforehand, causing their flesh to shatter and explode like crushed ice the moment the heavy hammer struck them.

Nothing caused loyalty better than fear. Perhaps this was why the residents seldom left Frosthammer, and why the few that visited never left. Somehow over the centuries, other kingdoms dismissed Frosthammer, and the less the city was mentioned, the quicker it faded from memory into that of mere legend. Because few Dwarves ever moved outside the mountains that housed Frosthammer, the city's population steadily multiplied.

From Boldair's estimation, Frosthammer easily outnumbered the combined populations of the three cities in the Dwarven Alliance: Nagdor, Damdur, and Icevale. Why did this magnificent kingdom isolate itself from the other Dwarven cities? Was it because the other Kings had shunned and forbade them from joining the Alliance? Or had King Dragonbane purposely withdrawn from a former alliance with the Northern Dwarven Alliance? If the latter was the case, evidence of such a withdrawal was stricken from the history ledgers and tomes.

Had Boldair not succeeded his father on the throne, he could have easily moved to Frosthammer without a single regret. But such a decision would have had to occur *after* he was too decrepit to explore Aetheaon in his quests to find more treasure and nearer the time when the mountains were ready to reclaim him.

He was still young for a Dwarf—too young to become King, he reasoned—and he thought it odd that his heart was being torn three different directions, as each of his strongest desires—being a king, treasure-hunting, and settling in Frosthammer—pulled with almost the same exact strength. However, now, being king ranked higher due to his responsibility to oversee his kingdom. With his father's execution near at hand, and Forboud not worthy to take the throne, it left Boldair to do so.

"Boldair!" Dwiskter said.

Boldair jerked and flicked his gaze at Dwiskter. Drucis had opened another goblin purse and stood examining its contents with eager eyes.

"Your mind has taken you elsewhere," Dwiskter said with a short laugh. "Are ye lost in your memories of your previous visit? Or are the issues with your father and Forboud still troubling you?"

"Apologies. A lot weighs heavily on my heart and my mind."

"I understand. With all the places to explore in Frosthammer—the beautiful monuments and fountains, the various merchants and shops— this is a city I could get lost in. I don't see why you never came back," Dwiskter said. "Is there a reason you've not disclosed to us?"

"I wanted to return," Boldair replied. He sighed and lowered his gaze. Again, his mind drifted. "I truly did. My heart and mind have battled fiercely with one another over the decision. Eventually my mind won, persuading me to lean toward my adventurous side." He chuckled. "It's true dat one can get lost in this city's beauty. One can also get lost in—" He cleared his throat and changed the subject. "And if one isn't careful, one might never leave. I grieved a long time after my departure, and dat's why I couldn't return. I felt a continual tug at me heart to come back though. Dat dull nagging desire never faded completely. My mind lost its strength to resist any longer. Perhaps dat's why I took the opportunity to cross through the city on our way to Meadwyrm Pass. I fear I might regret returning though."

Dwiskter gave Boldair a curious smile. "And why is dat?"

"I 'ave me reasons," Boldair said.

"My guess is he's avoided his return to Frosthammer because of me," a voice said from behind them.

The three Dwarves turned to see a female Dwarf standing near the center of the bridge with her muscled arms crossed. Like the guards at the gate, she wore icy-blue armor made from frost dragon scales. Her dark, bluish-black hair was tied with fancy knots down her back. She peered at Boldair for several long moments with anger flaring in her amber eyes. Then, without warning, her anger subsided and her gaze softened. Her eyes moistened.

"Wynneffin?" Boldair said.

"Did you think you could visit Frosthammer and I *wouldn't* find you? That I wouldn't sense your presence?" she asked.

Boldair smiled. The wrinkles at the sides of his eyes creased deeper. "I'm glad you found me, actually. I had no idea where to start looking for you."

"Is dat the truth?" she asked.

"Aye, it is."

Wynneffin sighed and shook her head. "I doubt I've crossed your mind over the years. I don't think you'd have searched for me, either."

"Wynnie, dat's not true."

Her attention moved to Dwiskter and Drucis. "Tell me, gents, has Boldair *ever* mentioned anything about me to either of you? One word even?"

Taken back by the question, Dwiskter pushed back from the rail, glanced at Drucis, and said, "It's time you and I explore the city. We don't want to tread into this ... long avoided conversation dat doesn't concern us at all."

"Aye," Drucis said. He chuckled. "The goblins we fought were mild to the battle Boldair's about to face."

"Hey—" Boldair said, pointing a stern finger at them.

Dwiskter laughed under his breath, and he winked. "Tis why I've not pursued a wife."

Drucis winked and whispered, "Seems she's pursuing him."

Dwiskter nodded. "I believe you're right."

Drucis offered a slight bow to Wynneffin. "Best tavern nearest us?"

"The Cunning Midget," she replied without hesitation. She pointed. "After you pass the third bridge on the other side, take the alleyway about three blocks back. You'll see it."

Drucis nodded. "We wait for you there, Boldair. Whenever you're done … *reminiscing*."

Boldair offered a sheepish smile. His face flushed red and his throat tightened, making it difficult for him to breathe. "Aye, meet up with you later."

After Drucis and Dwiskter walked away, Wynneffin placed her hand atop Boldair's muscled forearm. Her strong grip tugged him toward her. He didn't resist. She slid her hand into his and squeezed.

"I oft wondered what became of ye," she said, staring into his eyes. "And why you forgot me so easily."

"I've never forgotten you," Boldair said. The truth of the words hurt. Looking into her eyes, he realized how much pain he'd buried to stay away from her.

"So you've returned for me?" Wynneffin said with an optimistic gaze. "I knew you'd come back, but your visit isn't for me. It doesn't concern me at all, does it? The fact you never have mentioned me to your companions tells me all I need to know. It explains plenty."

She took his hands into hers.

"I didn't know how to explain—"

"Explain what exactly?"

Boldair sighed. "With the huge gap of time dat's passed, Wynnie, I—I figured you hated me too much for me to even hint dat you're the greatest treasure I've ever found. My extended absence got longer and longer because I didn't know how to face you. I'm ashamed I've waited this long."

"Have you returned to stay then? With me?"

Boldair sighed and shook his head sadly. "I'm only passing through. I wish I could stay. I do. But things for me have changed—"

"Passing through?" Wynneffin said. "To where exactly? Our city is far out of the way for any Dwarf or race to consider 'passing through.'"

"We're headed to Meadwyrm Pass."

"Why?"

"You see, there's a vendor who sells a drink made from a poisonous vine and well—"

"A drink!" She frowned and shook her head, appalled. The amber in her eyes flashed like flickering lightning. He tried to step back, but she held his hands tighter. "A drink? You've come all this way as a shortcut to get a drink? This stout, mead, grog, or whiskey means more to you than I?"

"Of course not," Boldair said. His brow tightened.

"So it appears, you had *no* intentions of finding me at all."

"Dat's not true," Boldair said. "If it were true, this—this conversation would be over and I'd join my comrades at the tavern."

"Then tell me. What do you see dat's wrong with me?"

"What do ya mean? The situations dat changed in my life aren't about you or us, but," Boldair took a deep breath and sighed, "but these are things dat affect my future and my friends' future for the rest of our lives."

"Do I not figure into your future? We shared our hearts the last time you visited, Boldair. Within your words and mine, we shared our dreams of a future together. You expressed how you felt about me. Have your feelings toward me changed?"

Vendors with drawn carts and other passersby pressed around them, ignoring them and their conversation, as citizens crossed the bridge from both sides.

"Could we *possibly* discuss this in a more private setting?" Boldair asked. "Perhaps over a tankard or two of stout?"

"Numbing the pain already?" she asked. Her voice deepened and the rage in her eyes blazed. "We've not even *scratched* the surface."

"No, it's not dat. My friends and I 'ave traveled a long ways to get here. We even fought and killed several dozen goblins in the cavern."

Wynneffin pressed her index finger against his lips. Her eyes widened. She looked around to see if anyone heard his statement before turning her attention back to him. "Shh. Don't announce such news in public. Are you trying to cause a panic?"

"You know 'bout them?"

She nodded. "I've heard the rumors, but what you've spoken lets me know dat it's the truth."

"Where can we talk?"

"The Dragon Pit is a tavern one level down, or there's the Dungeon of Dragons Pub if we walk the opposite direction your friends took on the other side of the bridge," she said. "I can assume your friends will be okay for a bit without you?"

"Sure."

CHAPTER 24

*A*llowed the choice for which tavern they should sit, drink, and catch up on the events in their lives, Boldair decided to visit The Dungeon of Dragons because he liked its name, and because he found himself missing Taniesse. She wasn't only his friend, but she was a great advisor. However, he doubted she'd have the proper advice to alleviate his current inner turmoil.

He understood why he'd avoided his return to Frosthammer the moment Wynneffin's voice caressed his ears and he looked into her eyes. The excitement of seeing her shot through him, as did the pain and ache of missing her that he'd kept secret and buried deeper than his most prized gems. His mixed emotions were nothing compared to the sudden fear that overshadowed him. He wasn't certain what her feelings for him were after all this time.

He thought it odd that he possessed less fear facing a dragon's fire or fighting a mob of crazed Vykings during battle than he did contemplating his future life with someone he truly loved. His reason for avoiding Frosthammer altogether sat directly across from him.

He could deny his feelings all he wanted, but Boldair knew without any doubt she was the strongest pull on his heart. A Dwarf's life changed drastically when he finally settled with a spouse. That was the main reason he'd fled. Although when he'd left to get gold from one of his coffers, he intended to return to her immediately. And he would've, had he not overthought the stirring feelings of love welling inside his heart and mind. These foreign emotions weren't something he understood. He didn't know how to work through them. Rather than confront them, he pursued other goals.

His decision to take a spouse was as daunting as assuming the throne of Nagdor. Settling with Wynneffin meant he must abandon his hunts for treasure. At the time he left her, he was younger, mentally immature, and couldn't acknowledge which he loved more—her or his freedom to scout for gold. Looking at her from across the table, he realized dat by leaving he'd made a foolish mistake. He had chosen wrongly. But her eyes and her voice still showed affection for him. She seemed willing to look past his childish hasty decision and perhaps, she'd forgiven him.

Boldair glanced around the quaint tavern. Sconces made from hollowed dragons' teeth were fastened to the walls with candles burning softly inside. The chandelier balanced similar sconces atop long, sharp dragon claws.

Where had they gotten these teeth and claws?

Dragons shed their teeth yearly, but their claws did not regenerate. He worried that dragonhunters in the past had sold these teeth after successfully killing a dragon in its lair. But that would have been ages ago. These relics were seldom seen in other kingdoms. In fact, Boldair had never seen so much dragonscale armor as was present in Frosthammer, and that disturbed him.

He understood why Taniesse and her sisters had chosen to disguise themselves as humans. Such usages for a dragon's body parts was savage, but until Taniesse befriended him, he'd never actually given it much thought.

A mural of raiding Dwarves rushing into an ice dragon's lair with shields and axes covered the wall across from them. The horrific scene most likely was recorded as a time in Frosthammer's history, The Dwarves in the picture wore mithral and steel armor, not dragonscale.

Fires softly roared in the corner fireplaces. Behind the large U-shaped bar stood the barkeep. His bluish-white hair flowed across his shoulders. He wore an onyx ring on his right hand and a ruby one on his left. A black headband kept his hair from falling over his face.

A female Dwarf bard stood near the hearth, singing tales of woe. The tone and pitch added more sadness to her story. Several elder Dwarves seated at the tables wept and wiped tears from their eyes as their bodies shook. Boldair hated hearing tales that offered no hope or lacked triumph. His tales were always about his travels and finding treasures. Such stories were hailed in the poorest taverns where only peasants gathered. For those without gold or adequate necessities, hearing the possibility of *finding* wealth beyond means often stirred the embers of hope enough to get them through another day.

His most popular tales were retold by other bards, and his reputation in Aetheaon often preceded him, making him popular at the taverns he frequented the most. He liked the recognition in some ways, but he hated it for other reasons. For one, others who hoped to find riches followed him after he departed for the next town. Theirs wasn't to befriend him necessarily, but they hoped to discover his secrets. A couple of times, thieves shadowed him. Once, he nearly lost his life to the blade of an overly greedy thief who demanded a coffer of treasure and in exchange, he'd allow Boldair to live.

Boldair could see by the glint in the thief's eyes that even if he gave the man treasure, Boldair's death soon followed. So Boldair took the thief to his largest coffer in a cemetery where he'd set numerous deadly traps. A skilled thief should know how to disarm any trap. This thief was more violent than skilled, apparently, and he didn't recognize the most obvious trap, which killed the rustler instantly.

Boldair shook his head, dismissing those thoughts, and turned his attention away from the singing bard.

The tavern patrons were sparse, so the barkeep took a broom and swept the area behind the bar. As he swept, he paid little attention to others in the tavern. His eyes were distant and deep in thought. By observation, Boldair knew this Dwarf had never labored in the mines, nor had he ever partaken in a bloody battle, which was a stark contrast to Dwarves in the other Dwarven cities.

The city lacked diversity. All the patrons were Frosthammer

Dwarves, or at least that was Boldair's conclusion. Unlike Hoffnung, Nagdor, Legelarid, and other cities throughout Aetheaon, where it was common to see almost every race except Vykings and the disease-ridden Ratkin, Boldair noticed few outsiders visiting Frosthammer. Of course, the vast city might have more attractive areas for Elves, gnomes, and humans to frequent and gather since Telsia had been rather blatant with her comment of how Elves were *tolerated* in Frosthammer.

All the resident Frosthammer Dwarves held common traits in their appearance, which were unlike any Dwarves in the other kingdoms of the Northern Dwarven Alliance. Regardless of their dominant hair color, their hair gleamed a bluish tint. Their eyes were various shades of amber. He had not yet noticed any difference. Their statures and physical characteristics made them unmistakably Dwarves, but their skin tone, eyes, and hair meant they were a separate race of Dwarves.

Two female Dwarves carried trays to different tables, with tankards of dark stout, bread loaves, and brie. Another server stood behind the bar and filled a tankard from a large balanced barrel of stout set on its side. A line of unopened barrels set near the storeroom door. A grayish-white mouse poked its head cautiously between the barrels.

With all the amenities this tavern offered, Boldair expected to see a larger number of patrons. Perhaps the tavern bustled later in the evening? Of course, the singing bard's sorrow-filled songs might have caused others to retreat. No being could withstand constant inner turmoil.

Boldair lowered his gaze, staring at the tankards of stout on the table. He grabbed the loaf of bread and ripped a corner off of it. Then he took the dull knife and sliced a piece of brie. He smiled at Wynneffin. She patiently waited for him to break the silence. He wasn't certain how to even begin the conversation.

"Wynneffin, the last we spoke, I explained that I am—I *was* a treasure-hunter. Marriage wasn't right for me. I wasn't ready to settle down. My heart and my devotion for hunting treasures prevented me from being a proper husband, and you deserved far better than I could offer."

"Shouldn't you have had enough courage to at least tell—" she said.

She cocked a brow and studied him for several moments. "Wait. You said, '*was* a treasure-hunter.' What's changed, Boldair? Are you ill?"

"Nothing like dat. More things than I've time to explain." He chewed the bread and brie and swallowed. "When I said that we're passing through, dat is true, and believe me, it's not to avoid this conversation we partake in now."

"There's always time. Nothing rushes you except yourself. You're more carefree than any Dwarf I know."

Boldair forced a smile. "At one time, aye, dat was true. *Not* anymore."

"What changed?" she asked.

He sighed and held up his palms, indicating for her to stop pressing the issue. "Please. If you'd give me a few moments to finish me thoughts—"

"Apologies."

Boldair tilted back his tankard and emptied its remaining contents, and then he held it up for the server to see. The maiden saw his request and nodded.

Boldair sighed. "I've been tasked with other major obligations dat will prevent me from hunting treasures the way I 'ave in the past."

"How so? What are these obligations?"

"I'm Nagdor's new King."

Her eyebrows rose and her mouth hung open. She took in his words and sat in silence, studying his face.

"It's not a farfetched tale, if dat be the reason for your surprised lack of words," he said with a wide grin. "It's the truth."

"No, your words ring true. Your honesty showed in your eyes when you spoke. I've always detected whenever your boasts were exaggerations. Your eyes have always revealed the truth to me."

The server set a tankard of stout in front of Boldair. "Thanks."

The server smiled and turned to clear another table.

Boldair stared at Wynneffin. "You think my tales are filled with lies?"

She shook her head. "No, not lies, but you inflate the stories for—how shall I politely put this? To add *gumption* to the story!" She pushed back into her chair, crossed her arms, and laughed heartily.

Boldair laughed for several moments, his face reddening. The beauty of her laughter was contagious. He roared from his gut in a fit of laughter, slapping the table with palm of his hand before pointing his index finger at her. "*Gumption*! Yes, dat be the word! Ah, Wynnie, for what little time we've known one another, you know me too well."

Her laughter ceased, and she wiped a tear from her cheek. Seriousness overtook her expressions. "Wait, your father was King. What happened? Did he die?"

"No," Boldair said, shaking his head. "Not yet."

Wynneffin sighed. "Dat's good."

"Actually, his death might've been far better for all of us."

"How so?"

He explained how his father had betrayed Hoffnung and that he was locked in Hoffnung's prison awaiting trial.

"Dat's horrible."

"Aye, and then me brother—" Boldair shook his head. "I'll leave dat story for another time."

She watched him with saddened eyes. "I've missed you so, Boldair. I realize dat we only spent those two weeks together, but not a day has passed when I've not thought of you. But I suppose those feelings were one-sided?"

"Not entirely," he replied.

"Not entirely?" She stared at her tankard for a moment, her eyes darted back and forth with mixed emotions, and then shook her head. She huffed. "Your flattery overwhelms me, Boldair."

Boldair shook his head. He reached across the table and placed a hand on hers and gently squeezed. "Apologies, Wynnie. I didn't mean dat like it sounded. I've thought of you often."

"But not daily?"

"Wynnie," Boldair said. "Recently, I've had some rough days and weeks at times. I was nearly roasted by a dragon."

She gave him a shrewd, almost questionable stare.

He grinned. "It's not a lie."

"I see dat to be true. You sure you weren't drunk at the time?"

Boldair frowned. "Of course not! Well, I was when she abducted me, but not when I awakened and she shot fireballs at me."

Wynneffin laughed softly. Her eyes sparkled brighter than any gem he'd ever unearthed. "I can still vex ya, after all this time."

"Aye, you do, and I suppose it's because you read me so well."

"I do, Boldair, and dat's why I should be your queen." Her face showed no hint of a smile, nor did her voice. He was stunned by her immediate proposal.

Boldair leaned back from the table and swallowed hard. His mouth felt dry.

She said, "Do you deny those feelings we shared when you last visited? It wasn't the effects of the stout dat caused you to say dat you love me. We hardly drunk anything."

Boldair nodded slightly. Fear rose in the pit of his stomach. "I know, Wynnie. I know."

"Has dat changed?"

"Circumstances have changed," Boldair said.

"But your feelings haven't?"

"Look—"

She shook her head, never taking her eyes from his. "No, Boldair, you're not changing the subject, no matter how hard ye try. I gave my heart to you dat night for many reasons. I can never share what I have with you toward another Dwarf. Either you've returned to propose or I *insist* you *leave* Frosthammer *never* to come back."

Even though her words were icy, her eyes remained warm and caring. Nervously, he tore a hunk of bread from the loaf and stuffed it into his dry mouth. As he chewed, she folded her hands on the table and stared into his eyes.

Boldair couldn't remember a time when he felt more pressure, or when his stomach twisted from intense worry like it did now. He swallowed but the dryness of his mouth and throat caused the bread to lodge halfway down. He grabbed the tankard and gulped a huge swallow. The bread washed down with the stout. He sputtered and coughed.

He stared at her for several more moments. "Wait a minute. Shouldn't *I* be the one proposing instead of you ordering it?"

"The decision's all yours, Boldair, but the last time you fled rather than propose. Remember? At least you hinted dat your interests in marriage were to be discussed when ya returned. Did I misread dat? If I did and ya can't ask me today, there's no tomorrows for asking in the future. Do you think I won't be a good queen?"

"I don't know dat I will be a good king," he replied.

Wynneffin smiled. "The greatest kings have always had strong queens to council them."

Boldair held his tankard between his two hands on the table and stared at the frothy head still stuck to the top. "I don't recall my mother."

"Not at all?"

He shook his head. "No. Father seldom spoke of her after her death. I was told dat she was a great person. I only wish I knew based on my memories. But those don't exist."

"Sorry."

Boldair shrugged. He gazed into her eyes and found himself lost in them. He smiled. His courage prompted him to finally tell her what he wished he'd said so many years before. But before he could let the words flow, they were interrupted.

"Boldair!"

He turned in surprise to see the Telsia's sprite, Frizt, fluttering at his ear. The sprite's voice was much deeper than he'd ever expected a tiny creature to emit.

Boldair's heart pounded. "What is it? Is Viorka okay?"

"Come quickly," Frizt said. "She's been taken."

CHAPTER 25

"Taken?" Boldair said, rising to his feet. He pulled gold coins from his belt pouch and placed them upon the table.

Wynneffin rose from her seat. "Who's Viorka?"

Boldair faced the sprite. Anger and fear stirred in his troubled eyes. "What do you mean she's been taken?"

"Exactly what I said," Frizt said.

"By whom?" Boldair asked, walking swiftly to the door. His steel boots thudded hard.

"Who's Viorka?" Wynneffin asked, following behind.

"Best I could tell," Frizt said, "Viorka was taken by two forest Elves."

Boldair frowned with fury. He remembered passing the Elves when he first entered Frosthammer. They'd seen Viorka in his arms, and their facial expressions indicated keen interest in the fynx. They were the only Elves he'd seen thus far.

"Boldair," Wynneffin said, "who's Viorka?"

"She's my friend!" Boldair replied with frustration. He glanced at Frizt. "Go quickly and tell Dwiskter and Drucis at The Cunning Midget."

Frizt cocked a brow. "Being a Dwarf, even you should know not to jest over height."

Boldair frowned. "It's a tavern."

Frizt laughed in a high-pitched squeal. "I know!"

Boldair's face reddened and darkened to near purple. Now wasn't the time for humor. If he didn't needed the pixie's help to retrieve Drucis and Dwiskter, he'd have smacked the pixie across the room with the back of his hand.

The pixie noticed Boldair's dark mood and quickly zipped out the door, disappearing into the alleyway. Boldair hurried as fast as his thick stubby legs could move. Wynneffin kept pace with him.

"Where are you headed?" she asked.

"Telsia's shop, if I can still find it."

"I know where it is," she said. "Come on."

She led him to the bridge and they headed across. "So who is Viorka exactly?"

"Are ye jealous?"

"Should I be?"

"No. She's a traveling companion of mine who set out with us for adventure. But she nearly died in the goblin caverns. I feel horrible because I 'ave only myself to blame."

"The goblins attacked her?"

"No, my wolf mount, Ember, did" he replied.

"Odd your mount attacked her."

"The damn wolf has tried to kill *me* twice," he said.

Wynneffin gave him a perplexed side-glance. "Really? Didn't you have a better trainer?"

A soured expression claimed Boldair's face. "The wolf was my father's, and he's more resentful dat I'm king than my father is. The wolf's loyalty to me is equal to dat of my brother. Neither, it seems, support my reign."

"Get a new mount. If Ember's determined to kill you and your female companion, the wolf's not safe and reliable enough to keep. I can't believe it'd attack a female Dwarf."

"Viorka's a *fynx*. I'm supposing dat since she often resembles a cat dat Ember didn't like her and dat's why he tried to kill her. Of course, she didn't go down easily."

"A fynx? That'd make more sense as to why someone would steal her. Few have ever seen them."

"I know," Boldair said. He formed fists and growled. "I knew not to leave her unguarded with Telsia. 'Trust me,' she said. I trust few individuals, and I foolishly let down me guard and ignored me gut."

"Boldair," Wynneffin said, placing her hand on his arm as they walked. "Telsia's a trustworthy soul. She wouldn't betray your trust. I'm certain she didn't 'ave anything to do with Viorka being taken."

"Maybe not. I'm not necessarily implying dat, but had we remained in the shop, we could've stopped these forest Elves from ever taking Viorka."

"They couldn't have gotten far," Wynneffin said. "And most likely, they've not gotten out of the city."

"In this city? They don't *need* to get far," Boldair replied. "There's so many places where they could hide. And they don't need to leave, either."

Wynneffin hurried through Telsia's shop door. Boldair followed her and drew his ax from over his back. She looked at Boldair and shook her head. "Dat's not necessary. The Elves aren't here."

"I refuse not to take precautions."

"Telsia?" Wynneffin cried out.

A muffled groan came from the small room behind the counter where Boldair had left Viorka. Wynneffin entered the room.

"Boldair, come quickly," she said.

With a bit of caution, Boldair stepped to the door and peered through with his hands tightened on his ax. Books, scrolls, and other objects were strewn across the floor. The blankets on the cot were tossed aside. Telsia sat in a corner with her wrists tied together and a cloth stuffed in her mouth. Her face was battered.

Wynneffin stooped and pulled the cloth from Telsia's mouth. "What—"

Boldair stepped closer. "What happened?"

Telsia took several deep breaths. "Two female forest Elves rushed me while I was tending to Viorka. I tried to fight them off, but one struck me in the face. I—I lost consciousness for a bit. When I awakened, they had taken Viorka."

Wynneffin offered her hand and pulled Telsia to her feet.

"Thanks, Wynneffin."

"So you hadn't treated her?" Boldair asked.

Telsia nodded. "I just started to spoon feeding her medicine."

"Where could they have taken her?" Boldair asked.

Telsia rubbed the bruise above her right eye and winced. Slowly, she shook her head. "Lower levels of the city, I suppose."

"I'll put on some tea," Wynneffin said.

"Thanks, Wynnie," Telsia said. She placed one hand to the wall for support. "Make twindle-root. It's in the—"

"I know where it is," she replied, walking past Boldair.

"Wait," Boldair said to Wynneffin. He gently took her hand.

Wynneffin turned and her brow furrowed with curiosity. "What is it?"

He eyed them suspiciously. "How do the two of you know one another?"

Surprised, Wynneffin said, "I've lived 'ere all my life, Boldair. I know hundreds of Dwarves."

"Well enough dat you'd know *exactly* where a particular type of tea was notched away in a cupboard? I know lots of folks in a lot of hamlets and cities, but I've never snooped their cupboards or closets to know where they store things."

Miffed, Wynneffin turned and walked out the door. Boldair followed with Telsia slowly making her way behind them.

"Oh, no," Telsia said, leaning against the counter while Wynneffin placed a kettle over the small fireplace. "They took my Fae stones."

Wynneffin glanced toward the table in horror where the crystals had set when Boldair first entered the shop. "Those will be impossible to replace."

Boldair frowned. "Worry less about your crystals and more about where Viorka might've been taken."

"Apologies," Telsia said, rubbing her temples. "Yes, she's top priority."

Boldair sheathed his ax and crossed his arms, staring intently at

Wynneffin. "Now, tell me what I need to know. The two of you … how long 'ave you known one another?"

"What's dat matter?" Wynneffin asked.

"I find it a bit odd dat only a few minutes after I left this shop, *you* found me, and during dat short amount of time, two forest Elves attacked Telsia and took Viorka."

Wynneffin's brow furrowed with confusion. "Are you implying dat this wasn't done by Elves and dat I had something to do with it?"

"No," he replied. "I'm certain forest Elves took her because I saw them when I entered Frosthammer. They couldn't hide their interest in Viorka. Dat much I believe. But as for the two of you knowing one another and Wynnie finding me so quickly in a population so vast? You cannot convince me of that being a coincidence. Like I told you, Telsia, I trust few individuals."

Wynneffin sighed, drooped her shoulders, and stared at the floor. "I met Telsia a few weeks after you left Frosthammer and didn't return. She used the Fae stones to look for you because I feared you had died."

Boldair glanced at Telsia. Telsia nodded.

"She was able to find you," Wynneffin said, "and dat you were okay, but you'd moved on to another city. My heart broke. So I paid her to check your whereabouts once a week, and Telsia and I soon became friends. Once I realized you probably weren't going to return, I stopped having her locate you and we spent our time talking. She taught me mystical ideology, but neither of us has the ability to cast magic."

"Then how'd you know I had returned?" Boldair asked. "Were you hiding in here when I brought Viorka?"

Wynneffin shook her head. "No, Boldair. But, like Telsia did for you, she linked me to a pixie. When you arrived, she recognized you from the Fae stone visions and summoned my pixie to inform me. Since I was already on my way to the shop, I wasn't far from where you and your friends were on the bridge. *Dat's* how I found you. I hadn't visited Telsia yet."

Drucis and Dwiskter stepped inside the shop door with their hands on the hilts of their axes.

Boldair stared at the caged pixies. "Could a pixie find where Viorka was taken?"

Telsia shook her head. "They'd have to drink her blood to become bound to her."

Boldair's shoulders slumped. "Then it's hopeless."

"What happened?" Dwiskter asked.

Boldair told them.

Telsia straightened and walked into the room where the cot was. She returned several seconds later with a wet cloth. She held it up. "I washed blood from the fynx's nose and mouth with this. I cannot promise, but I might be able to squeeze out enough blood for a pixie to drink."

She took a small steel bowl from a cabinet and wrung the cloth over it. The pinkish liquid was blood mixed with water. Boldair could only hope it worked.

Telsia set the bowl inside a cage that housed one greenish-blue winged pixie. "Hexis? Drink this and tell me if you can find Viorka."

Hexis lighted on the bottom of the cage beside the bowl. She cupped a handful of the liquid and drank it. She made an odd face and shook her head. "No, nothing."

"It's mixed with water, so you might need to drink more," Telsia said.

Hexis cupped more and drank, shook her head, and drank a bit more. Her eyes widened and she smiled, nodding.

Telsia opened the cage door, allowing Hexis to fly out. "Don't let Boldair lose sight of you, okay? He's the one who needs to find Viorka."

Hexis smiled at Boldair. "Better be moving those stumpy legs if you wish to keep up."

"Hexis," Telsia said in a scolding tone.

Hovering in place, Hexis held her hands outward and shrugged with a grin.

"Thanks," Boldair said to Telsia.

Telsia forced a smile, still holding her temples. "A word of caution, Boldair. Even if you find the forest Elves, don't kill them in Frosthammer. Although their kind is moderately tolerated in our city, you mustn't kill them. If you do, you'll stand trial regardless of what crimes they've committed."

Boldair nodded. He turned to Drucis and Dwiskter.

"And here," Telsia said, handing him a small vial. "This is the medicine I was trying to give her before they attacked me. If you find her in time, try to get her to swallow it. It won't completely heal her, but it should aid her recovery."

"Thanks," Boldair said.

"Boldair," Wynneffin said, "I'd like to accompany and help you."

"It's a shame those Elves stole Telsia's Fae crystals. You could've viewed the happenings without setting foot outside the shop."

"Boldair—"

"Wynnie," he said, "I don't like the thought of you spying on my whereabouts while I was gone."

"I wasn't *spying*," she said, angrily. "I was concerned and I needed to know you were alive."

"Once a week?"

"I stopped after I realized you weren't coming back," she said. "I didn't want to torture myself over you and your broken promises."

"Come on," Boldair said to Drucis and Dwiskter. "Let's find Viorka so we can leave Frosthammer."

"Do you want me to come or not?" Wynneffin asked.

Without glancing back, Boldair said, "Do whatever suits ya."

CHAPTER 26

Boldair stood in the center of the lift with Hexis seated on his left shoulder. Drucis stood to his left and Dwiskter was on his right. Wynneffin insisted on coming, even though Boldair hadn't given his opinion either way. Before the lift rose, she spoke to a pair of patrolling guards and informed them of the situation. While she talked softly, the guards peered over her at Boldair with a slight look of confusion. One guard stayed with Telsia and the other hurried to find a medic to tend to Telsia's injuries.

Wynneffin rode the lift near the front but didn't glance back at Boldair. He couldn't tell if she was angry or worried about how he'd reacted to the news of her using Fae stones to watch his activities. The tension between them stood like a towering steel wall.

Boldair sighed, while watching her from the corner of his eye. If she turned toward him, he could look ahead and pretend his mind was elsewhere. His heart, though, was torn. He still loved her, but he wasn't certain either of them could gain back an equal level of trust.

He admired the beauty of her bluish-black hair and the time she'd taken to fashion the knots. He found it odd she was dressed in armor, as he'd never gotten the chance to discuss her duties in Frosthammer during their brief romance. Was she a warrioress or one in training? She wore the armor but didn't carry a great ax or sword. Tucked into sheathes on her belt, she carried daggers.

When he last saw her, she favored libraries, and wore thick leather robes and a skirt. Her rough demeanor was the same. Her stubbornness reminded him of his father, which led him to remain cautious because the last thing he wanted in a relationship was someone to constantly butt heads with. He half grinned. She was spirited. He liked that but he'd learned not to trust what he saw on the surface; not when the true person was hidden inside. Often the worst monsters were the most beautiful in appearance, luring unsuspecting prey to its doom; and those with the purity of heart were quite the opposite sometimes.

Boldair placed his thumbs behind his belt, watching the floors slowly pass. He wasn't certain why he felt uneasy about Wynneffin seeking Telsia's help in spying on his whereabouts after his departure. What else might the two have conspired to do? Even though Wynneffin claimed she and the healer weren't capable of using magic, he wasn't quite convinced.

The pixies being used to track individuals after drinking their blood resembled a sort of dark magic often used by the dark Elves and sorcerers. What more was at Telsia's hand?

Boldair understood that he had wronged Wynneffin by promising to return and not doing so. He'd broken his promise and lied. He didn't view it as a deliberate lie because after he left, he simply changed his mind due to his fear and uncertainty. But the way he'd done so was still wrong. His actions had hurt her. He easily acknowledged that. He shouldn't have left her wondering and worrying; but even if he were capable of observing her everyday activities, he would've respected her privacy. What events had she witnessed Boldair doing? Did she suspect he was seeing someone else during that time? He'd not done anything except continue treasure-hunting and avoided his return, until Taniesse tapped him to lead a battalion into battle.

He didn't know why, but he was completely uneasy that she'd watched unfolding events in his life without his permission. She apparently didn't view it as spying, but he couldn't see it as anything less.

"Seems to be getting colder, the farther down we go," Drucis said. "Aren't we getting closer to the River of Steel?"

Hexis nodded. "We are."

"Then why does the temperature continue to plummet?" Dwiskter asked. Little white clouds puffed from his mouth as he spoke.

"Some believe it's the mountain's curse," Wynneffin said, without looking in their direction.

"Do you believe dat?" Dwiskter asked.

"Seems possible," she replied.

"I agree," Drucis said. "Icevale's inside a different set of frozen mountains, but it's nice and balmy near the forges. That heat warms the rest of the fortress. But not here. I find *dat* particularly odd."

"Where do you see Viorka?" Boldair asked the pixie, choosing not to join their conversation.

"She's somewhere below on the eighth level," Hexis said. "The area we call the Ruthless Pits."

"A bad place?" Drucis asked.

Wynneffin looked over her shoulder toward him, deliberately casting her gaze to ignore Boldair. "Not so much bad, but the entire level is under construction."

"How do ya mean?" Dwiskter asked.

"Each level of Frosthammer started as a mining quarry. As the ore is removed, steel beams and shaft walls are placed to support the city levels above. Once all the ore and excess rock has been removed, architects start the construction of buildings," she replied.

"Odd, I never noticed any beams or supports," Drucis said.

Wynneffin smiled. "They're good at concealing those in the city's construction."

"Then why would they take Viorka to the Ruthless Pits?" Boldair asked. "If there are no buildings?"

Wynneffin sighed and a worried expression came to her face. "There are hulls of buildings where shady trading occurs at night. It's a place where thieves and murderers gather. Darkness is the best shield for such activities."

"You think they're trying to trade her?"

"No. My fear is they're trying to find a way to sneak her out," Wynneffin said.

"How? The main exits are on the top floor where we entered," Boldair said.

"The old mining tracks haven't been removed yet. They lead out through various tunnels to ventilation traps. They'd have to figure a way to climb them, but dat wouldn't be easy for most. Thieves, though, are crafty and use ropes quite effectively."

"For what purpose? She's almost dead. If she dies, what good would she be to them?" Boldair asked.

"I hate to say it, but it's possible they could sell her body as a trophy for a hunter's collection," Wynneffin said. "Let's hope dat's not the case."

"Aye," Boldair said sternly. His jaw tightened and he formed fists. He wanted to find whomever had taken Viorka and cause them immense suffering and pain. He hated to feel helpless, and at the moment, not knowing how to find Viorka, frustrated him to the core.

The elevator slowed and stopped. Wynneffin stepped off the platform.

Boldair said, "This is it?"

"Yes."

A few sconces flickered along the massive steel beams that supported the city level above, but didn't offer enough light to see any clear paths. Instead, the wash of lighting created more shadows for those with unruly intentions to hide and carry out their illegal endeavors. Every major city housed a place where thieves and murderers gathered. Usually, they met in the darkest places. Only those interested in seeking to hire these underhanded scallions dared to abandon the safety of the light and enter uncertainty. Most first time visitors became victims robbed of their gold and tragically lost their lives.

Boldair was there to find Viorka. Anger built inside him. For several moments he thought about how much she'd aggravated him when they traveled with Taniesse gathering troops for the Battle of Hoffnung. Early on, he thought he'd be happier if they went their separate ways to never see one another again. But now, with her life in the balance, he'd risked his own to find and rescue her without giving it a second thought.

"Should we follow the sconces and see where dat leads?" Boldair asked, pointing.

"It's probably wiser, Boldair, for you to allow us to go first," Dwiskter said.

"No," Boldair said firmly. "She's my responsibility."

"She's all of *our* responsibility. If you're killed," Drucis said, "Forboud assumes the throne instead of you. Imagine what a disservice to Nagdor you'd impose upon them then."

"So be it," Boldair said.

"Boldair—" Wynneffin said.

His harsh gaze was a combination of anger and determination. He took a step toward the first massive steel pillar. What would eventually become alleyways and streets were crude walkways with jagged rocks protruding. Stacks of large granite blocks, carved into cubes, set upon flat railcars and would probably be used for building walls. Since the builders didn't have the greater luxury to access trees for large amounts of lumber, all the buildings were made from steel and granite, which reinforced the levels above better than wood. In regard to building materials readily attained, lumber was rare and more expensive than using steel.

The rough ground shook beneath them.

Boldair glanced at Wynneffin. "Blasting sticks?"

She nodded.

"Ye think dat's safe?" he asked.

She shrugged. "The city's fortified with massive columns of steel."

Drucis chuckled. "Doesn't mean those blasts aren't weakening it."

Gears and chains creaked. The lift rose behind them. Boldair turned and noticed the massive titanium wall that rose about forty feet high. "Is that the outer dam of the molten river?"

"Yes," Wynneffin replied.

"Whoa!" Drucis said, looking up. "Best hope those walls never give way while we're down here."

Dwiskter laughed. "Ah, now, you won't be remembering it should dat happen."

"Hexis, can you locate Viorka?" Boldair asked.

"Yes," she whispered.

"She's near?"

"Not near, but in the general direction to which you pointed earlier," she replied.

"Don't fly ahead of us," Boldair said. "I'll lose sight of you. Stay on my shoulder and tell me which direction to go."

"Straight ahead," Hexis said. "Follow the lit sconces."

"Wait," Dwiskter said. He grabbed something off one of the flat carts and caught up to Boldair.

"What did ya find?" Boldair asked.

Dwiskter said, "An extinguished torch a builder must've left behind."

Dwiskter walked to the nearest sconce and touched the torch to it. He turned with the flaming torch in his left hand, which allowed enough light to see the crude floor. "The only problem with this, Boldair, is dat a moving torch gives our position away."

Boldair nodded. "Under the circumstances, though, we have no other alternative."

"I suppose you're right," Dwiskter said.

Boldair pulled his ax. "Be on guard."

Drucis pulled both axes and readied them. Wynneffin slid one dagger from its sheath.

"Allow me to the front," Boldair said.

"Aye," Dwiskter said, stepping aside. "But I still think you should allow me ahead of you."

"Those behind me have need of the light as well. With you behind me, enough light spills out dat I can see."

"As you wish," Dwiskter said.

Hexis slid herself closer to Boldair's ear. "Follow the lit torches."

"Aye," Boldair said. "Let's find Viorka and bring her back safely."

CHAPTER 27

*B*oldair was glad his boots were steel-plated as he walked across the jagged rocks. Soon, however, he found himself upon the rails the miners used to push carts of ore and rock from their mining tunnels.

"Ah, dat's a bit better," Boldair said.

"Much," Drucis agreed.

"There's no end in sight to this pathway though," Boldair said.

"At least our path's marked by the line of sconces," Dwiskter said.

"That only means someone has traveled through here recently," Wynneffin said. "Or someone is intentionally leading us to them."

Dwiskter said, "I agree. Seems too easy for us to follow them, and dat's suspicious to me."

"Aye," Boldair slid his shield from his back and held it in his left hand. "I find it odd myself. Ready yourselves, we could be walking into a trap."

"Why take the time to light all the torches?" Drucis asked. "Dat would slow their process."

"Keep going," Hexis said.

"How far?" Boldair asked. The line of lit torches stretched endlessly ahead. Dozens of them, with each fire progressively appearing smaller until the last one in view was nothing more than a speck of light.

A wind encircled them. Boldair paused in mid stride. The sconces behind them extinguished in the blink of an eye. The one immediately ahead was snuffed and then the next.

"Run!" Hexis said into Boldair's ear.

"Which direction?" he asked.

"Follow the lights before they're gone, or you could lose Viorka forever," she replied.

Boldair leaned slightly forward and rushed into a slow sprint. As he approached each torch, the fire vanished like the snuffing of a candle. He hurried toward the next and the next, but before he entered the slightest edge of a torch's arc, the fire was gone.

Their need to stay with the lit sconces bordered on sheer desperation, which meant they were being led to an unknown destination by an unknown person or party. The one responsible might not even be associated with whomever had taken Viorka. Boldair believed their unavoidable trap was at the end of this chase, but he couldn't risk not knowing if Viorka was there, too.

The rest of his party followed with equal speed. Their boots and mail rattled as they sprinted to keep up.

"Be careful, Boldair!" Drucis yelled. "I fear we're being drawn into a trap."

"As do I," Boldair replied. "Fate will hand Viorka back to us or not, but we 'ave no other alternative."

The swirling harsh wind was tainted with magic. Boldair sensed this. The priest-blessed gems on his ax and shield glowed, detecting the essence of a sorcerer's touch, which flowed around them. But they'd come too far to turn back.

All of the torches suddenly extinguished. Other than Drucis' torch, a blanket of darkness surrounded them.

"Halt!" Boldair stopped running, leaning slightly to catch his breath. Drucis' torch burned, giving away their position. The wind teased and flickered the flame. "Now what?"

Drucis stood beside him and swept his torch across the floor where they stood. "We stand at a crossroads where two rail paths cross."

"So pixie," Boldair said. "Are we any closer?"

"Yes," she whispered.

"Directions, please," he said.

Before the pixie replied, a light brightened down the right pathway of the crossroads. The size of the light was too large to be that of a single torch.

"Dat way?" Boldair asked.

"Yes," Hexis replied. "It seems you've been given an invitation."

"Boldair," Wynneffin said. "You don't have to go."

"You're right, Wynnie. I don't *have* to. I *need* to go."

"Boldair—"

He turned to Drucis. "Put out your torch."

Drucis' brow rose. "You're not serious."

"I am. Now, put it out. We approach in darkness. The torch only lets them know where we are."

"And if their light goes out, too?" Wynneffin asked.

"Then we're on equal footing," Boldair replied.

"No," she said, "you're not. This is their territory for now. Slowly they will be squeezed out as the new shops, taverns, and homes are built. That could take a few years. Until then, this is *their* terrain."

Drucis placed the torch on the ground and gently turned it beneath his boot, quashing the flame.

"Thanks. Now let's go," Boldair said.

Boldair stepped ahead of the others, but Dwiskter caught up and walked to the left of Boldair. Drucis stood on the right while Wynneffin stealthily crept along behind them.

The light ahead dimmed.

"Is Viorka there, Hexis?" Boldair asked.

"Yes. We're getting closer."

"What's happening to the light?" Drucis asked.

"Not sure," Boldair said in a near whisper. "Walk quietly."

"In steel boots?" Dwiskter said.

"I know. It's not easy. But as quietly as possible, let's get closer, hopefully without their noticing," Boldair said.

The light dimmed even more, but still illuminated enough that they were able to slowly advance. Had they not been able to walk upon the tracks, their approach would have been more cumbersome with all the rough rock exposed.

Boldair gripped his ax tighter and eased his way nearer to the light. Its brightness hadn't actually dimmed but was in a deeper unlevel spot, apparently where miners must have found a deep ore deposit or gems embedded in hard stone and decided to pick the deposit until all of the valuable ore or stones were taken.

Voices whispered in the deep pit. Boldair looked over the edge but couldn't see anything except where the light shone from a small adjoining pit or room.

"Is Viorka down there?" Boldair whispered to Hexis.

She nodded.

"You mind getting a closer look?" he asked. "So we know what we're dealing with?"

"That wasn't my duty," she replied. "You only requested that I lead you to where she is. That I've done. I shall not risk my life for her or you."

And with those words, she whisked off into the darkness.

"Dammit," Boldair whispered. He couldn't rightly blame her, but his disappointment came in that he needed to know how many were in the pit below before he decided to climb down. What upset him more was whether or not the pixie had told him the truth about Viorka's location.

"Over here," Drucis whispered.

"What is it?" Boldair asked.

"A crude set of stairs."

Boldair eased around the edge of the pit to where Drucis stood. "Seems they already have another room dug out."

"It happens in large caves," Wynneffin said. "Sometimes areas are hollowed out due to underground water erosion. I'm sure it's the same in Nagdor, too."

"Aye, it is," Boldair agreed.

"Usually the houses or shops built over these pits have the luxury of a cellar that was naturally formed."

Drucis placed his index finger to his lips. Below, the whispering grew louder as two or more individuals argued. Drucis was the first to start down the steps. Boldair offered no protest. Reconsidering the advice the others had given, it was foolishness for a king to place himself directly into the line of attack. Even though he'd led a battalion into batlte, his experience as a warrior wasn't any comparison to Drucis and Dwiskter. They'd been trained for battle. Both wore battle scars with pride and honor. He was thankful that they were willing to fight and protect him.

After Drucis reached the third step, Boldair stepped downward, careful not to scrape the bottom of his steel boots against the stone.

Wynneffin stepped behind him.

"We seem to 'ave a problem, Boldair," Dwiskter said from the rear.

Boldair looked over his shoulder. "What's dat?"

Dwiskter stepped onto the steps with his axes held out and above his head. Behind him yellow eyes glowed. Sharp teeth gleamed in the faint glow of the light in the pit. The creature snarled and squealed, holding a long spear to Dwiskter's back.

"Goblins?" Boldair whispered.

CHAPTER 28

Boldair heated with intense anger. He wanted to charge past Wynneffin and decapitate the goblin. He was almost certain its blunt-tipped spear couldn't penetrate Dwiskter's armor, but it wasn't something he'd risk. And besides, more goblins might be waiting in the darkness above and possibly below.

The goblin's high shrilling voice sounded like an alarmed cat, but Boldair wasn't able to interpret what it said. The crazed goblin poked Dwiskter's back twice and then pointed for Drucis to go farther down the stairs. Drucis looked at Boldair with uncertainty. Boldair nodded.

Drucis continued down the steps. Boldair followed stepping sideways as he walked to watch the goblin.

The goblin chattered with a small fit of laughter, waving his spear in the air, as though in triumph, but the creature lacked the intelligence to disarm Dwiskter.

"The goblins 'ave found a way into your quarry," Boldair whispered to Wynneffin.

"So it seems," she said, sliding her hands over the hilts of two daggers.

"I hear rumor dat the undead roam these lower levels of Frosthammer," he said softly.

She frowned. "Really? By whom? I've heard nothing of the sort."

Boldair offered a firm grin. "You didn't expect goblins, either?"

"No, but who told you this?"

Boldair took another step and pressed his back to the wall. "A Dwarf we met on our way through the Lost Pass. Ice'ik is his name."

Wynneffin laughed and shook her head. "He's a bit touched about a *lot* of things."

"So it seems," Boldair said. "He's building a ship on the side of the mountain."

Her mouth gaped.

"It's true," Drucis said, grinning.

"Hold up, Drucis," Boldair said.

Drucis stopped. Boldair stood beside Wynneffin at the wide corner where the crude stairs turned and continued downward.

"Nah! Nuh!" the goblin shouted, poking the blunt tip of his spear against Dwiskter's back.

Dwiskter rolled his eyes, staring upward. He looked at Boldair, indicating he could kill the goblin, if Boldair okayed it.

Boldair glanced at Wynneffin's fingers as she slid a dagger from her belt. He nodded.

She turned and flung the dagger before the goblin or Dwiskter even noticed it leave her fingers. The blade sunk to the hilt into the goblin's left eye. Its body stiffened and then fell limp. It tumbled and almost dropped off the side of the stairs. Dwiskter grabbed its arm and pulled it onto the steps to prevent its splattering fall to the threshold below. He placed its dead body onto the stairs but the spear fell from its loose fingers and struck the rock below with a dull thwack.

No other goblins rushed down the stairs at them, but the voices below silenced.

Drucis readied his axes.

Boldair eased down the steps behind Drucis. Dwiskter stopped at the wide corner step.

"Get ready to charge," Boldair said.

"I wouldn't advise it," a voice said from above.

They turned to see a figure dressed in black robes, holding a short staff in his left hand. An onyx orb set inside the gnarled finger-like roots he used as the handle. He slid back his hood. He was a forest Elf, but by his complexion, he looked more like a dark Elf. Rune tattoos marked his face, which meant he was a sorcerer. But something more darkened him.

Dwiskter turned with his ax.

The Elf shook his head. "As I've already stated, I wouldn't advise it."

"Well," Boldair said. "We're not going to drop our weapons."

The Elf laughed and shrugged. "Your weapons are of no concern to me. I can shrivel your insides and kill you before you got near me." He glanced at the dead goblin. "Nicely done."

"He's one of yours?" Boldair asked.

"A goblin?" The Elf grinned and shook his head. "They stink to us as they do to you. We've no treaty nor do we bargain with their filth. Its inconvenient death came only because it entered the wrong place."

Wynneffin slid another dagger from its sheath.

The Elf pointed a stern finger. "You pull the dagger, and I inflict a slow agonizing death on all of you. Understood?"

She shoved the dagger into its sheath with her thumb and frowned. Her jaw tightened and her eyes flared.

"Now, move forward. I assume we have something you want. Otherwise, you'd not have entered *our* chambers."

"Ya 'ave a name, Elf?" Boldair asked.

"Rhuse," he replied.

"Fitting, no doubt," Drucis said.

"Go," Rhuse said, pointing to the doorway below. His eyes were completely black. The glow spilling from the room below revealed the deep festered pocks on his face.

"I suppose you're responsible for extinguishing the torches on our way along the rails?" Boldair asked.

"It got you here, didn't it?"

"So you wanted this meeting?"

"We have mutual needs we can help one another with," Rhuse replied.

"Doubtful," Boldair replied.

"Listen to our terms before hastily disregarding the offer."

Drucis stood at the doorway and waited for the others to step behind him before crossing the threshold. The room was much larger than Boldair anticipated. Small fires burned at each corner of the room.

In the center of the room was a large slab of rock that resembled altars Boldair had seen in other temples. Viorka lay on this rock with the two female forest Elves he saw near Frosthammer's underground entrance.

Boldair pushed past Drucis and walked into the room. The female Elves fastened their attention on him. One raised her hand and a glowing blue fire danced on her palm.

"That's close enough," she spat. Her eyes were solid black like Rhuse's.

"Release her to me," Boldair said, "and ye shall live to see tomorrow."

Rhuse appeared on the other side of the stone slab beside the two females. He laughed softly. "You're far bolder than you need be. Your threats are idle. You hold no power here. You're not native to Frosthammer."

"Neither are you," Boldair replied. "You a thief, and the fynx is my friend. She's not an object to negotiate over. She's injured, and I was given something to help heal her."

The one female Elf flicked her gaze to Wynneffin. A sly smile spread across her face. "You? I guess you found what you wanted, Wynnie." She glanced at Boldair and then to Wynneffin again.

Stunned, Wynneffin's hand jerked a dagger free of its sheath. "Myriel," she said in a low gruff tone.

"You know one another?" Boldair asked in surprise.

"Not in the manner you might think," Wynneffin replied.

Myriel laughed. "Yes, you stole his heart like you stole so many other things in the past."

Wynneffin drew back the dagger to fling it, but Boldair grabbed her wrist.

Rhuse and the other dark Elf shot waves of bluish flame at Wynneffin. Boldair brought his shield around and blocked both paths of flame. His shield glowed, absorbing the magical fire.

Drucis readied both axes, and Dwiskter gripped his ax with both hands.

Behind the protection of his shield, Boldair stared into Wynneffin's eyes for several seconds, trying to read her thoughts by her reactions, but he wasn't able to. She looked away. Boldair lowered his shield.

"One more misstep," Rhuse said, "and all of you perish."

"Not before I cut at least one of you down," Dwiskter said with a harsh glare.

Rhuse ignored Dwiskter and his eyes fastened on Boldair. "You're the one in charge of this party. What do you say?"

"Tell me what it is dat you want?" Boldair asked. "All I want is to take Viorka and leave. No blood needs to be shed. You let me take her, and we can forget this entire ordeal."

"You really think your weapons can harm us?" Rhuse asked.

Boldair shrugged. "As you can see, your magic has little effect on us."

"So we're at a standstill?"

"Doesn't 'ave to be. Why did you take her? Is it because of whatever sickness dat's eating you up from the inside?" Boldair asked.

Wynneffin gave him a puzzled expression and then set her gaze on Rhuse's face.

"How do you know about that?" Rhuse asked. His facial expressions softened by his surprise.

"The infection is coming out your pores. Death's trying to claim you, but it won't be successful."

Rhuse lowered his staff and cocked a brow with the briefest glimmer of hope in his eyes. "What do you mean?"

"You won't die. Not in a normal death at least. You've been cursed. The whole lot of you."

Rhuse rolled up the sleeve of his robe and revealed the black sores. Some of the festering scabs leaked pus. "You've seen this before?"

Boldair nodded. "It's as I feared. Mors has been here."

"Who?" Rhuse asked.

"Mors is the Plague-bringer."

"I've never heard of him," Rhuse said. His eyes darted as his mind thought.

"He's related to Tyrann," Drucis said.

The three Elves gasped.

Drucis nodded. "Mors released his plague in Glacier Ridge. Nearly all of them perished. A few of us, myself being one of them, were fortunate enough to escape with our lives."

"We have this plague?" Myriel asked.

"Aye," Boldair said. "Do you have any memory of how you might 'ave contracted this disease?"

Rhuse stared straight ahead as he thought.

"Not to throw accusations in your direction," Boldair said. He placed his attention upon Myriel. "But I gather dat you're thieves. Not particularly stealing fynxes, but perhaps pickpocketing those who are misfortunate enough to pass close enough to you? Like when you're warming yourselves by one of the fire pits?"

Embarrassed, Myriel swallowed hard and nodded.

"Did you happen to rob someone and find something unusual in the bag's contents?" Boldair asked.

Rhuse cringed. "Yes, but not from any of the city floors above. I found a bag on a corpse near our thieving guild hideout. When I opened it, a swarm of strange beetles scurried out, biting all three of us."

Boldair glanced at Dwiskter. "The Plague-bringer."

"Is there a cure?" Rhuse asked.

"If I may ask, have you seen wandering dead bodies down here?"

"No," Myriel said. Her eyes widened with fear and uncertainty. "None."

"Only the dead body I took the bag from," Rhuse said. His eyes widened. "But it was gone last I looked. You think it's wandering around?"

Boldair shrugged. "Quite possibly. But if you've not seen a large number of them, dat means the infected ones are most likely on the other side of the River of Steel. Why did you take the fynx?"

Myriel reached over to the other female Elf and gently placed her hand on the Elf's shoulder. "Syvil?"

Syvil cupped her hands together at her waist. She took a raspy breath and exhaled. Blood trickled from her nose.

Myriel stared with concern at Syvil, and then she said, "We hoped her blood might heal us."

Angry, Boldair took a step forward. "What exactly did you plan to do to her?"

"We weren't going to kill her. We just needed a small amount of blood to add to a concoction I hope can cure us," Myriel replied. "Then we were going to return her to the mystic shop."

"The fact dat you took her before she was healed nearly killed her."

Wynneffin said, "You almost killed Telsia in the process, too."

"Is that what you think?" Myriel asked. "*She* helped us stage the attack."

Boldair gave Wynneffin a sharp glance. Wynneffin shook her head.

"That can't be true," Wynneffin said.

"You might concern yourself with Wynnie's friendship," Syvil said. "Circumstances often aren't what they seem."

"You had a part in this, Wynnie?" Boldair asked.

She shook her head adamantly. "No, not in this. I swear it! Telsia didn't, either! They're lying."

Syvil laughed.

"Is there a cure that you know of?" Rhuse asked.

Boldair nodded. "One that never fails."

Rhuse looked hopeful for a moment. "And that is?"

"Your body must be burned."

Rhuse snarled. He held his staff tightly. Bluish fire glowed around the onyx orb.

"You asked. There's no other way," Boldair said. He raised his shield. "None dat I know. Not when it's progressed as far as it has with the three of you."

"You don't think Syvil's potion will work?" Myriel asked.

"Honestly, I've no knowledge of what potion might work. I'm not a herbalist," Boldair replied.

"Can we at least try?" Rhuse asked.

Boldair sheathed his ax and reached into a pouch on the side of his belt. He took out the vial Telsia had given him. "Allow me to administer this to Viorka first."

"What's that?" Myriel asked.

"It's the potion Telsia gave me dat should at least stabilize and help her heal faster," Boldair replied.

Dwiskter frowned. "You trust dat it's safe, after all they've revealed about Telsia's hand in abducting Viorka?"

Boldair held up the vial and studied it. "Good point."

Wynneffin placed her hand upon his elbow. "No, Boldair, Telsia wouldn't have given you something that'd kill Viorka."

"How can ye be sure?" Boldair asked.

"Because I know her. She's my friend," Wynneffin said. "And the accusations they hurled against her, saying dat she helped them take Viorka, are all lies. You must believe me. You know I tell you the truth."

"I used to think so, Wynnie."

The sting and hurt of his words brought tears to her eyes. "Boldair, think about it."

"I've been thinking about a lot of things since I arrived in Frosthammer. I find my disappointment is in distorted memories. Perhaps my gut warned me long ago and dat was why I chose *not* to return."

"Look," Wynneffin said. "Telsia has no reason to stage the attack they did to steal Viorka. Think about it. If she were conspiring with them, she had no need to let them take Viorka outside the shop, placing Viorka's fragile life into danger. Did she? If all Syvil needed is a bit of blood, they could've easily gotten dat in the shop and never had need to take Viorka away."

"Dat's true," Drucis said.

Dwiskter nodded. "Besides, Boldair, when have you ever known a thief to tell the truth?"

Boldair's mind raced, trying to discern what was truth and what were lies. It didn't take much logic to know that one could never fully trust a thief to tell the truth. If anything, they might tell partial truths padded with the deceptiveness of lies to lure one's trust. But nothing they ever said would be the complete truth.

However, Wynneffin was correct in her evaluation. If Telsia was involved with this trio, she had no reason to suffer a battering, be tied to a chair, and allow her precious shop to be torn asunder. Such a plot would have to be set up well in advance.

From the moment Boldair noticed the lustful greed in Syvil's and Myriel's gaze, he recognized their desire to take Viorka. The lustful stares was similar to that he'd seen in treasure-hunters. Short of death, little could be done to persuade them not to take her. These two must've followed him in the shadows without any foresight of where Boldair was taking Viorka. It could've been any medic or healer's shop. So it wasn't coincidence. These thieves were lying. With the disease consuming them, they were desperate to do almost anything to find a cure.

Boldair wondered if they only needed a little blood, as they insisted. Perhaps that much of their story was true. But what if a little amount didn't work? Would they have taken much more? Would they have drained Viorka of all her blood, consumed by their desperate need to be healed? After all, they were forest Elves, vile and underhanded, to say the least. The sacrifice of a fynx was nothing to them. And if the blood benefited them, and Viorka survived, they could have filled their pockets with gold by selling her.

Boldair walked to the edge of the stone slab. Viorka looked peacefully asleep, but she was so still that he worried she might already be dead. Her long tail curled around her left leg. He placed his hand to her stomach. Her chest rose and fell slightly. Her breathing was shallow.

Drucis and Dwiskter stood close behind with their weapons drawn, but Boldair wasn't too worried the dark Elves would attack. Their interest was on Boldair and the vial he held in his hand.

Carefully, he tilted Viorka's head back. He held the back of her head in his hand. With his teeth he yanked the cork from the small potion bottle. Her mouth was slightly open, so he gently used the top of the bottle to pry her mouth wider. He slowly tipped the bottle, allowing the liquid to trickle into Viorka's mouth. Her nose twitched and her whiskers moved.

He cradled her head with his hand so she didn't choke while the potion flowed down her throat. The small bottle emptied quickly. After he was certain she'd ingested the contents, he lowered her head carefully.

"Now what?" Syvil asked.

"We wait," Boldair replied.

"We don't have that much time." Syvil wiped blood from beneath her nose.

"If you need her blood, it's her permission you need. Not mine."

Rhuse frowned. "You want us to wait until she's awake? We'll die!"

"How else will you get her permission?" Boldair asked.

"What if we take what we need now?" Rhuse asked.

"That would not be in your best interest," a voice said from overhead.

Rhuse turned and looked upward.

Boldair and everyone else did the same. Several armored Dwarves stood on a narrow balcony. They must've found another way into the room.

"Is all well, Boldair?" he asked.

"Yotram?"

"Aye."

"How'd you know we were here?"

Yotram said, "Frosthammer's a massive city. However, not much occurs that we're not aware of, especially in the unfinished sections."

"Could it be dat Wynnie sent message to ya?" Boldair asked.

Yotram laughed. "Dat would be a better analysis. But we 'ave enchanted bats dat send out shrill alarms to inform guards when shady activities take place down here. Some things don't concern us, but abduction and sacrifices must be stopped."

Bluish flames engulfed the orb of Rhuse's staff. His eyes darkened and he shouted, "Enough! Syvil, take her blood!" He turned to Yotram and the other guards atop the narrow balcony. "I'll turn you all to ash if one of you interferes."

"Rhuse," Yotram said. "I strongly insist you abstain from what you're doing."

"By the time any of you reach me, the task will be done. Besides, your axes and swords cause me no fear," he replied. "Syvil, you've delayed long enough."

CHAPTER 29

*B*oldair shook his head. "Rhuse, we freely offer our aid to help you find a cure, but not like this."

Rhuse studied Boldair's eyes and offered a gracious nod. He rolled up his sleeve. "While I believe your words ring truth, time isn't something we have. You see the pustules on my face and arms. I feel the taintedness of the plague crippling my insides. We have no other hope."

Syvil stepped toward Viorka and slipped a dagger from the inside of her robe. Blood trickled from Syvil's nose and down the sides of her mouth. She coughed, paused in step, and reached a hand for the stone slap to steady herself. Her head wobbled. She peered at Boldair, disoriented.

Boldair could only guess that the undead plague was in its latter stage with her. She was more *undead* than alive.

"Syvil?" Myriel said, placing a hand on Syvil's shoulder. "You okay?"

Syvil staggered, gasped, and fell into Myriel's arms. Myriel hugged her, holding her limp body. A black arrow shaft protruded from Syvil's back.

"Perhaps, Rhuse," Yotram said, "you'll fear arrows?"

Rhuse scanned the balcony, confused.

Boldair did also. He'd never known a Dwarf to use a bow. Dwarves took pride in close combat because they could watch the fleeting life escape an enemy's eyes.

Myriel eased Syvil onto the floor. Tears of blood leaked from Myriel's eyes.

"I warned you!" Rhuse said, drawing bluish flames from the staff.

Boldair leapt on the stone slab and dove at Rhuse.

"Boldair!" Wynneffin said.

Boldair struck Rhuse with the side of his ax. The blow interrupted Rhuse's spell and his concentration. The staff fell and spun across the rock floor.

Drucis and Dwiskter rushed them.

Boldair reared back his fist.

"No!" Myriel said. "Don't strike him. Syvil's still alive."

Rhuse looked at Boldair's steel-gloved fist and his eyes widened. He must have read the rage in Boldair's eyes and realized the strike would've been a deathblow. Rhuse relaxed and allowed his arms to fall at his sides.

"Myriel," Wynneffin said in horror. "Syvil's *not* alive. Get away from her. She's undead."

Myriel scooted across the floor, trying to put distance between her and what had once been her friend. Syvil awkwardly forced herself to rise to her feet. Her mouth released strange gurgling sounds, and her attention fastened on Myriel.

Three arrows pierced Syvil's back, jolting her, but ineffectively stopped her advance.

"Myriel," Rhuse said, "move away! Hurry!"

Myriel rolled to her side and tried to stand. Before she could, Syvil clasped a tight hand around Myriel's ankle. Myriel shrieked.

"Do something," Rhuse said, trying to get out from under Boldair. "Please."

Several more arrows struck Syvil. One went through the center of her head, but still Syvil ignored the injury and held tightly.

"I told you," Boldair said, "only fire destroys the undead."

"Then allow me my staff," Rhuse said with tears in his eyes. "Please."

"I don't know dat I can trust you."

"Please," Rhuse pleaded. "It's the only way I can save Myriel and myself."

"Very well," Boldair said, pushing himself to his feet. He extended his hand to aid Rhuse to stand. "But know, if you do anything other than burn Syvil, I'm close enough to remove your head."

"You have my word," Rhuse said, scrambling across the floor to get his staff.

"For what dat's worth," Drucis said.

Rhuse grabbed the staff. "Everyone stand back."

"I cannot do dat," Boldair said.

Rhuse faced Boldair with fury in his eyes. Blue sparks glowed on his fingertips. Sincerity coated his words. "You must. If they think I'm casting to hurt others, they'll send an arrow through my heart. You're standing too close. The hazard is too great with this spell and will engulf you, too."

Drucis grabbed Boldair's forearm and nodded. "Come on."

Boldair walked to the stone slab, gripping his ax and standing ready to hurl it at Rhuse should it become necessary. The throw might not decapitate the sorcerer, but he figured the blow was enough to severely injure or kill Rhuse.

Viorka stirred slightly. The medicine seemed to be working. Boldair watched her from the corner of his eye, but kept his focus on Rhuse.

Rhuse placed both hands around the staff and thrust it against the rock floor. Blue flames rose around the onyx orb. Small strands of lightning and tendrils of fire spiraled and grew, spreading outward.

Myriel pulled her foot, trying to get free of Syvil's grasp.

Rhuse spoke deeply. The words were foreign but held a poetic melody that was pleasant to Boldair's ears. The blue flames flickered and hissed, rising higher from the floor and the staff and slowly built a wall around the sorcerer. The fire was cold like the purest blue ice found in the coldest regions of Glacier Ridge. The fire swept in a cylindrical wave, resembling a cyclone. Rhuse cried out in pain. His body convulsed. He leaned forward, pressing his body against the staff, which was now frozen into the rock.

Drucis looked at Boldair questionably. Boldair could only shrug.

He'd never witnessed such a spell being unleashed and wasn't certain what might happen. He readied his shield between him and the dark sorcerer. He hoped the hidden archers in the shadows held their aim on Rhuse.

The spiraling flames rose higher and higher. The circling wind rushed with a wailful whistle.

Rhuse's mouth moved, but his voice was absent. His brows narrowed. Frost thickened on his eyebrows. His skin turned dark blue, almost black. His jaws tightened. He continued leaning forward, but the pressure inside that wind column sapped him. His shoulders slumped and his knees bent. Boldair wasn't certain exactly what the sorcerer was doing.

Rhuse reared back his head and his intense gestures indicated he was shouting. The blue wall of fire blazed forward across the rock floor and settled over Myriel and Syvil. The frigid cold was consumed by intense heat, which caused Boldair to stand closer to Viorka to shield her helpless body.

Myriel screamed. Her eyes widened with confused fear. "Why, Rhuse?"

Her body dropped. She didn't move and showed no evidence she was alive. The flames engulfed Syvil. Her flesh and robes smoldered before fire burst out of her body. The intense magical fire dissolved her into a pile of ash before crawling up Myriel's leg and consuming her. Myriel didn't struggle. Moments later, her body was ash.

Rhuse dropped to his knees. Black tears streaked his cheeks. The wave of fire that had consumed Syvil and Myriel rushed toward him. He turned long enough to make eye contact with Boldair. His eyes were void of hope. He gave a slight smile and a nod of appreciation before the magical fire engulfed him.

Yotram and the other Dwarves from the balcony made their way down to where Boldair was. "Why'd he kill them and himself?"

"They contracted a disease that was turning them into the undead," Boldair replied. "He killed them out of mercy."

"At least he saved us the trouble of disposing their bodies," Yotram said.

Boldair retrieved Rhuse's charred staff, which still glowed in places. He stared at the onyx orb for several moments and grinned. Once he found a smith, he'd have the new stone fitted into his ax or a dagger.

"He understood dat he was altering into an undead," Boldair said. "Syvil had turned, which was why the arrows didn't affect her."

Brandrum stared shrewdly. "Is this one of your concocted stories? It's hard to tell with you sometimes."

"It's every bit the truth," Boldair said. "Ask Drucis and Dwiskter. We've seen it before."

Yotram and Brandrum looked at them. Drucis and Dwiskter nodded.

"Who's your archer?" Boldair asked. "Never known a Dwarf to use a bow."

Brandrum laughed. "Keerla is a forest Elf in our army, along with several hundred of her race."

Boldair searched the balcony and found her standing in the shadow of the doorway above. She nodded, holding her bow to her side.

"Are you preparing for war?" Boldair asked.

Yotram smiled. "One must always be prepared. That's why our alliance with these Elven archers is most beneficial. These thieves didn't expect range weapons, did they?"

Boldair shook his head, studying the three piles of ash. "Have you not found undead roaming these unfinished sections of the city?"

"From time to time, the miners have reported small groups of them," Yotram said.

"Undead Dwarves?" Drucis asked.

Yotram nodded.

"And dat doesn't concern you?" Boldair asked.

"Of course it does," he replied. "We're not certain how it happens since we don't bury our dead in stone like the other Dwarven kingdoms. We conclude each ceremony by placing the body into the River of Steel, where the fire consumes it."

Dwiskter and Drucis gave Boldair a stunned look.

Boldair frowned. "And you're fine with dat?"

Yotram shrugged. "Why should we not be? Since the majority of our steel is placed into the construction of our city's new foundations and buildings, our dead are part of the structure forever. It prevents necromancers from raising an army of our ancestors to attack us. That's why encountering undead Dwarves is troubling. We've no dead buried here."

"What do the miners do when they find the undead?" Boldair asked.

"They immobilize them with their pickaxes and then toss the wriggling bodies into the River of Steel. Why?" Yotram asked.

"Good. Fire's the only way to completely destroy them," Boldair said. "I suppose what Ice'ik told me is true."

Brandrum chuckled. "Don't tell me you spoke with the mad Dwarf? Bah! Half of what he speaks you gotta ignore. He's never been the same since he struck his head on a steel beam in a mining tunnel. The only reason the blow didn't kill him was because he was wearing an enchanted helm."

Boldair crossed his arms. "Dat's what happened to him?"

They nodded.

"All I can say is dat he's right about the undead." Boldair sighed. He glanced at Myriel's ashes setting on the stone floor. He wished he could've spoken to her before Rhuse had incinerated her. He wanted to know what she knew about Wynneffin. She knew vital information, and specific details Wynneffin didn't want him to discover. Wynneffin became uneasy when Myriel mentioned that Wynneffin had gotten her wish. Wynneffin's reaction was to silence Myriel with death, if necessary. Why else was Wynneffin eager to pull her dagger? What did Wynneffin *not* want him to know?

Had Wynneffin used a love spell to inspire Boldair's return to Frosthammer? With Myriel dead, he'd never know what information died with her.

Other than aiding Rhuse in taking Viorka, Myriel had posed no immediate threat at the moment Wynnie was ready to kill her.

Boldair sighed. What information had Myriel taken to her grave?

Yotram stood over Rhuse's ashes, sheathed his weapon, and clasped his hand on Boldair's shoulder. "Our business is finished here. How 'bout those drinks you promised us?"

Boldair nodded and a smile parted his beard. "I'm a bit parched myself, old friend. I could down a tankard or two."

"A tankard?" Drucis said with a hearty laugh. "After *this*, I won't settle for less than a barrel!"

"My pockets aren't dat deep," Boldair said, laughing.

Yotram frowned. "No? I've never known a poor King."

Boldair looked uneasy.

"Why didn't you share your good fortune with us upon your arrival?" Yotram asked.

"There's no need for a fuss, as the coronation ceremony has yet to occur," Boldair replied. "I'm not convinced dat it's good fortune to chain oneself to a throne."

"Never known a *modest* King, either," Yotram said. "Come, drinks be on me this night."

CHAPTER 30

While they waited for the lift, Boldair noticed a large titanium gate beside the River of Steel's levee. The massive gate's architecture blended with the surrounding fortified wall in such a way that Boldair had not noticed it when they stepped off the lift earlier. His focus and worry to find Viorka had probably blinded him, preventing him from seeing the obvious.

Seeing the gate now, he couldn't understand how he failed to notice such a huge object. Each rivet that held the massive gate in place was larger than a Dwarf. A giant chain hung halfway down the gate from what appeared to be the handle. The tallest Elf or human couldn't reach the handle from the floor without the chain. Even if it were within grasp, Boldair guessed a small army of Dwarves were required to open or close the gate, as the weight for this barrier was immense.

No guards were posted at the gate, which increased Boldair's curiosity.

"Is that a gate?" Boldair asked, adjusting Viorka in his arms. Her breathing was nearly normal, but she'd yet opened her eyes.

"Aye, it is," Yotram replied.

"Where does it lead?"

"I doubt that it's ever even used anymore," Yotram said.

"Its purpose then?" Boldair asked.

Yotram shrugged. "On the other side of that particular wall of our mountain, The River of Steel separates into various channels dat lead to various types of molds for support blocks, weapons, and gears and so forth. From my guess, the gate was fashioned after all the necessary equipment for the forges were installed. Since it's so deep inside our city, it acts as a reinforcement barrier to support the mountain wall. I'd say more than a hundred years have passed since it was last opened. It seals off the city from the forging processes."

Boldair studied the giant gate a bit longer, and then he noticed a small door in between the river's levee and the gate. Up several floors of the city was a balcony that crossed over the River of Steel. "I suppose your access to the forges is the smaller door?"

"Yes," Yotram replied.

"Perhaps you could escort me through those channels, so I can see how your process works?"

"Ah, I would but I don't have access to enter."

"Why not?"

Yotram smiled. "I'm not an engineer or a miner. I'm a guard. Only a few guards have ever gone inside."

"Just out of curiosity … How does one even open a gate dat size?" Dwiskter asked.

Brandrum laughed. "We've never seen dat occur. Like Yotram said, 'more than a hundred years have passed since it was last opened.'"

Boldair frowned while he studied the detail of the titanium gate's construction.

Yotram laughed. "Your curiosity eats at ya, eh?"

"All the time," Boldair said in a harsh whisper.

"I 'ave a pressing question at the back of me mind," Dwiskter said.

Yotram cocked a brow and looked at him. "What's dat?"

"How is it dat we're so close to the river, which is molten steel and yet, it's so damn cold in Frosthammer?"

"Mysteries abound everywhere, don't they?" Yotram replied.

"I suppose so," Dwiskter said. "I'll wager dat you don't know why?"

"It's something all of us in Frosthammer are accustomed to. It's been this way for my entire life. Since we know no difference, why should we let it plague our minds?"

"Very well. Though my curiosity remains, I 'ave no more questions."

Boldair kept wondering the same thing about the odd cold temperature. Yotram perfectly avoided answering the direct question, which made Boldair a bit suspicious. Being this far under the mountains, the temperature should increase. Dwarves favored cities underground because the mountains buffered the cold, but oddly, not in Frosthammer.

Yotram clasped Boldair's shoulder. "You're still troubled about the gate? You could stare at it for a year and never find the understanding to satisfy your curiosity. There be better things to spend one's time worrying over."

"Let's take some worries off ye, now dat you have your fynx back," Brandrum said.

"Then lead the way to the best tavern," Drucis said.

The gears of the lift squeaked as the platform thudded against the ground floor of the city.

"Drucis has the right idea," Yotram said. "Let's allow ourselves time to relax and forget our troubles for a bit, eh?"

Boldair nodded, half smiled, but he didn't take his eyes off the gate. He stepped on the lift platform. "Aye. I'm for dat!"

The lift chains rattled and the gears ground. Slowly they rose. Once they were above the River of Steel's fiery orange flow, Boldair said, "While we hunted for Viorka, we came to a crossroads in the rails. I must assume dat the ore is taken to the other end of the river?"

Yotram nodded. "Yes."

Boldair smiled and chuckled. "I suppose it's quite obvious dat I don't know a lot about the smelting processes. Not dat it bothers me because I'd rather explore Aetheaon and hunt for treasure and hire a smithy whenever needed."

Brandrum laughed. "Wouldn't we all? You probably won't believe this, but I've never been outside of Frosthammer."

"Never?" Dwiskter asked.

Brandrum shook his head.

"Nor have I," Yotram said.

"I've often dreamed of what it's like outside our mountains," Wynneffin said.

Boldair stared at her from the corner of his eye, but he didn't address her comment, nor did he look directly at her. Her blatant hint lingered in the air, but for the moment, he was unable to get past her use of magic to spy on him during his absence.

"Why would you stay in this city forever?" Drucis asked Yotram. "There's so much more to view in other cities and the forests."

"We're self-sufficient," he replied. "We 'ave no need to venture away. Since we keep to ourselves, and few visitors from other kingdoms ever pass through our gates, we don't have problems with the politics of war disrupting our lives. We 'ave chosen to be a peaceful city. But, should Frosthammer ever suffer attack, we 'ave a massive army dat prevents us from ever being defeated. An enemy's entrance is too narrow to send massive forces all at once. No offense, Boldair, but dat's why King Rigrim has forbade Frosthammer from being a part of the Dwarven Alliance."

"No offense taken," Boldair said. "However, Yotram, since undead are turning up, Frosthammer's already been attacked, albeit discreetly."

Yotram acquiesced a slight shrug. "If anything, it's a minor threat."

"No, it isn't," Boldair said. "You saw the three of the forest Elves. Syvil had *already* changed. She was undead. Had Rhuse not consumed himself and the other two with magical fire, they'd have infected others. It's a plague. Not one dat kills the entire body. Rather, it kills the mind and overtakes the body to spawn more undead by spreading the plague to others. It's not a situation to take lightly."

Yotram's jaw tightened. "Duly noted. I'll report this to King Rigrim. It's more his concern than yours."

"Yotram," Boldair said, shaking his head and raising a hand. "In no way was I admonishing you or trying to dictate what actions should be taken. Viorka and I have seen this plague overtake an entire hamlet. Drucis, Dwiskter, and I have seen an army of undead risen by Mors, the Plague-bringer. Should the number increase greatly within your city, the devastation would be unlike anything you've ever seen. You won't stop it."

Yotram turned and stared into Boldair's eyes. "I'll make a report, King Boldair. Perhaps the report will have a greater bearing if you accompany me to see King Rigrim.

After the lift stopped, Wynneffin stepped off and walked away.

Boldair watched her leave without offering any words. Although he truly wanted to speak with her in private, he didn't know how to start the conversation. He wasn't certain he could place his trust in her again, and perhaps their parting ways now eliminated the possibility of bitter words later.

"Everything okay?" Drucis asked her.

"I need to check on Telsia," she replied without looking back.

Drucis glanced at Boldair and whispered, "Perhaps you should go talk to her?"

Boldair cradled Viorka in his arms and shook his head.

"Ye sure?"

"At the moment? Yes," Boldair replied.

No anger echoed in Wynneffin's tone, nor did she sound saddened. She refused to make eye contact or to tell him goodbye. For him, it indicated that she either understood his lack of trust in her or she was too embarrassed for getting caught for spying that she didn't know what actions she should take. Either way, he needed to sort through his problems without adding more.

"Boldair?" a Dwarf said in his approach.

Boldair turned. "Yes?"

"I'm Burr, the stablemaster. I came to inform you about your wolf." Burr was a husky Dwarf with a wild unkempt beard and frazzled hair. He wore a coat made from striped bear pelts and a cape fashioned from bat leather, possibly from the giant bats that swarmed the swamps near Woodnog.

"Oh?" Boldair studied Burr. He wondered how Burr had obtained the pelts and leather for his clothing when the places to hunt such creatures were far from the Frosted Peaks. With so few visitors to Frosthammer and fewer residents leaving the city, how had Burr obtained such furs?

"Yes. He's strong and healing, but he's lost his left eye. The deep gashes caused too much damage. An Elven healer could remedy the eye much better than us, but by the time you journeyed to such a place, there'd be nothing an Elf could do, either. The wolf's shoulder where he was pierced should heal readily, provided he has no infection."

Boldair nodded. "Thanks for informing me. Ember, I'm afraid, has served his purpose for me. Do you think he'd be much use for you 'ere?"

The stablemaster cocked a brow. "What do ya mean? You don't want him?"

Boldair nodded at Viorka in his arms. "Dat wolf almost killed her. I don't trust turning my back to him. He's attacked me several times and nearly took my hand. It's best I part with him."

"Odd," Burr said. "He's well-behaved, considering the amount of pain he endured with the injuries he suffered. Quite gentle."

Boldair chuckled. "Aye, he's favorable to anyone other than myself. You see, he was my father's mount. After my father's imprisonment, I took the wolf for my own. But Ember despises me."

"If you're in need of a new mount," Yotram said, "I'm certain we'll have no problem finding you a new one. We have dire mount breeders and excellent trainers. Of course, there are rams as well."

"I definitely need to trade Ember for a new mount, but with only one good eye, I doubt anyone would take interest," Boldair said.

Burr said, "I've a young dire wolf mount I'd trade for Ember. He's trained well, obedient, and more loyal than any other wolf pup I've ever reared."

Boldair frowned, thinking about the offer. "Why would ya want a wolf with only one eye?"

"Breeding purposes, Boldair," Burr replied. "Ember has a remarkable fur coat. I'd like to see if his pups have the same coloring. If so, they'd be easily traded or sold."

"I see," Boldair said. "I've some important ... uh, pressing issues with Yotram and Brandrum first, but if it pleases you, I could view your wolf tomorrow to possibly work a trade?"

"Of course," Burr said with a slight grin. "There's no hurry. But if you decide to keep Ember, I truly understand. He's recovered enough dat he could leave tomorrow."

Boldair smiled. "Oh, don't worry. We'll work a trade somehow, as I hold no favor for Ember since he's unruly toward me and Viorka."

Burr grinned eagerly. "Good. I'll leave ya to your affairs."

With that, Burr turned and headed to the lift.

CHAPTER 31

Boldair sat at a corner table in Hogshead Splatter Grog and roared with laughter. The entire tavern was rowdy and filled with raucous chatter, so his hearty laughs weren't noticed by the Dwarves seated at other tables.

Some Dwarves challenged and dared others to compete in various displays of strength. While Boldair enjoyed listening to others tell tales and watching their feats of strength, he was happiest being in their midst without any of them knowing he was the new King of Nagdor.

He held up his tankard and clicked it against Drucis'. On the table was a stack of firm loaf bread and a fresh peeled wheel of hard cheese. Above the roaring fire was a young boar on a spit. A barmaid cut through its golden skin and sliced away big hunks of meat.

Across the room Dwarves covered with grime from the mining pits downed tankards and conversed with one another but with less energy than the off duty guards.

Viorka was curled on the bench beside Boldair. Despite their loud laughter, she remained asleep. Occasionally, she turned and adjusted herself. Her breathing was stronger and her ears twitched at the overzealous laughter.

"You told the stablemaster we had *pressing* issues?" Drucis howled, grinning at Boldair. "Ya don't even drink wine!"

Yotram choked and turned to spit his stout on the floor. "Wine presses? We don't serve Elven drinks 'ere!"

Boldair wiped a tear from his eye. His laughter subsided. "What else should I 'ave said? The whole reason we came this direction was to get to Meadwyrm Pass for drinks, but then no need to *press* on until we've had our fill 'ere first."

"Meadwyrm Pass?" Yotram said, setting down his tankard. "What's that place?"

Boldair shrugged. "Nothing but a narrow trail through the forest, but some vendors sell a rare drink that'll nearly burn your insides out. But the drink's not important. The journey was simply something to pass the time until I'm able to return to Nagdor for my coronation."

Brandrum frowned. "What prevents you from doing so now?"

Boldair sighed. "Word has reached me dat my life might be at risk when I return."

"Why's dat?" Yotram asked.

"Loyalty to my father," Boldair replied. "There are some, my brother included, who won't view me worthy of the throne."

"Your brother—" Brandrum shook his head and took a deep gulp of his stout. After wiping the foam with the back of his hand, he looked at Boldair. "None of us could ignore dat his beard was cut off. Was it you who cut it?"

Boldair nodded. "Aye."

"Was it because he doesn't favor you as King?"

"No. Well, partly. He tried to kill Viorka for slashing Ember's eye. She merely defended herself, but Forboud has undermined me ever since father was imprisoned."

Yotram rubbed his bearded chin. "You think he vies for the throne?"

Boldair cleared his throat and motioned for a barmaid to bring him a fresh tankard. "Father told me dat he wanted Forboud to on the throne, which is all the more reason why me brother should never become King. Father betrayed Nagdor. If Forboud became king, Nagdor would still lack a worthy king."

"What are your plans for him?" Brandrum asked. "Why not try him for treason and execute him."

"Dat's harsh, don't you think?" Yotram asked, glaring at Brandrum. "You're speaking of his brother."

"Aye, tis true and sad dat I've thought about doing just dat," Boldair said. "However, he suffers greater by remaining alive."

"If he lives, he's always a threat to your rule. He'll plot on how to overthrow ye," Brandrum said. "When it comes to ruling a country, your chiefest enemies can be family and those you trust the most."

"Where do you get this?" Yotram asked. "We've known only one king our entire lives."

"Aye," Brandrum said, nodding. "But King Rigrim's *lost* three sons in weapons training, too, hasn't he?"

"They died in training?" Dwiskter asked.

Brandrum nodded.

Yotram shook his head and set his tankard down. He lowered his voice. "You honestly think King Rigrim had something to do with the deaths of his own sons?"

Brandrum shrugged. "If you think it's mere coincidence—"

"Silence your tongue," Yotram said. "Or you give me no choice but to drag you away in shackles for treasonous accusations."

Brandrum glared at Yotram but bit his lip and cradled his tankard between his thick hands.

Boldair frowned and studied the growing tension between the two guards. Brandrum's jaw tightened. He tore a piece of loaf bread and dipped it in honey. Boldair thought them to be the best of friends, but it was obvious they tolerated one another; much like the Dwarves *tolerated* outsiders visiting Frosthammer. None of them had drunk enough to go to fists over minor arguments. If they were already at odds with one another, more stout was the last thing they needed.

"Ah, there ya be!" Kairun said, walking to their table. "Ya got room for two more?"

"Of course," Boldair said. He gently eased Viorka into a seated position in the corner, allowing her head to rest against his shoulder.

Kairun adjusted his ponytail and squeezed into the corner seat opposite Boldair, so he could view anyone's approach to the table with his right eye.

Bathil sat between Kairun and Brandrum.

Boldair said, "Have any of you ever ventured outside of Frosthammer?"

Yotram, obviously still perturbed by his brief argument with Brandrum, flicked his gaze toward Boldair. His glare softened and he shook his head. "I've not, as I've mentioned before."

Brandrum chewed his bread and said, "No."

Bathil simply shook his head and motioned for a bar maiden.

Kairun studied Boldair for several moments. "Nah, not interested in what lies outside Frosthammer. This is my home. I was born 'ere, and I will die 'ere, never once to gaze upon the sun. Why do you ask?"

"Is such forbidden?" Boldair asked. "Are you bound to remain in Frosthammer because you're guards? What permissions must you secure to venture to another city?"

"To request a leave is not forbidden," Kairun said. "But actually taking a leave … *dat* would draw scrutiny from higher level guards and of course, King Rigrim."

"Scrutiny, eh?" Boldair asked. "Is dat why Ice'ik's viewed as a mad Dwarf?"

Drucis reared back his head and laughed.

Bathil, Kairun, Yotram, and Brandrum stared at him, perplexed.

"Ice'ik has pretty much made himself look mad," Drucis said. "Building a ship on the side of a mountain is insanity at its worst."

Boldair laughed. "Okay, so he's not the best example."

The bar maiden set several tankards of stout onto the table, grabbed the emptied ones, and hurried away.

Kairun sipped his stout and set down the tankard. "Ice'ik's an odd one. Some say he was touched before his head injury. Always talking about Deities and what 'appens after the mountain claims our bodies. He had a good following and could've easily built a temple to cause an uprising, if he had chosen to do so."

"What happened?" Dwiskter asked.

"He warned of doom dat would be coming to Frosthammer," Kairun said.

"Doom?" Boldair asked. "Like what exactly?"

"The River of Steel would swell and rise above its barriers to consume us all. He caused terror for a while, but then he was exiled. I was one of the guards to escort him through the goblin cavern, along with six of his loyal followers."

"Only six?" Drucis asked.

"Aye," Kairun said, nodding. "He was heartbroken 'cause he thought *dozens* would follow him because of his prophecies. I suppose they were more afraid of the unknown outside our mountains. They remain inside the city. Ice'ik's message though, is still told in small circles. However, they're not as convincing with the message as Ice'ik was. But if he's building a ship on the side of the mountain, like you say, he's even madder than they've stated. Frosthammer's better off without him."

"His prophecy doesn't alarm you?" Boldair asked.

"No," Yotram said. "Not one bit."

"You don't think such could 'appen?"

Kairun shook his head. "No. The river's channels 'ave plenty of safeguards. Besides, we're the ones feeding the ore into the smelters. *We* control the levels of the river to ensure the molten steel never overflows."

Yotram set his tankard down and peered around for several moments. "Boldair, where is Wynneffin?"

"She went to tend to Telsia," he replied.

"Ah, I figured she'd be here by your side. You seem to have captured her attention."

"A bit *too* much, I'm afraid," Boldair replied.

Yotram raised one eyebrow. "What ya mean?"

Boldair explained what had happened after he left Frosthammer and Telsia using the Fae Stones to spy on him. "How would you fellows feel 'bout someone doing dat to you?"

Kairun rubbed his bearded chin. "Dat be a bit much. You hardly knew her at the time, correct?"

Boldair sighed. "Time-wise, aye. Only the couple of weeks. But, we'd grown rather close in a short amount of time. Too close, perhaps."

"Ah, she be scorned," Brandrum said. "You riled up her interest in ye, and then wandered away. But this might be more 'bout her than ye."

Boldair looked into Brandrum's eyes. "What'cha mean?"

Brandrum offered an uneasy smile. "The way dat you left without coming back or sending her an explanation could've made her believe dat she wasn't good enough or dat maybe you didn't find her attractive. You left her with a lot of unanswered questions. So perhaps dat is her true reason for consulting Telsia? You could've made her self-doubt her own qualities." Brandrum shrugged slightly and then reached for his tankard. "Dat's how I see it."

Boldair chewed his lower lip and nodded. "I never thought 'bout it like dat, but ya might be right. What I did and how I did it was unforgivable. Signs of a coward, now dat I look at it."

Yotram smiled. "I wouldn't go *dat* far. But, you should definitely sit down and discuss your true feelings with her to resolve whatever problems the two of ye 'ave. At least, if you don't feel the same way toward one another, you won't leave Frosthammer with unsettled business this time."

CHAPTER 32

oldair sliced a narrow piece of the wheel cheese and placed it on a torn piece of bread with a chunk of boar meat. Before shoving it into his mouth, he said, "So, this isn't the exact type of things we'd be talking 'bout tonight."

Yotram chewed some bread.

Brandrum said, "Ya don't think the advice is sound?"

"I'm not implying dat," Boldair said, "but what do the lot of ye actually know 'bout love?"

"I know we don't 'ave it," Kairun said with a shrewd grin.

"And ye think I do?"

"Better than the rest of us," Drucis said. "Not dat I'm looking."

"We're always *looking*," Yotram said.

Dwiskter shrugged. "Maybe. Maybe not. But what I've noticed is dat when you *stop* looking, dat's when it finds you."

Boldair chewed the bread and cheese before washing it down with stout. He set his empty tankard on the table. "Let's bring the subject back to something else."

"Like what?" Kairun asked.

"I thought your interests were in my telling of the treasures I've found since we last met," Boldair said with a gleam in his eyes, hopeful to change the subject.

"How 'bout the treasure you'll let slip away, if ya don't act upon it," Yotram said with a smirk.

Boldair frowned. "Like I said, let's bring the subject to something *else* for the time being."

"No greater treasure than love," Brandrum said.

Boldair formed fists and set them atop the table. He glared at them. "Okay, I can take a good jesting from time to time, but enough for the evening, if it suits you. Cause even if it doesn't, it suits me perfectly. So, no more."

Yotram glanced at Kairun and shook his head. "His defensiveness proves his heart aches for her."

"Aye," Kairun replied. "No denying dat."

Boldair leaned partway across the table with fury in his narrowed eyes. "Enough, while we're still able to call one another friends."

"Sorry, Your Highness," Yotram said, offering a slight bow.

Boldair pointed a stern finger at him and shook his head. "Dat's to remain a secret for now."

Kairun sat back against his chair and frowned. "Did I miss something?"

Brandrum whispered to Kairun, "Boldair is Nagdor's new King."

"Ah, ya see, I didn't know dat," Kairun said. "Then your situation's entirely different."

Boldair turned his attention to him. "What'cha mean?"

"I mean, Wynneffin could become your queen if ya don't mess this up."

Frustrated, Boldair lowered himself into his seat and sighed. "Ya not going to let this go, eh?"

Kairun chuckled. "We've not held a better conversation since your departure."

Boldair rolled his eyes and huffed.

Kairun adjusted the patch over his eye and said, "Look, I'm being serious, friend. The most valuable treasure you 'ave is the one your heart yearns for. Right? You want to tell us a story about finding your *greatest* treasure, but Boldair, your story's not yet complete. You must secure the treasure or ya 'ave no tale to tell."

"You're probably right," Boldair said softly.

"No, he *is* right," Viorka said, opening one eye to stare at him.

"Viorka," Boldair said, turning to her. A smile spread on his face. "You're finally awake."

She opened both eyes and slowly sat up. "Who can sleep with all this noise?"

Boldair cupped her furry face in his hands and stared into her emerald eyes. "You had me worried, lil' cat. I thought Ember had killed ya."

"He didn't hold back in his attempt," Viorka said, pulling her head from his grip and holding her side. "I'll be bruised for some time. I only hope I returned some pain to him. I don't recall what happened after his jaws wrapped around me."

"He lost an eye to your claws but ya missed his heart," Boldair said.

She shrugged. "Pity. Under better circumstances, I wouldn't have missed."

"Ember won't be traveling with us from this point forward," Boldair said.

"Won't see me weeping tears." Viorka sniffed the air and looked at the boar meat on the table. "Could I have some meat?"

Drucis set a juicy hunk of boar on the table before her. She retracted her long slender claws and took the meat in both hands. She sat back and gnawed it.

"So, Boldair," Yotram said, "when will you finish your quest."

"What quest?"

Viorka paused in eating and glanced at Boldair with a look of disbelief. "Overcoming your fears to tell Wynneffin that you love her. Sheesh. I've been asleep for hours and yet I even know what you need to do."

The Dwarves at the table laughed.

"It's not dat easy," Boldair said.

"Not if you continue to postpone the inevitable," she said.

"It's not supposed to be easy," Drucis said. "Probably be one of the hardest decisions you 'ave to make as king."

Kairun shook his head and laughed. "No, telling her is far easier than asking Wynneffin's father for her hand."

Boldair's eyes widened with fear. "What?"

"Aye," Kairun said. "Her father is none other than King Rigrim himself."

"What? No-o-o," Boldair shook his head. "Ya putting me on. Dat cannot be true."

"Oh, but it is," Yotram said.

Brandrum nodded.

"She never told me dat," Boldair said.

"Perhaps she thought telling you would scare you off," Kairun said.

"And then he fled," Yotram said with a wide grin, followed by a bellowing laugh.

Brandrum nodded. "Now, it's making more sense."

"What is?" Boldair asked.

"She might think you left her because you found out dat her father is the King of Frosthammer."

"Dat's something she should've told me, don'cha think?" Boldair asked.

Kairun laughed. "She never makes a big issue out of her royalty, much like yourself."

"Hey!" Boldair said, "I've not even had a coronation ceremony yet, so it's rather foolhardy to announce it to anyone I come into contact with."

"Then ya need to talk to Wynneffin 'bout everything dat's happened," Kairun said. "If she decides to become your wife, you can join the two kingdoms."

"O-oh," Yotram said, shaking his head.

"What?" Boldair asked.

"As much as King Rigrim hates immigrants, I wonder how he'll view such a marriage proposal?"

Kairun glared at Yotram. The patch over his missing eye made the stare even more intimidating. "Don't scare Boldair off a second time."

"You think *dat's* why she didn't tell me earlier today?" Boldair asked.

"Possibly," Yotram said with a shrug. "Rigrim can be quite ... overbearing and frightening, even to her, I imagine."

"Did you tell her dat you were Nagdor's King?" Brandrum asked.

"Aye," Boldair said, nodding. "And she practically *asked* to be my … Queen."

"Ahh," Kairun said. "She's not lost interest in you or the fact she's a princess. I can tell by your reactions dat you're not over her, either. What's holding ya back?"

"I—I don't like dat she spied on me," Boldair said.

"Do you not think it's because she might have been worried dat something happened to ya?" Brandrum asked. "Or, like I said before, she might've thought you found fault with her?"

Kairun shook his head. "I think it might be dat she feared Boldair had learned she was a princess more than dat. And at the time, he wasn't a king."

Brandrum said, "Since you're a king, at least you'll be on equal levels with her father when you ask for her hand in marriage."

Drucis roared with laughter. Everyone stared at him in question. He quieted himself. "Apologies, but no one, King or otherwise, is ever on equal ground when asking for a daughter's hand in marriage. Suitors are *always* met with the utmost scrutiny. Few ever meet a father's expectations on the first meeting."

Boldair swallowed hard. His eyes revealed his nervousness.

Viorka swallowed the boar meat and licked her paw-like hand. "Ya know, Boldair's never going to find out why she chose to spy on him unless he gets brave enough to *go talk to her*! Stop speculating and go find her, Boldair. Have the courage to ask her. Clear the air. Worry about speaking to her father *afterwards. Not* before."

Kairun laughed. "Couldn't 'ave said it better myself. Boldair, go find her. We'll still be here if she rejects and runs you off. I'm betting she won't. But if she does, we'll buy a barrel of stout to drown your sorrows."

Boldair took a deep breath and his eyes met each Dwarf's individually as he scanned the table. Each Dwarf displayed the same eager hope that he'd act on his heart and feelings and express those to Wynneffin. He rose and nodded. "Wish me luck."

CHAPTER 33

Boldair entered Telsia's shop. At first, he thought no one was inside. Glass shards rustled and clinked on the other side of the bookcase. He walked to the other side of the bookcase to find Wynneffin sweeping up broken glass vials and dried herbs.

Boldair cleared his throat. "Here you are. How—how's Telsia?"

Wynneffin set the broom against the bookcase. She shrugged. "She's with another healer. I don't know yet."

"Look," Boldair said softly. "I think it'd be good for us to talk."

"I agree." She nodded.

"When can we?"

"Now's as good a time as any."

"Here?" he asked. "The place's a mess."

"I'll tend to cleaning it up while we talk."

"Dat's no job for a princess."

She frowned and released a small gasp, which could've been from shock or relief. "Who told you?"

"Is it such a grand secret? All the guards at the tavern who sat with me knew. Did you think they'd not tell me?"

Wynneffin shrugged. "It no longer matters."

"And why not?"

"I've thought a lot about you since you arrived. But I view our situation in a different light now."

"How so?"

"For one," she said, walking to the front counter. "You didn't return to Frosthammer for me. You made it clear that you were only passing through the city as a shortcut to get a drink." She shook her head and looked away. Tears started to form in her eyes, but she took a deep breath, and with determination, she prevented them from maturing. "A drink! In importance to you, I fall behind a measly drink. You 'ave any idea how *dat* makes me feel? Dat you'd venture to our grand city, not to find and visit me, but to pass through to get a rare drink?"

Boldair lowered his gaze to the floor and nodded. "Aye, I understand how dat makes you feel now. Again, when I had spoken those words, they didn't come out like I intended."

She glared at him. "You never intended to find me when you arrived, did you? Don't lie. I'll know. I'd rather be hurt over the truth than angered over a lie. The hurt I'll survive and can forgive you for. A lie? Never."

"From the moment I told my companions dat we were going through Frosthammer, I thought about you," Boldair said, looking in her eyes. "But understand, as vast as the city is, I never thought I'd find you, even if I scoured the each level of the city, looking for you. Truthfully, I didn't 'ave the time for such an endeavor. I was surprised when you approached me on the bridge."

"I could tell," she said.

"But it was a good surprise, Wynnie," Boldair said. "It stirred my heart and all the feelings I've held for you awakened."

She closed her eyes. "It's good dat you can tuck them away into slumber whenever I'm not around."

"Wynnie—"

She shook her head. "No! I've *ached* for you, Boldair. I've stayed up nights wondering about you and why you chose not to return. Treasure-hunting outweighed your feelings for me. A drink does, too? How many nights 'ave you stayed awake thinking and wondering about me?"

Boldair frowned while his mind raced.

"Dat's what I thought," Wynneffin said, brushing past him and heading for the door.

He gently placed his hand on hers and turned her. "Look, Wynnie, I don't profess to be an honorable Dwarf in how to court a lady, especially a princess, but I think I've matured a bit since I returned."

"No, Boldair, you haven't. The distance between us is too great to bridge the gap."

"I'm sorry my shallow stupidity hurt you. Dat was never my intentions. Honest," Boldair said.

"While dat may be true," she said, "my heart no longer yearns for you."

The coldness in her voice cause his skin to pimple from the chill.

"Fine," Boldair said softly, nodding in surrender. He sighed. "Perhaps it's best this—whatever it is we had between us—ends this evening, then. Might I ask you something before I leave?"

Wynneffin nodded.

"How long 'ave you been practicing magic?"

She was taken back by the question. "I've not."

"Wynnie, you 'ave. The fact dat you had Telsia use the Fae Stones to spy on me is enough proof."

Her face tightened with anger.

"Wait, I'm not trying to offend you," Boldair said. "But the use of such stones *is* channeling magic. Using those sprites to keep tabs on one's whereabouts by having them drink the blood of the person they're required to watch is dark sorcery. You realize dat, don't ya?"

She sighed. "The sprites ... I could see dat as dark sorcery, but dat's something *she* did. I've no part of it. But it really bothers you dat I chose to have Telsia use the Fae Stones to see if you were okay?"

He nodded. "Yes, it did and still does a little now."

"Why?"

"Because it was an invasion of my privacy."

"You 'ave something to hide?"

Boldair shook his head. "No, but it still makes me uncomfortable, like you were hoping to discover me doing something unruly. And—" His eyes widened.

She stared at him curiously. "And what?"

He turned away from her and ran his hand along his beard. "How often did you spy on me?"

"I told you."

"No, how often? How many times? What was I doing when you viewed my activities?" He asked, turning toward her with anger in his eyes.

She was taken back by his sudden anger. "I don't recall."

"Give an estimate then," he said.

Wynneffin crossed her arms. "A few dozen times, I suppose."

"Are you able to use these stones by yourself or did Telsia summon their power for you?"

"She did. I told you dat I know no magic."

"Dammit," Boldair said, shaking his head.

"What?"

"Dat means *she* could've been watching me on a daily basis without you being present."

Wynneffin frowned. "Why would she want to do dat?"

"Tell me what I was doing when she viewed me," he said.

"Different things, why?"

"It might well be dat she knows where I've stashed some of me treasures."

"So?"

"Wynnie," Boldair said with a firm stare. "*Where* is she?"

"Why?"

"I don't think the forest Elf was lying when she said dat Telsia had a hand in Viorka's disappearance."

Wynneffin frowned. "Why must you assume the worst about her? You don't know her."

"I don't think you know her as well as you think you do."

"You barely know anything about me," Wynneffin said.

"Aye, you 'ave secrets of your own, too, dat we've *not* discussed yet."

"You believe she'd actually allow them to pummel, gag, and leave her behind like they did?"

Boldair nodded. "I'd wager my entire cache of treasures on it."

"You realize the degree of your paranoia?" she asked.

"It's a gut feeling dat she's taken advantage of the information she's gathered 'bout me in her supposed *offer* to help you."

"Preposterous."

"Where is she?"

"I'll not tell you," Wynneffin replied.

"Then you're in on it, too."

"Boldair!" Fury blazed in her amber eyes. "How dare you—"

"Either you take me to where she is, or I'll have no choice but to believe that she and you are in cahoots to rob me. Dat's an offense I won't take lightly." His eyes narrowed as he awaited her answer.

"Fine," she said, coldly. "I'll take you to the healer where she's at. You'll see dat I've been honest with you. When you see dat, I want you to leave Frosthammer and never come back. Is dat understood?"

"Either way, Wynnie, I've no intention of ever setting foot inside Frosthammer again." He motioned toward the door. "Lead the way."

CHAPTER 34

If Boldair had thought he'd seen Wynneffin at her angriest, he quickly learned that he had not. She fumed as she marched across the bridge and they descended three floors on the lift. Her fists were so tight that her knuckles whitened. The entire way, she refused to glance his direction, and worse, she was so silent that he could almost hear the brassiness of her thoughts.

Anger radiated energy and the harsh vibes undulating from her let him know to keep his silence. If he were wrong about Telsia, he'd readily accept a verbal thrashing afterwards. No need to sample her desired unrelenting tirade beforehand.

But now, Boldair was certain that the forest Elf had not lied. Elves and Dwarves were never the closest of allies, but in the search to better one's knowledge in the realms of magic, barters and schemes were common to advance to a higher plateau, regardless of race. With thieves, this was also true. Stealing a magic scroll from a sorcerer without being detected and killed was richly rewarded by other wizards and sorcerers. This was the situation he assumed Telsia had involved herself in. These forest Elves had been supplying her with scrolls, potions, and rare herbs to advance Telsia's knowledge and power in a tradition better known by Elves than Dwarves. With the possibility of gaining greater riches, Telsia must have offered them a substantial amount of gold and gems to increase her abilities, only *she* didn't possess that kind of wealth.

Although Boldair wasn't absolutely certain this was Telsia's arrangement with the forest Elves, his strong premonition linked their mutual benefits of their working together. The Elves needed Viorka, or at least her blood, to concoct the perfect potion to rid themselves of the plague. But the disease had already gone past the point of healing, slowly consuming their minds.

It seemed by chance that Boldair entered Frosthammer at the exact time with Viorka to allow the forest Elves to abduct her. But the only way that was possible was if Telsia was an oracle or had direct access to one. If so, that explained how the forest Elves were lying in wait when he and his party entered the gates. Viorka suffering great injury and her need of a medic didn't matter. What mattered was that Telsia knew he was coming with a fynx. The Elves would've still found a way or attempted to take Viorka even if she'd been healthy.

Because Wynneffin completely trusted Telsia, Telsia needed to make herself appear innocent when the Elves took Viorka. A feat she pulled off with success.

After the lift stopped, Wynneffin brushed past Boldair, shoving her shoulder into him to push him aside. Her lips curled in a snarl. All the loveliness he'd once seen in her was gone. Seeing this side of her was hurtful, as had it not been for his gut accusation toward Telsia, Wynneffin would not openly display such countenance.

Even if his instinct about Telsia was correct, Boldair was finished with Frosthammer for good. Too much contention divided Wynneffin and he. There was nothing that could mend their severed friendship.

Wynneffin's anger caused other Dwarves along the street to step aside and allow her to pass. Who she was, a daughter of King Rigrim, was not a mystery to the citizens of Frosthammer like it had been for him. They knew who she was, and if the King's daughter held intense anger, none were safe should anyone unintentionally cross her path or inconvenience her.

Boldair realized asking her father for her hand in marriage might be a lot easier than surviving a lifetime of walking on brittle eggshells, hoping not to provoke her darker side. In her defense, Boldair could not picture a more perfect queen whenever the situation with a neighboring city became hostile. Any other ruler would think twice and perhaps a third or fourth time before acting undiplomatic.

They walked past a vendor shop that reeked of strong cheese. The aroma caused Boldair to hold his breath until they were several shops away. The sulfur in the deepest pits near a smoldering volcano was far more pleasant. It didn't surprise him that the shops on either side were empty. How anyone went inside the shop to purchase a wheel of cheese was beyond him.

A carved picture of a vial and herbs was posted above a door a couple of blocks from the cheese shop. Wynneffin stormed to the door and flung it open. Several birds in a steel cage chirped their alarmed cries and thrashed against the bars, trying to escape.

An old Dwarf with silvery blue hair adjusted his brass-rimmed goggles and frowned at her intrusion. She crossed her arms and glared at the birds and then at the old Dwarf. When he recognized her, nervousness widened his eyes. "Yes? How might I help you, Wynneffin?"

"Xyle, I need to speak with Telsia," she replied firmly, walking to the polished countertop and setting her tightened fists upon it.

"Telsia?" he asked, lifting his goggles and rubbing his eyes. He adjusted his goggles again. "She was only here for a short time."

"She was injured and said that you'd attend her injuries."

Xyle shrugged. "A guard escorted her here, but soon after he left, she told me all was well and headed outside."

The anger vanished from Wynneffin's face. She was instantly pale. "Did you give her any remedies? Salve?"

"No, nothing. She didn't act injured in any respect."

"When I last saw her, her face was battered. She could barely walk."

"Well, she sorta limped into the store with the guard but afterwards, she didn't."

"Was she faking her injuries?"

"That would be my assumption, Wynneffin," Xyle said.

Shocked, she turned to Boldair.

"I told you," Boldair said. He turned on his heels and exited the shop.

"Wait!" Wynneffin said, rushing out the door to follow him.

Boldair marched with abrupt steps. "I'm gathering my party together and leaving Frosthammer. I'm good for my word this time, Wynnie. I won't return. Not for you or anything else. I hope ya understand dat."

"Look, Boldair, I really didn't think Telsia would do something like this."

"None of dat matters now," Boldair replied. "I have me safeguards in place to protect my treasure. After my coronation, I'll send troops to gather all my treasures and have them stored in Nagdor's vaults where no one can possibly steal them."

"Boldair," Wynneffin said in a softer tone. "We shouldn't part ways like this."

He turned with fierceness in his eyes. "You were fine with it a few minutes ago, weren't you? When *you* were right and I was wrong! Now, dat it's the other way … We should never 'ave crossed paths again. And in the future, I hope we never do."

She grabbed his forearm.

He yanked it free. "I'm warning ya. I'm in no mood to discuss this further. You couldn't even consider my advisement concerning the underhandedness of Telsia until *after* you discovered the truth. If ye think so little of my observations, why should I ever consider any future with you? There's no trust between us, nor will there ever be. Dat's *not* what I need in a Queen."

"I was hasty in my actions, Boldair."

"In every single way, Wynnie. First by spying on me, which probably gave Telsia enough information to attempt to steal some of my treasures. And then, regardless of what I said, you deny her of any possible wrongdoing."

"I thought she was my friend, Boldair. I trusted her and she was always loyal to me."

"Is dat right?"

"Aye, it is!"

Boldair kept his gaze straight ahead as he walked. The strength of his anger was enough that he didn't even notice the stench of the cheese shop as they walked past. "Tell me something."

"Anything, Boldair," she said, hurrying along beside him.

"Did you know her before you decided to try to find out more about my whereabouts? Now, I mean *know* who she was and not in name or reputation only. Did you?"

"No. But we became quick friends."

Boldair nodded. "I imagine so, once she learned about my passion for hunting gold and treasures."

"She never mentioned anything about your treasures or where you kept them hidden," Wynneffin said.

Boldair paused to glance angrily at her and then continued walking. "Do ya really think dat she would? If her goal was to get wealthy by somehow robbing my caches, she's not going to clue ya in 'bout it. Just like she let you believe she needed to see another medic when she didn't."

"You need to remember dat you told me you were going to return," she said. "Dat's why I consulted her in the first place."

"I would've returned eventually. Dat was never a lie. Not returning quickly was wrong. I've admitted dat. But I would've returned like I promised. Now, though, I regret ever having come to this city in the first place."

"You really mean dat?"

"You bet'cha I do."

She halfway growled in frustration. "Turn around and talk to me."

"I'm done talking," he replied. "And to think I had come back to Telsia's shop to discuss our future together."

"You really came to talk about dat?"

"Aye, but then you showed me how little you believed in my observations. I can't have a queen who doesn't believe in me."

She huffed. "Gut feelings are not absolute."

"Mine are. They've always been. They're the reason I'm still alive. I've survived against some insurmountable odds, and it was due to what I felt in me gut."

"What's your gut telling you now?"

"To get as far from this frozen hellhole as possible," Boldair replied.

"Without me?"

"Without you."

"Why?"

Before Boldair stepped onto the lift platform, he turned and faced her. "As I promised when we left Telsia's shop, I'm leaving Frosthammer either way. Whether Telsia was where she told you or not, I was leaving. And I am. A promise is a promise."

"Sorry dat I caused you to possibly lose your treasures."

"The issue isn't about the treasures, but more about your lack of trust."

"You can't talk through our differences?" Wynneffin asked, folding her arms.

"After your display of anger earlier when I expressed my concerns about Telsia, I don't logically see any benefit in trying to discuss anything with you. You're not rational."

She shook her head in exasperation. "And *you are*? Boldair, I'm sorry. I felt you were challenging me and I reacted in kind. It was as if you didn't believe I was capable of discerning the true motives of ... my friend."

He shrugged. "How does it make you feel now dat you know the truth?"

"Humiliated," she replied. "As well I should be since I was wrong. Not only did I misjudge her, I misjudged you. And for dat, I'm truly sorry."

"I'm sorry, too, Wynnie, but to be honest, it's dat kind of misjudgment dat lets me know you could never be my queen. A queen must have the ability to read others effectively in order to council me about decisions. You've failed miserably." He stepped onto the lift and turned to face her. "This is goodbye ... forever."

Fury heated her gaze. Her amber eyes brightened from her rage. "You'll regret walking away from me. You'll return to Frosthammer to face your doom."

Before the lift rose, he was certain her fingertips glowed like he had seen wizards right before they summoned a spell into action. Did she know how to cast magic? Had she lied about that? Were her capabilities something she and Telsia had learned to accomplish together? Few

Dwarves held the ability and knowledge to become sorcerers or wizards. And if she were lying, she was holding back far more information than he ever had.

Regardless of her potential powers, he realized by her quick temper that she and he would never remain compatible enough to marry. One of them would surely die, and he was certain it wouldn't be her.

CHAPTER 35

*B*oldair returned to the Hogshead Splatter Grog and was hailed by Dwiskter, Drucis, and the Frosthammer guards. Still seated at the table where he'd left them, they raised their tankards at him before downing the contents.

Their broad grins shrank as he walked to the table. His anger and disappointment weighed his facial expressions. The heaviness of his footsteps hammered his frustration.

"I take it things didn't go like you hoped?" Kairun asked.

"It went as badly as I expected *before* the lot of ya convinced me to go talk to her. I'd 'ave been better off never seeking her out," Boldair replied. He glanced at Dwiskter and then at Drucis. "It's time to gather our belongings and travel on."

Yotram frowned. "So soon? Boldair, at least sit and drink. Stay the night and be fresh for your travels on the morrow."

"No. I appreciate the offer and invitation, but we really must be heading onward."

Yotram stood and placed his hand on Boldair's shoulder. "The nights are far colder than the days in the Frosted Peaks. Even a hardy Dwarf can freeze to death quite quickly. Not to mention, predatory animals roam in the darkness, so even if you found a place to set up a campfire sheltered from the blasting frigid winds, these beasts would rip you apart in the dead of night."

"What sort of beasts?" Drucis asked. His thick eyebrows rose. "I like a good challenge. Besides, it might be nice to have some new trophies on Nagdor's dining room walls. Eh, Boldair?"

Boldair grinned and nodded, but his eyes never met with any of the other Dwarves. Inside, a harsh whirlpool of emotions tugged his thoughts downward into his aching memories. Had he done the right thing in how he left Wynneffin? Were the words that escaped his mouth been from his heart or from the rashness of his building anger toward his father and brother for their betrayals? Add Telsia's deceit to the mix, and perhaps his anger was misplaced. Wynneffin had been betrayed by Telsia as well. Boldair had lashed out at Wynnie without fully letting her explain.

Boldair stood and was about to leave the table when Kairun gripped his shoulder and pulled him back to the table. He placed a tankard on the table before Boldair. "Here, don't go yet. Drink up!"

Yotram looked at Drucis. "What sort of beasts, ye ask? Some say dat they're part human and part bear. Others have spoken of strange Owl-beasts dat roam during the night. Both of these creatures are blood-thirsty terrors. Along the cliffside are ice spiders dat blend in with the snow and icicles. The extreme cold doesn't bother them, but the heat of the living attracts them. They slowly spindle down their silk strands to drain travelers of their blood while they sleep."

"Bah! You've never even left Frosthammer. Ya said so yourself," Boldair said. "How do you know such is true?"

Yotram laughed. "Expeditions are sent out for logs dat we saw into lumber. We can't make *everything* out of steel. We do trade with other peddling caravans from time to time, and these are the kind folks who offer their tales of terror. Some have survived the attacks and have the scars to prove it."

Boldair sighed. "I'd rather face those odds than—"

"Look, rejection's difficult for the best of us."

"No. She didn't reject *me*. I rejected her and walked away. And dat's what I want to do now. I want to leave Frosthammer."

Viorka slid from behind the table and came closer. "*Why* did you reject her?"

"It'd take too long to explain," Boldair replied. "Besides, I'd rather not get into the particulars. But, let's just say dat Telsia did more than help Wynneffin spy on me."

Drucis frowned. "What do ya mean?"

"Telsia used the Fae Stones to view where I stashed some of my treasures."

Kairun took a sharp breath. "You're sure?"

"Aye. I'm positive."

Dwiskter said, "Did she tell you dat? I thought she'd been injured by the forest Elves."

"Dat's what she wanted us to believe. Wynnie and I went to see the medic Telsia was to get treatment from. He said dat Telsia had already left. According to the medic, she wasn't hurt like she implied. She wasn't hurt at all. My guess is she'll leave Frosthammer to seek my closest hidden treasures."

"Not if we can help it," Yotram said. "We only have three gates dat lead out of the city. I'll inform the guards to not allow her to pass and to retain her. Dat way, your treasures remain safely hidden."

Boldair grinned. "I appreciate dat, but I 'ave you know dat even if she finds my stashed treasures, she can't release the traps without dying. If she's somehow managed to get outside of Frosthammer, her life will be short."

"Boldair," Yotram said, "no residing Dwarf in our city would dare attempt to leave during the coldest hours of night. I assure you. We know the fate of doing so. Please, have a seat and your tab tonight is on me, new King."

Yotram waved at two guards from the bar and met them halfway between their table and the bar. He spoke to them briefly before returning. The two guards left their tankards and exited the Grog.

Boldair sighed and reluctantly took his seat with his back to the wall. Yotram motioned a bar maiden. She brought him a tankard. Boldair wiped the excess froth from the top and he pressed the tankard to his lips. He tipped it and downed half the contents.

Dwiskter sat beside Boldair. "I'm sorry things didn't work out."

"Ah, don't worry over it," he replied. "I tell ya dat I've a better understanding of her than what I've pictured in my mind all these years. I like a strong female dat's spirited. I do. She's one dat can stand her ground against the worst ruffian, but she can't control her temper. Much like myself. Worse even is dat she didn't believe me when I attempted to tell her the truth about Telsia. Instead, she hurled her anger and mistrust toward me until *after* she realized Telsia wasn't the friend she believed her to be. Then her demeanor softened as though I'd forget the fiery anger she'd displayed minutes before. Suddenly, she wanted to side with me as though she was as much a victim as me."

"But wouldn't anyone think that way?" Viorka asked. "Wouldn't you place stronger trust in someone you've known for a long time over someone you didn't? In some ways, Telsia's betrayal cut Wynneffin worse than your suffering, as you saw what she could not about Telsia."

Boldair shrugged. "Perhaps. And it'd depend upon the circumstances. But Wynnie's always butting heads with me. Her stubbornness doesn't allow her to trust me and my instincts. She'd rather oppose me until she's proven wrong. As King, I can't 'ave dat in a Queen. Our kingdom would be quickly divided."

"Dat's true," Drucis said.

Boldair sighed. "Ya know, I truly hoped for a better outcome with Wynnie. I did. Like a fool I believed what all of you had convinced me."

Viorka's eyes narrowed. "Boldair, things between you and her might yet change. I don't think she's ever deliberately set out to hurt you. Give it time. You might see the circumstances differently tomorrow."

Boldair turned up his tankard and emptied its contents. "The damage between us might be too great to repair. I'll bear the sorrow for a time."

Dwiskter held his tankard up firmly, nodded, and finished off its contents. "Not everything goes as planned."

"Aye," Boldair said softly. "But it's good having friends who 'ave ya back regardless of the disappointments. And those of you gathered 'round this table with me, I count you as the closest of them all."

Kairun, Brandrum, and Yotram grinned.

Boldair looked at Yotram. "If ever the three of you decide to adventure outside of Frosthammer, I invite you to visit me in Nagdor. Dat's a King's invitation. We can hunt or you can enjoy the finest ales and stouts our city makes."

Kairun nodded. "Dat's an invite worthy of examining, friend."

"Agreed," Yotram said.

Brandrum looked at the door with an uneasy expression. "I must say dat we have some unexpected company."

Kairun said, "Royal guards? Never seen 'em enter here."

Two Dwarf guards were dressed in heavier ice dragon armor. The sharp tusks on their pauldrons were gold-plated, making them more distinctive in appearance from the regular guards or soldiers.

They approached the table where Boldair sat.

"King Boldair," the one guard said.

"Aye?" Boldair said.

"King Rigrim requests your immediate presence."

Boldair glanced toward Yotram. Yotram shrugged.

"If you would accompany us—"

Boldair rose slowly. He wanted to decline the invitation, but since it was the King of Frosthammer, he couldn't. Refusing a King's invitation was a direct insult. As a new King, Boldair couldn't afford making enemies, especially not that of a king he needed for an ally.

Yotram exchanged nervous glances with Brandrum and Kairun.

Boldair offered a quick wink to those at his table. "Save some stout for me for when I return."

CHAPTER 36

King Boldair entered King Rigrim's private library behind the two royal guards. King Rigrim sat in a fine cushioned, high-back chair with his frost warhammer propped against the chair's right arm. He wore a nightshirt and bearskin leggings. Boldair guessed Rigrim would soon retire for the night.

Rigrim's thick hands gripped the armrests of the chair. Swollen veins on his forearms resembled small ropes. His frost-blue, long beard curled onto his lap. For an elder Dwarf, he lacked any signs of age or weakness. His amber eyes reflected his vigor and his intense stare brought chills to Boldair. Wisdom bore in his eyes, and for several antagonizing moments, Boldair believed Rigrim was trying to invade Boldair's mind to read his thoughts.

Bluish-white waves of frost filtered into the air from the magic of his weapon. A thin layer of frost formed around the warhammer's head where it touched the floor.

Boldair had seen magically enhanced weapons before but none quite as intimidating as this one. Such a weapon combined with the brutal appearance of King Rigrim would make an Orc army momentarily freeze in their advance.

"Have a seat." Rigrim extended his hand toward the chair opposite his. The coldness of the statement indicated it wasn't a request.

Boldair nodded. The cushion sank beneath his weight, and the sensation was similar to floating on air. Boldair adjusted himself, and after finding the perfect balance, he observed the bookends on the bookshelves.

Above the books were large heads of strange beasts, which adorned the top shelves where no books collected dust. Some of these head mounts resembled the creatures Yotram had spoken about just minutes earlier in the tavern. They were intriguing beasts but their fangs, beaks, and claws could easily inflict the damage like Yotram described. Yotram did not exaggerate the accounts.

After Boldair finished admiring the different mounted heads, his gaze froze on Rigrim's piercing eyes.

Rigrim studied Boldair in silence for several moments. He offered neither a smile or a frown. His peering eyes, though, spoke volumes. The quietness made Boldair even more uneasy. The room grew icy cold, despite the small fire in the hearth. Rigrim looked at the two escort guards and motioned them away.

"Leave us," Rigrim said.

The guards bowed and backed through the door, promptly closing it behind them.

"King Boldair," Rigrim said in a thunderous voice. The high ceiling allowed the deep resonance of his words to echo, which made Boldair wonder if the room's architecture was deliberate for such intimidating reasons. "I find it odd that a king would enter Frosthammer without making an announcement of your arrival. Isn't that the proper way kings should behave?"

"My apologies. Aye, you're right. But my reign as king is not yet official, King Rigrim."

Rigrim frowned and peered at him. His amber eyes glowed and his gaze could bring fear to almost anyone captured within it. "What do you mean, *not* official?"

"My coronation has yet to occur."

Rigrim tilted his head back, keeping his gaze firmly locked on Boldair. "I see. What brings you to my kingdom?"

Boldair explained how he and his party simply wanted to pass through Frosthammer to reach the other side of the mountains more quickly.

"How is it that you know of Frosthammer in the first place?" Rigrim asked.

"From a map I found in a vault. Directions and the proper pattern of knocks to get inside were written on it. Due to my overpowering curiosity, I came to investigate and stayed a couple weeks."

"Is this when you met my daughter, Wynneffin?"

"Aye," Boldair said, nodding slightly.

Rigrim frowned. "What are your intentions with my daughter?"

"I have none."

"I was told you had come to ask her hand in marriage. Is that true?"

"Not officially, no."

"Is anything ever *official* for you?" Rigrim asked. His brow tightened and his eyes gleamed. "Was your intention to join our kingdoms through marriage?"

"No," Boldair replied.

"No?" Rigrim's brow narrowed.

Boldair shook his head. "I had no knowledge until a few hours ago dat Wynnie was even a princess."

"She never told you?"

"No."

"What are your intentions now?"

"My intentions are to continue on my journey with my party. We set out tomorrow morning."

"Without her?"

Boldair nodded. "Aye."

"If I may ask," Rigrim said, "had you ever considered marriage to my daughter?"

"Yes. For a long time after I left Frosthammer, I considered the possibility. When I first met her, there was an attraction between us. A strong one, but I was too young to settle then. I sought adventure, as I can see you have as well, with all your mounted trophies. I've always sought treasure to pass me time."

Rigrim formed a bridge with his fingers and rested his chin upon them. He leaned forward. A slight smile spread on his lips. "You and I should hunt sometime."

"I've not done much hunting, but I would find the opportunity to hunt with you quite enjoyable," Boldair replied.

The library door opened. Boldair glanced toward it. A servant brought in two tankards. She handed one to Rigrim and offered the other to Boldair. He took it and nodded his appreciation. The servant smiled before turning to leave.

Rigrim waved his hand toward several of the beasts' heads on the wall. "Hunting creatures such as these proves one's courage, as the next worst thing to hunt is a dragon. Not many of those nowadays, are there?"

Boldair met Rigrim's eyes and didn't flinch. "I've seen a few."

"Lately?"

"Aye."

Keen interest claim Rigrim's facial expressions. "Might I ask another question regarding my daughter?"

"Depends upon the question," Boldair said, smiling slightly.

"Aye, I suppose so." Rigrim chuckled and eased back in his chair. "What changed your opinion about marrying her?"

Boldair explained how Wynneffin had Telsia use the Fae Stones to spy on him. And how Telsia had taken the opportunity to learn where Boldair stored his treasures, and that he believed Telsia had fled in order to find and steal some of them.

"So you've lost your trust in her?"

Boldair nodded. "For dat, yes. But, she apparently holds little trust in me and my assessments anyway. As King, I must 'ave a wife who backs me instead of haggling me over every detail. Besides, any relationship without trust is doomed for failure."

"Yes, quite true and I understand your reasoning. Marriage consists of equal footing, even for a king. Too many struggles exist outside the throne room for a king to have to deal with strife within his marriage."

"Aye," Boldair said.

"Wynneffin!" Rigrim said, looking toward the dark corner of the room. "Present yourself."

Wynneffin stepped from the shadows of the corner bookcases. She looked at her feet while she walked to stand between Rigrim's chair and Boldair's.

Boldair felt the blood drain from his face. His heart dropped at the thought she'd been hidden in the shadows the entire time he had spoken to her father. His mind raced, wondering if he might have implied an insult toward her, which he had not. But still he worried. He felt hollow inside, partly because it seemed Rigrim had betrayed his confidence. He was fearful of what Rigrim was about to do and say. But, by the look in her eyes, she seemed as fearful about what might happen next as was Boldair.

"Is it true, Wynneffin, that you sought the counsel of a known sorceress to spy on your potential suitor?" Rigrim asked.

Known?

"Yes, father," she replied.

"For how long?"

"Months."

Anger rose inside Boldair but he fought to rein it in.

"And Telsia betrayed you?" Rigrim asked.

She nodded.

"What magic do you know?" Rigrim asked.

Wynneffin dared to look into her father's amber eyes, but she didn't answer.

"Are you capable of using magic?" he asked.

"No less than you are," she replied, crossing her arms.

Boldair gave an incredulous stare at Rigrim but Rigrim offered a dismissive frown and shrugged. For the moment, he kept his attention on Wynneffin.

"So Telsia did teach you?"

"Aye, father," she replied.

"Why abuse such power as to watch the activities of someone without their knowledge? What had you hoped to gain?" Rigrim asked.

"At the time, I never viewed it as abusing my magical abilities. I was genuinely concerned about his welfare in the beginning because I thought he planned to return immediately. He promised me he would."

"So you know how to use the Fae Stones to view others' activities?" King Rigrim asked.

"Yes, father."

"Return to Telsia's shop and use those stones to find where she's hiding. Have two of my guards escort you. When you locate her, send them to apprehend her."

"I cannot," she replied.

Fury tightened Rigrim's brow. "Why not?"

"The Fae stones were taken. Telsia probably packed them away."

"Then report this to each guard at our entrances," Rigrim said. "Give them orders to not allow Telsia to leave."

"Yes, father." Wynneffin offered an embarrassed smile to Boldair in passing. Her smile spread into a sly grin once she turned from her father's view. Her eyes darkened with threatening mischief.

What's she up to?

Boldair watched her leave, offering no words and wondering how he'd failed to see her true nature from the beginning. Perhaps subconsciously he'd detected it and that was the reason he had chosen his treasures over her. And *she* faulted him for lying when she had denied having the ability to use magic when he had asked?

After she left the library, Rigrim shook his head. "King Boldair, I offer my apologies. Should Telsia somehow escape Frosthammer before we arrest her and she steals any of your wealth, I will recompense your losses."

Boldair waved a dismissive hand and shook his head. "Dat won't be necessary. Most likely, the first trap she encounters in my troves will kill her."

"Nonetheless, my offer has been made and I stand behind it."

"Appreciated," Boldair said. "Might I ask you something?"

"Sure."

"In the Dwarven kingdoms I've journeyed to, I've seen only two other Dwarves capable of wielding magic. Yet, you, Telsia, *and* your daughter have this ability?"

Rigrim smiled, but not pleasantly. "I'm convinced that most races possess the ability, if only the individuals seek to tap into the well. For Dwarves, since we're capable of using runes to nullify the effects of magic, most Dwarves are conflicted by seeking to channel magic as a weapon." He placed his hand on the handle of the warhammer. "As you can see, magic has great benefits for me."

"You're the one who enchanted the weapon?"

Rigrim nodded. "Yes. The magic that flows into this weapon comes from the core of our great city. The city is named after my weapon, Frosthammer, and is connected only to me. No other individual can wield this warhammer. Doing so is instant death. The frost magic courses through the body of anyone else's touch and turns him or her into a block of ice, which is why I always keep the weapon close at hand. Curious folks often don't think before acting, and an eager hand is death awaiting."

Boldair smiled. "Good to know."

"Another thing I need to ask you about my daughter, Wynneffin."

"What's dat?"

"She's the only daughter that I have who has never married. In beauty, none of them are fairer, but in temperament … I wish my living sons held half the stubborn zeal she displays in weapons training. I've watched her defeat every one of my sons in practice duels. Believe me, they didn't hold back. Their frustration in trying to defeat her was too great, and not one of them has ever bested her. Because of her dominant display to outdo those around her, she has a way to repulse male Dwarves who courted her in the past. Has she done such with you?"

"Her zeal and spirit were the reasons I often thought about her while I journied and explored. Those are traits dat attracted me to her. But never 'ave I seen someone who could go from gentle to burning hatred within the blink of an eye."

Rigrim's brow rose. "She did that?"

"Aye. She spoke—practically insisted—of becoming my Queen. But when I discovered Telsia's underhanded plot to steal my treasure,

Wynnie turned utter disdain toward me. Volcanoes burn with less intensity. The moment after she learned the truth about Telsia, her hate-filled attitude vanished as though she'd never gotten mad. She made no excuses for her behavior."

"That explains a lot."

King Rigrim rose and Boldair followed suit. They firmly clasped hands. "King Boldair, I've kept you long enough from your affairs with your friends, but note that you're welcome in Frosthammer at any time."

"Aye," Boldair grinned and nodded. "Once I reach Nagdor, I shall send word by raven. If you'd accept the invitation, I'd be honored for you to attend my coronation ceremony."

"I appreciate the invitation and shall consider it. I've not made any journeys outside the Frosted Peaks for half a century or more." He released Boldair's hand and waved toward the door. "Please enjoy the remainder of your stay."

CHAPTER 37

Boldair awakened the following morning. His vision was blurred and his thoughts murky. He blinked several times, trying to clear the fuzzy blur clouding his vision, but still everything around him remained unclear.

He rubbed his eyes and viscous tears etched from the corners, meandered down his cheeks, and soaked into his beard. Squinting, he saw the hazy flickering of a torch at the edge of the wall.

"Bloody hell!" he said, swinging his feet over the side of his bed. "How'd I get 'ere? More importantly, where is *here*?"

Boldair massaged his temples. The last thing he recalled after leaving King Rigrim's library was returning to join his party, Yotram, and the other guards in the tavern. They had drunk, sang, and he told some of his more popular treasure tales while standing atop the table. The other patrons gathered around, listened, and cheered to his triumph during his ordeals, but then … He had no idea.

He certainly hadn't drunk enough to lose consciousness. The strongest drink he consumed was the frosty dark stout Yotram insisted to be the best brew under the mountains. How could he refuse such a boast? It was good, Boldair recalled, but cold like swallowing huge chunks of ice. The drink gave him a tremendous headache, like frozen icicles were thrust into his brain from all sides. But after those harsh effects wore off, he drank other stouts with better taste and less unpleasant effects.

"Behold, the King! Morning, brother."

Boldair turned in the direction of the familiar voice and opened his eyes. His vision was a bit clearer. Boldair rose to his feet, stunned. Bars separated him and his brother, Forboud.

"What the—" Boldair staggered to the cell bars. He was in the prison cell beside Forboud. "How'd I get in 'ere?"

Forboud grinned, clearly amused, and chuckled. "Doesn't set too well, does it, oh King brother of mine?"

Boldair frowned. "What happened? Why am I in 'ere?"

Forboud shrugged. "No entirely certain, but those guard friends of yours dragged you in during the night, despite your adamant protests."

Confused, Boldair gripped the cell bars and fought to remember. "What did I do?"

Forboud laughed and shrugged slightly. "You were a raving lunatic, madly shouting, kicking, and fighting to break free. Dat soon passed after they tossed you into the cell and locked the door. I don't recall ever seeing you quite so hostile. It took three guards to haul you inside dat cell."

Boldair released the bars, turned, and placed his hands over his face. It hurt to think. "Where are Dwiskter and Drucis? Were they arrested, too?"

"No," Forboud said. "Not dat I know about, at least. They weren't down here when you were arrested."

"Did Yotram say anything to you or me when they locked the door?"

"No, but *you* said plenty. I've never seen you so angry."

Boldair shook his head. "This makes no sense."

"You were a bit tipsy."

Boldair shrugged and waved Forboud off. "I've been dat way plenty. I've been arrested before, too, but usually I recall the reasons for why. But not … this time."

"Like I said, brother, you were quite angry, and they looked none too pleased with you, either."

Boldair sighed and returned to the cot. He plopped down. He grumbled and kicked the straw on the floor. The last time he found himself in such a predicament was when Taniesse had taken him prisoner. Only then, he'd been shackled to the prison wall while she threw fireballs at him until he promised to return her treasure.

"Brother," Forboud said, softly. Boldair glanced in his direction. "How'd we get to this place?"

"What do ya mean?"

"At such odds against one another."

"Bah!" Boldair said, shaking his head and waving him off. "Brother, my head hurts too badly to discuss this right now."

"Boldair, we've shared many adventures together. I've always admired your free spirit and how you roamed the lands seeking wealth. Such is a skill I don't possess, which is why I was honored whenever you allowed me to go with you. I truly would never cause you harm. I'd give my life to save yours. What are your plans now? Will you have me face death like our father does?"

"Father's situation is far more different than yours. I didn't place father into custody. The Dwarven Alliance Kings did."

"I realize that."

"Father dealt himself his own fate. You've dealt yourself your own as well."

"Death?" Forboud asked quietly.

Boldair frowned and looked at Forboud. Seeing his beardless brother tensed Boldair's stomach. He fought looking away, because then it'd appear Boldair's actions had been rash. Perhaps he had been too irrational in cutting Forboud's beard. It was a harsh punishment, but something drastic that needed to be done in order to get his brother's attention. His constant undermining infuriated Boldair, and Forboud had tried to kill Viorka, even though Forboud knew the catlike creature was one of his closest friend. That was a crossed line Boldair could never ignore nor forgive.

Boldair sighed. "Brother, I don't know. Death comes for all eventually."

Forboud held a meek appearance, like an animal that had been beaten down by a stronger animal, but that didn't mean his brother had lost his bite or that his teeth had lost their edge. Serpents, when cold, accepted the warm coddling of a compassionate human, only to turn and bite their savior when they regained strength.

"Boldair, I must confess dat it does bother me for the Alliance to have chosen you to replace our father when my qualifications—"

Boldair raised his palm toward Forboud and shook his head. "Not now."

"Please, it's the only time we can talk heart to heart in privacy."

Boldair sighed, rubbed his temples, and nodded. "Carry on, then."

"Thanks. Even though my qualifications are greater because father taught me diplomacy—"

"To the point, brother. My head aches."

"Yes. Sorry. I accept my place beneath you to serve you as my King." Forboud knelt on his cell floor.

"Come off it," Boldair said. "Dat's not necessary. Rise."

"Is there any way I can prove my submission to you?"

"Look, our journey after we leave Frosthammer is long yet. Prove yourself during our travel back to Nagdor, and perhaps I can see dat you've had a real change of heart. Your actions dictate the trueness of your heart and mind. But, I must tell you dat after you tried to kill Viorka, it'd take a mountain's worth of proof to ever bend my mind in your favor."

Forboud rose to his feet and held the bars. He nodded. "Quite right, brother. I should've never gone after her, but unlike you, I helped father rear Ember from a pup, which makes me feel like he's my own."

"You understand dat Viorka was only defending herself?"

"Aye, I've thought about dat since they put me in the cell. When I reacted in the cavern, I wasn't thinking. She or no one else had any reason to simply let Ember kill her. I'm truly sorry. How is she?" Sadness dampened his eyes. "She did survive?"

Boldair nodded. "Aye, but barely. A lot transpired after we got her to the healer, but we did get medicine into Viorka and she awoke a while before I was placed in this cell."

Forboud looked relieved. "That's good news. Again, I'm sorry."

"Something you should express to her," Boldair replied.

"Yes. If we ever get out of these cells."

Boldair stood and walked to the door of his cell. Outside their cells was a large circular room and in its center were several hanging crow's cages. Two of those cages held Dwarf prisoners. More prison cells encircled these cages. From the two prisoners' tattered clothing and their thin, emaciated faces, they seemed to have been there for quite some time. "We shouldn't be here too long."

"Why do you say dat?"

"Cause we seem to have better boarding than others."

"Ah, ya mean the cages outside?"

"Aye."

"I suppose so," Forboud said. "They've said nothing and haven't as much as rattled their cages. I'd say they've been there for quite some time."

"I agree, brother."

"Can ya ever forgive my transgressions?" Forboud asked.

"In time, I hope to be able to do so."

"I'll do all I can to prove myself to you."

As much as Boldair wanted to believe his brother enough to forgive him, Boldair knew doing so this early was premature. Before their father lost the throne, Boldair never viewed Forboud in a negative fashion at all. They were, at least to his knowledge, close. But now? The divide was vast and nowhere near capable of being joined. The fondest memories between them were tarnished and the luster might never gleam brightly again. To Boldair, that loss was worse than Telsia finding and stealing his treasure. One could always find new treasure, but one could never replace the loss of a sibling. And worse, it seemed, was an estranged sibling.

Footsteps echoed from the stairwell beyond the cages. The determined thudding steadily descended. He hoped it was Drucis or Dwiskter and that they could somehow aid his release. Try as he did, he still had no knowledge of what actions he was guilty of that led to his arrest. The footsteps stopped outside his cell door.

"Morning," Yotram said from the other side of the barred cell door.

He yawned and pulled a ring of keys from his belt. "Have you calmed down enough for us to release you?"

Boldair stood. "Calmed down? I've no idea what I've done to be locked away."

Yotram smiled curiously. "Not at all?"

Boldair shook his head. "No. My memories of what transpired escape me. *Why* was I arrested?"

"Please don't think this as an arrest. No charges lie against you."

"Then why?"

Yotram unlocked the door and swung it outward. He motioned Boldair to step out. "More for your safety than anything else."

"My safety? From whom?"

"Aye, dat last story ya told angered quite a few of the tavern patrons. Several guards wanted your head for your insulting comments."

Boldair frowned with confusion. "For what? What did I say dat was so offensive?"

"You belched a long tirade over Frosthammer's dragon ornaments and our armor," Brandrum said from the outer prison hall. He laughed. "And you mentioned something about being friends with a trio of female dragons and how you'd have them set Frosthammer ablaze for our atrocities."

"Good job, brother," Forboud said, shaking his head.

Boldair ignore his brother and frowned. "I said all dat?"

Yotram and Brandrum nodded.

Yotram shut the prison door and smiled at Boldair. "I 'ave to say dat was quite a story you told. We tried to convince the other guards dat you had drunk too much strong stout. It took me buying them several rounds to calm them down. We took you here to stay the night to ensure your safety. Since you and your party are leaving today, we'll escort you through the gates before the other guards 'ave slept it off."

Boldair leaned his back against the wall and shook his head. "I never meant to offend the other guards. You know me. I'd never do something like dat."

"We know," Brandrum said. "Again, you did drink a *lot* last night."

In thought, Boldair frowned with confusion. "I did, but no more than I normally do. So tell me, what did I drink dat would make me totally forget what happened after my telling stories? The event of the tavern crowd becoming offended escapes me. My being dragged to the prison cell … I have no recollection of dat, either. So which drink could've caused me to lose consciousness or for me to spout off offensive words to those not interested in my stories?"

Yotram thought for several long seconds and finally shook his head. "I don't know. I don't recall you drinking anything stronger than the rest of us. What do you think, Brandrum?"

Brandrum shrugged. "I agree. Nothing comes to mind for me, either."

Boldair rubbed his eyes. "The last story I remember telling was the one of the kobold trying to kill me in a mine. You say the guards became offended about my statements over their armor?"

"Aye," Yotram said.

"Hmm. I don't even recall mentioning dat. You know, when I first arrived yesterday and while I sat in the Dungeon of Dragons tavern, I noticed a lot of dragon parts were used for the sconces and the chandeliers. And all the guards' armor, of course. I never spoke a word about it though. Might I ask where you came upon so much dragon scales and claws?"

"Dat, my friend," Yotram said softly, "is something we've been sworn to secrecy by Royal Order of King Rigrim."

"I see. But the scales for your armor are from Frost Dragons, are they not?" Boldair asked.

"Aye," Yotram said with a nod. "More than dat, we cannot say."

"My apologies for my behavior last night," Boldair said, still baffled by his lack of memory. "I don't recall those outbursts."

"We've all had too much to drink at times," Yotram said.

"While I'd agree with your assessment, I assure you dat I've drunk far more without forgetting my actions."

Yotram nodded. "Perhaps, in time, all will become clearer."

"I hope so. I hate to feel like I've lost time."

Yotram turned toward Brandrum. "Shackle Boldair's brother securely and meet us at the stables."

Brandrum nodded.

"Boldair needs to find himself a new mount this morning," Yotram said. He turned to walk across the room with Boldair to get to the stairs. "Indeed, quite a story you shared last night. I wish the other guards hadn't so easily taken offense by it."

Boldair forced a smile, but inside, he knew that what he supposedly had said—though he didn't remember saying it—were words he would've freely spoken *without* drinks, as he took offense to any race using dragon claws and scales as ornaments.

Before meeting Taniesse, he'd have never given it a second thought. He wondered why the guards were sworn to secrecy over how they obtained such large quantities of dragon parts. He couldn't risk saying more without angering King Rigrim. Boldair wanted to be as far from Frosthammer as possible, and the sooner, the better. He certainly didn't want any animosity between himself and Rigrim. Nagdor had always sought peace, especially with other Dwarves. The longer he stayed in Frosthammer, the more likely he would do or say something that could cause worse damage than what happened the night before.

CHAPTER 38

Boldair met Burr, the stablemaster, at the stables. Unlike most Dwarves who took pride in their appearance with the proper grooming of their beards and long hair, Burr spent no time primping his. In many ways, his wildly frayed beard and hair reminded Boldair more of a beast than a Dwarf.

Burr ran a hand through his beard. His dark eyes were unlike the other Frosthammer Dwarves. Only a pinpointed speck of amber glowed at the center of their inky black. He studied Boldair with eagerness. "Welcome. Have you come to consider my offer?"

Boldair nodded. "I have. Might I see Ember beforehand though?"

"Sure," Burr said. "This way."

The stables were housed inside a long bored tunnel that went deep into the mountain wall. Overhead lanterns glowed brightly. At the corner of every stall were smaller lanterns.

The harsh smell was as unpleasant as any other stable he'd ever visited. Nothing dispelled the thick soured aroma of urine and fecal matter. Often the acrid stench hit one like a sledgehammer long before reaching the stalls and pens.

Not even magic could put a dent in dat, Boldair thought, snarling his nose in protest.

Several young Dwarves with short beards used rakes and shovels to clean the stalls. The smell didn't affect them, but Boldair guessed they'd worked in the stables long enough to ignore it.

Boldair passed several individual stalls where large mountain ram mounts chewed straw over their troughs. The rams gnawed with bothersome expressions because visitors entered the stable hall. They were annoyed.

"Your wolf mount's in the next stall," Burr said, pointing.

Before Boldair came into view, Ember caught Boldair's scent. The dire wolf snarled, curled its upper lip, and turned toward Boldair with an indignant growl. A patch covered Ember's left eye.

Burr shook his head. "I see he's not too fond of you."

"The feeling's mutual," Boldair replied, leveling a shrewd glare at Ember.

"You cannot place your trust in such a beast. A good mount's one that protects its rider, not turn on him." Burr climbed over the gate. For a moment, Boldair almost yanked Burr back, fearful that Ember would rip the stablemaster apart. Instead, the massive dire wolf wagged its tail and licked Burr's face and hand.

"Traitor," Boldair whispered.

Ember turned and growled fiercely at Boldair. The wolf stood between him and Burr, acting protective of the stablemaster he'd only met the night before. Boldair shook his head.

Burr rubbed between the wolf's ears, calming it. "I've never seen a mount act this way toward its rider."

"It's evident he doesn't view me as his rider," Boldair said, softly. "I doubt he ever will since my father and brother reared him."

"Aye," Burr said, nodding. He scratched the sides of Ember's head. The motion of his fingers brushing through the wolf's unique fur looked like a gentle breeze arousing the red fire in dying coals. "Those early years of rearing a mount are crucial, but even so, a mount should adapt quickly to accepting a new rider. Wolves are sociable, so if you treat them right, you'll gain their loyalty."

"No one's told 'em," Boldair said, pointing at Ember with his thumb. "I've never given him a reason to be hostile toward me."

Burr climbed back over the stable gate. Ember chuffed and wagged its tail. "Come, I'll show you some of our other wolf mounts. They're young, but they've been trained. Each wolf has multiple riding trainers so the wolves don't imprint to one rider. They're less temperamental, too."

Boldair laughed. "An immediate plus."

Burr joined in with an odd cackle. "Yes. I'm surprised Ember's allowed you around him for as long as he has."

"I agree."

Burr walked away and Boldair stepped closer to the stall. Ember bared his teeth.

In spite of Ember's attempt on Boldair's life, Boldair still viewed the great wolf with admiration. He hated exchanging the wolf because of its brilliant fur and magnificent stature. Ember was an incredible beast, but Boldair couldn't see a mutual understanding ever developing between he and the wolf, regardless of any satiating Boldair offered. The wolf was hostile toward Boldair and would always challenge Boldair's authority, never allowing Boldair to be his rider or master. The wolf was a true alpha with a mule's stubbornness.

Boldair whispered, "I truly wish you could've had a change of heart, Ember. I hate leaving you 'ere."

The wolf's growl ceased. It panted and sadness overwhelmed its facial features, as though it fully understood what Boldair said. It whined a long, sorrowful cry.

"Look, Ember," Boldair said, "sorry 'bout your eye. Viorka was only defending herself. You should've never attacked her. You could sense dat she was a part of our group."

Ember chuffed softly and then licked his chops.

"When I return to Frosthammer, perhaps you'll hold a different attitude toward me, eh? I might even trade for ya back."

Boldair stared into Ember's eye for several long moments. The wolf cocked its head to the side and then lowered its nose in submission, something Boldair had never seen Ember do before. For a moment, he considered rubbing behind the wolf's ears like Burr had, but then he thought better against it. As surely as he placed his hand through the gate, the wolf would probably try to rip his arm off.

"I'm on to ya ploy," Boldair said with a crude grin. He laughed. "You *almost* had me convinced."

"Ya coming?" Burr asked from several yards away.

"Aye," Boldair said.

"Ah, good. For a second, I thought perhaps ye had changed your mind."

"No. Trust doesn't exist between Ember and myself, at the moment. I'm finding myself in dat situation more and more lately."

"I understand. Any relationship can become strained, whether it's blood ties or friends. Even riders and mounts won't necessarily form a strong necessary bond. When dat occurs, it's time to look elsewhere to find a new one."

Boldair nodded.

"Since wolves are pack animals, they have a tendency to include their riders into their family, which is why they're far more loyal than rams. Rams are great as long as their riders are on them. However, once the rider dismounts, rams obey their stomachs, often chewing through their ropes, and wandering off in search of food. I've known many Dwarves who've lost their mounts in the wild, due to this."

Boldair laughed. "The only other thing I dislike about a ram is the horrendous odor they 'ave."

Burr laughed and nodded. "There's dat, too. But like working in the stables, ya get used to it after awhile."

"Bah! I never could. I figure ya nose probably quits working so the smell can't affect you."

"Dat's probably true. I no longer enjoy food because nothing smells right anymore."

The stable hall took a sharp curve to the right and opened into a large room with several larger stalls. Inside these stalls female mounts nursed their pups.

Across the room in another wide stall were three large wolves. They were almost the same size as Ember, except thinner, which was the tendency with the younger dire mounts. The longer they carried a rider, the more muscle they gained, making their muscular girth wider and the wolves stronger. Those were necessities when traveling through the rugged, snowy mountains because riders had to carry extra packs for supplies to go longer distances.

One of the young mounts stood out from its two gray siblings. This wolf's fur was icy-blue, with darker blue streaks that ran along both sides of its back. Its eyes were white like fresh snow not yet been blemished. Its ears perked when it met Boldair's gaze. It wagged its tail vigorously and chuffed. Boldair felt an immediate attraction to this wolf.

"Dat one," Boldair said, pointing and trying not to allow his excitement to resonate in his voice.

"Ahh, yes," Burr said. "Dat's the finest one in its litter. He seems to 'ave taken a liking to you right away. Dat be a good thing."

Burr snapped his fingers, catching the attention of a young Dwarf near the stall. He instructed the lad to bring the wolf for Boldair to inspect.

"What's his name?" Boldair asked.

"We leave dat to you," Burr replied.

"You've not named 'em?"

"Most of the time when we've named a mount before it's taken by a permanent rider, the new owner's displeased with the name we've given. So, with dat litter, we've not named them."

Boldair scratched at his bearded chin while studying the wolf. "Frost. Dat's the name he'll 'ave."

Burr smiled and a renewed wildness came to his eyes. "Dat be a good name."

"His fur reminds me of the frost dat appears on the surface of the snow after a morning fog disappears," Boldair replied.

"I'm confident the young dire mount will give you many years of devoted service, unlike Ember."

"Ember's certainly taken well with you," Boldair said.

"Aye," Burr said. "But the majority of animals tend to be drawn to me. They feel safe in my company. I'm not entirely certain why."

The young Dwarf brought Frost to Boldair. The young wolf leaned downward in a submissive stance, allowing Boldair to scratch behind Frost's ears.

"Do we 'ave a trade?" Burr asked.

Boldair nodded and laughed as Frost licked the side of his face. "Aye!"

"Get Boldair's saddle," Burr said to the lad. "And get Frost ready to ride." He glanced at Boldair. "You're leaving this morning, correct?"

"Aye," Boldair replied.

"In dat case, I'll 'ave someone ready your party's mounts," Burr said.

"Yotram's already doing dat," Boldair replied.

Burr offered his hand and Boldair shook it fiercely. "In a year or so, I invite you to return to see what Ember's offspring look like. I'm sure we'll have a few more litters by then."

"I look forward to dat," Boldair said. "But, if I might request, I'd like first choice in any of them dat favor Ember."

"And you shall 'ave it," Burr said.

oldair rode Frost to where Dwiskter and Drucis stood with their mounts. Forboud sat atop his ram with his wrists chained together. Forboud eyed Boldair and paled. He peered frantically behind Boldair.

"Where's Ember?" Forboud asked.

"I traded 'em for Frost 'ere," Boldair replied.

"Don't you think you should've consulted me first?" Forboud asked, angrily.

Boldair shook his head. "Why should I consult *you*? You didn't own Ember. I did."

"You didn't spend years rearing and training him like I did with father," Forboud said. "I'd 'ave bought the mount ye 'ave now and paid you twice Ember's worth, just to keep 'em."

"Ember has proven himself too dangerous to trust during our travels. He tried to kill Viorka and me, so we don't need dat while we ride."

"Boldair, please reconsider," Forboud said.

"Sorry, brother, but I cannot. Our trade has already exchanged." Boldair sighed. "I understand dat Ember meant a lot to ya—"

"King or not," Forboud said, "you had *no* right to trade 'em."

"I had *every* right," Boldair said with narrowed eyes. His hands tightened into fists. "One more outburst or calling my decisions into question will ensure dat you ride gagged for the duration of our journey. Is dat understood?"

Dwiskter and Drucis exchanged shocked expressions.

Boldair leaned in his saddle toward Forboud. "Is dat clear?"

Forboud's jaws tightened. Tears of heated anger burned at the edges of his eyes. His face reddened. His hands tightened, and it was obvious Forboud was flexing and straining against the metal cuffs. In spite of his fueled temper, he bit off a quick, "*Yes.*"

Hatred echoed in Forboud's voice. His eyes narrowed with unrelenting fury. Were Forboud not a prisoner, Boldair and the others knew Forboud would've dismounted and grabbed the nearest weapon to attack Boldair. Dwiskter and Drucis slid their axes partially from their sheaths.

Having noticed the extreme tension, Yotram walked to the side of Frost and gazed up at Boldair. "You can always leave your brother in our prison and return for him at a later date, if you please."

"No. I've not time," Boldair replied.

Wynneffin stood outside the main gate of the stables. Boldair caught her gaze, which was a bit frostier than when he'd seen her in the library. Whatever memories he held of her beauty withered, and it saddened him. He doubted he could ever revisit the fonder memories they once shared. She was different and he couldn't deny that he had changed, too.

Boldair said, "Thanks, Yotram, for your welcome and the drinks. Please extend my thanks to Brandrum and Kairun as well."

"Aye," Yotram said with a broad smile. "I look forward to your next visit."

"As do I," Boldair replied. "Remember my extended offer for you to venture to Nagdor. Now, if you'll excuse me, I think Wynneffin wishes to speak to me."

"Good luck with dat," Yotram whispered with a slight grin.

Two Dwarves opened the gate to allow Boldair and his party to leave the stables. Boldair rode Frost to where she stood.

"Wynnie?" he said with a slight nod and a partial smile. "I didn't expect you to see us off."

"I'm not here for dat purpose," she spat bitterly. "Father insisted I tell you what I saw in the Fae Stones."

"You found them?"

She nodded.

"Where?"

Wynneffin remained silent for several moments. He realized that she would not be there at all, except for Rigrim's orders. She glanced at a Frosthammer guard who stood nearby. His interest was on her and Boldair.

"Well?" Boldair asked.

"She covered the stones with a cloth and tried to hide them on a bookshelf."

"Ah, good, I suppose. She didn't keep them."

"Look," Wynneffin said, "I don't want to speak to you any longer than necessary, but being as father sent this guard to ensure I find and tell you, I've no choice in the matter. It's my hope dat after today, our paths never cross again."

Boldair stared stoically in an attempt to prevent her from seeing how her words affected him. They cut him to the core, but he didn't want it to show. He couldn't allow her to see his pain. Not as King. Inside, he was coiled bed of mixed emotions; partially angered, hurt, and ready to spout vehement words at her for betraying his trust. Instead, he held himself in check. "What did you see?"

"Telsia has not yet left Frosthammer," she replied.

"Where is she?"

Wynneffin shrugged. "Somewhere dark, so possibly in the tunnels beneath Frosthammer or on the floor where the three forest Elves had taken Viorka."

"Thanks," Boldair said. He nudged Frost's flank gently and the wolf turned away from her.

"So dat's it?" she said.

"It's as you asked," Boldair replied. "Or at least how you implied, is it not? You don't want to talk to me longer than necessary, or did I mishear dat?"

She huffed and nodded. "Those were my words, yes."

Boldair regarded her for a few moments. "Okay, then."

"You can turn off your feelings, just like dat?"

"Seems you already did dat well before me," Boldair said. "Ya can't 'ave it both ways. Now, if you'll excuse me, we must get on with our journey. Although seeing you again wasn't as I hoped, I wish you … a happy life."

Wynneffin fumed and walked in front of Frost, grabbed the wolf's bridle, and clung tightly. In a low voice, she said, "One should never leave their differences unresolved. As a new King, you've much to learn."

"You've taught me lessons dat will last a lifetime, but those also prevent me from repeating *mistakes* I don't need to fret over."

Her eyes narrowed. "You leave without resolve, and I assure you, you'll be back in Frosthammer quicker than ye imagined. I'll see to dat."

Boldair sighed and shook his head. "Wynnie, I don't want any hard feelings between us. We could talk for days 'bout the situation, but it'd do no good. It won't change how our relationship was severed. You desire to craft magic. Dat's fine, but don't abuse your powers and turn them against me. We simply should say our goodbyes and when I leave today, know dat I won't be back. Dat's the finality you didn't get when I left the first time, but it's not the same outcome this time around."

"Then *leave*," she said harshly. "But, you'll come back. I assure you."

Wynneffin released Frost's bridle and stormed away. A cold breeze funneled through the stables and gusted around him. An impressive exit but Boldair found himself wondering if the breeze was merely a coincidence or was it a product of her magical abilities?

After she left the stables, Yotram opened the large steel gates that allowed riders to exit Frosthammer. Although Frosthammer was frigid for a city, nothing prepared Boldair for the biting cold winds that swept through those gates. He'd forgotten how severe the outside temperatures were, and in retrospect, he was thankful they had not left during the middle of the night. The night beasts would've been the least of their concerns.

Boldair wrapped his bear hide around him, offered his thanks to Yotram once more, and led his party through the gates.

CHAPTER 40

oldair and his party rode in silence for the better part of an
hour. The whipping cold winds lashed while whistling
banshee shrieks of coming doom. On occasion, some of the long bluish-
white icicles broke free of the jagged, icy cliffside and shattered on the
rocky bottom like glass. At other times, snowy rocks cracked and
popped, causing Boldair to suspiciously watch the ledges because he
was certain they were being watched or perhaps followed.

He pulled the bearskin tighter around himself to block the harsh
wind. Tiny icicles coated his beard around his nose and mouth. The rest
of his beard was white from captured snow.

In spite of the cold, Boldair felt a rush of heat from the hot angered
stare of his brother riding behind him. Even without looking, Boldair
could picture Forboud's indignant glare, which made him uneasy. The
wedge between them cut deep with no amicable feelings left.

In ways, he didn't blame Forboud for his anger. He understood the
reasons, but after what Ember had done to Viorka, Boldair simply could
never allow the wolf to travel in their company. Besides, he still wasn't
certain what Boldair's fate should be for his disrespect and disobedi-
ence. But it was a decision Boldair needed to make *before* they reached
Nagdor.

With Ulthor's fate still in the hands of Queen Taube, sentencing Forboud to death for his underhanded traitorous behavior was not in Boldair's best interest. Boldair couldn't imagine handing down such a verdict anyway. Doing so made Forboud a martyr for those still loyal to King Ulthor. After all, Forboud was his brother, and even if Boldair chose to imprison him, Forboud's imprisonment would have to be in another city. Otherwise, Nagdor would be in constant unrest. Regardless of what actions Boldair decided, or if he chose to pardon his brother altogether, he didn't see any chance the two could fully trust one another again.

Boldair sighed. He had yet to have his coronation and already enemies were surrounding him. Estranged family and friends were enemies he never expected. He wasn't certain if King Rigrim was an ally or not, based on their short meeting. Rigrim seemed more displeased with Wynneffin's actions and scolded her outright for her behavior in front of Boldair.

In turn, Wynneffin focused her anger and resentment on Boldair, perhaps merely magnifying her feelings from her earlier frustrations, but he couldn't help but view her last words as a direct threat. How she actually *planned* to deliver that threat remained unclear. Boldair hoped that by putting distance between him and her, her festered anger might eventually diminish and she'd forget about him.

He doubted things between them could end so easily or in a peaceful resolve, because she'd never forgiven him for his departure the first time. His apology about his behavior was sincere and heartfelt, but she remained unconvinced. What he said to her was correct. Regardless of how much more time he spent in Frosthammer trying to mend their differences, nothing fruitful could ever be gained. Her biases, as well as his own, were set. The undertones of bitterness and their lack of trust prevented them from moving forward. The best thing was to separate and move on with their lives. But her threat ... she wasn't finished and she seemed to be scheming a plot. Perhaps revenge?

Boldair sighed and adjusted in the saddle. Viorka, who was curled under the bearskin behind him and asleep, straightened into a seated position.

She peered through a slit in the bearskin. A yawn escaped her mouth. "We're still in the snowy mountains?"

"Aye," he whispered. "Go back to sleep."

"It's too cold to do anything else," she replied. "I certainly have no wish to *walk* in this snow and ice."

"Is all okay?" Dwiskter asked. "You've been quiet since we left Frosthammer."

Boldair shrugged.

Drucis rode up beside Boldair. "It'll get better once we're out of this cold."

"I'm glad you can be so optimistic," Boldair said.

"Looking around us," Drucis said, "I can't see anything getting much worse."

Dwiskter shook his head. "Don't jinx us."

"Jinx us?" Drucis said. "Merely words of observation, friend. Fate deals whatever it wishes regardless of my words. I'm no sorcerer or wizard or witch."

"Thank the gods for dat," Dwiskter said dryly. "The white skies indicate more snow and our path is becoming increasingly more narrow. Doesn't seem many travelers ever come this direction. Is this the route you took before, Boldair?"

Boldair studied his surroundings for a few moments. He nodded. "Aye. The path will serpentine downward and after that, a short line of trees. The cold will lessen, as will the snow. We're on our way out of the Frosted Peaks."

"Sorry things didn't work out between you and Wynneffin," Dwiskter said. "What did she tell you before we left?"

"Dat Telsia was still in Frosthammer."

"How's she know dat?"

"The Fae Stones."

"She can use them?" Drucis' brows rose.

Boldair nodded.

"When did you learn of her ability to consult them?" Drucis asked.

"Last night when I spoke with her father in his private library."

Drucis frowned. "Something's amiss."

"How so?" Boldair asked.

"It's not normal for any Dwarf to read Fae Stones," he replied. "It's *not* possible. I say dat because we Dwarves are no kin to the Fae or the Elves. Nowhere near one another at all. Regardless of how one learns magic or draws upon it, a Dwarf should 'ave no access to the magic of the Fae."

"Aye, I agree," Boldair said. "But Telsia held the same abilities."

"I know Wynneffin swore dat Telsia had the ability, but I've thought long and hard over this," Drucis said, shaking his head. "It's still not possible nor does it bear any logic. We Dwarves craft and consult runes to protect us against magic. But wielding it? Few ever 'ave. And certainly not *Fae* magic. Our bloodlines have never crossed with Fae or Elves. Besides, even if any Dwarf wished to marry an Elf—"

Dwiskter spat on the ground.

Drucis nodded. He pointed a stern finger. "Rightly so! No offspring could ever be birthed between the two. Our bloodline can never be tarnished by the Elves or vice versa. Humans and Elves, now dat be a different matter altogether. We encounter half-elves all the time, as humans 'ave no problem tarnishing other races with their substandard blood. But half human and half Dwarf? 'ave ya ever seen one?"

Boldair shook his head, as did Dwiskter.

"I'm not certain I'd *want* to see one," Dwiskter said. "A combination of our traits into one being? Talk 'bout deformities."

"Aye. There's a reason for dat," Drucis said. "We're a proud race, but our creation apparently was far different than either of theirs. We cannot blend our bloods to form a half with the others. Not to say I've not ever been attracted to a female human or Elf, because I 'ave. Some of their beauty is far greater than anything I've ever beheld, but more than admiration, I don't possess the desire."

"So you don't believe it possible dat a Dwarf could effectively use the Fae Stones to view the future or to search for lost loved ones?"

"I don't see how," Drucis replied. "I know you've been fretting over a lot since we left Frosthammer, but 'ave you ever considered dat Wynneffin lied to you about *seeing* anything?"

"It has crossed my mind."

"Understand, Boldair, dat Frosthammer's an unusual city and not even commonly known to the rest of Aetheaon. For a place with a river of molten steel, it's colder than a tomb. Dat river should billow heat throughout the entire city and yet, it doesn't lessen the frigid air at all. The surrounding mountain should be like a volcano without a flake of snow gracing its peak. It's contrary to what it should be."

"Aye," Boldair said. "King Rigrim also has tapped into magic, too."

"How do ya know?" Dwiskter said.

"He admitted such. The frost warhammer he wields is how the city obtained its name, and it seems to be the very heart of the city. The entire time I sat in the library, the weapon constantly released a stream of cold frost dat seeped down through the floor. Everything in the city looks like it's been bitten by frost. Every Frosthammer Dwarf's hair and beards all are tinted blue."

Drucis nodded. "I noticed dat as well. I hope you've no intention of ever returning."

"No immediate plans," Boldair replied.

"Good. Too many things don't settle well, but I can't quite place a finger on what exactly troubles me the most," Drucis said. "How comfortable do you feel about Yotram and Brandrum?"

"I consider them friends, but not anywhere as strongly as I do about you and Dwiskter. Why?" Boldair asked.

"When you were arrested—" Drucis said softly.

"Yes! Please, tell me what happened?" Boldair asked. His eyes widened from his curiosity. "I've no recollection of my outbursts dat they insist I did."

"Dat was no exaggeration," Dwiskter said. "You did."

"For what reason?"

"Yotram said something about taking you on a dragon hunt," Drucis said, "and to be honest, from his tone of voice and sly grin, it was all in jest. But something about it set you off. Yotram insisted it was one of the drinks you had while seated at the table. But, Dwiskter and I drank the same drinks. Nothing altered our states of mind."

"A dragon hunt?" Boldair asked.

Drucis nodded. "Yes, but he wasn't being serious."

"Ya see, though, I don't recall dat," Boldair said. "And you drank everything I did?"

"Aye," Dwiskter said.

Boldair frowned for several moments before suddenly realizing something he'd forgotten. "Bloody Hells!"

"What is it?" Drucis asked.

"When I was in the library with King Rigrim, one of his servants *brought* me a drink."

"You think it was spiked with something?" Dwiskter asked.

"Quite possibly," Boldair said, nodding. "Wynneffin was hiding in the shadows, listening to my conversation with her father. She had every opportunity to do so."

"Would she actually do that?" Viorka asked from under the bearskin.

"She's quite bitter and angry at me," Boldair said. "She's set on revenge."

"Then most likely, dat's what happened," Drucis said. "But *why* would she do dat?"

"The last words she spoke were more a threat than anything," Boldair said.

"And *I'm* the one shackled?" Forboud said.

"For entirely different reasons," Dwiskter said, turning in his saddle and frowning.

"I've done nothing wrong," Forboud said.

"You've done plenty," Drucis said. "Undermining a King is a capital offense, worthy of death."

"He's not *my* King."

"Ah, he's the King, whether you admit it or not, dat doesn't change anything," Dwiskter said. "Treason is a quick death in most cities."

"Ignore Forboud," Boldair said. "Can we get back to discussing what happened in the tavern?"

Drucis nodded. "Not much more to tell. Your outrage sparked the surrounding guards into a rage dat made them draw their weapons. Yotram, Brandrum, and Kairun are the only reason you weren't attacked and possibly killed."

"For several moments, though, it didn't appear they were in any mood to protect you," Dwiskter said.

"Really?"

Dwiskter and Drucis nodded.

"I wonder why?" Boldair said.

"I can think of several reasons," Forboud said under his breath.

"It appeared as though they no longer recognized you," Drucis said. "Perhaps the spiked drink was also bewitched with a spell? Something dat altered your outward appearance?"

Boldair frowned. "Dat's possible, I suppose."

"Yotram must 'ave some persuasion with the other guards or maybe he has greater authority, as he was able to talk them down."

"But did I lose consciousness?" Boldair asked.

"No, never," Dwiskter replied.

"I told you dat you were flaring mad when they dragged you into your cell," Forboud said.

"You did," Boldair said, nodding. "I just wish I remembered what happened."

"Shh!" Dwiskter said, rising in his saddle.

"What is it?" Boldair said.

"Ya smell dat?" he asked, scrunching his nose. "Smoke."

"Now dat you mention it, yes," Boldair said.

Drucis nodded and then pointed. "There's a stream of smoke drifting through those evergreens."

"Approach with caution," Boldair said.

"Perhaps you could remove my restraints?" Forboud asked. "In case we are forced to fight?"

"I don't think any of us trust handing ya a weapon at the moment," Drucis said.

Boldair glared and placed his forefinger to his lips. Then he pointed forward.

CHAPTER 41

Dead, now frozen, goblins were sprawled around the smoldering, charred sections of the firs. Seeing the carnage, Boldair hesitated any further approach. He scanned the area for what might've recently killed these goblins. The fire wasn't produced by natural means. The scorched goblin flesh resembled the results of a wizard's magical flames, as though their bodies had been engulfed in sudden balls of flame.

The goblins appeared to have been taken by surprise. Their wide eyes, frozen by death and the cold, revealed as much. Their fallen bodies lie as though they had turned to run. with their heads turned, looking over their shoulders at what was hurling fire at them. They weren't grouped in an attacking formation. They had been trying to flee.

From whom or what?

None survived the fire. If any survived their burns, they'd have died from the elements in a matter of minutes.

Due to the extreme cold of the Frosted Peaks, a live thin-clothed body could freeze in a short amount of time, but a dead body ... the frigid winds turned the flesh into a block of ice in a matter of minutes. Since the trees still smoldered, the fiery attack had occurred within the past hour.

In a grim, soured tone, Forboud said, "So much for the goblins being driven out of Aetheaon."

"Aye." Boldair nodded and glanced at Drucis and Dwiskter. "Worse. The goblins 'ave come to the surface. We're in graver danger than I imagined."

Dwiskter nodded. "The good thing is dat they're all dead. The bigger problem is dat we don't know what killed 'em."

"I was thinking the same thing," Boldair replied, sliding off his mount.

Drucis and Dwiskter dismounted as well.

They stood a good thirty yards from the melted snowy path that had refrozen into a vast circle of intense heat. Boldair took a step forward. The ice beneath his boot crunched like a dried brittle leaf. Its echo amplified between the two high mountain ridges. He paused before taking another step. They needed to approach the goblin corpses without being seen or heard, but the ice-crusted snow made that impossible. The slightest movement caused the ice to protest.

Boldair slid one of his axes from its sheath.

"Ya see something?" Drucis asked.

"Only the dead," Boldair replied.

"Maybe we should mount up and ride on?" Dwiskter said.

"Either way," Boldair said, "we still 'ave to pass through these dead goblins."

"True, but my mount is far faster than my legs can run," Drucis said.

Frost tilted his massive head upward and howled, sending a colder chill down Boldair's spine.

Boldair turned his head, keeping his feet still, hoping to understand the reason for wolf's howl. Almost invisible in the white cloudy sky was a massive dragon in flight. Its wings straightened and it glided over the mountainside outside of view. The magnificent giant beast made no sound and was mesmerizing to behold.

"Dragon," Boldair whispered and pointed. "A *snow* dragon."

"Where?" Dwiskter asked.

"It flew over the ridge and out of sight. Mount up," he replied. "We need to scurry, in case it returns."

They hurried to their mounts and saddled up.

"How many goblins?" Viorka asked.

"I counted thirty-five," Dwiskter said. "Not a massive amount, but enough to inflict a lot of misery and damage on a small village."

"More than we'd want to fight right now," Forboud said.

"Ah, dat's what *you* think," Dwiskter said. "Me ax could take out a dozen in a few minutes."

Drucis reared back his head with a hearty laugh. "It'd be a worthy challenge."

Forboud sighed, looking down. "What has brought them back?"

Boldair tapped Frost's flank gently. "Perhaps they never left. The Dwarven Alliance slaughtered thousands of them and the survivors retreated into the mountain caverns. After dat? Who knows? No stories 'ave been told of our generals sending in troops after them."

"Legends are often exaggerated," Forboud said. "Especially after Dwarven stout."

Boldair nodded his agreement.

"There must be a reason they've returned to the surface," Drucis said. "Something's obviously disturbed them."

"Aye," Boldair said, nodding. They rode past the charred trees and dead goblins. His mind returned to when he had led the troops with Taniesse along the Fae Barrier Pass between the Black Chasm and the Woodnog Forests. The Pass was a neutral zone between the opposing magical forces. However, whatever creatures were hidden within the darkness of the chasm constantly tried to break through the Fae magical barrier. Some had grabbed some of his troops and pulled them into the chasm, eviscerating them. If ever the Fae magic that protected the Pass lessened or failed, he feared what dark forces inside the chasm would be unleashed. The dam of magic was the only reason the Black Chasm had not spread closer to the mystical forests of Woodnog. Boldair suddenly wondered if Tyrann might be responsible for the goblins' return to the surface.

"Keep alert," Boldair said, softly. "The dragon must have killed the goblin forces in one engulfing ball of flame. As white as dat dragon is, it could easily blend into the ice and snow along the peaks. It took them by surprise."

Dwiskter nodded. "I noticed dat, too."

"Aye, whatever killed those goblins saw them before they saw it," Drucis said. "There might be more than one dragon lying in wait."

A loud fierce roar pierced the air, originating from the peak where Boldair watched the dragon descend. Although he was friends with Taniesse and had witnessed her transformation into her dragon form, he mainly interacted with her human form, so he wasn't certain if the roar was a forewarning of its coming attack, or a rally cry to gather other dragons together.

According to Taniesse, other dragons still existed. They were hidden from the general population. He assumed she had meant the other dragons were magically transformed to look human in order to pass through cities undetected.

"Ya heard dat, too?" Dwiskter asked.

"Aye. Let's pick up the pace," Boldair said.

"I'm with ya on dat," Drucis said. "A few dozen goblins we could handle, but I'm afraid on our best day, we're no match for an angry dragon."

They rode down the winding mountain trail. The ice and snow lessened. More trees lined the edges of the slope and the road. Boldair wondered if the snow dragons were the dragons that Yotram had invited Boldair to hunt. But the scales of the Frosthammer Dwarves weren't from snow dragons. The scales were blue and from frost dragons. They were two different species altogether, but no travelers had mentioned seeing frost dragons for nearly a century.

Of course, few *survived* their encounters with snow dragons and lived to tell the tale. Could the two types of dragons even coexist peacefully?

They rode hard until they left the permafrost level and the terrain was greener.

"Do snow dragons spew fire?" Dwiskter asked, breaking the silence. "I mean, frost dragons don't. They spew icy breath, freezing their victims. Their name comes from dat more than from the color of their scales."

Boldair straightened in his saddle. "I don't rightly know."

"Cause if they don't," Dwiskter said, "dat dragon didn't kill those goblins."

Drucis' eyes widened. "Never thought of dat. Dat's worrisome. Could be a sorcerer or wizard."

"Aye," Boldair said, scratching his beard. "Once I find Taniesse, I'll ask her."

"We might be dead before we ever see her," Forboud said.

Drucis cocked a brow, gazing at Forboud. "*One* of us might."

Forboud frowned. "Look, if ye want me dead, as seems to be the hopeful verdict each of you deem for me, end me life 'ere and now! Do it! I'm fine with it. It beats being dragged through frozen mountains, dragons and wizards, and being shackled while you torment me with degrading words."

"Bah!" Drucis said. "Don't tempt me."

"No hold yourself back," Forboud said. "I know ya want to use dat ax. It's itching at ye. Your need to shed blood."

Drucis frowned. "Nice try, but the greatest punishment is keeping your alive. Dat's why you're needling me to end your life. But, keep talking and I'll find something to stuff in your mouth, like bitter moss. Hard to speak when your mouth is shriveled like a prune."

"Brother," Forboud said, with a tired sigh. "Please, simply end all this? You'll never trust me enough to allow me freedom, so execute me. I'm no use to you or Nagdor. Regardless of any actions on my part to better our relationship, nothing will rectify the chasm I've created between us. I'd rather die than—"

Boldair turned at Forboud's sudden silence.

"There!" Viorka said, jumping off Forboud's ram mount.

Forboud's eyes widened and his face scrunched. Sticking out of his mouth was a large wad of yellowish-green moss she had shoved into his mouth.

"Long overdue!" Drucis said.

Boldair tried to hide his smile but couldn't. "Sorry, brother, but my ax could never take your life. I'll not 'ave your death on me conscious. But your fate is something I'm still unsure of. Perhaps, in time, I can better understand what needs to be done. We're less than a day from Meadwyrm Pass, and a few more days from reaching Nagdor. I will 'ave made me decision by then."

CHAPTER 42

Their good fortune was that the snow dragon never pursued them. A day later, and without incident, Boldair stood at a vendor table in Meadwyrm Pass in the forest to the northeast of Bridgebarrow. He watched with anticipated amusement as Drucis and Dwiskter stared at their drinks. While they'd never admit their uneasiness at drinking the brew with the potency Boldair endorsed the drink for possessing, their eyes indicated their slight nervousness.

Drucis' hesitation didn't last long. He made quick glances to each of the Dwarves, took a deep breath, and smiled. He grabbed the tankard, turned it up, and downed the contents.

"Blasted!" Drucis shouted, slamming his tankard on the table beside his steel helm. He wiped froth from his beard with the back of his gloved hand. His eyes widened. "That, me friends, be a mighty potent liquid!"

"Aye," Boldair replied with a hearty laugh. He clapped his hand against Drucis' back a couple of times. "I told ya. You'll never guess what the secret ingredient is."

Drucis coughed with tears blurring his vision. He beat his chest with his fist. Sweat cropped his brow. His voice rasped. "Gah! The heat's getting worse. Not sure I *want* to know. Molten steel?"

"Bah-ha!" Boldair exclaimed a moment before turning up his drink. He held his breath for a moment, bracing himself. Tears formed in his eyes. He beat a hearty fist against his chest-plate. He hiccuped and belched.

"Whew! You might 'ave wilted a few plants with dat one," Drucis said, pinching his nose and coughing. He rubbed his throat and flicked a hardened gaze at the barkeep. "What *is* this?"

The barkeep smiled. "Briarthorn Firespit."

Boldair winced and patted his chest. "Made from the poisonous barbed vines in the forests. The ones I told you had nearly killed me."

Drucis' eyes watered. He nodded at Boldair and cleared his throat. "Aye, ya did. So what now? We've all been poisoned? That's what this little side trip be all about. Ahh, just what we need. A drink to end all sorrows."

Boldair shook his head and wiped away a tear. He and Drucis watched Dwiskter grab the handle of his tankard.

Dwiskter eyed his drink, frowned momentarily before closing his eyes, and then he gulped down the liquid. He slammed down the tankard, almost gagging, but he forced the harsh bitter drink down against his throat's obvious protest. He expelled heated breath and shook his head. He steadied himself against the table. "Whew! Damn!"

Boldair and Drucis offered raspy howls of laughter.

The barkeep grinned. "And … what of your unbearded companion? Shall I pour him one as well?"

Boldair glanced at Forboud. Forboud shook his head. "He indicates, 'no.'"

The barkeep stared at Forboud for several quiet moments. "What crime has this Dwarf committed? Isn't that the reason a Dwarf has his beard removed?"

"Most of the time," Boldair said.

"And his fate?"

"Not known at this time," Boldair replied.

Dwiskter rubbed his throat. "This is made from a poisonous plant?"

The barkeep nodded.

"We've been poisoned?" Drucis asked, rubbing his stomach. "Is there an antidote? Feels like the flames of Hell are burning from my stomach into my throat."

"We distill out the poison," the barkeep said with a sly smile. "The heat, however, is something that settles in its own time. It's that fiery kick Dwarves crave the most."

"Aye," Boldair said with a shrewd smile. "No lie there. I've found myself wanting another tankard for some time."

The barkeep nodded. "Tis true with a lot of travelers. Once they've gotten a taste of this, they eventually come back for more. Of course, they tend to forget how painfully harsh it is until after they drink it again."

"Aye," Boldair said, nodding. "Still stings and burns as badly as my first consumption."

"I imagine," Drucis said, squinting. "Tomorrow I'll need to take a dump in a creek to prevent setting the forests on fire. Might need the cold water to relieve my arse, too."

The barkeep laughed.

Dwiskter plopped a gold coin onto the crude booth table before the strange barkeep. "Aye, give me a second."

A devious grin spread across the old man's face. "You sure, Dwarf? Few can handle more than one."

"Dwarves can drink any human or Elf under da table," Drucis said, shaking a firm fist.

"Ah, but surely nothing as potent as *this*," the barkeep replied. "No human has ever drank a second, and those Dwarves who've drank two never asked for a third."

Dwiskter frowned, placing his hand atop the gold coin. "Then why give away the first for free?"

"Tis charity to weary travelers," the man replied.

"Ah, now, *is* it?" Dwiskter asked. "I be thinking it more an opportunity for you and your surrounding vendors in this little forest to take advantage of inebriated customers. A new type of highwayman. Get passersby drunk and then rob 'em."

Viorka stood behind Boldair with a large hunk of boar meat she had gotten from a neighboring vendor. She chewed while she watched the

Dwarves drink. Her interest seemed intent on the barkeep, and Boldair assumed she did so because of how their last meeting had gone. Either the barkeep hadn't noticed her, or he simply had forgotten about her stealing the orb from Sissrow when they visited Meadwyrm Pass before.

The old man's eyes narrowed. "Dare you make such an accusation against me, *your host*, in this secluded, off the beaten path, tavern?"

Drucis howled with laughter. "Tavern? *This?*"

"The whole lot of you Dwarves dare to offend me? *Us?*" the old man said, waving his hand toward the other covered vendor tables. "Your insults are the reasons why folks like us isolate ourselves so far from any civilization. We seldom make a profit, *scrounge* to survive with barely a roof over our heads. What crime have we done, other than freely offer a rare drink no other tavern in Aetheaon is capable of making? Nothing else compares to it! You're nothing more than wretched Dwarves who spit in our faces!"

Dwiskter placed his hand on the handle of his ax. His face hardened and he held the gold coin between his thumb and forefinger. "I offered you gold for me second round."

"Moments before outright accusing us of thievery," the barkeep replied. "When your first drink was free."

"Aye," Dwiskter said with a firm nod. "But even a Dwarf understands nothing comes for free. Everything has a price, no matter how small." He glanced at Drucis. "No pun intended."

Drucis chuckled.

The barkeep's eyes darkened. "So if you drank one and kept traveling on down the forest path, what price is required of thee?"

"A sword in me back to rob me of me gold?" Dwiskter said.

The old man's jaw tightened. Fury set in his dark eyes. It was almost like staring into the eyes of a venomous serpent moments before it struck.

Boldair placed his thick hand on Dwiskter's shoulder. "Easy. He never showed any ill will when I was here before."

The barkeep flicked his gaze from Dwiskter, and he eyed Boldair curiously.

"You were not King when you passed by before, either," Drucis said softly to Boldair.

"King?" The old man gasped. He gave Boldair a shrewd stare. "I see no crown."

"The coronation has yet to occur," Forboud said.

"Of what city?"

"Nagdor," Boldair replied.

The barkeep shook his head. "Ulthor is their King."

"Not … anymore," Boldair replied.

"So the King has fallen?"

"In ways unexpected."

"Pray tell, how?"

Boldair's face tightened. "I'll not be discussing the affairs of my kingdom with outsiders, especially *human* ones."

"I remember you now," the barkeep said. His eyes widened with recognition and he pointed a crooked finger. Beads of sweat glistened on his bald head. "Not too long ago, you traveled to my booth, had one of these drinks while *your* Fynx companion robbed one of my patrons. Ridiculous, your companions this eve accuse *me* of being a thief and trample my hospitality. As I recall, Sissrow was nearly killed in the forest after he tried to get back the orb your Fynx friend had stolen. We offered our aid, but he denied us and he pursued the two of you on his own. I have to assume that you later murdered him, as he's never returned. He was a devoted customer, a true friend, and his absence remains a mystery. Nagdor is doomed to disarray if their new king is a murderous thief!"

"What be your name, barkeep?" Drucis asked. His bushy eyebrows rose. His black eyes shimmered.

"Cadell Prowell. Why?"

"You make treasonous remarks about our King, which is worthy of immediate death," Drucis replied in an angered whisper.

"He's *not* my King. But what I speak is the truth. Ask the other vendors in our pass. We're all witnesses of what transpired that night. None of us drink in the presence of patrons, but *your King* drank at least two. Perhaps he doesn't remember?" He turned his glance to Boldair. "Do you deny killing Sissrow?"

Boldair's jaw tightened but he held his gaze. His voice was gruff. "I didn't kill him."

"Is he dead?" Cadell asked.

"Aye. He is."

"How?"

"The Fynx killed him."

Cadell cocked his head to the side with a mocking sneer. "See? *You*, a *King*, robbed the man and then killed him. Who are the real highwaymen?"

Boldair formed fists and shook his head. "No. His death and the situation are not so easily explained."

"And how's that?"

"For one, the orb we took from Sissrow was one *he* had stolen first. He was the farthest from being noble than an imprisoned assassin thief. We took the orb because of the danger it posed, not for Damdur or Icevale or Nagdor but for all Aetheaon."

"What threat did that orb impose?" Cadell asked.

"Sissrow possessed the Dark Orb of Misthalls," Boldair replied.

Cadell's eyes widened. He salivated and swallowed hard. His voice lowered to a whisper. "The Dragon Conjuring Stone?"

"Aye, the same."

"But we've no dragons in Aetheaon."

Drucis laughed. "You've been hidden in this forest far too long."

Cadell cocked a brow while studying each Dwarf's stern face. "Wait. The dragons are *not* dead?"

"They live and reign in the skies once more," Boldair replied. "The Fynx and I worked with the great dragon, Taniesse. She sent us to retrieve the orb."

"You're fr-friends with a dragon?" Cadell wiped sweat from his brow.

"Aye," Boldair replied. "And we're closely aligned with Hoffnung."

"I see. And the orb? What of it?" the barkeep asked.

"Destroyed. Smashed to a thousand bits."

Regret claimed Cadell's face.

Boldair stared at him harshly. "You seem disappointed dat the orb was destroyed."

Cadell flinched slightly and his eyes narrowed. "No. Not at all. Just taken back, tis all."

"About the stone or the dragon?" Drucis asked.

"Both."

"It's our duty to protect Hoffnung and the great dragons," Boldair said. He pointed to the silver pendant riveted to his chestplate. "Not only am I King of Nagdor, but Drucis, Dwiskter, and myself are all Dragon Skull Knights."

"How does a Dwarf get ... such an honor?" Cadell asked.

"We were the driving force that aided Lady Dawn in reclaiming her throne," Boldair replied.

"And this one?" Cadell asked, giving a nod toward Forboud.

Boldair shook his head. "Ah now, well, he wasn't in the battle."

"Is that the reason for his shorn beard? Was that his shame?"

"Again," Boldair said sternly. "Nothing dat concerns ye."

Cadell's eyes set on Forboud. "Perhaps you'd like to tell me of your dilemma?"

Drucis, Dwiskter, and Boldair looked at Forboud with their hands on the handles of their axes. Forboud took a sharp breath and swallowed hard.

"I serve my brother," Forboud said, "and support him as our new King. Our kingdom's affairs are none of yours."

Cadell's shrewd stare at Forboud mellowed at a moment's notice. The fear in Forboud's eyes was obvious. He faced Boldair and his eyes subtly glanced from each Dwarf's hold on their axes. Cadell bowed deeply at the waist toward Boldair, and greatly exaggerated lifting his left arm into the air behind his back, which looked more theatrical than sincere. "My apologies, dear King of Nagdor. I had no knowledge that you weren't a commoner Dwarf. Please forgive me."

"*None* of us are commoners," Drucis said with a fierce glare. "We be warriors through and through."

"Yes. Sorry." He waved his hands pleadingly. "Dragon Skull Knights.

Please, accept this gift as a token of my goodwill." He placed a large flask on the table.

Dwiskter frowned. "What's dat?"

"A flask of Briar-thorn Fire-spit. Anytime you or your party travel through our pass, all drinks are on the house."

"Acceptable terms, if you ask me," Drucis said, grabbing the flask with a broad smile.

Dwiskter placed his hand over Drucis' and then yanked the flask from Drucis' grasp. "The terms aren't yours to accept."

"Aye," Drucis replied, releasing the flask.

"Sire?" Cadell said.

Boldair eyed Cadell harsh and long until the barkeep broke their gaze and fidgeted uncomfortably with his wool tunic. "Tell me why you set your *tavern*, as you call *this*, on the forest pass and not in Bridgebarrow?"

"Bridgebarrow?" Cadell scoffed. "Surely you jest?"

"No," Boldair replied. "It's a reputable little village with an ample number of travelers passing through daily. You'd make, if you pardon the quip, a King's ransom of more gold than you do 'ere along the narrow wood pass."

A sly grin spread across the Cadell's face. His eyes narrowed, making it impossible to hide his greed. "King's ransom, you say?"

"Indeed," Boldair replied. "Perhaps even more."

"All the same," Cadell replied, "we prefer the tranquility of the forests and less with the bustle of traders, merchants, and competitive vendors."

"You 'ave no fear of highwaymen?" Drucis asked.

"No. Most are enticed by free drinks and move on. Not something one can do in Bridgebarrow. A free drink to a weary traveler is far different than offering a free drink in a tavern filled with greedy farmer peasants. I'd be outta business in hours."

"The more people learn of your powerful concoction, the more gold you'll make. You'd never 'ave to give them for free," Boldair said.

"You're probably right, King, but Bridgebarrow doesn't have the proper ingredients necessary to make our brew, and our ... distillery, it's impossible to uproot that. Besides, we have a limited clientele, barely able to keep the supply equal to the demand." He pointed to the flask Dwiskter held. "Take that, please, as my apology for misjudging you and the Fynx about Sissrow. I never knew him to be a thief. He always seemed such a kind fellow whenever he visited."

"Looks can be deceiving," Boldair replied.

"So very true. I suppose it shouldn't surprise me though."

"By chance did you ever meet Sissrow's father?"

Cadell shook his head. "No, I never did. He never spoke of his father. Why?"

"Long story," Boldair said.

"Beware, barkeep," Drucis said. His blue eyes sparkled in the faint light. He ran a hand along his white-knotted beard. "Boldair's known to weave long tales *before* he became King."

Boldair shot Drucis a sharp glance beneath a harsh frown. "Not this evening, I won't. We must travel onward to reach Nagdor. But ... to make a *long* story much shorter, Sissrow and his father were once one person unified."

Cadell eyed him curiously. "You only drank one shot of the Briarthorn, right?"

"Aye, I did."

"'Cause it sounds like you might've already drunk the entire flask."

"No, me senses are keen. Wylard was Sissrow's father, in a sense of the word, but Sissrow was actually the product of Wylard's wish at the Well of Misfortune where he pleaded to have a son. The child he received was conceived and molded by taking all of Wylard's bad traits and containing them in flesh. His wish became his curse and ultimately, his death."

Cadell nodded. "That seems right. The well, that is. Only a fool makes a wish there. Sissrow, however, never tried to cheat or steal from us. Always the perfect vendor. Now, about the flask. It's yours. You may enjoy it here or wherever you venture next."

Boldair took the flask from Dwiskter and set it on the vendor table before Cadell. "I appreciate your hospitality, and know I've no hard feel-ings against ye. But, I cannot accept your gift."

"What?" Drucis and Dwiskter turned toward Boldair in shock. Each Dwarf's lower lip quivered.

"No, it's best we keep our wits about us as we travel," Boldair said with a firm nod. "But when we pass this way again, we'll be taking you up on your offer for a few more rounds."

"Your Highness, *please*," Cadell said.

Boldair looked fiercely into the man's eyes before grinning. "As you clearly pointed out, I'm not *your* King, and while a gift is a gift, taking it makes me indebted to you."

Cadell's eyes widened for a moment and he shook his head. "No, it's not intended as such. I swear."

Boldair nodded with a gracious smile and gently placed a hand the Cadell's shoulder. "I believe ya. All the same, we must go."

With disappointment in the Cadell's eyes and a slight degree of offended agitation, he set the flask down, giving a shrug. "Be safe in your travels, new King."

"Aye."

CHAPTER 43

$\mathcal{B}$oldair led the way down the forest path with Drucis and Dwiskter grumbling under their breaths until the covered vendor tables were out of view. Boldair chuckled at their mild fit of anger, but his gut told him that Cadell held a darker intent with his *gift*.

Frost's ears perked. Something drew his interest from the right side of the path. Boldair wondered if they were being followed. Dwiskter's accusations had angered the barkeep, but Boldair believed the man's anger stirred more from being identified for what he and his companions actually were: Highwaymen.

And while Cadell had insisted that he never knew Sissrow to be a thief, such an admission was most likely a lie. Thieves protected one another. It was an unspoken code, even if they were members from different guilds. Being a backstabber or a snitch marked a thief and often set a bounty on the tattler by other thieves. Since thieves were masters of hiding and deception, the last thing a thief wanted was to worry over being hunted by one of his own. So Cadell was willing to lie about Sissrow's true character.

A lie was a small transgression. Theft and murder were simply a part of the occupation for some thieves. The majority weren't murderers, as they prided themselves in being able to purloin items without the victim realizing his valuables had been taken. Killing a victim to take his belongings actually proved the thief inadequate in his skills. No thief wanted a tarnished reputation amongst other thieves. Pride was almost as great a reward as fencing the best loot.

A branch crackled in the underbrush to the right side of the trail ahead. Frost sniffed in the direction of the snapping branch but didn't slow his pace, nor did he offer the slightest of growls.

"Bah!" Drucis said. "What'd ya do that for? A *whole* flask of that stomach-kicker could've been ours."

"It'd have been our deaths," Boldair replied evenly.

Dwiskter cocked a brow and looked at Boldair. "What'd ya mean?"

"Poison."

Forboud nodded. "My thoughts exactly. I don't see why any of you even tempted your fates by drinking the Briarthorn Firespit to start with. How could you trust dat their distillery process worked? They're hidden on a dark trail far from any decent civilization. That in itself should 'ave been your first warning. No doubt the flask is as my brother has said. Filled with poison."

"Those shackles giving you a change of heart, Forboud?" Drucis said with a glare. "Now you hope to offer counsel to Boldair?"

Forboud frowned. "I only offer what I believe to be the truth. With you and Dwiskter's insults, Cadell would have reveled in your deaths."

Dwiskter looked at Boldair. "You really believe dat? He'd have poisoned us?"

Boldair nodded.

"How can ye be sure?" Drucis asked.

"He switched the flasks," Boldair said.

"What! When?"

"Moments before he offered the flask to me, his hands lowered beneath the table. He lowered the flask in his right hand but when he brought his hands up again, the flask he offered was in his left."

"Slight of hand?" Drucis asked in a near whisper, more to himself than to the conversation. "Like a street magician?"

Dwiskter shook his head slightly. "Bah! Doesn't mean it was poison."

Forboud shook his head in disbelief. "Never let your cravings for the hard drinks override your rationality."

Dwiskter pointed a stern finger at Forboud. "Look, you keep ya trap shut or I'll find more moss to shove in your mouth!"

Viorka leapt off the back of Boldair's saddle. "Would you all stop bickering? Your fiery belches have continued since we left the vendor tables, along with your grumbling complaints of ailing stomachs. Now, all this fighting over whether or not a flask of liquid was poison or not? If it wasn't poison, you'd be happy to contend with your insides being torn asunder? Perhaps that would be the *least* of your concerns. But what if it was filled with poison? If it were, the lot of ya would be on the forest floor gasping your last breaths of life."

"I still 'ave me doubts, lil' cat, that it was poison," Dwiskter said.

"That's the risk you'd be willing to take?" she asked.

Dwiskter's lips tightened but he held his silence. His eyes indicated he was mulling over the possibilities more than before.

Drucis gave Boldair a confused expression. "Dwiskter's right. What makes you certain it was poisoned? Ya could be wrong."

"And your loyalty to Boldair as your King?" she said. "What of that? You'd turn on him for a decision he made that might just have saved your lives?"

Drucis' eyes narrowed in anger, he opened his mouth to reply, and then as quickly, he lowered his head in shame. "You're right, lil' cat. My greed for dat drink has clouded me judgment."

Dwiskter sighed and looked away. "Aye, my apologies, Boldair."

Boldair shook his head. "Like she said, I was looking out for all of us. But Dwiskter was right about his earlier point, but not about the flask being filled with poison."

"What exactly was I right about?" Dwiskter asked with curiosity.

"About their plot to get patrons drunken out their wits in order to rob them. The reason they don't fear highwaymen is because they *are* highwaymen. Rather than hiding in the shadows to attack unsuspecting passersby, they lure them in for food and a powerfully strong drink. Your insinuation angered him because you saw through their guise." Boldair ran a hand along his knotted beard. "Cadell made mention dat the poison's distilled from the brew, which made me wonder what they did with all the filtered poison afterwards? He was insistent dat we take an *entire* flask. His true intentions were deeply shady and reflected in his eyes. Either to kill us, so we didn't alert others to the possibility of these traders being highwaymen, or to rob us for what we have. We Dwarves have a high tolerance for the strong stuff, but I'll tell ya, that Firespit rendered me almost unconscious the first time I partook of it."

"Drat!" Drucis said, forming fists. "All I got was the one shot in me ale. Nothing more! More fire than jarring my senses."

"Perhaps this time dat was best for all of us," Boldair said. "The first time I drank a direct shot."

"Did the ale soften the potency of the Briarthorn, then?" Drucis asked. His brow furrowed.

Boldair shook his head. "No, not at all. Ye'd think it would've, but I tell you, it heaped its fiery kick throughout the brew. In fact, adding it to the ale probably intensified it!"

Dwiskter shook his head. "Ah, no wonder me stomach is still throbbing."

Viorka rolled her eyes and shook her head. "And you wanted an *entire* flask of it?"

"Now dat I think 'bout it, not so much anymore," Dwiskter said. "My gut is rumbling."

Drucis cackled. "Aye! I'll be finding a shrub soon to drain me insides. It seems to 'ave unsettled everything else!"

"Aye," Dwiskter agreed. He belched and waved his hand to disperse the odor.

"Cadell seemed quite amused by your King's ransom statement," Dwiskter said.

"He did entertain dat notion, didn't he?" Forboud asked, glancing at Boldair.

"Aye, he did. Had we drunk from the flask, we might all be dead."

"King's ransom?" Drucis howled. "If only they knew how much poorer you are since you gave the dragons back their treasures."

Boldair winced slightly. "I lost a lot, tis true, but all those gems and gold were never mine to begin with. Now that I'm King, the tradeoff is worthwhile. Besides, Taniesse rewarded me handsomely for leading the troops into battle and by keeping me alive."

"No King is ever poor," Forboud said, eyeing Drucis sharply.

"I be far wealthier than I've ever been in my life," Boldair said softly. His eyes drifted into thought.

"How so, brother?" Forboud asked. His eyes narrowed with the question.

After a few minutes, Boldair turned his attention at Forboud's question. "Father never told you?"

"Of what?"

"The gold and silver ore veins abandoned by the Dredgemen?"

Forboud's bushy eyebrows rose. "No."

"Never?" Boldair asked.

Forboud shook his head. A stunned expression froze on his face.

A gleam came to Dwiskter and Drucis' eyes.

"This be another of your tales?" Dwiskter asked.

"It must be," Forboud said, angrily. "Father *never* mentioned these rich ore veins to me."

"So he kept secrets from you, too?" Boldair asked with amusement in his voice. "And you thought he favored you highly? Seems there were some things he didn't trust you to know."

Forboud's jaw tightened. Through gritted teeth, he said, "Surely, you're jesting at me expense."

"No, brother," Boldair shook his head. "I wish I were. But if our father was telling the truth . . . Of course, he has lied about so many things and might've been partially responsible for King Erik's death. So, if it be not true, tis not my doing, only my speculation on the words he boasted before King Thorgum, King Staggnuns, and myself. After we reach Nagdor and after my coronation, I plan to send a mining exploration to survey Snowloch. Drucis, I want you and Dwiskter to accompany me."

"You plan to go?" Drucis asked.

"Aye, why wouldn't I?"

"You're our King," Forboud said.

"I am, but I'll not have my ass welded to a throne. And, if the gold and silver are there as father said, it was deeded to him and is Nagdor's property now. I want to oversee the initial mining operations."

"It's hard to protect a traveling king," Forboud said.

Boldair frowned with curiosity. "Brother, are you having sympathies toward me now? Or is it because we're so close to home dat you want to find yourself in my good graces."

Forboud shook his head. A partial smile curled on his nearly beard-less face. He raised his cuffed hands. "I've had a lot of time to think along our out of the way journey."

"Cuffs chaffing ya wrists, eh?" Drucis said with a sly smile.

Forboud frowned. His held back his agitation to reply to the comment and kept eye contact with Boldair. "Things might never be the same between us, but you still hold the throne by all rights. I can never ignore dat. Especially not when the Dwarven Alliance has placed you there. If I chose to remove you, they'd kill me and destroy half our kingdom in the process. When we arrive at Nagdor, I'll openly voice my support of you before the council and the entire city. You 'ave my loyalty, and I hope dat you'll be able to one day trust me again."

Boldair studied Forboud's eyes for several long moments. His voice indicated his sincerity, and his eyes never flinched from looking into Boldair's. Although it was possible Forboud had undergone a change of heart, Boldair couldn't allow complete trust immediately. Or ever.

Trust couldn't be rebuilt in a day's time, perhaps not in a year or a lifetime. Boldair would simply have to study Forboud for some time to come. One's consistent actions indicated the trueness of one's heart. Their father was a master of telling lies and hiding the truth, and Boldair couldn't ignore that. Since Forboud had been under their father's training and tactics, and his direct influence, it was possible Forboud had discovered the ease of telling a lie without the slightest tell escaping. He wanted to believe his brother held allegiance toward him, but Boldair had met too many swindlers during his travels.

Of course, Forboud had not drunk any of the Briarthorn Firespit, either. He might simply be hoping that Boldair was in a stupor and could disregard Forboud's behavior during their journey. Boldair chuckled slightly at the thought. He had not ingested enough of the brew to alter his perceptions.

Boldair's prolonged silence brought a look of confusion on Forboud's face. He frowned, prompting Boldair to speak.

"I appreciate dat, brother," Boldair said.

"I still believe it's not in your best interests to travel into those mines so far from the city," Forboud said. "The dangers would be far too great. Like I said, it's difficult to protect a traveling King."

"I haven't any enemies," Boldair replied.

"Aye, not yet," Dwiskter said. "Queen Taube didn't either, but she was almost killed by Waxxon and he was one of her personal council. Your enemies are sometimes disguised as close friends or can be family." He leveled a frown at Forboud. "Jealousy causes more murders than anything else, especially amongst royalty."

"That be true," Boldair said. He looked over his shoulder at the darkened forest. Frost's ears remained perked. The wolf slowed its pace.

"You keep looking back, brother. Do you think Cadell and his companions are following us?" Forboud asked.

"I do," Boldair replied. "I've heard the occasional branches snap along the forest floor near this trail. Frost is on high alert, too."

Viorka nodded. "I've not said anything, but I've heard those same noises."

Forboud peered over his shoulder. "No one seems to be following us."

"We're not out of the forest yet," Boldair replied.

"If they're excellent thieves," Viorka said, "you'll not see them until *after* it's too late. But the snapping branches indicate that they're not the greatest at stealth."

"You think it's possible he'll come after us?" Drucis asked. He slid his ax partially out of its sheath.

Boldair shrugged. "Depends on how greedy he is and what more he thinks he can part from us."

"Aye," Dwiskter said, placing a hand on his broadax. "I be parting his head from his shoulders should he pursue us."

Drucis laughed. "That we will. Journey's been uneventful thus far. We missed out on slaying more nasty goblins. It's time for a bit of sport."

Faint light from the moon spilled through the trees, not enough to see clearly, but the right amount to make the shadows more ominous, stretching into slender figures that seemed to move as the Dwarves rode.

"Any forest Elves in these woods?" Drucis asked.

"No Dwarf has ever reported such a sight," Boldair said. His eyes studied the shadowed canopy. "Of course, they're the masters of stealth, especially at night. So, unless forest Elves sought to kill travelers, no one would know of their presence. Besides, we're in between two major Dwarven cities. It's unlikely. Why do you ask?"

Drucis placed his thick hand on the hilt of his ax. "Aye, 'cause there be eyes a watching us. I've never felt such a feeling that it not be true."

"Then keep your wits about ya," Dwiskter said. "Tis good we *didn't* drink more."

"That be true," Boldair said.

"I hate to admit such a bold admission," Drucis said, "but I agree."

Off the path in the darker recesses under the massive trees, leaves crunched. Occasional birds fluttered, chirped, and darted past them. Boldair pulled Frost's reins slightly. The dire wolf stopped and peered in the direction where the birds had fled.

"A forest Elf wouldn't make any sounds in her approach," Viorka said. "They're more stealthy than the best thieves."

"Aye," Dwiskter said in a near whisper. He slid his ax from its sheath and nodded at Drucis. Drucis pulled his ax and slid one leg over the saddle, so he could drop to the ground in a moment's notice.

"Any idea what Cadell and his companions do with their victims after they rob them? You think they kill them or simply rob 'em of their gold and goods and send 'em on their way?" Forboud asked, still looking over his shoulder.

"For a Dwarf, you have a lot of jitters," Drucis said. "There be worse things in the caverns we traveled through than here."

Forboud rolled his eyes and held up his cuffed hands.

"Aye," Boldair said. "I don't rightly know. My guess is they kill them.

We have no proof. But you know how often I've been at the Bridge-barrow Tavern. Never once heard a tale about someone getting robbed. That's why the flask probably holds poison. To kill us."

"You mind releasing my hands of these?" Forboud asked. He frowned at Drucis. "You'd have jitters, too, if you had no good way to defend yourself."

Drucis glanced at Forboud's cuffed wrists, huffed slightly, and then looked at Boldair for an answer.

Boldair nodded. "Unshackle him. He's right. If we're soon to be attacked, we'll need all the help we can get."

Drucis' eyes narrowed. "If ye recall, he never showed any resourcefulness in the Battle for Hoffnung."

Boldair shrugged. "All the same. If he fails to defend us, kill him first."

Forboud's eyes widened at the threat.

Drucis took a key from the pouch on his belt and grinned. "Gladly."

Perplexed, Forboud said, "How 'ave I become your enemy?"

Unlocking the cuffs, Drucis leveled a glare into Forboud's eyes. "Undermining the King is a great offense. None greater in my book. So prove yourself in defending Boldair and my disapproval of you will lessen a tinge."

Forboud rubbed his wrists and nodded. A few seconds later, he reached for his beard and found stubble instead. Hurt filled his eyes.

Another branch snapped, but from the opposite side of the path.

"What was that?" Dwiskter asked, sliding from the saddle and pointing with his broadax.

Boldair stopped. "Don't know."

A spark of blue light flashed farther down the path.

"Did you see that?" Viorka asked.

Boldair nodded and whispered, "Aye. A wisp?"

Drucis shook his head. "No. Too large and too bright to be one of those."

The blue light flashed again.

"Much too large," Viorka said softly. "Shimmers with strong magic, too."

The leaves rustled in the dark canopy. The wind, although warm, brought chills to Boldair. With the breeze came the scent of musk and aged sweat.

"Be on alert," Boldair said sternly. He gripped the ax handle tightly. With his free hand, he took Frost's reins and led the massive wolf. "Let's go see."

"Brother," Forboud said. "Allow me to lead the way?"

Boldair turned toward Forboud and stared at him momentarily. Drucis and Dwiskter nodded their agreement.

Boldair sighed. "Very well."

"To rebuild your trust in me," Forboud said, "I must prove myself to you and the others."

Drucis elbowed Dwiskter and whispered, "Dying honorably is an unyielding trust."

Boldair stepped aside, allowing Forboud to pass. Forboud led his ram and held his ax ready to attack should something or someone emerge from the shadowed edge of the forest.

Where the winding forest path ascended and turned at a sharp rising curve, a dim blue dome of light shimmered through narrow slivers of leaves and branches. The vibrations hummed steadily with an odd pulsing sensation that softly shook the ground beneath their feet.

Forboud nervously glanced back at Boldair, swallowed hard, and returned to leading them toward the mystical object.

Drucis and Dwiskter exchanged nervous glances with Boldair. He shrugged and returned to following Forboud.

Curiosity forced them to approach with their axes and daggers drawn. As they came closer, the light cast a bluish tint over a pile of skulls and skeleton bones.

Forboud stopped and pointed. "Look."

"Blasted," Drucis said softly. "You think these are the skeletal remains of the highwaymen's victims?"

"Could be," Dwiskter replied.

"Fresher corpses over 'ere," Boldair said, pointing. An arrow zipped past his head, striking a massive tree trunk with a sudden thud.

"Elves?" Forboud asked, flicking his gaze toward Dwiskter.

"No," Dwiskter replied. "Elves aren't *dat* foolish!"

"Or dat *bad* a shot!" Drucis said, readying both axes.

"Give us the Dragon Conjurer Orb," Cadell said from the shadows of the trees. "And we'll let you live."

"But a greedy barkeep t'would be," Drucis said through grinding teeth. His hand tightened around his ax.

The bluish light brightened. In the shadows of the trees the faint outlines of three more men stood behind Cadell with bows trained on the Dwarves.

Boldair turned. Anger tightened his brow. "The orb was destroyed. It was as I told ya."

"You lie," the barkeep said.

"You dare threaten the King of Nagdor?" Boldair said, now holding an ax in each hand. "I told you the orb was smashed into a thousand bits. It's useless and I certainly won't tote worthless shards of glass in me pockets!"

"Then Nagdor shall be seeking a new king," Cadell said, pulling back the bowstring.

In the blink of an eye, Dwiskter and Drucis removed their thick shields off their backs and swung them into defensive positions, placing themselves in front of Boldair. Arrows plinked off the shields and before the highwaymen could fire again, one of the men screamed and went silent.

Boldair frowned.

Cadell looked behind him. One of the archers was dead in the underbrush. Another archer cried in pain, dropped his bow, and clamped his hand to the back of his knee. The man tried to scramble forward but fell flat on the ground with his leg too severed to support him.

"*You!*" Cadell gasped. "So the King of Nagdor *still* uses the thieving little Fynx to fight your battles?"

"What?" Boldair asked, stepping forward. His brow furrowed, but Drucis and Dwiskter stopped his approach.

Viorka sprang from the thick underbrush and raked her long jagged claws across Cadell's face. He dropped his bow and flung his hands over his slashed cheek. He growled. Blood coated his fingers.

"Take him!" Boldair said.

Dwiskter rushed Cadell with the pointed spike of his ax aimed for the barkeep's throat.

Cadell dropped to his knees. He pressed the flayed flesh of his cheek to the side of his jaw, trying to hold it in place. "Stop! I'm not armed. She's killed the other vendors. I'm no longer a threat."

"Ya never were to start with," Dwiskter said in low gruff tone. He pressed the tip of the ax spike against the softness of Cadell's throat. "So we were right 'bout ya all along. You get patrons drunk, kill them, and take their loot. Tried to poison us as well, eh?"

Cadell didn't meet Dwiskter's gaze. He stared toward the ground with his hand pressed against his flayed cheek.

"Tis a good scheme you had going," Boldair said, walking to the barkeep. "I'm surprised you hadn't done the same to me when I came 'ere before."

Cadell's dark eyes flicked to Boldair. "We'd have 'cept the Fynx became the distraction."

"And now, you've sealed your fate. Tis no wonder you hid your tables on this forest path far from any civilizations," Boldair said.

"And you, a proposed King, set out with your Fynx to steal from passersby like before. I realize Dwarves have greedy eyes and hearts that lust for gold, but using a Fynx to help you steal—"

Boldair holstered his axes. His wide muscled hand wrapped around Cadell's neck. With one quick motion, he heaved the man to his feet and lifted him off the ground. Cadell's feet dangled and kicked slightly. Boldiar squeezed the man's throat tighter. "I 'ave you know I've never stolen from another. While I hunted treasures throughout Aetheaon, I sought treasures in ancient caves and ruins. I didn't rob people. I found three large dragon lairs filled with gems, jewelry, and gold and silver coins; dragons believed to be long dead. Their treasures made me richer than all the Dwarf Kings combined for a time. But when Taniesse revealed to me who she was and her two sisters, I gave back all the treasure I had taken from their lairs. I detest any thief."

Cadell struggled to breathe but couldn't. Strange gurgling sounds sputtered as he moved his mouth.

"And more than that, I abhor a murderous swindler. As for the Fynx, she's a mind of her own. She could've filleted your throat instead of your face in less time than ya could sneeze, which is a suitable punishment, don'cha think?"

Cadell gasped for air and tugged against Boldair's hand with both of his. But there was no loosening the King's tight hold. Veins swelled on the barkeep's forehead, and his eyes widened.

Boldair glared at Cadell. "Now, what to do with you?"

Viorka stepped closer. Her humanoid figure was slender. Her excessively long claws extended to sharp tips. The backs of her hands and arms were covered with fur as was her delicate face. The claws and fur prevented her from blending into a crowd unnoticed. Her emerald eyes peered like a cat. She placed her sharp claws to the back of Cadell's neck.

His body stiffened.

"Like the King of Nagdor told you, the orb is gone. Do you think if he'd kept it intact that he'd be roaming the countryside? He could conjure his own dragon to do his bidding, and most likely, he'd ride the dragon through the skies. He'd have no reason to visit here, riding upon a dire mount, now would he?" She pressed her claw harder until she broke the skin. A thin line of blood trickled.

Boldair flicked his gaze from Cadell's nervous gaze and looked into her eyes. For a moment, he didn't recognize her. The wildness of a hungered beast had taken over. She looked like a massive cat about to pounce on its prey.

Slowly, Boldair lowered Cadell and then he lessened his grip. Cadell gulped in several deep breaths, sputtered garbled words, and fought to remain standing.

"What of your fate now?" Boldair said.

"Please spare me, Your Highness," Cadell replied.

"Oh, it's Your Highness now?" Drucis said. "Earlier, as I recall, you stated dat he wasn't *your* King."

"Clearly, I was wrong. My apologies. I was brash."

"Judging by those corpses, he's killed several dozen travelers recent-ly," Viorka said. "Probably hundreds have been murdered over the years at his party's hands. You release him and he'll continue doing this. Put him to death and you'll spare the lives of his future victims."

"Never known you to resort to violence so readily," Drucis said with a broad grin. "I'm beginning to like you more."

"One does what's necessary," the Fynx replied. Her eyes flickered and glowed like glistening gems, making it difficult for Boldair to look away.

"You missed the battle." Boldair released Cadell. The barkeep didn't attempt to flee. He fell to his hands and knees, gasping desperately for air.

"Hoffnung?" she asked.

"Aye."

She shook her head. "I was there. Don't forget how well I blend into my surroundings."

"I cannot kill Cadell in the forests," Boldair said. "It's not proper without a trial."

"He tried to kill you," Forboud said.

Viorka jabbed her slender, needle-tipped claws into the side of Cadell's throat without any hesitation. The man looked up in horror, clutching a tight hand to the wound. Blood spurted between his fingers with each heartbeat. He opened his mouth to speak, perhaps to curse, but nothing escaped his lips except the gurgling sound of blood in his throat. Within minutes, Cadell was dead.

Boldair eyed the Fynx, cocking his head to the side. She had never been so darkly violent in her decisions, even though she was correct. If Cadell lived and was set free, he'd continue killing and robbing innocent patrons. "You killed him?"

She shrugged, wiping blood off her claws onto the path's soft moss. "He'd have slowed our journey, and undoubtedly caused more problems along the way. A token of appreciation would be nice."

"For *what*?" Boldair asked.

"Saving your life."

"What? We had things quite under control."

"Three archers had their arrows trained upon you. Close up, you could have killed them quickly as they wear only cloth, but not from their vantage point. I took out all three of them," she said with a wide grin and twitching her whiskers.

"No arrow they fired could've pierced our shields," Drucis said with a firm brow. "You did give an element of surprise, which was necessary and much obliged."

"Don't embolden her!" Boldair said.

"So I shouldn't have gotten involved? Is that what you're implying?" Her voice sounded like a fragile girl. She looked hurt and peered down. "I thought we were friends, and I feared you were in a deadly situation, so … I helped the best I could. I suppose you being King has changed all that?"

"No, not at all. We … we're friends," Boldair said. "And you did good, little cat. You caught me off guard is all."

"When we were here before, this man and those around him had been determined to protect Sissrow, which made me wonder their true intentions," Viorka said.

"Aye," Boldair replied. "Cadell implied that Sissrow was a trust-worthy individual."

"Perhaps Sissrow was one of them?" Forboud asked.

"Could be, brother," Boldair replied. He exhaled a gruff sigh.

Viorka leveled a stern frown. "Cadell did say Sissrow was the *perfect vendor*. Perhaps a slip of the tongue?"

Drucis' eyes widened. "Dat he did!"

Boldair shook his head. "Ah, well, it's best we head on. The worst part of their deaths is that the secret of their firespit brew died with them."

All four Dwarves lowered their heads sadly and pounded solemn fists to their chests.

"Dat's truly a loss," Dwiskter said.

"And what of their corpses?" Drucis asked.

"We leave them for the crows and worms," Dwiskter said. "The same way they left all their victims."

Boldair turned toward the shimmering blue light at the edge of the sloped path. "What do ya make of this, Viorka?"

She took several timid steps toward it. "It wasn't here the last time we passed through."

"I know. Tis why I asked."

"I don't know." She came closer but paused outside its edge.

Dwiskter took his ax and sliced away the low leafy branches that partially concealed it. The discus radiated a faint blue light. Upon closer inspection, glyphs weaved together in a unique pattern, pulsing bright energy into the center of the circle.

"Does anyone know what these mean?" Boldair asked, rubbing his bearded chin.

"No," Forboud said, shaking his head. The others shook their heads as well.

"I've never seen anything like this," Boldair said. "And I've been all through Aetheaon."

"Aye," Drucis said, studying the bluish glyph. He took his ax and brought it overhead. "We could smash it."

"No!" Boldair said, gripping Drucis elbow.

"And why *not?*"

Boldair shook his head. "Haste brings death. I almost learned that the hard way when I came through these forests before." Boldair placed the tip of his boot onto the platform. Whatever magic controlled the disc could quite possibly be far worse than the poisonous barbed plants.

"Ye sure?" Drucis said.

"No," Dwiskter said. "Let us inspect it."

"A king must be unafraid to lead," Boldair said.

Boldair placed his foot onto the platform but nothing altered. He allowed a partial nervous grin, shrugged, and then he stepped fully upon the blue disc. He took a couple more steps.

"What's it feel like?" Forboud said. His brow furrowed with a mixture of concern and partial fear. "Does it hurt?"

"No. No pain," Boldair shivered. "Lots of energy though. Makes the back of my neck tingle."

Viorka stepped onto the disc. Her fur stood on end. She giggled. "Tickles!"

"Ah, come now," Drucis said, joining them. "Aye, tis strange energy it is. Wonder why it's here and who's responsible?"

Dwiskter frowned. He placed a timid step onto the platform, and tapped his steel boot twice before walking beside them. "Sorcery?"

The bluish gleam brightened around them, making their images look like apparitions caught between two realms.

"Could be," Boldair said.

"Then you should get off!" Forboud shouted.

The light intensified around the Dwarves and Viorka.

Boldair laughed and shook his head. "Ah, brother, you worry too much!"

A moment later, the blue light shone brightly around them. They all vanished on the platform, leaving Forboud alone on the forest path. The disc darkened.

CHAPTER 44

The Meadwyrm Pass forest faded from view. The last image Boldair saw was his brother rushing off the path toward the glowing disc. Boldair didn't remember a time he'd seen Forboud consumed by fear.

In the blink of a wisp, Boldair's stomach plummeted with an odd sensation similar to the time he dove off a high bank into the cool waters of the Shade River. The feeling was the same, like he was continuously falling, but the endless fall he currently experienced was in complete darkness. He didn't know if Viorka, Drucis, and Dwiskter were still with him.

Even though his body lofted downward like a bird's lost feather, every muscle in his body tensed as he braced himself for the inevitable landing he expected to occur.

Ye can't fall forever, can ye? he asked aloud. No reply came.

If the others were with him, he didn't hear them. He figured at the least, Drucis and Dwiskter would be shouting obscenities at whatever taken them from the forest.

Whenever and wherever Boldair finally landed, he was uncertain. He awoke lying on a cold stone floor, and slowly opened one eye. When his vision cleared, Viorka was staring at him. She lay prostrate nearby, apparently awaking at the same time.

"Where are we?" Boldair asked. He pressed his hands against the broken stone floor. Before pushing himself up, he scanned the floor and walls beyond Viorka, in case they were in a hostile place.

No sunlight beamed, and there were no lit sconces. Instead, the place was dimly lit from luminous mushrooms nestled in the cracks and crevices along the walls and rocky ceiling. For several moments, the walls seemed to have glowing eyes.

Viorka rolled and sat up, rubbing her head. "I don't know. I was going to ask you."

"What kind of hellhole is this!" Drucis said in a gruff whisper. He walked to Boldair and offered his hand and helped the King to his feet.

"Thanks." Boldair craned his neck, popping it and wincing. "No idea, but I've a feeling it's a long way from Nagdor."

"Aye," Dwiskter said, combing his beard with his hand.

Boldair glanced at Drucis and sighed. "I'm afraid your luck has shriveled."

Drucis frowned. "How's dat?"

"There be no taverns here," Boldair said with a slight grin. "No taverns … no stout."

"You don't think I know dat?"

Dwiskter chuckled. "Our greatest concern is in discovering where *here* is?"

"Aye." Boldair nodded. "Magic brought us to whatever this place is. But for what reason?"

Viorka shook her head. "Which was clearly our fault."

"How's dat?" Drucis asked.

She shrugged. "It was sheer foolishness to walk onto that disc."

"She's right," Dwiskter said.

"Bah!" Drucis said.

"Nothing'll change dat now," Boldair said. He pulled one of his heavy axes from its sheath. "Our travels now are on foot. We've no food. Nothing to drink. And no idea which direction we should take."

"It appears we're in a cavern," Dwiskter said. "One dat's drier than a bone, too. If we can find a water source, like an underground stream, we can follow it to find our way out."

"It's odd for a cavern to not have water," Drucis said.

Viorka shivered. "As cold as it is, the water should be ice."

Dwiskter sighed and his breath fluffed like a white cloud. "Aye, I agree wit ya, little cat."

Boldair nodded, and looked both directions. After a few seconds, he sniffed the air and scrunched his nose. "The smell of death is in the air."

Viorka sniffed the air and frowned. "My sense of smell is far greater than yours, and I don't smell anything rancid. All I smell is musty stale air and earth."

Boldair glanced at her. "Aye. Those who 'ave died here, died long ago. The smell that lingers in the air is only present in the oldest sealed tombs."

"Ya think dat's where we are?" Dwiskter asked. "In a tomb or mausoleum?"

Boldair shrugged.

"Where are the vaults?" Drucis asked, looking around.

"Nearby," Boldair said. "But it's a gamble which direction we should take. It seems we're in the middle of a tunnel."

Drucis scratched his bearded chin, pondering. "Either direction has equal chance of leading to nowhere."

"Or to an exit," Boldair said.

Frustrated, Dwiskter said, "I'd be satisfied knowing where we are."

"Aye, me too," Boldair replied. "I wonder how long dat magical disc was in the forest?"

"Perhaps it was a snare to capture you," Drucis said.

Boldair shook his head. "For dat to be true, the summoner would've had to know I was in Meadwyrm Pass."

"You think coincidence?" Dwiskter asked.

"I don't know. For once I should've heeded my brother's advice," Boldair replied.

"And what of your brother now?" Dwiskter asked.

"Aye," Drucis said. "He was left behind."

"He was fearful we faded," Boldair said. "No telling what became of him."

Dwiskter's eyes widened. "Forboud could easily return to Nagdor and take the throne. All he need do is tell the council dat you're dead and since your father's in the Hoffnung prison, the throne is rightfully his."

Boldair's jaw tightened.

"He's yellow-bellied and underhanded enough to do it," Drucis said.

Viorka's emerald eyes narrowed. "We need to find the surface and figure out where we are."

Boldair shook his head. "Although Forboud might attempt such deceit, he doesn't possess the crown. Without the crown, the Dwarven Alliance Council will reject his ascent and hold him in contempt."

"You 'ave the crown?" Drucis asked. "It's not in your saddle pack?"

"No. I have it with me," Boldair replied. "It's tucked behind my axe sheaths. When King Staggnuns handed it to me, I vowed to never keep it outside of me grasp."

"Dat's good!" Dwiskter said with a broad grin.

"Ever since my brother's outrage in Hoffnung for leaving our father behind, my trust in him diminished," Boldair said. "I never said anything, but I watched him rummaging through my saddle pack several times when he didn't know I was watching."

"He was trying to find it?" Viorka asked.

"I believe so." He chuckled and pointed. "Now, I say dat we go this way."

CHAPTER 45

With his ax drawn, Boldair led the way down the narrowing tunnel. Viorka followed with Drucis and Dwiskter immediately behind her. The air became colder, even though the path didn't rise or descend.

"If the path gets any narrower," Boldair said, "we need to turn back."

Drucis laughed. "Aye, this tunnel wasn't hewn out by Dwarves. Dat much is certain."

"Then by whom?" Viorka asked.

"No idea," Drucis said. "But whomever did, they took enough time to mine little pockets of ore from the walls. The path's only getting smaller."

"Perhaps we're going the wrong direction," Boldair said, stopping.

A deep growl rumbled ahead of them. The short growl turned into a sudden cry of pain.

"Did you hear that?" Viorka asked. Her emerald eyes widened.

"Aye. What *is* dat?" Drucis asked.

"I'm not certain," Boldair replied. "The sound isn't from a small creature. I can't tell what the beast is."

"Shouldn't we go see?" Viorka asked.

Boldair placed his hand against the rocky wall. Water dripped. "Seems we've moved away from the vaults of the dead. There's water here."

Viorka scrunched her nose and covered it with her furry hand. "Now, *that's* rancid."

"Aye," Boldair replied. "The smell's getting worse but in a different way."

"Blood, excrement, and rotten carcasses," she said, gagging.

"Whew!" Drucis said, covering his mouth and nose. "Smells like a sun-scorched battlefield days after the battle's ended."

The large animal dispelled a weakening growl, and oddly, the sound pleaded for rescue.

"Should we keep going, Boldair?" Drucis asked. "Or would you prefer to turn back?"

Boldair huffed, tightened his hand around the ax hilt, and said, "Something's being tortured. Without knowing what it is, I cannot justify turning back. Plus, I'd like to know what's at the end of this narrow passage."

"Then lead the way," Dwiskter said, pulling his second ax.

The ceiling lowered, causing Boldair to stoop in order to keep walking. His boot struck a metal object, which clicked slightly. He looked to find a pickax and the skeleton of a Kobold. Its dry leathery skin hung loosely on its bones. Small chunks of silver and other ores were spilled from its pack. Boldair pointed down. "Dat explains why the tunnel's so crudely carved."

"It's been dead for quite a long while," Viorka said.

"Agreed," Boldair said. "That doesn't mean more aren't nearby."

"This one appears to have been fleeing right before it died," Dwiskter said, kneeling beside its corpse.

"Kobolds might not be our biggest worry," Boldair said. "The good thing is the tunnel opens into another room."

"Please," Drucis said, stepping beside Boldair. "Allow me to enter first."

Boldair sighed with regret, squeezed against the wall, and allowed Drucis to pass. One thrill Boldair savored was discovering new places.

As a king, he realized those days were few.

After Drucis cleared the small opening, Boldair followed through and stood. He stepped aside for Viorka and Dwiskter to join them. He marveled at the height of the lofty ceiling in this section of the cavern. With perfect symmetry, the large round stones with rough oval bumps stood in long lines. A narrow walkway wound through them. Delicately carved, each gray stone was larger than the Dwarves.

"Such majestic detail and precision," Boldair said, running his hand against the bumpy side of the closest stone. "What artist carved these? Unusual texture."

"We'd best turn around and go back," Viorka whispered.

"Why?" Boldair asked.

"These are dragon eggs," she said softly.

Boldair stepped back. His mouth dropped in awe. "Indeed, they are. I was so fascinated by their beauty. I thought these were carved stones." He ran his hand along the bumpy surface and grinned.

"There must be a hundred of 'em," Drucis said. "Maybe more. We can't see past them, so dat's a crude estimate. No dragon lays dat many for one nest."

"We're in a den of dragons," Dwiskter said. "We be no match for one angry mother dragon. Even less should there be more."

The pain-filled cry echoed on the other side of the eggs.

"Come on." Boldair walked through the winding line of dragon eggs. "Let's see what's making dat noise."

"No," Drucis said. "We should leave."

"Not without seeing what's happening." His foot slid in a small pool of a thick sticky substance. He raised his boot and grimaced. The viscous pink, greenish goo stretched between his foot and the floor.

"Ugh," Viorka said, covering her nose. "What's that?"

Boldair leaned against an egg and wiped the bottom of his boot on the rough cavern floor. He winced. "Whatever it is, it has a powerfully rotten odor."

"Look," Dwiskter said, pointing.

They looked and discovered the broken halves of a dragon egg on the path with more of the goo spreading from where the dragon had hatched and crawled away. The top section of the egg was large enough for a Dwarves to crawl inside and hide. A serpentine trail of the goo was visible from when the little dragon left the egg and slithered away.

Boldair scanned the area around them. "Where's the dragon? It must be nearby."

"Perhaps dat's what made the earlier noises?" Drucis asked.

"Perhaps," Boldair replied.

"And if so, the mother dragon won't be thrilled to find us here," Dwiskter said.

"Keep alert," Boldair said. "As large as these eggs are, she'll be one hell of a dragon."

Several gruff growls and tiny roars erupted on the other side of dragon eggs. Boldair stepped between the eggs as quietly as possible. When he reached the last row of eggs, he stopped and held up his hand for the others to slow their pace. He peered around the egg and anger overtook him.

"Bloody hells," he whispered.

"What?" Drucis asked.

He nodded. "Take a look."

Drucis glanced in the direction Boldair indicated and a growl rattled in his throat. "I'll not stand for dis!"

"Wait," Boldair said, reaching to grab Drucis' shoulder but missed. "We don't know how many are here."

"Doesn't matter at this point," Drucis said. "I'm angry enough to take on a small battalion."

"I'm with ya," Dwiskter said, pulling his second ax from its sheath.

"You there!" Drucis yelled. "Stop what your doing!"

Two armored Dwarves turned in surprise. One was tugging the baby dragon, which was the size of a large dog, by a thick chain attached to the dragon's muzzle. The dragon fought, pulled, and tugged, trying to break loose. The second guard flailed it with a long whip. Several welts swelled on the infant dragon's rear flank. It emitted small agonizing whimpers of pain.

This newborn dragon was wingless and resembled a massive serpent with legs. Its claws were thick and sharp, cutting into the stoney cavern floor. Although small, it was incredibly strong. If it had wings, it'd have been too strong for these two Dwarves to control. But this wasn't a dragon like Taniesse and her sisters. It was a drake. Although wingless, its poisonous bite could kill any Elf, Dwarf, and human in a matter of minutes.

"Who let you in here?" the one Dwarf asked, releasing the dragon's reins and reaching for his short sword. His eyes glowed amber. His short beard was black with a bluish tint.

Frosthammer guards? Boldair shook his head. Surely, they weren't in Frosthammer again.

Boldair stepped forward with both axes in hand. "We sorta arrived unannounced and against our wishes. Pardon our intrusion, but I must insist dat you not torture the young drake any longer. It's in your best interests."

The other Dwarf held a whip in one hand and a sharp serrated dagger in the other. "Mind your business, intruder. You didn't answer his question. Who let you in here?"

"No one."

"Then how'd you get here?"

"Dat's something dat puzzles us more than it does you," Boldair said.

Dwiskter and Drucis nodded.

Viorka flexed her paws, exposing her long sharp claws.

"There's no way you got past our guards," the first Dwarf said, walking toward them, but never allowing his eyes to move from Viorka. He didn't fear her, but seemed more interested in her possible attack. The anger in his voice matched the rage glowing in his eyes. "Even if ye got past them, you'd have never gotten through the massive gate."

"Like I said, 'it puzzles us more than it does you,'" Boldair replied.

"Are you saying dat you simply *appeared* in our cavern?"

"Aye," Boldair said, nodding. "Exactly like dat."

The Dwarf laughed and looked briefly at his comrade. "Whipped in here like magic, eh, Cerphid? Ya believe him?"

Cerphid shook his head. "No, Lukrean, I don't. They must've entered the tunnel by the Sepulchers of Twilight. But dat entrance was buried under a massive landslide of heavy snow and ice."

Viorka leaned forward, laughed heartily. The madness of her cackles caused Boldair, Drucis, and Dwiskter to turn their attention toward her instead of the two Dwarves. After her laughter subsided, her eyes narrowed, and she lowered her clawed hands to her sides, ready to sprint toward them.

"What do ya find so funny, cat?" Lukrean asked.

"How else would *you* explain our arrival, if not by magic?" she asked. "Or are you so daft?"

The two Dwarves frowned. "Hurling insults will get your little tongue cut out."

"You don't think before you speak, do you?" she asked. "I could split both your tongues from your mouths before either of you could stop me. Don't make threats you've no ability to carry out."

The statement jolted Lukrean. The anger in his eyes turned to fear as he regarded her claws again.

Her emerald eyes narrowed. Any sign of amusement she displayed vanished. "You admitted we couldn't have gotten past your guarded gate and the only other entrance is buried … so how else, other than magic, could we gain entrance into this dragon nest?"

The two Dwarves exchanged confused glances.

Boldair studied them for a moment. "By your appearance and dragonscale armor, you're Frosthammer guards."

Confused, Cerphid said, "Aye. How'd you know dat?"

"We departed Frosthammer over a day ago, but we never expected to return."

"And yet, here you are," Lukrean said.

"Much to our displeasure, if ya don't mind my saying," Boldair said. "So we're in Frosthammer?"

"You are," Lukrean said, "but trespassing in an area dat rewards your immediate death."

"Before you get hasty," Boldair said.

"I dare him to come at us," Viorka said.

Boldair tried to stop his smile but failed. "Perhaps you could send word to King Rigrim dat the King of Nagdor has returned."

Lukrean lowered his weapon and frowned at Boldair for several long seconds. "You know King Rigrim?"

"Aye, and he knows me. So before it's your heads placed on pikes for threatening an allied King, you might want to reconsider your next words," Boldair said.

"He gave you access to our drake breeding grounds?" Cerphid asked.

"No. What I said is the truth. I've no idea how we returned. We were on our way to Nagdor for my coronation. We stepped on a glowing disc in the forest and were teleported here. We never intended to return. It places us days behind our return home. But, after seeing your mistreatment of this young drake, I'm apt to say our return gives me insight to your kingdom's wickedness. I knew Rigrim held dark secrets, but I never imagined something so cruel. Is this how you get the scales for your armor and the bones and teeth dat you decorate your buildings and taverns with?"

"You dare slander King Rigrim?" Lukrean asked.

"No slander and no accusations. Only my deductive observation," Boldair replied.

"You might be the King of Nagdor," Cerphid said, "but Rigrim's our King. You've no right to dictate rule over us. Doing so is enough reason for us to kill you where you stand."

Viorka took a nimble step forward. Cerphid and Lukrean stepped back.

"Then by all means," Drucis said, "come forward and—"

Boldair chuckled. "You're no match for us. I've no doubt in Viorka's quickness to slit your throats. Allow us passage to see King Rigrim and no blood will be shed between us. You get to live another day."

"You hurl insults and threats at us and *think* we'll step aside. You're trespassers and as such, King Rigrim won't hesitate to reward us for killing you."

"What reward comes from your own deaths?" Viorka asked.

"We might be trespassing, but not at our own doing," Boldair said. "Like I said, we 'ave no knowledge of how we were brought here."

"Lukrean and Cerphid, he speaks the truth. I'm the reason for their return."

Boldair, Dwiskter, and Drucis turned in the direction of the familiar voice.

Wynneffin and six of her guards stepped from the shadows. Her narrow gaze bore into Boldair's confused stare. "Drop your weapons, King of Nagdor, or it will be the deaths of you and your friends."

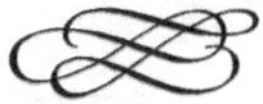

CHAPTER 46

"You!" Boldair said, with fury rising in his voice. "You used magic to summon us back here?"

"I did," Wynneffin replied.

"Can you not understand dat the interest I once held toward you is no longer the same?" Boldair said.

Hurt and anger stirred in her eyes. The hardness of her jawline indicated she hadn't gotten past her scorn. Her words were sharp and cold. "I do."

Viorka whispered, "If you wish, I can disarm her."

Boldair shook his head.

Wynneffin flicked her gaze at Viorka for a moment and then she regarded Boldair once more. Her stance held defiance, even though she looked like she wanted to say something.

"Then why use your sorcery to bring me back when you know I never wanted to return," Boldair said through his teeth. "Ye can't let it go, can ya?"

Cerphrid and Lukrean exchanged puzzled looks.

"You two know one another?" Lukrean asked. Confused, he lowered his weapon, as did the guards standing beside Wynneffin.

"Unfortunately, I've had the displeasure," Boldair said.

"The displeasure was all *mine*," she spat back.

Drucis grinned at Lukrean and shrugged. "Lovers' quarrel."

Boldair glared at him. "*You* keep outta this!"

Drucis's grin shrank and he nodded.

Boldair returned his attention to Wynneffin. "I wanna know why you'd interfere with my return to Nagdor? Ya know my business in Frosthammer was finished. For good, I had hoped."

"Don't make this about you," she replied.

"Then *what* should I make this about?"

"I brought ya back because of a more important problem dat doesn't concern what we once felt for one another. So if you hold what a true king possesses, set aside your distaste for me and help us with the real issue."

"And what is dat?"

"The dead are rising," she said. "They're becoming undead. And they're nearly impossible to destroy."

The news sent a cold chill down his back. "Where?"

"On the lower floors, where I went with you to find Viorka." She narrowed her eyes at Viorka. "Who seems to have no gratitude for me aiding her safe return."

Viorka sneered. "You seem to have caused more ill-fated consequences for Boldair than you *ever* aided in my rescue. Or have you forgotten so quickly?"

Wynneffin took a deep breath and held it. Her face reddened. Boldair realized she was several seconds from allowing her anger to overtake her.

Boldair waved his hands, trying to calm the situation between both sides. "Aren't Frosthammer's dead tossed into the River of Steel?"

She nodded. "Most are. Some Dwarves died under unusual manners in the mining pits. By the time they're found, they're already undead, possessed with an urge to kill. You can't reason with them."

"How do you think I can help?" Boldair asked.

"You said dat you've dealt with this before. You know who's responsible."

Boldair nodded and sheathed his ax. "Aye, I do. The Plague-bringer."

"Then *please* assist us? I'm not asking for myself. I'm asking for Frosthammer." Wynneffin lowered her dagger and tucked it into its sheath. Her eyes softened. He read the pleading in them, which was even greater than her pleading tone. For her, simply saying *please* was more difficult than asking anything else.

Boldair sighed. He understood how painful it was for her to swallow her pride. As much as he wanted to be angry that she'd used her magic to track and trick him into returning, she expressed the truth he couldn't ignore. Frosthammer's population might be in jeopardy. This wasn't about her or him.

Finding and destroying the Plague-bringer benefited all of Aetheaon. The more he thought about it, the more he wondered why they had all departed in different directions after Hoffnung's was regained for Queen Taube. They had essentially won one major battle, but in the celebration of their victory, they ignored the greatest danges. No kingdom was safe until the Plague-bringer was defeated.

"If you don't wish to aid us," she said, "I'll send you to Nagdor immediately. I swear to never bother you again."

Boldair crossed his arms. "Before I agree to aid your cause, I need some answers first."

"What answers do you seek?"

"You never hesitated to summon me and my two best warriors when your father has a vast army at his disposal. Why hasn't King Rigrim done *anything* about the undead? He has thousands of troops at his command."

Wynneffin turned to her guards. Waving her hand dismissively, she said, "Leave us."

The Frosthammer guards nodded, turned on their heels, and walked away.

Once they were were out of sight, Wynneffin said, "Father doesn't believe me or any of the guards I've sent to consult with him concerning this epidemic. He dismisses it as a minor problem. But he has since posted guards to patrol the mining and construction areas."

"You believe it's much worse?"

She nodded.

"How?"

Her eyes grew distant for several moments. A slight tinge of fear flickered before she focused on him. "The last few found in the lower levels were not undead Dwarves."

Boldair frowned. "What were they?"

"I should say they weren't *normal* undead Dwarves," she replied. "They were … mummified, and somehow brought back to life. The conditions their bodies were in, they should never have been able to move. Their flesh was harder than stone."

"Where would these have come from?" Drucis asked.

"The Sepulchers of Twilight dat lie on the other side of the entrance where you emerged," Wynneffin said. "Dat's the only bodies mummified to my knowledge. Ours aren't."

"So you planned to 'ave us teleported into the narrow passageway?" Boldair asked. "Dat's why you were nearby when we approached Lukrean and Cerphrid?"

"Yes."

"If we'd 'ave gone the other direction, instead of this way?"

She allowed herself a half-grin. "You'd have seen firsthand what our miners chopped to pieces in the lower levels."

Boldair shook his head and his jaw tightened. "Ya know, every time I'm close to forgetting the reasons for my anger toward you, you make certain to rekindle dat anger."

"I'm sorry," she said, shaking her head. "The reason I'm in the drake hatchery with my personal guards is so we could make certain you were okay. We were preparing to enter the passage to find you."

His narrowed eyes studied her.

"It's the truth, Boldair," she said. "I swear it."

"Why not close off the tunnel dat leads to the sepulchers?"

"We plan to," she replied. "But first I wanted to get your assessment."

Boldair chuckled. "What's to assess? If you 'ave undead stumbling out of the sepulchers and invading your city, you blast the tunnel until enough rock and debris prevents another undead from getting through."

Wynneffin sighed. "I realize dat, but those tombs hold the history of a former civilization dat occupied Frosted Peaks before Frosthammer was founded by my father. They're known as the Twilight Stoneshapers. Often, histories of past cities are the keys to future cities' survival. We need to study and learn what we can from those before us. I expect tomes and scrolls line the insides of some sarcophagi. Blasting to collapse the only remaining opening could prove costly in losing precious knowledge."

"Dat's true," Dwiskter said.

"Aye," Boldair said, nodding. "Such knowledge should be gathered and placed in your father's royal library. What 'ave you learned about the previous settlements?"

"From the appearance of the undead corpses, they're our Dwarven predecessors. The resemblances cannot be denied, but they were more primitive. Dat's why I want to examine the sepulchers to learn all we can from them. You rob tombs, so I thought you'd know more about the histories of past civilizations."

"I don't rob tombs," Boldair said. "You cannot rob the dead. They 'ave no need for trinkets and treasure after they're buried."

"Dat's my point. The greatest treasures in the tombs are the tablets, tomes, and scrolls dat contain valuable history, which is all the same to me," Wynneffin said. "Accompany me and help explore. Anything you consider treasure, other than written tomes and scrolls, is yours for the taking, as payment for your troubles."

Drucis and Dwiskter's exchanged excited glances.

Boldair sighed. "I don't know, Wynnie."

"Are ye mad?" Drucis asked. "We could loot a fortune."

"Gold and silver hold no value when I beheld how Frosthammer's guards are treating these baby drakes," Boldair replied.

"What do you mean?" she asked.

"One of your guards whipped a newly hatched drake hard enough to leave welts on it. You called this a hatchery. Tell me how you possess all these eggs? And why your guards tortured the newly hatched one?" Boldair asked. "Are you slaughtering these drakes to use their scales for your armor?"

"No." Wynneffin shook her head. "A guard actually struck one of the babies?"

"Aye," Boldair said. "We all witnessed it."

Drucis and Dwiskter nodded. Anger filled their eyes.

Boldair pointed to the Dragon Skull pendant on his armor plate. "Ya see this? Lady Dawn knighted me, Drucis, and Dwiskter into the Dragon Skull Knights. We're the first Dwarves ever to be initiated into dat Order. I'm friends with three dragons, and as such, I never tolerate mistreatment of any dragon or their lesser relatives. So tell me what's going on? How did you come to possess so many eggs? And what are you doing with the babies?"

Wynneffin's eyes grew colder. "Tell me which guard struck the dragon. His punishment will be harsh, I assure you. The whips are only to be used for their sound to frighten them, never to harm them."

"Instilling fear into a dragon dat has yet imprinted is harmful in itself."

"I agree," she replied. "None of these drakes are ever to be harmed. I'd never allow it."

"Then explain where you got all these eggs and how your entire army and guards wear armor made from the scales of these drakes or from dragons," Boldair said. "I've seen the sconces, the chandeliers, and other ornaments carved from dragon bones throughout the taverns and shops. Dat's a lot of scales and bones, which means shiploads of dead dragons and drakes, especially if every floor of Frosthammer displays them."

Wynneffin sighed. "Come with me."

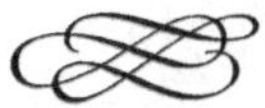

CHAPTER 47

Boldair's hardened frown looked chiseled like carved stone.

Wynneffin's face reddened. She waved him and the others to follow her.

"What kind of drakes are these?" Boldair asked.

"Rime drakes," she replied.

"How'd you obtain hundreds of their eggs?" Boldair asked.

"They're entrusted to our care," she replied.

"By whom?"

"The drakes."

"Really?" he asked.

"Yes."

"I find dat odd."

"Why?"

"Your father invited me to go dragon hunting," Boldair said. "He didn't indicate any friendliness toward them. He didn't mention drakes. He was specific in saying *dragons*. Even he'd know the difference."

"I bet he grinned when he said it, too?"

Boldair shrugged. "Sorta."

"Dat's because he enjoys seeing the terror on Dwarven warriors' faces any chance he gets," she said with a forced grin. "Let's just say dat it's far worse should he ever entertain visiting Elves. Most are so paralyzed by fear dat when they leave Frosthammer, they never return."

"Is dat so?" Boldair asked.

Wynneffin smiled and nodded.

"Sounds more like a jester than a King," Drucis said with a harsh laugh.

"Don't mock my father," she said.

"Mock him? I like him already! Dat's the same thing I'd do," Drucis laughed harder. Tears moistened his eyes.

Dwiskter wailed with laughter. "Yes, Drucis, I could see you do such a thing."

Wynneffin laughed and shook her head. "Do you realize how many suitors I've lost because of those *supposed hunts*? If any Dwarf was serious in his effort to ask for my hand in marriage, they abandoned the idea after agreeing to hunt with my father."

"He made it difficult for ya?" Boldair asked.

"Always," she replied.

"The way he talked to me about ya, he's quite proud of your toughness and zeal," Boldair said.

"Perhaps," Wynneffin said, motioning the guards to hoist the chain winches to pull open the massive door. "But actually complementing me isn't something he does. Regardless of my skills or how I've performed while dueling, he points out my mistakes in spite of my victory."

"So he only invited me to hunt dragons to discourage me from asking for your hand in marriage?"

She shrugged. "*Dat's* not a matter needful of discussion anymore, now is it?"

The coldness of her words pricked his heart no easier than a frozen spike might. In spite of her sarcasm, her eyes held pain and disappointment. He found himself wanting to console her, but with greater issues at hand, now wasn't the time. He knew it, and he figured she did, too.

The metal gears groaned, pulling the massive steel door up. Two giant serpent-like heads rose from the floor. The creatures stood, showing their full height, but like the hatchling, these full grown drakes didn't have wings. They chuffed. Small clouds of ice crystals puffed from their mouths and their long forked tongues licked their lips, as they eagerly expected food.

Their narrow serpent eyes appeared colder than their breath. Much like a viper or a dragon, their mesmerizing eyes were almost seductive in their gaze, enticing others to sacrifice themselves as prey should they stare too long.

The drakes fastened their gazes on Boldair, Drucis, and Dwiskter, apparently not noticing Viorka scrunched behind Boldair. Their pupils narrowed. They took deep breaths, possibly trying to get the Dwarves' scent. A harsh gargling rumbled in their throats, and Boldair feared the sound came from hungry stomachs.

Dwiskter, Drucis, and Viorka froze, immediately holding their breath.

Licking their massive chops, the two drakes craned their necks while inspecting their new guests.

"Uh-uh," Wynneffin said, shaking her head. "Look at me."

The drakes blinked and looked away from Boldair and turned their attention to Wynneffin. She smiled and walked closer to them. She extended her hand and the smaller one leaned its massive head down to her. She patted the underside of its scaly chin.

"By the gods," Boldair whispered. "Why are these imprisoned in there?"

"Imprisoned? No." She shook her head. "It's not a prison, Boldair. Dat chamber is where the two eldest Frost Drakes live. They're free to leave, if they ever choose. But they realize dat we need them, and they need us. We have a mutual need for one another."

"Need them? For what exactly?" Dwiskter asked, slowly running his hand along his beard. His eyes stared intently at the dragons.

"The heat off the River of Steel would prevent our survival, making the air too hot for us to breath at the higher levels of the city. Without these drakes cooling the river's barriers at both ends of its flow, the molten steel would rise and spill over the barriers, effectively killing us."

"So there are more of them?"

Wynneffin nodded. "On the other end of the river are two more elder drakes that aid in keeping the river cooler."

"I see. What do they *need* from you?" Boldair asked.

"Protection from the Frost Dragons that live in the Frosted Peaks. Those dragons have sought to kill them throughout time," Wynneffin said.

"The Frost Dragons kill drakes?" Dwiskter asked while still studying the two drakes with great interest.

"Yes. Dragons have a greater advantage since they have wings," Wynneffin replied.

"Why would dragons kill them?" Viorka asked.

Her small voice immediately caught the attention of the two drakes. They looked from Wynneffin and twisted their long necks, slinking closer to Boldair, trying to locate Viorka.

Boldair took a deep breath and swallowed hard. Despite Wynneffin's obvious control over the scaly drakes, the worst thing he could do was show fear.

"No!" Wynneffin said, snapping the drake's attention back to her. Its head lofted upward and slowly moved back to her soothing hand. Without looking at Viorka, Wynneffin said, "Drakes and dragons compete for their food. Since both cannot survive long outside the frozen environment of the Frosted Peaks, they must fight for whatever prey exists. Drakes are weaker, so the dragons often prey upon the drakes. Not for food necessarily, but as a sign of dominance."

"So they share the same territory?" Boldair asked.

She nodded. "Yes. Dragons actually have a better range for finding food as they can fly over the ridges and peaks with ease. Drakes must resort to ambushing smaller animals between the ridges where they can corner them. Humans dat raise sheep have killed more drakes than dragons because dragons attack from the sky."

"I never thought about human herders," Boldair said.

Wynneffin forced a slight smile, still rubbing the drake's scales. "Have you known a time when humans have ever befriended drakes or dragons?"

"Actually, I know several humans who hold dragons sacred," Boldair replied. "One former King, his living Queen, and Lady Dawn, to name a few. Might as well say the entire City of Hoffnung reveres dragons."

"How about other kingdoms?"

He shrugged.

She said, "Most kings view them as sport, a prized trophy to mount in the city's square to show the King's power."

"Frosthammer boasts the same," Boldair said coldly. "With your dragonscale or drake-scale you're wearing, I'm surprised these two massive beasts don't take offense and kill you and your guards where you stand."

"Dat will never happen," she said. "They know the truth and therefore, they'll never turn on us."

Boldair studied the eyes of the closest drake. Each time Wynneffin spoke, the drakes' eyes glowed with obvious affection, as though mesmerized by the sound of her voice. Was she using magic to keep these massive beasts in check?

Drucis frowned. "What do ya feed 'em?"

"Sheep," Wynneffin replied.

"Sheep?" Drucis shook his head in wonder. "Dat's a *lot* of sheep."

"It's their food staple and another reason why they're safer here than along the edges of the mountainsides killing herders' stock. In the past, disgruntled farmers have hired wizards or small armies to rid themselves of the great dragons. The majority of humans deem all types of dragons to be the same thing." She shook her head. "What they don't realize is dat wizards have limited power against the greater dragons. Most wizards kill drakes, because it's easier. They drag its head to the village as *proof* of the kill. Farmers don't know the difference based on the head alone and are in such a state of relief dat they pay the wizard anyway. While some, like myself, behold them in spectacular beauty and reverence, others view them as hostile pests. They had ruled the sky for generations, until they vanished almost within a day. Without dragons being visible in the sky, the drakes perished faster."

Boldair was fascinated by the two drakes. Both were captivated by Wynneffin and remained submissive to her. He'd never witnessed such a strong creature, which was mightier than Rigrim's best fifty warriors, being controlled by one person. He had no choice to believe Wynneffin had somehow bewitched these drakes to remain docile. He also didn't doubt for a single moment that she could say the proper words and command the two drakes to rip him and his comrades to shreds in a heartbeat.

"They seem loyal to a fault," Boldair said with a smile.

"Shouldn't they be, since we're protecting them?" she asked.

He shrugged. "It still doesn't explain the scale armor or how you 'ave a den of hatching eggs."

"In time," she replied.

"If what you said about the undead is true, we might not 'ave a lot of time."

Wynneffin placed her thumb and forefinger into her mouth and shrilled a loud whistle. She motioned to a guard at the bend of the chamber and he nodded, unlocking a small cage. He led several sheep from the pen and headed toward where Wynneffin stood.

"It's best we leave the drakes alone during their feeding," she said. "It gets a bit … messy. Come and I'll show you more."

CHAPTER 48

*B*oldair walked in near silence as Wynneffin exited the massive chamber where the two drakes resided. Guards lowered the door, but not before the sheep bleated their terror. Their cries ended quickly but the Dwarves winced at the sounds of bones snapping and pelts being torn apart.

Was Wynneffin's sudden willingness to reveal the Frosthammer's mysteries sincere or was she using her magical control over the drakes as a subtle threat of her power? He recalled the power to summon a dragon through the magical Orb he had taken from Sissrow. Wizards and mages could enchant items to lure control over others and great beasts, but Wynneffin didn't seem to possess such an object.

She walked along a narrow path at the outer edge of the hatchery. The path was almost hidden in the shadows. Like the other recesses in the tunnel where Boldair and his companions had arrived, large luminous mushrooms lit the cavern. No flaming sconces offered heat or light. Midway across the hatchery, they came to a metal door guarded by two Frosthammer Dwarves.

"We need entrance," Wynneffin said.

The guards glanced at Boldair momentarily before nodding. One unlocked the door and pulled it open. She entered with Boldair and the others followed close behind.

This cavern room was lit by large torches and oil lanterns. Tables were carved from rocks and seamstresses sat on both sides of these long tables about ten feet apart. The tables stretched at least a hundred yards. Piles of dragonscales were stacked between each seamstress. These scales weren't the same as the drakes'.

These were icy blue dragonscales like the guards and Wynneffin wore.

"As you can see, these aren't scales from the drakes," she said.

"I'm aware, but they *are* dragonscales. Where—"

"You'll see where we found these." Wynneffin walked in between two long tables toward the gated door on the other side of the room. None of the seamstresses bothered to look up from their work.

A Dwarf pushed open the door from the other side and backed through, pulling a two-wheeled wagon with several bundled stacks of scales. After he passed, Wynneffin held open the door and motioned Boldair and the others to pass through.

On the other side of the door, they stood at the ledge overlooking a deep circular gorge below. A smooth pathway outlined the edge of the pit and spiraled all the way to the bottom. Flaming torches lit the pathway.

"What is this place?" Boldair asked.

"At the bottom are piles of dragon remains," Wynneffin replied. "Scales, much like bone, don't deteriorate quickly. This is where we've gotten dragonscales to make our armor and the bones you inquired about as ornaments in various taverns and other decor."

"Why are so many dragons' remains at the bottom?" Viorka asked.

Wynneffin shrugged. "We assume this was a dragon burial ground. A place they came to die with their ancestors." She pointed to a narrow crevice at the edge of the cavern's domed ceiling at the other side of the room. "Dat's where they must've crawled through."

"How'd you know you'd find their remains at the bottom of the pit?" Viorka asked.

Wynneffin smiled. "My dear, dat's how far down we've excavated. At one time, their scales and bone were level with where we stand."

Boldair's eyes widened.

Drucis and Dwiskter exchanged astonished looks.

"Dat's a lot of dragon carcasses," Drucis said.

"I never imagined so many had flown the skies," Boldair said. "It's sad to know their numbers have dwindled."

"Yes," Wynneffin replied, "and it'd be a shame to let them set there useless."

"How many have you unearthed?" Boldair asked.

"Fifty-seven so far," she said.

"Dat's all?"

She nodded. "I imagine there's at least dat many more the deeper down we dig. They're huge beasts. Eldest dragons would be my guess. One's thick hide and massive bones take up a lot of space. Do you realize how many suits of dragon armor can be made from a single dragon alone?"

Boldair shook his head. "No idea."

"Since these dragons died without suffering injury from weapons or sorcery, fifteen to twenty chestplates and leggings can be made from one dragon. Depending on the length of a great dragon's neck, several shields can be made."

"Fifteen to twenty?" Drucis asked.

Wynneffin nodded. "The scales from an elder dragon dat size are quite large. If the seamstress is frugal and precise with her cuttings, she can make a lot of armor. I never lied about dragons being spared. We never killed any of them."

"I see dat. It's good dat you're using the dragon carcasses though," Boldair said.

"Why?"

"The Plague-bringer can bring dead dragons back to life. We've witnessed it before."

"When?" she asked stunned.

"The Battle of Hoffnung. It was a Frost Dragon dat the Plague-bringer resurrected, but it was only bone. The remains in this deep pit would look like real living dragons if resurrected. It'd be impossible to tell the difference."

"The majority of their scales are pristine."

"Any idea why they're so well preserved?" Drucis asked.

Wynneffin shrugged. "Probably the frigid cold temperature inside Frosthammer. It could be because these are Frost Dragons, too. Their unique powers make them resistant to freezing. The armor keeps us warm, even when we venture outside into the Frosted Peaks."

"Don't brag," Boldair said with a sly grin. "You're making me envious. Even the heaviest bear pelts fail to keep me warm while riding through the Frosted Peaks."

"Aye," Dwiskter said. "'Tis why I crave hard stout on those long cold rides. Gotta 'ave something to warm me insides."

"For the troubles I've caused in bringing you back to Frosthammer," Wynneffin said, "I'll make certain each of you get undershirts and under-leggings made from Frost Dragon skin. You'll be amazed at the warmth such a thin layer of their skin adds. They don't chaff, either."

Boldair shook his head. "While I greatly appreciate your offer, I must decline. Such would not be viewed favorably by our dragon allies. They would be greatly offended by knowing we wore clothing made from their kin."

Wynneffin frowned. "I see."

"So tell us about the drake eggs?" Boldair asked. "You've well over a hundred dat will hatch. As large as the elder drakes are, you cannot possibly house and feed dat many inside Frosthammer."

"I know," she replied. "We're attempting to find a place where to release them when they're old enough to fend for themselves. A place where no farmers will try to kill them."

Viorka shook her head slowly, deep in thought. "You have four elder drakes?"

Wynneffin nodded. "Yes."

"There's no way four drakes produced a clutch of eggs as large as you have in the hatchery," Viorka said. "How did you acquire so many?"

A flicker of anger flashed in Wynneffin's eyes. "We have younger breeding pairs of drakes."

"How many pairs?" Viorka asked. "May we see them?"

Wynneffin shook her head. "Dat is not advisable."

"Why not?" Viorka said, almost defiantly and with a demanding tone.

"The younger drakes are far more aggressive than the elder pairs," Wynneffin said. "I cannot control them as easily."

Boldair regarded the information with curiosity, but didn't ask further questions. He wondered why Wynneffin had withheld that information and why Viorka's questions obviously angered Wynneffin. Were they only being shown what Wynneffin wanted them to see? If so, what more was she hiding?

"Anything else you wish to know?" Wynneffin said sternly.

"No," Viorka said. "I'm satisfied. Boldair?"

Boldair shook his head. "I've nothing more. Now, let's examine the Sepulchers of Twilight so I can determine whether we've a reason to continue our affairs in Frosthammer."

Wynneffin nodded but held a firm stare into Viorka's eyes. A daring smile curled on Viorka's lips, which caused Wynneffin to turn away.

"If you will," Wynneffin said, "let's make our way back to the hatchery."

CHAPTER 49

*B*efore Boldair and his companions were led back to the narrow cavern passageway where they'd been teleported by Wynneffin's magic, Wynneffin left them long enough to gather eight heavily armored guards from the outer chambers to accompany them.

"Keep your guard up," Boldair whispered to Drucis and Dwiskter.

"Ya think she's up to no good?" Drucis asked.

Boldair shrugged. "I don't know. Just because she's shown us the drakes doesn't mean she won't turn on us later."

"You still don't trust her?" Dwiskter asked.

"More than I did," Boldair replied. "A part of me wishes I could fully trust her, but for now, I don't. She has darker secrets she's not telling us. Besides, we're outnumbered and those passageways we're about to enter are narrow. Quite easy for her soldiers to run a short sword through our backs."

Wynneffin nodded at Boldair in passing and led the way to the narrow tunnel with her guards pressed close behind her. She placed her steel helm on her head.

Boldair shook his head. He, Dwiskter, and Drucis had left their helms with their mounts, which was a worrisome regret. He didn't know the glowing disc would transport them or he'd have been better prepared. He'd have never stepped onto the platform in the first place.

"I'll send my troops ahead, in case more undead have arisen," Wynneffin said. "Once we're through the tunnel and into the crypts, we'll 'ave room to spread out."

"Aye, good," Boldair said, somewhat relieved. Had she insisted he and his group go first, he'd have known his suspicions were accurate.

Drucis stepped between Boldair and Wynneffin's last guard. He waited until after the guard had left the narrow tunnel and entered the room filled with crypts.

"Well?" Boldair asked.

"One second," Drucis said, pulling his ax.

Dwiskter stepped in between Boldair and Drucis and drew his axes.

Drucis gave a firm nod and walked through the carved doorway into the crypts. He cautiously peered to each side to make certain Wynneffin's guards weren't ready to attack them. The guards stood in the center of the large room. They were mesmerized and silent. They weren't concerned with Boldair.

Boldair scanned the walls from the floor to a ceiling that was too high to see. The room was dim except from the glow of the numerous mushrooms growing in the recesses between each sepulcher.

He regretted not having an herbalist in his party. Those mushrooms and the grave soil providing nutrients were no doubt quite valuable to a wizard or sorcerer. He leaned down to Viorka and whispered, "Can you gather some of the mushrooms and dirt to carry with us?"

She nodded.

Boldair returned his attention to the walls of stacked, sealed sepulchers and whispered, "By the gods. There must be a legion of dead entombed here."

Wynneffin walked to him and nodded. "See? Dat's why it'd be disastrous to totally close off this area."

Boldair nodded. "We could spend an Elf's lifetime excavating and never examine what's hidden inside."

"I know. But a brief search might be enough to discover whether or not a wealth of knowledge is buried with the dead," Wynneffin said.

Dwiskter said, "They might've been too primitive to have a written language though."

"Dat is true," Wynneffin replied.

"But the architecture," Boldair said in awe. "Delicate artwork and detail is more like the Elves than human or Dwarven."

She nodded.

"I don't see any undead," Dwiskter said.

"Nor I," Drucis said.

"Are you certain the undead roamed out of here?" Boldair asked.

"I know no other place," Wynneffin replied. "I can't see how the Plague-bringer would know about these tombs."

"He's a dark sorcerer," Boldair said. "Being a necromancer, he must 'ave some connection to where the dead are buried, especially massive graves like this."

One of Wynneffin's guards rushed to where they stood.

"What is it, Filgam?" she asked.

"Voices on the East side of the sepulchers," he replied.

"Did you see anyone?"

Filgam shook his head. "No, I thought it best we go as a group."

Wynneffin nodded and then she glanced at Boldair. "What do ya think?"

"The undead do not speak," Boldair said. "We need to investigate. Understand dat the Plague-bringer, should he be here, has powers unlike any wizard you've ever encountered."

"In what way?" she asked.

"He possesses bags of carrion beetles, flies, and other insects that quickly spread his diseases to claim more undead followers," Boldair said. "Should he toss a bag at us, flee. I don't know if we'd be able to kill the insects before they infected us."

Wynneffin motioned all her guards toward her. When they gathered around, she said, "Proceed silently. We need to know if the Plague-bringer's here—" She glanced at Boldair, not certain what to say.

"If he's here," Boldair whispered, "we exit and blast the tunnel."

"What?" Wynneffin asked, perplexed.

"Wynnie, we 'ave no choice. None of us carry range weapons,"

Boldair said. "If we had an Elven archer or two, we could attack. Without range, we're no match against his magic. He'll infect all of us. Believe me, there's no undoing the infection."

Wynneffin chewed her lower lip while she thought. She nodded. "We do as Boldair suggests. If the Plague-bringer's inside the Sepulchers of Twilight, don't make a sound. Retreat for the safety of Frosthammer." She shook her head. "I've never longed to befriend Elves any more than I do now."

"Approach cautiously," Boldair said, looking at each Dwarf. "And silently."

They all nodded.

Boldair looked around and sudden fear twisted his stomach. "Where's Viorka?"

CHAPTER 50

The wall of stacked sepulchers adjacent to the front wall of the chamber caused Boldair to gaze in disbelief. By his estimate, several thousand sepulchers formed the visible wall. Due to time, a few had broken loose and crashed to the floor. Behind this wall was another wall of tombs. A half million or more were buried here.

Fires flickered in the sconces lining the lower sections of the chamber. The thought crossed Boldair's mind that the former civilization housed inside the mountain hadn't been a primitive society, not with the detail dedicated in persevering their dead. What secrets were buried inside the sepulchers with the corpses?

Several fire pits, which should have been buried underneath layers of dust and cobwebs from nonuse, blazed high and hot. Six individuals dressed in black hooded robes stood with their backs to Boldair and his company. Wynneffin's eyes widened with curiosity. She glanced at him.

Boldair imagined his facial expressions reflected her sudden shock, which wasn't her normal expression. The voices were the constant hum of these six individuals chanting the same words over and over.

"What are they doing?" Wynneffin asked.

Boldair shook his head slowly. "I don't know."

These priests or monks or whatever they were, might be summoning the Plague-bringer, as his black carriage and hellish beast of a horse were nowhere to be seen. Then again, the Plague-bringer might've already been in the tombs and left, leaving behind his loyal necromancers to raise the mummified remains of a long dead civilization to add to his massive army. Resurrecting a half million undead to infect the million or more Frosthammer residents was an army too large to defeat.

An army that size could defeat every major city in Aetheaon without suffering losses. But under the Plague-bringer's command and his swift ability to summon the dead warriors into undead warriors, no mass of armies could ever defeat him.

The Plague-bringer could rule the entire continent of Aetheaon without opposition, which was an odd accomplishment. What purpose did it serve to rule over a world of undead humans, Dwarves, and Elves? They obeyed whatever the Plague-bringer instructed, but he'd have no intellectual intimacy with any of them. What good was it to be a King over a continent of undead races?

Or could it be the Plague-bringer hated the living so much that he'd rather destroy all humanity in their realm?

The black robed chanters raised their hands before them. A crudely hewn altar set against the mountainous wall of stacked crypts. The chanters' low-toned chants were in a language Boldair didn't recognize. Plumes of black spiraled from the ground. The earth shook.

"Stop them!" Dwiskter shouted, running with his axes drawn. "They're summoning the Plague-bringer! The black carriage is teleporting in front of them."

"What?" Panic furrowed Wynneffin's brow. She looked at Boldair.

Boldair nodded. "He's seen it before. He knows."

Drucis pulled his axes and darted across the rough cavern floor. Boldair did the same.

Wynneffin commanded her guards to kill the summoners. The wheels of the black carriage were visible.

Boldair rushed at the closest summoner. As he approached, he swung his double-edge ax over his head and kept his focus on the back of the summoner's head. He brought down the heavy blade, but the summoner sidestepped, causing Boldair to swing at empty air.

"Bloody hell!"

How had this practitioner seen him? The hood covered his head and his back was to Boldair. Even if the summoner heard Boldair's footsteps, he couldn't have known where Boldair aimed the ax. The summoner moved at the last second with the steel ax less than an inch from splitting flesh. Somehow, the summoner moved faster than Boldair could adjust his attack.

The unyielding power of the downward strike pivoted him forward, off-balance, and Boldair scrambled to find his footing against the rough, uneven cavern floor. His steel boots scraped the rock, striking a solid jagged stone, which tripped him. He hit the floor hard on his side. The air dispelled from his lungs and pain rattled through his body.

Boldair grunted, glancing back, and helplessly watched as the summoner's crimson red eyes glowed like a demon rising from the flames of Hell. Bluish waves of fire flowed from this unusual summoner's fingertips. It was that moment when he realized they weren't fighting anything human, Elven, or Dwarven. These *were* demons. Not anything like the occasional ones he'd encountered in taverns or those exploring the countryside that wanted to escape their shunned reputations by hoping to blend in with the other races.

These demon summoners were the vile-natured creatures that longed to harm and destroy the races in the Aetheaon or any continent. Without question, the eyes of this one spewed unspoken hatred for the living. Was this the reason the Plague-bringer sought to slaughter all kingdoms and resurrect them as undead minions? Afterwards, he could easily open the pits of Hell to free the chained and caged demons to roam the realm unchallenged by priests, paladins, and demonhunters. Everything pure in nature would be destroyed forever.

The blue flames spread and encircled the summoner's hands like balls of fire. The runes on Boldair's ax glowed. Their power wasn't enough to block the fire's blast when the demon unfurled them. His shield could possibly thwart the magical fire, but it was still strapped to his back.

He rocked back and forth on his side, trying to roll his body trapped under the weight of his own armor. His lungs ached and his side stung. He coughed and winced. The pain, no doubt, was the result of bruised or broken ribs.

"Blasted!" he shouted, unable to twist over and free his plated shield.

The blue flames shot from the summoner's fingertips like bolts of lightning, spreading outward in a broad swath and then narrowing their aim directly at him.

Tears heated his eyes. He glanced momentarily at Wynneffin. Her eyes widened with genuine fear and sadness. She flung a dagger, but at the speed the fire approached, the dagger wouldn't strike the summoner before the flames consumed Boldair.

Boldair closed his eyes, ready to accept death as an uncrowned King. He never thought his fate would be such, and in those final seconds, his anger toward Wynneffin ignited. She had teleported him and his companions back to Frosthammer. Otherwise, he'd be riding through Nagdor's gates. But even his anger wasn't enough to strengthen his resolve to somehow push himself to his feet. The pain in his side was too great.

Metal scraped the cavern floor, chiseling a groove several inches deep. Boldair opened his eyes to see two broad shields block the fiery attack of the summoner. Dwiskter and Drucis stood side-by-side thrusting their combined weight behind their shields, sending a wall of blue flames upward. Seconds later, the flames ended.

Dwiskter and Drucis each offered a hand to Boldair. Boldair clasped his fingers tightly around Dwiskter's hand and both Dwiskter and Drucis yanked Boldair to his feet. Boldair winced and growled in pain.

Leaning against his ax, Boldair expected to see the summoner lying dead on the ground from the dagger Wynneffin had flung, but he had somehow maneuvered outside its path. The summoner turned toward her, and cast a blue fireball. She rolled. The blast of fire struck a crypt behind her. The rock split and a chunk of the vault fell with a loud thud, followed by the shattering of stone.

Three summoners kept their attention on the swirling circle of magic, continuing their pursuit of pulling the black carriage with the Plague-bringer into the Sepulchers of Twilight. The plumes of black smoke lessened, instead of growing darker. Their power was weakening due to their focused circle being broken.

Wynneffin's guards attracted two of the summoners toward them. But her guards were unable to land any blows with their short swords.

Wynneffin pushed herself to her feet.

"Wynnie!" Boldair shouted. "Watch out!"

The summoner cast a second blue ball of flame at her. Before she could react, the flame stuck her chest, lifted her off the ground, and slammed her against the broken sepulcher.

Despite his pain, Boldair pushed off the handle of his double-edged broad ax and scrambled for her. Dwiskter and Drucis rushed the summoner, pulling their shields in front of themselves. He turned to face them with two huge balls of fire engulfing his fists. His crimson eyes glowed like boiling blood. His face creased with a wicked grin. Deep laughter rolled from his mouth with mockery. He raised his hands ready to cast.

Viorka leapt off the side of the sepulcher wall over thirty feet above. She extended her long sharp claws during her descent and thrust them into the back of the demon's neck. The long tips of her nails protruded all the way through his throat. His laughter ended and his fiery flames died in an instant. The demon staggered, attempting to reach around to yank Viorka off. She pulled her right claws free and rammed them through the side of his throat.

Dark blood spilled from his mouth. He sputtered and gurgling sounds rumbled in his throat.

After he dropped to his knees, Dwiskter said, "Move!"

Viorka withdrew her claws and kicked off the summoner's shoulders.

Dwiskter swung his ax in one swift arc, separating the demon's head from its shoulders. The wet plop of its head struck the cavern floor and rolling past the three demons summoning the Plague-bringer, breaking their concentration.

The Plague-bringer—setting on his carriage before them seemed only moments from being fully teleported—angrily shouted, "No!"

Seeing the crimson glow of the Plague-bringer's eyes left no question that not only was he a necromancer, he was also a demon, which explained far more than Boldair had known. Fury tightened Mor's tattooed brow and brightened his eyes. His hands tightened on the reins of his hellish horse. Spittle dripped from his sharp yellow teeth. "Kill them and then resurrect them! Bring their undead bodies to me at the edge of Woodnog Swamp near Fae Barrier Pass!"

Drucis decapitated another demon summoner before it could turn to attack.

After the two demons were killed, the image of the Plague-bringer faded, and then vanished completely.

Boldair knelt beside Wynneffin, ignoring the pain pinching his ribcage. She sat slumped with her back against the wall. He carefully slid her helmet off her head. Blood trickled from her nose and down the sides of her mouth. He took her hand into his and squeezed.

"Wynnie," he whispered. He dared a glance toward the other Dwarves as they sought to kill the four summoners without any success. He patted her cheek. "Wynnie!"

She didn't respond, so he yanked off his plated glove and pressed two fingers to the side of her neck. Her pulse was strong, so she was alive. When she might awaken, he didn't know. *If* she awakened …

Boldair pushed himself to his feet. Saddled with pain and a sudden fear that Wynneffin might have sacrificed her life to spare his, he pulled free his other double-edged ax from its sheath, twirled each in his thick hands, and growled through clenched teeth.

Although he'd openly admitted to Forboud that he'd never had much experience with hand-to-hand combat, he was too angry to allow himself to doubt his fighting skills. He was impressed to see these demons dodge each ax and sword blow from his companions and Wynneffin's soldiers. They glided effortlessly and even with attacks coming from multiple sides, they suffered no minor cuts at all. Not an ax or short sword touched them. Their reactions indicated their ability to predict which direction and the timing of each weapon's thrust, allowing them to fight unscathed.

Dwiskter and Drucis were better trained than Boldair, but he wasn't going to be a spectator. He walked slowly, advancing from the blindside of the closest summoner that was entangled between two of Wynneffin's soldiers. It was time to end this invasion before the summoners somehow gained an upper hand and managed to kill them.

CHAPTER 51

Boldair rushed rapidly at the summoner, ignoring his injuries. He approached without any battlecry, which was difficult to do with the increasing fury rising inside him.

The demon within Boldair's sights somehow kept dodging the blades of the two Frosthammer soldiers, slowly wearing them down. It moved so swiftly, at times, its appearance was more a blur than a steady image.

To Boldair's advantage, the demon ducked and darted past the Dwarves' blades and the occasional swing of their heavy shields, but it kept its back to Boldair. Boldair plowed forward. The two Frosthammer soldiers noticed his approach, slightly backing away from the demon. When it noticed their retreat, it spun a one-hundred-eighty turn, but not fast enough.

Its eyes widened a moment before Boldair pummeled the demon's head with the flat side of his ax. The impact smacked the demon hard enough to send it spiraling through the air. It dropped hard and sprawled onto the floor, barely moving. Boldair pressed the edge of his blade against the softness of its throat, forcing it to open its eyes and gasp.

"Fool!" it sputtered. Blue flames flickered on its fingertips.

One guard brought down his short sword in one swift motion, cutting off the demon's right hand. It howled in pain, cursing and writhing. Black blood spilled from its wrist and its urge to cast spells was buried by its pain.

Boldair pressed the pointed tip of the ax head against the demon's throat. "Why's the Plague-bringer going to Woodnog?"

The demon sneered and then laughed. "He's already there."

"Why?"

"Why else? Destroying Woodnog unleashes our kindred from the Black Chasm, allowing the plague to consume the living and Mors will rule Aetheaon. Anyone he gifts with remaining life will give their allegiance to him."

Boldair frowned. "Tyrann rules the Black Chasm. Not Mors."

"Aetheaon shall be Mors. Tyrann will bow to him or die as will you and your comrades on this day."

Boldair shook his head. "*Not* this day." He pressed the sharp spike through the demon's throat and twisted. "Not *ever*."

The demon's legs twitched and thrashed. When its body no longer moved, Boldair yanked the ax spike up. He nodded to one of the Frosthammer soldiers and almost grinned in his triumph when a cold blast struck the middle of his back, tossing him into the soldier with enough force that both he and the soldier were hurled halfway across the room.

Boldair's axes hit the rock floor and skidded. He and the other Dwarf landed hard on their sides, facing one another.

"What was dat?" Boldair asked.

The soldier shrugged. "No idea."

Boldair groaned and pushed himself up. Two Frosthammer Dwarves lie facedown on the cavern floor, not moving. Blood spilled into a circle around their heads. Boldair winced. Most likely, those two were dead.

He extended his hand to the Dwarf beside him and helped him sit.

"How bad are ya?" Boldair asked.

He shrugged. "I can manage."

Boldair pointed at an altar. It was partially deteriorated, but was high enough to block any magical blasts the summoners could cast. "Can you make it there?"

The Dwarf nodded.

"You go first, and I'll try to protect us with my shield," Boldair said. He slid his shield off his back and around until he was able to adjust his left arm into place. He nodded. "Go, now!"

The Dwarf crawled until he reached the long side of the sepulcher. Boldair held his shield steadily until they reached the crypt and slinked out of sight.

Another demon howled and then fell silent. Drucis laughed. "Ya can't dance and dodge forever."

Boldair risked peering around the side of the crypt to see how Dwiskter and Viorka were coping. Both were trying to get close to one of the demons, but neither had any luck.

Boldair took a deep breath and gently placed his hand to his ribs, even though armor prevented him from checking his injury. He gritted his teeth. Pressing his back against the crypt, he used his feet to push himself into a slight crouch.

A leathery hand grabbed at his shoulder. He noticed it from the corner of his eye, and the movement forced him to turn. From the crypt an undead creature attempted to pull itself over the side, but even though undead life had crept into its corpse, its hardened, mummified flesh prevented its joints from bending easily. Mobility was nearly impossible.

Boldair yanked his shoulder forward. The undead's hand gripped the air, opening and closing, blindly trying to grab anything. Boldair hurried and found one of his axes and returned, chopping off the undead corpse's head. The body spasmed.

He turned his attention to the spot where the black carriage had partially materialized. With four of the summoners dead, and the other two sparring to stay alive, the magical portal no longer existed. Tired and aching, he heaved his heavy ax on his shoulder and walked to where Drucis and Dwiskter tried, unsuccessfully, to strike deathblows on the summoners.

"What? You've returned without inviting us to share in the sport?"

Boldair turned to see Yotram with a broad smile. Brandrum stood beside him, as did Kairun.

Kairun laughed. "You look worse for wear, King."

"Aye, I imagine so."

"We're fresh for battle," Kairun said.

"As am I!" a voice thundered not too far behind them.

They all turned, stunned. King Rigrim stood, dressed in full armor, and held the Frosthammer in his thick muscled hands. He amber eyes glowed like fire through the slits of his winged helm.

"Everyone stand back!" he shouted.

Drucis, Dwiskter, and Viorka retreated from their attacks on the two summoners. Once they were out of Rigrim's line of sight, the King brought the warhammer overhead and slammed it hard on the cavern floor.

The rocks split apart. The cracks splintered across the floor like icy spider webs. Ice crept from the head of the warhammer straight toward the two summoners. They were too stunned to move or contemplate casting any spells. Their eyes fastened on the path of ice. The ice formed around their feet, up their legs and down their arms, leaving the demons' necks and heads unfrozen.

King Rigrim marched to them with fury in his glowing amber eyes. The two demons' eyes widened with greater fear than a demon should ever display. Their jaws shivered from the layers of ice cocooning their bodies and the fear of King Rigrim's approach.

"I sensed demons lurking in Frosthammer," Rigrim said. "Since you're demons your death will be painfully slow. The ice freezes your flesh to the core. If you were human, you'd already be dead."

The demons opened their mouths in what appeared an attempt to speak, but clouds of icy crystals were all that came out.

"Tell me why you're here, and I'll end your life quickly," Rigrim said.

"To re-re-resurrect an army," one demon said.

"Who sent you?"

"M-m-mors," the demon replied.

Rigrim's brow furrowed and he glanced at Boldair.

Boldair said, "Mors is the Plague-bringer. He's a necromancer, as are these two. But Mors has powers far greater. Had they succeeded in bringing this ancient race that is sealed in these tombs back to life ... they'd 'ave destroyed Frosthammer in a matter of days."

Rigrim's jaw tightened. His lips curl in anger. In a swift swing of his warhammer, he shattered the demons' bodies into small frozen bits of frozen flesh. Their heads fell atop the frozen mounds of demon flesh. For several seconds, they blinked. Confusion tightened their brows.

Rigrim set the head of the Frosthammer onto the cavern floor and faced Boldair. "I thought you left my city."

"Aye," Boldair said, nodding. "I had."

"What brought you back so soon?"

"I brought him back," Wynneffin said, staggering toward them with her hands rubbing her temples.

"Wynnie!" Boldair said with a broad smile. "You're okay!" He walked to her and wrapped his arm around her back to support her. She didn't protest and graciously leaned against his side. He groaned in pain.

"I'll survive," she said with a half grin.

"Did King Boldair come at his own freewill?" Rigrim asked. "Or—"

Wynneffin shook her head. "I used a bit of deceit and his curiosity lured him back."

"I see," Rigrim said through tight lips. He shook his head with disappointment. "Why the deception?"

Wynneffin sighed. "Father, he knows far more about this Plague-bringer than I or anyone else in Frosthammer does. I sought his help."

"Why didn't you consult me first?" Rigrim asked.

"I have tried before."

"When?"

"Many times. You've shrugged it off each time, as if the undeads' presence wasn't a threat. With Boldair's help, we stopped these summoner demons."

"Summoners?" Rigrim asked.

She nodded. "Yes. They were performing a ritual to pull the Plague-bringer into these sepulchers. We interrupted it in time, or matters would've been far worse."

Boldair nodded. "Yes, they had formed a portal. Mors was moments from materializing within your mountains. He's the reason Glacier Ridge ceases to exist."

"What?" Rigrim asked with a stern expression. His amber eyes flickered. "What happened to Glacier Ridge? Last I heard, Riese was the overseer."

"He was," Drucis said. "But the Plague-bringer appeared in Glacier Ridge. He released pestilence on the town, and I lost me brothers. Damn near lost me own life."

"How do we find this Plague-bringer?" Rigrim asked. "Is there any way of knowing where he might appear next?"

"Usually, no," Boldair said. "But this time, we know where he awaits."

"Where?" Rigrim asked.

Boldair grinned. "Woodnog."

"The city of Elves," Rigrim said with bitterness in his tone.

"They're my allies," Boldair said.

Rigrim's brow rose. "Allies? Elves? How could you ever offer complete trust to them?"

Boldair pointed to the Dragon Skull Pendant on his chest. "Because I've fought side-by-side with them at the Battle of Hoffnung. To defeat Mors, we'll need the aid of every race, even if we must set aside our scorn and differences."

Rigrim sighed and a rumbling low growl came with it. He thought for several moments before nodding his agreement. "It's been ages since I've emerged from our mountain city. I've hermitted so long I've lost touch with the outside world. Have things changed so much?"

"They 'ave," Boldair replied.

"Then it's time," Rigrim said, placing his hand atop Boldair's shoulder, "Dat my army aids all of Aetheaon by finding and destroying the Plague-bringer."

"Dat would be an incredible army of power," Boldair said.

"Mors must be stopped," Rigrim said. "He was near to invading my city. Such cannot be allowed. Besides, if you and my daughter can set aside your differences for a joint cause, I can ally myself with other cities and races for a greater purpose."

Wynneffin and Boldair exchanged glances, as she was still pressed against his side. He stared into her eyes, and as he did, they found themselves smiling at one another.

Rigrim laughed. "See? Dat's what I thought. Perhaps our kingdoms will one day join after all."

Boldair almost protested. He and Wynnie had not verbally settled on any proposal and only aided one another to survive.

"Now, Wynnie," Rigrim said. "Since you hastily brought Boldair and his companions to Frosthammer without their consent, you'll accompany his party by scouting ahead to Woodnog. It'll take the passing of at least two full moons before my armies are equipped to join the battle. Once you arrive at Woodnog, inform them dat help is on its way."

"Two full moons?" Boldair said. "Mors might be gone by then or already attacked the city."

"He'd have to raise an army capable of attacking Elves, who are rangers and archers with magic and nature on their side. He'd be a fool to attack with a meager army."

Boldair nodded.

Rigrim turned toward the others. "Yotram, Brandrum, and Kairun, all of you are to journey with Boldair and Wynnie to Woodnog."

They nodded. "Aye."

Boldair sighed.

"Is there a problem?" Rigrim asked.

"Word needs to be sent to Nagdor. I've yet to be coronated, and my brother's traveling to the city alone. He might tell them I'm dead so he can take the throne. Send word dat I'm alive and I want my best warriors sent to Woodnog."

Rigrim smiled. "Dat I can do. I assure you dat your brother will not protest, and if he does, he'll sorely regret it."

"Send messages to Icevale and Damdur, too. They'll aid our cause."

"Consider it done. The two of you need to see a medic before you leave Frosthammer."

"A medic?" Boldair asked.

Rigrim nodded. "The two of you took somewhat of a battering."

"Nothing more than I can handle," Boldair said.

Wynneffin nodded. "A headache, father, is all."

"Still, see a medic," Rigrim said. He glanced at Boldair with a grin. "Good news is dat we captured Telsia but the bad news is dat she's not in prison."

"She escaped?" Boldair asked.

"No, I'm afraid not," Rigrim replied. "She drank a potion before the guards reached her. She was dead before they could shackle her. She poisoned herself."

Sadness filled Wynneffin's eyes. She shook her head and looked away.

"I'm sorry, Wynnie," Boldair said with genuine concern. After the words escaped his lips, he realized his heart ached because of Wynneffin's loss. Even the death of estranged friends hurt.

She shrugged. "It's for the best, isn't it? At least you don't need to worry about her stealing your treasures."

"Her death isn't for the best," Boldair said. "Surely you don't think dat's how I feel. If she could've been taken alive, dat benefited all of us more."

Wynnie smiled. "She betrayed both of us, Boldair. I'm sorry I had not seen dat earlier on."

"I'm sorry I overreacted," Boldair said, taking her hand into his.

"The both of ya," Drucis said, waving his hand at them as he turned and walked away. "Get a room!"

The other Dwarves burst into laughter.

Rigrim laughed along with them. "No, they need to see a medic. Preparations need to be made. Woodnog's quite a journey. You'll need mounts, too."

Boldair nodded and looked at Wynneffin. "Aye, your father's right. Let's see what the damage is."

"Perhaps dat's it," Drucis said. "You both got hit in the head too hard. Turned their brains and words to mush. As for me, I prefer stout to mush me brains. Who's for a tankard?"

Dwiskter and the others cheered.

CHAPTER 52

Boldair rode Ember along the Lost Pass. Surprisingly, when Boldair returned to the stables, the dire wolf greeted Boldair with a chuff and wagged its tail with vigor. The wolf even licked the side of Boldair's face when he came closer. Somehow, Ember had taken a change of heart, possibly due to Burr's brief training. Boldair hoped the wolf's radical new behavior wasn't a ruse.

The moment Boldair saw Ember in the stable, his heart sank. A part of him loved the obstinate wolf and inside, he held no doubt Ember was worthy of being a king's mount. The wolf's temperament was equal to the stubbornness of almost any mule or Dwarf. Boldair couldn't fault the wolf for its disdained independence, but he understood that keeping the wolf as his mount meant to be on guard for occasional sudden outbursts.

Burr, the stablemaster, didn't offer much of an argument when Boldair asked to buy the wolf to regain ownership, especially since the wolf tried to maul Burr after he'd snapped the whip one too many times while giving Ember commands.

With his arm in a sling, Burr said that he loved the beauty of the wolf, but he'd never seen one as strong-willed and ill-tempered as Ember. Burr expressed that he'd rather not risk life or limb by keeping the wolf inside the stables. The stablemaster expressed his relief with a heavy sigh when Boldair offered to buy the wolf back.

Boldair chuckled. Perhaps that was why Ember set his newfound affections upon Boldair. The wolf actually *wanted* to ride along steep cold trails more than it wanted to be housed inside a stinking stable stall taking commands.

The harsh wind sliced across the frozen pathway, carrying sharp ice shards with it. Boldair covered his face, preventing them from slicing his skin and cutting his eyes.

Viorka rearranged her position behind the bear hide draped over them. She spoke little since Wynneffin joined their group. They weren't serious about reestablishing their relationship, but since they were traveling together on the long journey to Woodnog meant the possibility still existed. The little cat chose to let her objections be known by her silence.

Wynneffin rode alongside him with Drucis and Dwiskter on their new ram mounts behind them. Wynneffin's soldiers rode in pairs behind them with shields up and their weapons ready. At total, they were a dozen strong, which were good odds against traveling caravans or highwaymen, but not so should they encounter the Plague-bringer and his minions near cemeteries.

Due to the whipping freezing wind, none in Boldair's party said much. Their silence caused Boldair to evaluate the length of the treacherously long ride they needed to endure in order to reach Woodnog. Two more days of riding through the Frosted Peaks lie ahead before they even reached a warmer climate. Two days in the subzero temperatures seemed an eternity. He sighed.

"Ahoy!" a voice shouted in the wind.

Boldair and the others glanced over their shoulders but saw no one. They searched the cliff sides and then directly overhead. The huge ship gliding on the breeze several feet above their heads caught their attention.

"Do my eyes deceive me?" Drucis asked, rubbing them and looking again. He shook his head. "Nah, I'm past what I drank last night. Probably could use a few more tankards *now* though."

"Ice'ik!" Boldair shouted in surprise. He hailed the captain with his right hand.

"Bloody hells!" Dwiskter said.

"Lay anchor!" Ice'ik shouted. A hearty Dwarf tossed an anchor, which dragged along the trail ahead of Boldair and his company.

The anchor uprooted several large trees before finally catching the edge of a heavy boulder with enough weight to stop the ship from flying any farther.

Two Dwarves on the deck turned a winch, which was attached to the long anchor chain. Turning the winch steadily lowered the airship until its keel rested on the Lost Pass.

"Where ya headed?" Ice'ik asked, looking over the ship's rail.

"Woodnog," Boldair replied.

"Woodnog?" he asked, frowning. "I thought you were going to Nagdor."

"Changed agenda," Boldair said.

Ice'ik rubbed his bearded chin. "I see. Hmm. Sounds adventurous. Would you like to fly to Woodnog with us as our official maiden voyage?"

"To get out of this painful cold quicker? Yes. Provided you have room for us and our mounts," Boldair replied.

Ice'ik laughed heartily. "More than plenty of room. Mind you, now, the cost of the flight is dat each of ya have to contribute with the labor. Are ya up to dat?"

They nodded.

"Even the King?"

"Aye!" Boldair said with a fierce grin.

"Good. Once they lower the bow door, ride up the ramp."

Boldair studied the ship with curiosity. "Ya never said dat you were building a ship dat could fly."

"What'd ya think? Dat we were going to melt ice and float our way out to sea?" Ice'ik said with a sly grin. "I'm daft from time to time, but I'm *not* crazy."

"But how?" Boldair asked.

Ice'ik pointed to the oblong balloon floating over the sails. "We tapped into a flow of odd gas. When trapped into small pouches, I learned dat it caused the pouch to float. So I tested a wineskin with the gas, which was better sealed. The darned thing floated away. Being an engineer, my mind clicked with this grand idea of making a ship dat could float over the land instead of 'aving to sail across the sea. Fabulous idea, eh?"

Boldair nodded. "Indeed!"

Wynneffin grinned and shook her head.

"Ya find dat funny, Princess?" Ice'ik asked.

"No," she replied. "But it answers a lot of questions about your sanity. You're not crazy. You're a genius."

"I'll settle for crazy genius," Ice'ik replied with a wink.

She laughed.

The bow door creaked open slowly. When the top settled on the frozen path, Boldair rode Ember up the steep ramp. The wolf's curiosity and slight fear surprised Boldair. The dire wolf took timid steps walking into the hull.

After a quarter hour, all the mounts were tethered inside feed stalls built by Ice'ik and his team. Ice'ik seemed to have thought about all the possible needs his potential passengers might have.

They lifted anchor. Two crew members changed the direction of the ship's sails. The flying ship rose, turned, but instead of following the frozen path, they flew over the mountain ridge.

Boldair stood beside Wynneffin at the edge of the railing, watching the world beneath them expand. The mountains and trees got smaller as the floating ship gained altitude. They could see for miles.

Viorka stepped beside Boldair and pulled herself upon the rail, swung her legs over, and sat down.

Boldair clutched the railing tightly until his knuckles whitened. "Don't do dat!"

"What?"

"You could fall," he said, shaking his head. "Aren't ya afraid of getting dizzy and falling?"

"Nonsense," she replied. "I'm a fynx. Heights don't bother me, and besides, I have claws. My claws are slightly fastened into the wood now."

"Well, unless ya are capable of sprouting wings, it's a daring thing you're doing," Boldair said.

"Look at dat." Wynneffin pointed and her voice rose in awe.

Boldair looked to where she pointed. As the ship moved, the terrain altered quicker than they'd notice traveling on their mounts. The white mountainside and ice covered trees changed into lighter whites and then various shades of green as they crossed the descending slope. The wind rustled harshly against them, causing the Dwarves' thickly knotted beards to ruffle like the sails.

Boldair shook his head in wonder, having never seen Aetheaon from overhead. Taniesse had allowed him to ride on her back a few times, but she'd never flown to the heights of this floating ship. The changing terrain was stunning, but nothing compared to what they noticed before they left the Frosted Peaks.

The roars captured their attention. Then they spotted the magnificent Frost Dragons soaring below, almost as if they were escorting the ship from the Frosted Peaks. And perhaps they were, because the moment the ship left the frozen mountains and drifted over massive green conifers, these dragons lofted, suspending themselves in place for several moments before diving and turning back. The scaled giants glided in unmatched beauty.

Boldair sighed with tears burning his eyes.

Wynneffin cautiously placed her hand atop his, perhaps fearful he'd yank it away, but Boldair like having her hand resting there. She turned toward him. "What's troubling you?"

His jaw tightened, and his cheeks reddened. "Look at all dat beauty for as far as we can see."

"Glorious," she said softly.

"Aye. All the more reason to not allow the Plague-bringer to defeat us. If he destroys the City of Woodnog, his power increases, and being dat Woodnog is beside the Black Chasm, those two cities combined cannot be stopped."

"We're not going to let it 'appen," Wynneffin said.

"You bet we're not," Dwiskter said with a growl rolling in his voice.

"I'd 'ave stopped him on the Hoffnung Docks had he not vanished before I could get to him."

Ice'ik rolled a large barrel to the center of the deck, hammered a spigot into its side, and motioned everyone. "The ship successfully left the Frosted Peaks and we're all alive. Let's celebrate!"

Boldair frowned. "You didn't expect to get this far?"

Ice'ik shrugged. "Bah! Who knew? Eh? It's not called a maiden voyage for nothing. Never had a chance to test the kinks, either. So drink up!"

One of the crew brought a crate of tankards and set them beside the barrel.

The Dwarves cheered.

Ice'ik laughed. "Drink plenty. I've dozens of barrels below deck dat we might need to empty soon."

"Why's dat?" Boldair asked.

Ice'ik rubbed his eyes for several moments. His face flushed with embarrassment. "We might've already had a problem and don't know dat it can be rectified."

"What sort of problem," Drucis asked, wiping the froth off his beard and mouth.

"Dat gas in the balloon," he replied, pointing.

"Yeah?" Boldair and Drucis asked in harmony.

"An odd thing occurred dat I had no foresight in expecting."

"What's dat?" Wynneffin asked.

"Seems dat now we're in warmer air … we keep rising. It wasn't like dat in the frigid air. But now, we keep climbing," Ice'ik said. "Don't know what to do ta lower it."

"Ya can't get us down?" Boldair asked.

Ice'ik pointed toward the tankard. "Don't get all rigid on me, King of Nagdor. Down a tankard or two while I try to figure this out."

Dwiskter studied the large air-tank above the sails. He pointed. "Were the ropes tied around the balloon that tightly?"

Ice'ik shook his head, and then frowned. "It seems the balloon's swelling."

Dwiskter nodded. "If ya don't stop its growing size, it's going to rupture. And if it does, I don't care how good your sails are, we're going to crash."

Ice'ik motioned to a Dwarf at the top of one highest mast. "Release some of the gas from the balloon. Just be careful not to release all of it!"

The Dwarf did as commanded. After several minutes, the balloon shrank and the ship steadily lowered.

Boldair sighed with relief. "I think I'll get a tankard or three."

The others around him also sighed.

Ice'ik laughed nervously. "How was I supposed to know dat would happen? No one else has fashioned such a ship to my knowledge. Some inventions cost lives before they become successful."

"Might I take back my *genius* complement?" Wynneffin asked.

Ice'ik's face withered. "We're not dead."

"*Yet,*" Drucis said, waiting to fill his tankard again.

"All's going fine," Boldair said. "Let's not give our captain and host grief. Thanks for your hospitality, Ice'ik, and for giving us a quicker route to Woodnog."

ONE DAY in flight passed rather quickly. The airship didn't suffer any further mishaps. The most frightening ordeal, which was even greater than the possibility of the balloon rupturing was when the ship flew within sight of the Black Chasm.

The purplish-black veil prevented anyone from seeing what was beneath this unusual atmosphere. It wasn't composed of clouds, but lightning and thunder were present nonetheless. The most worrisome thing was not knowing what lie beneath the rolling cloud-like wall, which seemed an entity in itself. Again Boldair recalled the strange long tendrils that had reached out of the chasm, grabbed soldiers, and killed them within seconds. What other ominous horrors existed below?

Apparently, Ice'ik was also disturbed by the swirling black mass and fearful for the airship to pass through. At his order, the ship diverted southwest to fly outside of its range.

Boldair and his companions couldn't take their eyes off the chasm. His mind continued wondering what forces lie in wait. He couldn't shake the sensation of being watched. He held no doubt that if the ship flew into the chasm's territory, something horrible would attack. Twice, black wings poked through the clouds and then disappeared.

Less than an hour later, Ice'ik and his crew released more gas from the giant balloon, lowering the ship slowly over the swampy territory of Woodnog, which was south of the great City of Woodnog. Upon descent, Ice'ik and his crew lowered thick rope ladders. Because of the forked trees, landing on the ground was impossible. To unload their mounts, some of the trees needed to be cut down.

After the ladders rolled out and touched the soggy ground, Boldair and the others noticed several horsemen approaching on the miry road. As close as these horsemen were, he knew Ice'ik couldn't possibly get the ship to rise before these riders reached them. If they were Elven archers, rising wouldn't matter. They'd easily puncture the balloon with a hail of arrows. Repairing the balloon would not be an easy venture.

Boldair and Wynneffing exchanged puzzled glances. Dwiskter and Drucis pulled their weapons, stepping to the rail of the airship.

Boldair returned his gaze to the horsemen. His eyes widened with sudden recognition. He knew two of the riders: Roble and Lehrling. Boldair turned toward the others. "Allies, my friends."

"Allies?" Dwiskter said, frowning and squinting to better see.

"Aye, Sir Roble and Sir Lehrling. Fellow Dragon Skull Knight brethren," Boldair said. He waved his hand widely overhead. "Let's go greet them!"

<h1 style="text-align:center">CHAPTER 53</h1>

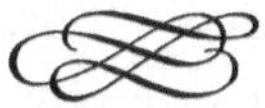

Boldair, Wynneffin, Drucis, Dwiskter, and Viorka hurried down the rope ladder while Ice'ik instructed his crew to chop down several trees, so they could land the airship.

Boldair grinned as he hurried toward Roble and Lehrling. Shawndirea, in faery form, sat on Roble's shoulder. "What brings you to this discarded muddy excuse of a road?"

"We've scoured the Woodnog swamps for days. I could ask the same question of you," Roble replied, offering his hand to Boldair. Boldair clasped it eagerly.

Shawndirea looked at the airship with sheer fascination. "What's that contraption?"

"Ice'ik's invention. Got us 'ere in less than a day from the Frosted Peaks," Boldair replied. "Why are ye here? 'ave ya come to help defeat the Plague-bringer?"

Roble nodded. His gaze was even. "That's why you're all here?"

"Aye," Boldair said, nodding. "King Rigrim's gathering his troops and preparing to dispatch them to join the war."

"King Rigrim?" Shawndirea asked. "Of Frosthammer?"

"Aye, de same."

"The city still exists?" she asked.

Wynneffin nodded. "It does."

"She's Rigrim's daughter," Boldair said.

"I see," Shawndirea replied. "For generations we had believed your Dwarven race was no more."

"As have other kingdoms in Aetheaon, I'm sure," Wynneffin replied.

"So you learned of the Plague-bringer from Boldair?" she asked.

"In part," Wynneffin replied. "But, we've encountered undead wandering the lowest levels of our city. Boldair and his party helped destroy summoning demons that attempted to teleport Mors into The Sepulchers of Twilight. A few million are buried there."

"Millions?" Lehrling asking, scratching his short beard.

"If it weren't for Boldair's aid," Wynnieffin said, "Frosthammer would've been destroyed and our numbers would've joined the undead armies."

"I'm afraid we're not free from that threat yet," a voice said from the darkly shadowed swamp trees. He stepped forward with a gnarled staff. A silver crystal, a black crystal, and a ruby red crystal were fashioned into an orb clutched inside the tight gnarled roots of the staff.

"Zauber?" Roble asked in surprise.

Zauber offered a slight bow and a haunted grin. "From my tower I traced Mors' emergence somewhere on the outskirts of the City of Woodnog."

"Won't the City of Woodnog be shrouded by magic so he cannot enter the city?" Roble asked.

"To those unfamiliar with magic, the city's always hidden," the wizard replied. "To someone with death and darkness and the ability to raise a fleet of undead … Mors won't have trouble locating Woodnog's hidden gates."

Galloping horses approached from the Barrier Pass between Woodnog's forests and the Black Chasm. Roble and Lehrling drew their swords. Boldair and the Dwarves readied their axes.

"Allies, my friends," Zauber said, raising his hand. A blue raven landed on his hand. Zauber brought the raven closer and stroked its feathers. "I've sent word to all the Dragon Skull Knights and the kings of the other kingdoms, in hopes that we can destroy Mors once and for all."

When the three horses came into sight, the riders were Lady Dawn, Sir Caen, and Odlon. Surprise registered on their faces when they noticed the airship and the party of Dwarves. They studied the ship with intense interest.

Zauber smiled. "Right on time."

Boldair frowned. "How is it dat you knew Mors was coming to Woodnog before the lot of us knew? Magic's one thing, but predicting the future … bah! No wizard can do dat! And yet, here you are."

Zauber smiled. "You're right, young King. I cannot predict the future but I've an ally who can. She's the one who showed me the pestilence Aetheaon will suffer should we fail to stop Mors in Woodnog. If he shatters the magical veil of Fae Barrier Pass, the Black Chasm will consume everything the Elves hold sacred. After that, the swamps of Woodnog will give up their dead at Mors' command. Most likely, his massive army will travel south and destroy Oculoth before resurrecting them into undead soldiers. Nothing shall stop his reign after that."

"We're the last hope before worse things befall Aetheaon?" Roble asked.

Zauber's eyes narrowed. "Yes."

"That's quite a burden to carry," Roble said.

Intrigued, Zauber rubbed his chin and approached Roble. "There's something … different about you, Overlander. You're veiled by protective magic, but not the faery's. Not the magic of any Fae. Be careful what magic you draw upon for protection." His eyes flicked to Shawndirea. She glanced away. "You know what the magic it is, don't you?"

"I do," she replied. "I've offered the same warning."

"As have I," Lehrling said, somewhat angrily. "Like any human from the Overlands, he's too stubborn to heed our advice."

"Overlander," Zauber said, "while dark magic can protect you, it comes at a price. Sometimes a greater price than you're willing to pay."

"I know," Roble replied.

Zauber looked amused. "Do you now? Tell me where you received this protection."

"We don't have time for the full details," Roble replied.

"Actually, we do. Because if there's one thing we cannot afford, it's for a bumbling fool to give Mors forewarning of our arrival. If I can sense this strange dark magic that enchants you, so can he. That's why I insist you tell us where you got this blessing and whom it was that gave it to you!"

Boldair rolled a log from the edge of the muddy pathway. "This sounds like it shall take some time. Might as well sit. Ice'ik, ya 'ave another barrel of stout you could spare? I'll pay ya for it."

Ice'ik nodded.

"Drinks all around," Boldair said.

The Dwarves cheered, but Lady Dawn, Caen, and the others were less celebratory. Boldair shook his head and grinned at Roble and Shawndirea, "Every Dwarf knows dat tales are much *better* with several tankards of stout. Now, Overlander, tell the tale. Your audience awaits."

THE END

Read Roble's tale in Shadowfae (Aetheaon Chronicles: Book Four).

ACKNOWLEDGMENTS

A special thank you to KC Riley-Gyer for the extra set of eyes to catch my mistakes, and her friendship from the opposite of the earth. Hobbits live near her.

ABOUT THE AUTHOR

Leonard D. Hilley II grew up a quiet, shy kid with an inquisitive mind. Learning to read at an early age, he fell in love with books. He read every book he could get his hands on and stacks of dark comics about ghosts, monsters, and creepy things that stalk the night.

Like a lot of boys, he caught beetles, wooly bears, butterflies, and had an ant farm. When he was ten, his interests in science increased even more after seeing a professor's insect collection. Soon he set out on his quest to build his own collection. He also learned to rear butterflies and moths to obtain perfect specimens. He learned botany, gardening, and set his goal to become an entomologist.

At eleven, he saw Star Wars. His imagination soared. Soon after, he discovered Roger Zelazny's Chronicles of Amber. Six months later, he had written the first draft of a novel. A novel he later discarded, but the characters stuck with him. Years later, these characters came to life in Shawndirea, which Hilley intended to be a novella for Devils Den. The characters, however, refused to be ignored and took the opportunity to unveil Aetheaon in their first epic fantasy. Lady Squire: Dawn's Ascension was quick to follow.

Shawndirea was Hilley's farewell to butterfly collecting, and those who have read the novel understand why. He has taken Ray Bradbury's advice to heart: "Follow the characters." He does. He follows, listens, and take notes—often never knowing where they're going to take him, but he's never been disappointed in the results.

Hilley earned a B.S. in Biology and an MFA in Creative Writing to combine his love of science and writing.

Sci-fi Titles: Predators of Darkness: Aftermath, Beyond the Darkness, The Game of Pawns, Death's Valley, The Deimos Virus.

Epic Fantasy: Shawndirea (Aetheaon Chronicles: Book One), Lady Squire (Aetheaon Chronicles: Book Two), Frosthammer (Aetheaon Chronicles: Book Three), Shadowfae (Aetheaon Chronicles: Book Four), and Devils Den.

UF/PR: Succubus: Shadows of the Beast (Nocturnal Trinity Series: Book One), Raven (Nocturnal Trinity Series: Book Two), A Touch of the Familiar

YA UF/Paranormal: Forrest Wollinsky Vampire Hunter; Forrest Wollinsky: Blood Mists of London; Forrest Wollinsky: Predestined Crossroads.